Dusk Runner
Dark Arrow Trilogy
Book 1

Mathias G.B. Colwell

Published by
Melange Books, LLC
White Bear Lake, MN 55110
www.melange-books.com

ISBN: 978-1-68046-164-0

Published in the United States of America.

Cover Art by Stephanie Flint

Dedication

"The road is like a snake."

Since the day I began writing, I promised myself that I would dedicate a book to my uncle. This is for you, Kerry. Thank you.

Prologue

Djumair Silverfist had been a traitor for nineteen long years and a coward for most of his life. He was the most dangerous type of coward there was, a bold one. He reflected idly on his life as he awaited the final orders for his next mission. Djumair let his thoughts drift even further from the next task and more upon his own being. He was not someone to question the decisions of the past. They were gone and could not be remade, so why bother with them? However, he was not above succumbing, every now and again, to the self-reflective melancholy, one reserved for time spent sifting through memories over a goblet of wine and a good view. Djumair looked off the edge of the platform, not five feet from where he sat, at the plains interspersed sparsely with copses of trees beneath him. Even though he was alone, and had nobody with which to share his thoughts, he allowed his mind to continue its backward journey. He was a solitary person after all. In many ways, he preferred to be alone and it seemed fitting to reminisce by himself.

Permission granted, he continued to remember. Not for the first time, nor for the last, his mind pondered the curious tandem of cowardice and courage that was Djumair Silverfist. He knew exactly what was required of a person to be on the winning side of conflicts in life, and he did whatever was necessary to ensure that he never lost. That fact, in and of itself, was his craven fault. Yet it simultaneously lent credence to his arrogant understanding of his own dangerous competency when it came to vanquishing a foe. He feared the price of losing so greatly that he knew he was a coward to the very core of his being. However, he was bold enough to know which decision or action, in the right circumstances, would be enough to ensure that he avoided failure, pain, and any other unpleasant consequences of defeat. Sometimes those decisions were difficult, but he made them all the same. Therein lay his courage, the ability to make challenging decisions.

His mind flashed back to that fateful day nineteen years ago, when he unleashed the flood of water that burst open Verdantihya's fabled gates—ripped them open from within. Bleeding and broken, he had sacrificed everything to avoid death, to avoid losing. He had joined the winning side—that much was clear. While he now sat and sipped wine freely on a slaver's deck, his former kinsmen fought, died, bled, and were captured. He thought of them as 'former' because one couldn't really claim to belong to the very people who they had betrayed. This sense of un-belonging defined Djumair, but it was a fair price for his own freedom, though not without pain.

Djumair had spent the better portion of the last two decades fighting a war for a king who he did not love and a Grand Marshal who he did not respect, and it had all been by his own choice. Many long years ago, when he had first felt the icy fingers of fear twisting in his belly, he had chosen this path. The first invasion had been sudden and swift, and the humans had established such a strong foothold on the continent that he had known his people had no hope of triumph. He had done the only thing possible, he had defected to what he knew would be the winning side. It had been a decision motivated by fear, but the choice in and of itself had not been one that was without the need for courage. It was a strange internal parallel in which he lived; fearful enough to betray his people and avoid defeat, and brave enough to make the hard choices in life, the choices that cut ties to one's heritage.

He broke from his reverie as he watched a servant approach from across the open-aired room. The wind swirled gently, high up on the eastern most Pillar in the land. Djumair reclined in a lounging seat with a view. It was a seat reserved for the slave captains who frequented this last outpost before heading north to begin a raid, or heading east to deliver the latest batch of captives to the humans. The wind was a dry breeze billowing up from the southeast. It carried the scent of smoke from the Camps and the dust from the land further beyond them as it curled up over the edge of the platform, leaving the ground far below it, hundreds of feet down. It was still strange to Djumair, even after his long years in this southern land, that the air could be so dry. This wind had a strangely familiar smell to it, a scent for which he felt the inklings of recognition. However, just when it felt he was about to lay hold of the memory of that particular scent's origin, it slipped away from his mind's grasp. He didn't like that. Djumair couldn't shake the odd feeling of importance for whatever it was he could not remember. It never paid to forget important information.

He took another swill of the white wine that sat chilled in his goblet, the contents creating tiny droplets of condensation on the exterior. It was not the most popular of beverages among his southern compatriots, but it was light and tangy. It soothed his dry throat and reminded him of the pleasures of this land, pleasures he was not likely to forget seeing as they were, in large part, the reason he had chosen this course in life. Wine of this vintage had been impossible to find in the north even before the invasion, let alone now, with the northern people of Andalaya scattered to the four winds across their mountain lands.

The servant finally reached the small, stand table to Djumair's right. He carried a silver pitcher polished to perfection, full of wine no doubt, should Djumair require more. It was the joy, and the nuisance, of being important. People to do his bidding, and at the same time, those same people were the ones who often interrupted the few quiet moments he had to himself. The swallow of wine tasted sour as Djumair grimaced slightly at the bothersome servant. The boy should be able to see that his wine glass was still half full and in no need of refilling.

The servant was young and dark haired like all of his people, and as he drew closer, he must have seen the dangerous glint in Djumair's eyes. The boy hesitated as if considering retreat, but then continued once he realized that he had come too far to leave without offering more wine. Fear shone in the boy's eyes as he approached. Djumair knew the fright that his name inspired in others. Just because he knew he was a coward, didn't mean that others did. In truth, most people were cowards at their core; he was just one of the few who admitted it to themselves. He embraced it and let it become a strength rather than a weakness. He let his fear push and prod him until it became a source of ingenuity and boldness rather than a reason to run from a fight. But this boy didn't know he was a coward. Instead, this servant saw one of the most feared warriors in the land, someone known for chopping off his own hand in order to win a battle. It was good the boy feared him. He liked it that way.

Djumair Silverfist watched the boy's eyes glance down at the immaculately forged silver fist attached to the end of his left arm. It was sculpted to perfection to resemble the very likeness of a living hand closed into a fist. It lay, along with his left arm, on the armrest and it glimmered in the setting sun.

"Would you care for some more wine?" the servant stuttered, his black hair hanging down the back of his tan, brown neck. All of the boy's kinsmen were tanned and brown, courtesy of this southern sun. For a brief instant Djumair felt bad for the boy. He was a servant, not a slave, but in this society of warriors and conquerors, once you accepted the role of servant, it was yours to fulfill for the rest of your life. The boy would never escape it. The pity was fleeting as Djumair remembered the boy's interruption of one of the few moments of solitary respite he had to simply enjoy the little things in life, like a sunset and a glass of wine.

He shook his head curtly. "Would you have me become drunk and susceptible to any sellsword who wishes to come my way?" He barked in response. "One glass of wine is enough for anyone who calls himself a warrior. Once you have had more than one, you cease the right to claim that title. You then become a drunkard and just another body for your captain to throw at the enemy." His words might have been a little harsh, but the boy had annoyed him.

"Yes, Silverfist, I mean, Sir," the boy spluttered quickly to repent, "what do I know of battle and fighting? Of course, you are right." He spun too quickly as he turned to walk away, and the pitcher flew from the tray, spilling its contents all over the ground.

The servant spun back to face Djumair, clearly expecting a tongue scathing remark at the very least, if not a command to the whipping post or worse. Djumair sneered slightly as he sat on the lounge chair, still reclining through the entire interaction, and watched the boy as he clutched the tray to his chest in fear, awaiting the consequences for spilling the wine.

His own image as reflected in the tray caught Djumair's eye, and he gazed upon his reflection as he pondered how he should punish the servant. From the polished, gleaming surface of the tray, light blue eyes stared back at him. Pale features, unlike the servant's, looked at him, and blond hair adorned the top of his head. The sides of his head were shaved in the manner of the warriors of the south, and his long, flowing locks of blond hair flowed off the back of his head just past his shoulders like a white-gold mane. It was not held in a braid, but it was gathered at intervals by loose, rawhide ties to keep it from getting in his way as he moved or fought. The hairstyle left the sides of his head clean, revealing ears that were pointed at the top, protruding in the manner of both his northern heritage and the servant's people. Dark or light of skin, the pointed ears were a common feature between the two races.

Djumair had a small, silver ring in his right nostril, but the most distinctive marks upon his face were the three blood red tears tattooed on both of his cheeks as if falling from the corners of his eyes. Traitor's Tears. They marked a person who had betrayed Andalaya in order to serve the King of the South. A decision Djumair Silverfist had made long, long ago. The tattoos were on his cheeks by choice. He had been the first to betray and had been the first to be tattooed. What was now required of the northerners who chose to give their lives to serve their new masters, he had pioneered as a twisted memorial to whom he had once been. In a strange way, everything about him was defined by choice, from the biggest decision to the smallest decoration on his body. Nothing had been forced upon him, and nothing would be.

He stood up slowly, faced down the servant with a penetrating gaze, and then backhanded him across the face as hard as he could. The boy dropped in a heap, and by the time he managed to pull himself together, Djumair had long since sat back down on his chair. He could hear the boy's sniffles, and feel the sting on the back of his good, right hand from the impact. It set his pulse racing and his blood buzzing. Even the slightest hint of combat made his whole body feel as if it were on fire. He was a warrior through and through. He feared death, but it did not keep him from the challenge of the fray. This however, was a simple disciplinary action and he calmed his fighting instincts.

"Go. Now. Get a rag, or better yet, remove your shirt and wipe up that mess," Djumair said flatly, as he gazed at the view before him. Maybe he could recapture some of the serenity that had preceded this unfortunate encounter—unfortunate for him, since it had interrupted his quiet. Djumair cared not a whit for the pain the boy was suffering. And suffering from the blow he was. Djumair could hear the pain in his voice as he responded that he would clean it up and intended do so immediately.

Djumair nodded at the boy's response but did not break his observance of the sunset painting the sky in front of him. He expected nothing less than immediate action when his commands were issued. This far from Dark Harbor and the Camps, he had the most power and authority of anybody on this Pillar.

Thoughts of Dark Harbor, the heart of his masters' domain, clouded his mind and he knew the peaceful moment from earlier had passed. He sighed to himself and let the worry, that he knew his thoughts of Dark Harbor would bring, come. What was Half-Mask planning? Something was in the works, some plan was being hatched, and Silverfist was not privy to the details. He hated not knowing. How was he to ensure the best possible outcome for himself if he did not know what was going to happen? True, his job was to follow orders. He gave them, as often as not, especially in a mid-point location such as this slave post—this Pillar was nearly halfway between Dark Harbor and the human forces, which were known as the Camps. However, when orders were issued by Half-Mask himself, even Djumair obeyed without question. Nobody frightened him like the Prince.

Footsteps, quick and quiet, approached and Djumair steeled himself for action, tensing his body in preparation to explode into action should the person behind him prove to be an assassin. It was not unheard of for people in positions such as his to fall at the hands of a sellsword ordered to kill them on behalf of a competing slave captain. Competition for honors in the land was fierce, and the higher your reputation among the slavers, then the higher prices you could charge at the auction block. A man such as Silverfist was always on guard.

As the person approaching him flickered into his peripheral vision, he relaxed. If it had been an assassin sent to kill him, the person would have attacked without allowing himself to be seen. Or at least he would have tried. If it had been an attacker, he would have been dead right now. Silverfist slipped the dagger that he carried tucked up the right sleeve of his silk coat, back into place before the person beside him could see that he'd had it out. It had slid into his hand freely, and the weapon returned to its place of concealment just as smoothly, with a quick flick of his wrist.

"So," Djumair drawled in a relaxed voice, "message from the capital, I take it?"

The soldier nodded his head and bared his teeth in a grimace of affirmation. Most people in these parts preferred fighting to running messages, and he, no doubt, had little reason to appreciate his duties as a courier. He was muscled and lean, with tan, brown skin and black hair. His head was shaved on the sides in the same manner, as was Djumair's, and his hair fell back from the top of his head in a tightly woven braid. His bared teeth were not a smile; it was more like what appeared to be a constant snarl, an expression with which he probably lived. The upper row of teeth in his mouth was filed to points that were sharp enough to rend flesh. It looked ridiculous to Djumair, and was one of the few affectations of this southern culture that he absolutely refused to adopt. He supposed that to some it might appear ferocious, especially when facing them in the heat of battle. The soldier's uniform was made of tight-fitting, forest-green pants and a sleeveless, black leather shirt. He was dressed for running, as a courier should be, and was only carrying a short axe at his hip and a long dagger tucked in one boot.

Djumair Silverfist eyed his opponent. They were almost certainly not going to enter into combat against one another, however, once you had fought in enough battles you ceased to allow yourself to be taken by surprise. It paid to be ready with a strategy to fight anyone, anywhere, anytime.

The soldier eyed him warily as well. He sneered as he looked at Silverfist, who was reclining in the seat with a view. Djumair, himself, was wearing tight, black hose and a well-cut, crimson silk coat. The coat hung loosely, unbuttoned, revealing his bare torso. He wore no shirt underneath, and the cool breeze danced lightly across his strong, toned chest. He tilted his head slightly as he watched the soldier appraise him, allowing a hint of menace to enter his expression as his own clear-blue eyes met the black ones staring back at him. He smirked as the soldier broke the stare first and looked away. It appeared that once again his reputation preceded him. Not many chose to fight him of their own accord. And of course, this soldier had no real reason to do so. The stare had merely been a byproduct of what happened when a war-like culture plunged headlong into the depths of conflict, chaos, and the continual hunt for slaves. Combat was natural these days even among allies, especially in times such as these when allegiances were shaky and often forced. It paid to be on guard.

"Well, what message have you for me?" Djumair waited after he spoke, allowing the messenger to produce a small scroll from his pocket. It was sealed with a crest in the shape of a face that was half covered by a mask. The seal of the Prince of Darkness himself, Half-Mask. Not a seal to be idly broken and certainly not one to be forged.

Djumair took the proffered parchment and reluctantly opened it. He had sworn allegiance to his current masters many years ago, yet he hated being sent on errands for which he was not given full information. Missions such as this, where he had been instructed to travel to this Pillar, the easternmost Pillar, and to await further information here, drove him to the furthest edges of his frustration. It galled him to no end to be kept in the dark. But he understood it. Djumair was accounted as a clever adversary by many and a dangerous ally by some. It was common for Half-Mask to keep him at arm's length, at least until he was ready to use Silverfist to achieve his own ends. Djumair Silverfist always got the job done, he was known for his competence, but even those who now owned his allegiance didn't trust him completely. Nor should they. After all, he had already switched allegiances once in his lifetime. In their eyes, that was reason enough to keep him at a distance. He knew they wondered whether betrayal might happen again.

The note was terse and whatever quill had been used to ink the words onto parchment had been pressed very firmly. It most likely signified the Prince's annoyance at having to send one of his most deadly weapons, Silverfist, on errands for the humans. Silverfist liked carrying out military objectives on behalf of the humans who had invaded his land as little as the Prince did, yet he knew it must especially vex his royal master to have to succumb to the wishes of a race he deemed inferior to his own. Half-Mask hated the humans, yet he was forced to work alongside them; at least for now. For the present he, and subsequently Silverfist, would politely accede to the requests of their allies and bide their time, waiting for the day when their people would rid themselves of the yoke they had accepted nineteen years ago.

Djumair read the instructions silently. They told him to proceed to the northernmost camp of the humans and upon arrival, to follow the instructions given to him by the Grand Marshall. Half-Mask made reference to the fact that Djumair would most likely be dealing with a particularly vicious rash of raids that the Camps had been experiencing this spring. He was to make himself available, in whatever way necessary, to the needs of the humans. Silverfist seethed quietly inside that he would have to obey direct orders from the human commander, but there was nothing to be done of it. For now, they held the tether. The sea of humanity that had arrived on the shores of this land years ago had swelled even greater in the years since their invasion. They were bolstered by new recruits from their distant homeland and had secured plenty of slaves, plucked from the rotting carcass of Andalaya to do the work deemed unfit for their human soldiers. They had entrenched themselves deeply along the eastern shore of the continent. The human military camps ran along the coast, from the fabled ruins of Akan Deraiya far to the south, all the way up the coast to where the East Mayn River met the sea. The mouth of the East Mayn, where it met the great sea known as The Fracture, was a perfect place for their northern camp. It was the last stop for ships sailing north, hugging the coast as they made their way toward Hope's End, the final staging point for slaves who were taken from this land and trafficked back along the Great Bridge to the home continent of the humans.

Silverfist crumpled the note in his good hand and tossed it aside to the floor in disgust. He was not pleased with the instructions.

"Something displeases you in what you read?" The soldier opened his mouth full of sharply filed teeth into an even wider grimace. "Should I report your displeasure to the Prince of Darkness when I return?" He threatened menacingly.

Silverfist snorted disdainfully. "I'll tell old Half-Mask myself when next I see him," he bluffed with a touch more bravado than he truly would have done if the Prince had actually been there to hear. His nonchalant words seemed to take the soldier aback. Not many dared speak in such a cavalier manner about the heir to the southern kingdom. He was without doubt the most feared person in all the land, the only exception possibly being the Prince's father. To be honest, they were both fearsome. The King of the South was midnight on a starless night. He was terrifying in the manner that only madness could steal the breath from your soul. But the Prince of Darkness was frightening in an entirely different way. He was what remained when light had been leeched away. Pure, unbridled darkness and terror. The King of the South had chosen darkness for his reign, but the Prince, Half-mask himself, had been raised in it. He had absorbed the darkness from the moment of his birth. And Silverfist served both of these dark masters.

However, Half-Mask's father, the King, had taken to seclusion for much of the time these days, and truth be told, Djumair had not seen him in years. It was rumored that the seeds of madness had recently sprouted in his brain. Djumair wasn't certain the seeds hadn't been there all along. Either way, like father like son, Half-Mask, or the Prince of Darkness as he was formally known, was concocting a plan. And Djumair Silverfist wished he knew the depths of it. Oh, he had hints of the plan, glimpses of what might come, and the little that he did know left him feeling edgy.

Silverfist waved the soldier away as he considered his orders thoughtfully. He heard the soldier leave as quietly as he had come, the softly retreating footfalls barely heard above the whirl of the wind. A distant, terrified shriek from a slave from across the other side of the Pillar cut through the air. Even the minds of the hardiest of souls could shatter when faced with the reality of a lifetime of imprisonment and forced labor at the mercy of a cruel master. The holding cages of the slaves reeked of waste and fear. Silverfist was glad he was upwind from them.

He heard a noise behind him and he leaned forward then and stood quickly. He turned to give the soldier a tongue-lashing he would never forget for returning after he had been clearly dismissed. But fortune shined upon him as a knife held in a black-gloved hand slashed through the air where his head had been when sitting. The attacker, who was in fact not the messenger who had just left him, quickly righted his balance and pulled a second dagger off his hip, holding the two weapons lightly and easily in his well-studied hands. The assassin advanced slowly, calmly. He was dressed all in black, with a deep cowl pulled so low over his forehead that his face was obscured by shadows.

Silverfist's own dagger appeared in his right hand and he readied himself to defend. Not for the first time, he thanked himself for the wisdom of choosing to slowly sip a glass of wine rather than swill it down in a rush. Drunkards rarely survived long in this world and he had survived close to his fortieth name day. The two opponents circled each other warily, and from the corner of his eye, Djumair saw the corpse of the messenger lying in a pool of his own blood, his throat slit before he'd had a chance to react. *So, this assassin had some skill, did he?* Dispatching a soldier that soundlessly was not easy.

The assassin closed the distance between them suddenly and his two blades flashed as he spun them in an intricate dance, weaving and slashing towards Silverfist's face and neck. Djumair Silverfist blocked the attacker's first knife with his own dagger, and used his metal fist to knock the other from his would-be killer's hand. People always underestimated his silver fist as a potential weapon. Little did they know how dangerous it really was.

His attacker didn't give up at the slight hitch in his plan. Determination could be seen in his decisive movements of continued assault. He slithered his way nearer to Silverfist again and in a surprising flurry of fists and steel, he managed to close the distance between them enough to actually deliver a shallow cut on Djumair Silverfist's chest before Djumair crashed his metal fist into the assassin's face. The impact sent a spray of blood and spit flying across the room to splatter upon his wine goblet. Dots of red contrasted against the light of the setting sun reflected through the crystal clear surface and its pale-golden contents. The assassin was stunned for a moment, which allowed

Silverfist to grasp and pull him toward the edge of the platform, before slinging him up over the rail and casting him off with a pitiful wail as he plunged through the empty air towards the ground far below. In truth, he had been just as dead when Djumair's fist had crashed into his cheek, as he would be from the impact of the fall, whenever he finally landed. Djumair had his metal fist crafted with tiny, sharp ridges along the silver knuckles. They were enough to break skin every time upon impact and were laced with a particular poison from the deserts far away to the south, beyond the Drylands. It was a convenient way to deliver a poisonous touch of death to an opponent's blood stream after striking them. It was a secret he kept as closely guarded as any other. Many looked upon his silver fist as a weakness. Only he knew just how truly lethal it could be.

The body finally struck dirt far below in a tiny puff of soil. It was a shame he couldn't be questioned, but Silverfist had no doubt that if he had been able to talk to the would-be killer, all that would have been discovered was that a rival slave captain had tried to thin the competition and drive up his own prices. Such was the price of fame and success. Besides, an attempt on one's life was needed sometimes to remind a person that he still lived and breathed. The racing pulse, the rush of blood to the head, it was a drug unlike any other, and Djumair Silverfist was no more immune to its treacherous grasp than any other warrior he had ever met.

He touched the long, dueling dagger hanging at his hip in remembrance. All battles could set the fire flowing in his veins, but only one fight had ever truly crossed the line into giving him real pleasure. His lips curved in a slight smile at the thought of that old victory.

North he thought. To deal with the raids and shadow tactics that his former brethren were using to harry the human troops and supply lines as the humans ferried their soldiers, slaves, and food stores between one staging area to another.

He knew he should feel frustrated with the Andalayan resistance. He was after all, being sent to deal with it. And deal with it he would. The resistance was shaky at best, disorganized, and lacking cohesion, and Silverfist always produced results. Yet there was a tiny part of him that felt glad they were giving the humans such trouble, that they were dealing just a small amount of death and destruction to the intruders—the humans. The emotion was not because of his lost heritage. No, he had given up every right to even think of himself as Andalayan long ago when he had chosen this traitorous course. He simply enjoyed the fact that the humans were having a difficult time of it. Whatever he was—whether he considered himself one of the pale-featured Highest from the shattered northern kingdom of Andalaya, or one of the dark-skinned Departed as his former people called their cousins to the south and who he now served—it made no difference. Even though for now, he fought alongside the humans and enslaved his former kin as part of the tentative alliance his new masters had struck with them, it changed nothing. Either way he was born of this land, and bred of its people. He was an elf and proud of it. He reached his hand down to feel the shallow wound on his chest. His fingers came away bloody, and he touched the tips to his tongue, savoring the metallic flavor of blood. He was a coward, and a traitor—there was no disputing that fact. But he was still an elf.

Chapter One

Spring had come to the Lower Forest. It was late arriving this year, but Elliyar Wintermoon could almost feel the land finally budding into life around him. The leaves on the oak tree in which he sat crouched and waiting, were a vibrant green, a stark contrast to the winter chill that had pervaded the land, long past when winter should have run its course. Elliyar breathed deeply, tasting the air, letting the wind rush into his lungs. It was a south wind. It was warm and carried a strange scent. He didn't like it. It pulled on his senses, tugging at his mind, as if trying to get him to remember a long forgotten tale. Elliyar had the uncanny sensation that whatever tale his mind was striving to recall carried some kind of warning. It frustrated him that he could not remember. The wind was not crisp and fresh like a wind should be. Wind in the mountains of Andalaya was never this warm and humid, and it never carried with it whatever scent it was that was triggering his internal alarm. This was almost a sour scent, like something rotting not far away. But Elliyar had scouted the area before taking his post and had seen nothing dead that could be emitting the smell. He shook the question from his mind and focused on what he could do, which was to take heed of his surroundings and watch. It would not be long now before the events of the evening began.

The shadows of sunset were creeping steadily across the outskirts of the Lower Forest, where Elliyar and his family lay in wait patiently. Each one of his family members were in a separate tree, ready to ambush the wood cutting detail that would be passing by shortly. The detail would be heading back towards the Camps from a day of logging. The slaves would be pulling heavy wagons laden with timber, while the cutters would be strolling along with the guards who were protecting them. This close to the Camps, not a half day's walk away, the cutters would not be nearly as alert as they would be if they were deeper into the forests of Elliyar's homeland. It was a bold attack. The Highest did not reach far outside the depths of their land anymore, but there were still those who fought. Elliyar and his family were some of those. Raiding this close to the Camps was bound to be dangerous. A simple cutting detail, consisting of lesser soldiers and slaves, would be fairly easy to eliminate even if the enemy outnumbered Elliyar's family. However, squads of the Departed had taken to patrolling the land near the Camps in an effort to minimize the havoc that some of the Highest had been wreaking for the last few months. The Departed were much more dangerous than this cutting detail. But that would not stop Elliyar and his people. The fight must continue, and continue it had. Recently they had stepped up the number of attacks they had been executing. Strike and move. Hit supplies, hit weak points, and move on. That was what a resistance did when they fought a war in which they were vastly outnumbered. Elliyar was proud of those of his people, the Highest, who still fought instead of running. The enemy would pay for his homeland, step by step, with their blood.

The shadows grew even fuller as the sun sank lower in the sky. It hung suspended above the horizon, its lower portion covered by the tops of trees in the Lower Forest. The only reason Elliyar could even see the sun was because this part of the forest had been thinned by logging over the last decade, allowing openings for the light to slip through. There were gaps in the canopy of leaves around him and above his head. All the trees that were deemed easy, quick cuts had been logged, leaving only the thick oaks too dense to chop through in a short time. Eventually these old, oak trees too would go. But for now, the humans thought of these trees as an unnecessary risk. When raids were common, as they were these days, the humans thought first and foremost of quick resources. They would extend their control with another campaign, perhaps this summer, and when these lands lay fully and safely under their control then they would take the time to cut every last one of these trees without the fear of taking unnecessary casualties in the process.

It was a shame that the humans destroyed the land, as well as its people. They were a forward thinking race, Elliyar conceded, with their contrivances and war weapons, the likes of which the Highest had never seen, yet they cared not for the land upon which they lived. In that regard, they were not so different from the Departed. The Departed were his people's dark cousins to the south, strong and proud, warlike and without mercy. They butchered the land and people alike, whatever got in their way. In some ways, with that similarity in mind, Elliyar supposed it was not surprising the humans and Departed had struck up an alliance so many years ago, although the pain of that alliance still cut Elliyar deeply. It was the source of woe for his people, the Highest, since the Departed made up the main body of slavers, which penetrated Andalaya and enslaved his people.

Elliyar pulled his concentration back to the moment at hand. Speculating on the nature of the alliance between the two races did nothing for him in this moment. The wind gusted again, filling his nose with a sense of wrongness. He ignored that too and focused on the sound of a wagon wheeling over the uneven forest path in his direction. He was the last and farthest from the deep forest, closer to the edge of the woods, leading to the Camps. He could not see his family, but he knew where they were.

Elliyar unlimbered his bow as he listened for the sound of his uncle leading the attack. They were all cued to follow his uncle. Elliyar's bow was black yew from the heart of Legendwood, the forest that lay to the north and west. Black yew was strong wood, yet supple; it was the right material for a good bow. The bow was a longbow, powerful, and well made. It had been cut to perfection by Elliyar's grandfather in an era when time spent on crafts and building had not been considered a luxury, but rather an expectation of excellence. Not like now. There was no time to create anything of such beauty any more. Elliyar ran his fingers over its smooth surface from tip to tip, feeling it become one with his body like only a weapon could. The grip was made from deer hide and fit his hand exactly.

The enemy wheeled into site and Elliyar drew an arrow from his quiver and knocked it to the bow. The arrow was black as well, crafted from Dreampine, the black pine trees on the distant northern slopes of the mountains, which were far from here, in a still-frosted, chill corner of the world. The black of his bow and arrows matched the shadows; they had been created to blend in with the dimness of the forest. Elliyar's hose and hooded tunic were a deep green, mottled with dark brown and black dyes. There had been a day once, when the Highest had not been forced to fight from the shadows, a day when they had stood proudly on the battlefield in the light, the sun gleaming off their breastplates, swords, and shields. They had been a sight to behold, the armies of Andalaya. At least, that was what he had been told. It had been before his time. Not now. Now, his people moved furtively and slid from tree to tree. They fought from the sides of paths and from the branches of trees. They fought and then retreated swiftly into the darkness. The Highest were light wrapped in shadow, good masquerading as darkness, because it was the darkness that concealed and protected them.

Elliyar heard a bow twang far to his right. That would be his uncle starting the raid. As he was about to join his family, the wind wreathed around his head in another surly gust, and the scent so agonizingly familiar assailed his nostrils once again. *Bonewinds* he realized suddenly in shock! The thought brought confusion and consternation. The Bonewinds were a legend so old that no member of the Highest who were living today knew much about them.

They were more superstition than anything else, a quaint story told to scare children. Elliyar had never smelled them before today; he doubted any living elf had. They were just a myth. Yet the strange scent fit the description in the tales.

Legend said that in the First Days the Bonewinds had blown almost incessantly, surging down from the northern marches and the Broken Tree range. They had blown sharp and cold, carrying with them the scent of dark tidings, the reek of death and decay and evil, heralding foes to come. This smell was different, not so crisp nor cold, yet the same. Elliyar had only heard of the Bonewinds in legend, but if a scent could carry decay upon it, then it was this fell, southern wind, dry and dusty. It gusted up from the south with the slight stench of something spoiled, a hint of danger and tragedy to come. The Bonewinds were new to him, Elliyar had never smelled them in his life, but he could sense their age. They were old, an ancient warning repackaged by the land into a new alert for those who knew how to heed their senses and the history of the world. Superstition or not, Elliyar shoved them forcefully from the front of his mind, cursing the seconds wasted thinking instead of acting and helping to attack.

Elliyar surveyed the scene below him. The enemy had also heard the arrow loosed by his uncle, and they formed into ranks as best they could. Elliyar could see the look of fear on some of the faces of the enemy men as they looked apprehensively into the trees around them, waiting for the hail of arrows they were expecting. They were not disappointed as Elliyar and his family loosed shaft after shaft into their midst. He knocked, pulled, and loosed. Knocked, pulled, and loosed. Five times, he shot his arrows before the enemy pinpointed his location in the oak tree and began firing small shafts of their own at him. Elliyar's five arrows had felled five men. He was an archer at his core and he rarely missed. It was a safe assumption to believe that his other family members had been similarly accurate with their own shafts. That meant at least twenty or so of the enemy, which was well over half, were already incapacitated or dead. It was time now for close quarter fighting. Elliyar launched himself from the tree in a ferocious leap, leaving his bow and quiver resting in the branches. In midair, he pulled free his long, dueling dagger, which was longer than his forearm, slender and slightly curved at the tip. He landed amongst the woodcutters and slaves, drawing blood with his first slash across a cutter's throat. *One more down* he thought in satisfaction.

A quick glance at the slaves around him showed that they wore copper collars. They would not fight. That meant all he had to do was focus on the cutters. Three surrounded him and he pulled free his second knife, a small belt knife, and held it point down, opposite to his dueling dagger. He shifted his weight to the balls of his feet, feinted one direction and then lashed out in another, and cut one human deep to the bone of his arm, following up the slash with a thrust into the man's gut. Elliyar spun then, crouching as he did to avoid the decapitating slash of a short sword in the hands of a different cutter. Elliyar exploded upwards from his crouch and tackled the man who had just narrowly missed cutting off his head. They collided in a heap of bodies and Elliyar's small belt knife dug deeply between the man's ribs, forcing breath and blood from his mouth in a fountain. The spray of red caught Elliyar's face and he rolled free from the dying man with his face painted in blood. The last remaining human cutter looked at him in terror as Elliyar pulled himself to his feet, holding the man's gaze. The man was frozen in shock. A man by himself like this, facing a warrior of the Highest, was normally easy meat and he knew it. The advantages of the humans were in their numbers and their weapons, especially the weapons crafted by the Makers, who were the sect of humans dedicated particularly to research, creation, and advancing their weaponry. All alone however, a solitary human soldier was hardly impressive.

Elliyar advanced slowly, like a predator stalking its prey, relishing the chance to show his enemies that he did not fear them. No, in fact *he* was the one to fear. Elliyar was young, having had only eighteen name days, the day each year commemorating his birth and naming, but he was a seasoned veteran of war.

The man shook off the terror that had held him frozen, turned, and sprinted into the underbrush on the side of the path. Elliyar swiveled his head to look behind him at the rest of his family fighting, checking to see if they needed his help or whether he could pursue and finish off this human coward.

Elliyar saw his uncle, Dacunda, cut through a man's sword arm with one vast stroke of his long sword and then promptly skewer him on the blade. His eldest son and Elliyar's cousin, Dahranian, fought at his father's side with a duplicate long sword. In fact, the two of them were a near match for one another. In one, you could see the past of one and the future of the other. Light brown, almost blond hair graced their heads. Both had their hair pulled from the front and woven into a giant braid, a warrior's braid that hung down behind each of them to nearly the middle of their backs. They were identical in motion and action, death made manifest with hands and swords if Elliyar had ever seen it, their grim faces locked in concentration as they fought in tandem.

In a moment, Elliyar's eyes caught a glimpse further down the path of his other cousin, Ryder, fighting with a long axe. The weapon had a narrow shaft, and a thin but wide blade on one end of the haft. He cleaved with one end of the axe and struck with the butt end as well, wielding that end almost like a stave. He was less fluid in motion than his elder brother and father, but he was nearly as effective. Surrounded by two human cutters, he fended them off easily and Elliyar could see he would make quick work of them. Ryder's hair was light brown as well, divided into two narrow braids hanging over either shoulder. The braids swung and danced behind him as he swirled and fought. Elliyar thought he heard laughter. *It would be just like Ryder to laugh at danger.* Ever the jokester, he had a hard time taking anything seriously, even fighting.

Elliyar's gaze found the last member of his family. His sister was lean like the rest of his elven family, yet her frame was even slimmer, in the fashion that many females often take. Valerihya's dyed, green hair hung loosely just above her shoulders. She wore her hair short. Rihya had never been one to conform to tradition, preferring flash and distinction, hence its color and style. Slashing and flinging knives, she dispatched one woodcutter with deadly grace and then turned to the guard who was advancing upon her, his shield held out in front to fend off another dagger toss. She could take care of herself, particularly when facing only a solitary man. Rihya was a very competent fighter. Elliyar glanced at his own bare wrist revealing a scar that his sister had given him when he had provoked her anger. She never held back her wrath and it was unwise to elicit her ire. Her temper was usually not serious, but Elliyar did have a number of different scars on his body resulting from arguments with her. He smiled coldly. His family could take care of themselves. It was time to hunt the coward who had fled into the underbrush.

Elliyar turned and sprinted into the forest following the guard who had run. He couldn't have gone far in the moments that it had taken Elliyar to survey the skirmish. A broken twig here, a footprint there, and Elliyar had no problem following the man's path. These humans came with numbers and weapons, with fire and war machines, yet they were city folk to their core. They were more adept with a fork and knife than with their hands, more accustomed to cobblestones beneath their feet than the feel of soil and dirt between their toes. It was one advantage the elves had in this fight. The Highest were born of this land, bred of its streams and lakes, its forests and game trails. He pursued lithely with the grace any elf could muster by his tenth name day.

The escaped man finally came into view, staggering and panting in exhaustion, as he clutched a tree. He glanced back and seeing Elliyar in pursuit, let out a squeal of fear, primal like terrified prey, a hare before the wolf, and spurred his tired body forward.

Elliyar readied himself for a final sprint to catch his fleeing enemy and finish the battle once and for all, when the stench of death hit his senses followed quickly by an elf tackling him from the tree above him. The elf was dark in complexion compared to the fair skin of Elliyar; he was tanned and brown from years spent in the southern sun. His ears were pointed at the top like Elliyar's own; in that regard, they were alike. But there were differences between the northern and southern cousins in more than just skin and hair color. Dark and light were not the only contrasts. The Departed, the southern elves, were ever so slightly more heavyset, not quite as lithe and graceful as their northern counterparts, the Highest, and many shaved the sides of their heads are. The Departed warrior caste also filed their top row of teeth into points, resembling a predator's fangs. Stories of battle said they even bit their enemies, tearing flesh with teeth as well as blade. Elliyar believed it, as he saw flakes of dried blood on the chin and lips of the dark elf, an old meal or the forgotten remnants of battle on its face.

Elliyar noticed oddities in the dark elf's behavior almost immediately because it seemed different from many of the Departed with whom he had fought during his years of raiding. In some ways, it seemed more of a *thing* than an elf such as he was accustomed to seeing. It still moved rapidly in the manner of elves, but there was definitely something *wrong* with his opponent. Some of the differences were subtle, such as the way it moved slightly jerky instead of smooth and measured, and the manner in which its eyes seemed to see him yet look right through him as well. Dead eyes. A blank stare. However, other distinctions were quite apparent. The dark elf seemed to carry a disease of some sort as he circled Elliyar, his curved scimitar pitted and stained, indicative of multiple uses without cleaning. The shoulders and arms of the Departed were bare and Elliyar could see that they were pocked and cracked, leaking with puss as if a wound had been left to fester. The odor of death accompanied it. The left side of its face looked raw, like new skin with the top layers gone.

The dark elf feinted and weighed his reactions before continuing to circle, testing Elliyar. It cocked its head slightly as if thinking some far off thought, then for the first time, life seemed to truly come to its eyes, dark and gleeful, as it rushed in to kill. In that moment, Elliyar wished it would return to the glazed look its eyes had been carrying before, because as much as the stare had spooked him to see, it was nowhere near as dangerous as the look the dark elf carried in its eyes as it truly engaged in combat. The blankness of before was replaced by cognition, as if it had suddenly switched back to being what Elliyar was accustomed to seeing in one of the Departed.

They fought swiftly and furiously, Elliyar using all of his speed and reflexes to stay out of the way of the scimitar singing its deadly tune as it whistled to and fro in the air around him. The jerky motions of the dark elf were hard to match for speed, it did not lack for power that much was certain, yet there was a smooth quality it did not possess. Elliyar used his grace and balance to slide in and out of range of the dark elf's weapon, ducking in low to slice a thigh, weaving right then left to nick a vein in one arm, loosing blood to flow freely. As Elliyar cut the vein in the Departed's arm, it slowed, the loss of blood affecting its power and pace.

Strangely, no fear showed in the eyes of the dark elf, just a shadowy passion, and a heat of battle that Elliyar had never witnessed. Elliyar had no time to ponder though, as it required all of his wits and fighting ability to finally finish off the dark elf. Elliyar still couldn't shake the feeling that the Departed he now faced in battle was somehow more of a creature than an elf. Elliyar feinted right then left, then ducked back to the right ahead of the creature's reactions. Sliding in close, he buried his belt knife into the Departed's guts, and saw the elf's grip on its scimitar loosen convulsively as it dropped the weapon to the ground.

Elliyar whipped his long, dueling dagger up to its throat and spoke softly to it. "One more of your kind dead, and I couldn't be more pleased." Elliyar punctuated the statement by sawing brutally through its windpipe. The elf thrashed and snarled through the blood that was clogging its throat. He gnashed his teeth bestially as he slid to the ground at Elliyar's feet. Dark blood, almost black, smeared Elliyar's hands and the sleeves of his tunic. The southern elves bled a darker red than Elliyar's own people, a rust color, but the blood of this elf was even darker than usual.

Elliyar pushed back his deep hood, finally allowing himself a moment to breathe in the air in the faint and failing light of the evening. The sun had sunk beneath the trees and would soon slip beneath the horizon altogether. It felt good to enjoy the last glimmer of ambient light upon his face before night fell completely.

He looked at the path ahead of him, where the human guard who he'd been pursuing had gone, and then back down at the corpse at his feet. He could probably still catch the man, but doing so would waste precious time. His uncle would want to move fast now that the fight was over and the objective accomplished. Cause as much mayhem in and around the supply lines and projects of the enemy as possible, then move on. That had certainly been accomplished this afternoon.

After all, it was the way of the Highest now. The fair northern elves, the race to which Elliyar belonged, were no longer able to fight pitched battles with their enemies because they were drastically outnumbered. It was now shadow tactics and viper quick attacks. Lightning strikes and just as fast retreats were the staples of their survival. Hit and run, hit and run. Strike with speed and then run to live and fight another day. Their main goal as a race was survival, but there was a price to pay for anyone who would try to lay claim to ruined Andalaya as their own. It was as if all of the Highest had an unspoken code to which they adhered. Strike hard, strike fast, and then retreat with as few casualties as possible. Retreat and run. If you ran long, and did not fight for a time, well then, when fate spun your course back into combat, then you struck a few more times or perhaps a bit harder to make up for the time spent resting. It was not a precise method. The bitter truth was, it was a losing effort and all knew it. But honor dictated that blood be paid to defend their land. Andalaya might be lost, but its people were not yet subdued. Spread to the four winds and scattered like dust they might be, many dead, many enslaved, but there were still enough of them left to at least bleed the enemy, bit by bit, every step of the way. Elliyar took some satisfaction in knowing that.

His family would move soon, he knew, but what to do about this body? Normally he left the dead, but this elf had looked like he was sick—plagued. Elliyar was not inclined to let a disease sweep the land. It would likely hit his people as well as the enemy and he couldn't allow that to happen. Plagues, once they ran rampant, were nearly impossible to contain. Allowing the Highest to lose precious people to a plague was a price Elliyar was not willing to pay, no matter what the cost might also be to the enemy. That was, if it really were a disease. In truth, he had never encountered one before today, only heard of them, so he had reason to question his own certainty on the matter.

Elliyar reached down and touched the face of the dead elf almost involuntarily. Prodding the dead unnecessarily was morbid, he knew, yet there was an attraction he did not quite comprehend. As he touched the face of the dead Departed, a shiver ran deep within his body, and a sensation of power he could not describe, welled up inside him. The face of the dead elf returned to normal, the skin healthy, and the slightly sunken half of the face filled out. Elliyar blinked in surprise. When his eyes flashed open, the body was back to its sickly looking state. Elliyar shook his head to clear his mind of whatever fancy had just run through it. This body was dead and it certainly looked diseased.

Thinking as quickly as he could, he gathered some dead, dry branches from the ground and piled them on the body. Striking flint, he lit the moss and lichen on top of the branches and watched the tiny funeral pyre go up in smoke and flame.

He felt no sadness for the death of his southern cousin; no, he had killed the Departed before and would kill them again. But this had been a strange encounter nonetheless. The way the elf had seemed different than most of the Departed he had previously encountered, how its eyes had seemed almost lifeless at times, and its actions bestial at others, was beyond odd. Not to mention, whatever he had imagined happening to its face as he had touched it a moment ago. He would need to think on it. Elliyar had never been one to process his thoughts aloud before spending as much time as possible sorting through them on his own. And sort through this encounter he must.

A horn sounded. It was a clear, bell-like tone, and Elliyar knew it was time to return to his uncle. The haunting note resonating through the forest was the call to leave. His family was probably waiting for him already. The fire from the burning body lit the woods at night, since the sun had finally disappeared beneath the horizon, ushering twilight in its wake. Using the moss from a tree, Elliyar wiped from his hands the dark elf's blood and then ran lightly, swiftly, back towards his family. This night they would run, and run fast toward safety, most likely to the north. They had been raiding hard for several months now on the eastern side of the continent. As much as Elliyar's blood sang during battle, he could admit to himself that he needed rest. It would be good to breathe the air of his homeland again. They were close to home here on the outskirts of the Lower Forest, but this was not Legendwood, this was not Andalaya proper. Home. It had been a while since he was home. *Wherever home truly was* he thought wryly. They had been raiding and wandering a long time now. And in truth, they had never stayed in one spot long enough to consider it a real home. But the mountains were as close as it came for him. He wanted to see the whole world, but nothing would replace Andalaya in his heart. Elliyar moved swiftly through the forest towards the horn and the battle he had left behind. He dreamed of home as he ran.

Chapter Two

"Do you have any more Source Water?" His uncle asked quietly yet urgently as Elliyar slipped out of the bushes and onto the aftermath of the raid. Dead men lay all around and it would not be long before the smell of death began to override the natural scent of the forest. Elliyar shook his head solemnly in response and tilted his head in question at his uncle's tone of worry. His uncle, Dacunda, caught his unspoken question and jerked his head toward his eldest son, Dahranian.

"Your cousin took a sword stroke to the thigh as he finished off his last man." Dacunda pursed his lips in frustration at the injury, then brightened somewhat as he continued. "It was the last of his four opponents." The concern at seeing his son wounded gave way to a pride only fathers experience when speaking of the feats of their children. Not for the first time Elliyar grimaced inwardly at the still gaping hole left in his life by the absence of his own father. He shoved the emotions down and ignored the pain.

Elliyar nodded seriously at Dacunda. "Dahranian has always been a great fighter, Uncle. Of that there is no question." His uncle nodded in unspoken agreement. They walked together towards Elliyar's eldest cousin, Dahranian. Ryder was looking over Rihya's shoulder as she tended the wound pointing out one thing or another, and Elliyar's sister was slapping Ryder's hands away.

"I don't need your help! I need space and room to work." Rihya tossed her green hair in frustration, her similarly emerald eyes flashing in anger. Dahranian wouldn't be the only one with a blade wound if Ryder didn't give Elliyar's sister some space. Rihya was quick with her knives. She wasn't stupid enough to do serious harm to a friend, but a nick here, a small jab there, and she could make her displeasure known to you.

Dahranian looked up grimacing. "Please brother, let her work in peace, I beg you." His low, clear voice was laced with pain. The wound he bore was deep enough to cause alarm. No wonder his uncle had been after him for some Source Water. It was a pity he had run out after the last raid. It was long past time they moved north to replenish their supplies and renew their vigor. One could not fight a never-ending war without the occasional respite.

Ryder huffed and stepped a few paces away, but before long he was back again, hovering over his brother and cousin, doing his best to be helpful and to not get in the way, but failing miserably at both. Rihya cleaned the wound with a wet piece of cloth torn from the tunic of a dead man lying on the ground not far away. She wiped away blood and did her best to wrap the wound. Dahranian moaned in agony as she cinched the makeshift bandage tightly around his leg.

"It will hold for a time," she said directing her speech at Dacunda, "but he needs rest and time to recover. And of course, a little Source Water would not be amiss," she muttered after the fact. Source Water was never amiss. It was a prized possession this far from Verdantihya.

Dacunda nodded solemnly. He was not a man given to many overt displays of emotion. When things went well, he rarely smiled. When circumstances were less than favorable, he wore the same stony face. It was his way.

"Fine," he said, "we move north a few hours tonight, just to get clear of this battle zone, then we rest until morning." Dacunda continued, "When morning comes, we push for the East Mayn and hopefully the river will be able to quell the worst effects of the wound. From there we'll move swiftly back into Legendwood."

Elliyar shook his head at his uncle. "There's no time, Uncle. We must push hard now." The four, older members of his family looked at him in question.

"This is no time for your arguments, Elliyar," Dacunda said with resignation in his voice, "your cousin needs the rest. This is the best course of action."

"No, you do not understand," Elliyar responded, his voice tinged with frustration. "There is no time."

Dacunda opened his mouth to retort forcefully, but Rihya put a staying hand on his arm.

"What do you mean, Ell?" She asked, bobbing her head forward and raising her eyebrows so that her face mimicked the verbal question with body language as well. Rihya always called him Ell instead of Elliyar. And to be completely honest, he was more comfortable with Ell as well. It just felt right. "Explain yourself," his sister flipped her hair behind one ear as she waited for his response.

Ell took a deep breath, and told his portion of the fight. The men he killed, the one who ran away, and his pursuit.

"Yes," his uncle said impatiently, "I saw you follow the cutter. I assume you dealt with him?" The query hung in the air for a moment before Ell was forced to respond.

are of shame was red hot as Ell was forced to explain how he scape. "He got away, and will most likely report this attack e could have a whole patrol on our trail, hounding us if we do nd now."

closed his eyes. Yes, he understood and was vexed that Ell had let the man escape. Take no prisoners and leave no man to carry tales. That was their attack motto. The only humans they spared were the slaves with collars. Collared slaves were the least trusted of all slaves, and would not fight to protect their human masters. But neither would they raise a hand against them. They did their best, typically, to melt into the forest surrounding a battle as quickly as they could. Most would eventually be retaken by their human masters. The slaves without collars however, would and could fight well. They had to be put down as soon as possible.

Ell spoke further, "That is not all, Uncle." He thought back to his confrontation with the southern elf, the Departed. He'd had a glazed look in his eyes, something akin to madness. "The human escaped because I was set upon by another."

His uncle looked at him sharply. "Go on, Elliyar."

Ell continued. "One of the Departed joined the fray."

"You killed him?" Dacunda interjected.

Ell responded. "He ambushed me from above and was almost more than I could handle. I killed him in the end, but it was a close ordeal. I was only just able to defeat him." Ell felt satisfaction at recalling the death of his enemy. If he felt bitterness at the teeming sea of humanity that occupied his land's eastern borders, he felt nothing but pure hatred for the plague of dark elves on its southern frontier. They were an infection that needed to be surgically removed from his people. Ell burned inwardly at their betrayal nigh on nineteen years ago now, though it had been before he was even born. Nevertheless, it had dictated the outcome of his life, the constant warfare and battles. The substance of his existence was a product of that betrayal and he would not lightly forget it.

His uncle was nodding in agreement now; he saw the truth of it. They had to move soon. If one Departed was near, the odds were good a whole band of them were also. They would move much more swiftly in pursuit than the humans would. Dahranian's injury was looking to be more of a hindrance by the moment.

"That is not all, Uncle," Ell was forced to continue. "After I killed the elf, the woodcutter was long gone. I piled up some sticks and I burned the body. With night having fallen, the fire will point almost directly to our location. We must move *now*." Ell emphasized his last word. It was imperative they move. Injury or not to his cousin, they could not stay here.

Four sets of eyes appraised him in the moonlight. His uncle, Dacunda, flicked a surprised glance at him when he recounted how he had burned the body. His uncle knew that his story made no sense. Lighting a beacon by burning the body was so far from the ordinary, normal circumstances, and was such a poor decision, that his uncle didn't even mention it yet. They would eventually speak of it, Ell knew, but for now Dacunda was content just to do what needed to be done. Later the questions would come. Ell was content to wait as well. He was still processing the events of the afternoon.

"You heard Elliyar," his uncle responded brusquely, "it's time to move. Son, can you make it?" He placed a hand on his son's shoulder. It was a rhetorical question. Dahranian had to be able to move. They all knew it.

Dahranian swallowed then nodded. He grimaced as he pushed himself to his feet. Twenty-three name days was more than old enough in this day and age to have dealt with an injury or two. In times of war, you did what needed to be done. Dahranian was nothing if not a good soldier.

They gathered up what few possessions they had, Ell making sure to retrieve his prized, black yew bow and quiver of Dreampine arrows from the tree in which he had started the ambush, and moved out. The pace was steady at first. They ran lightly, yet more slowly than they usually would, Dahranian's wound slowing them all down. There was one thing on which family could be depended on to do, and that was being there by your side through thick and thin. They would stick together, fight together, and if need be when the time came, die together. That was the life they led.

Breaks were short, only pausing long enough to sit for a moment on a soft, moss-covered rock, drink a gulp of water or a mouthful of food. They were the Highest, elves of the mountain strongholds and cool rivers, they were built to run and run they did, but that didn't mean they never tired. Of course, they could outrun a human company nine times out of ten, but even elves needed rest at times.

On one of these respites, Ell sat crouched down on the heels of his feet, back leaning against the bowl of an oak tree. He thought bleakly about the dire circumstances of his people and their endless struggle to survive. His face must have betrayed his bitterness at their plight, because his uncle approached and squatted next to him.

"You must not let the anger devour you, Nephew," his uncle said. Ell put on his most impassive face. If anyone had a right to be angry, it was he. Youngest in this group, Ell was often treated as impulsive or as having a loose rein on his emotions. But if one couldn't feel anger at the loss of their family then what merited anger? Surely a father, mother, and sister dead, and never known to him, were cause for resentment.

Dacunda continued. “I can see it on your face, Elliyar. You bury your hate so deep inside of you that I fear it will burn a hole in your heart.”

He shrugged off his uncle’s warning. “Shouldn’t I be angry, Uncle? They have taken everything from me.”

“Yes, you should be angry. Anger is a natural emotion,” his uncle paused, searching Ell’s eyes. “But you cannot let it consume you. Let it fuel you, yes. Let it spur you on in battle, always. Yet you cannot let it become your sole purpose in life.” He put his hand on Ell’s shoulder. “Anger is an untrustworthy guide, at best.”

“We do nothing, Uncle!” Ell finally let his rage from the last few months spill out in a low-voiced rant. “We kill woodcutters and raid wagons full of supplies for the humans. We kill scouts by the Pillars and then we run. Nothing comes of it!”

His uncle blinked slowly as if he understood but did not agree. However, Ell was now in full force and was not about to let his uncle get a word in until he was finished. The fire of anger burned in his belly, slow and steady. It was the one constant he had in life. Sometimes it raged fiery hot in the heat of battle, and at other times it sat cold, an icy fury in the pit of his stomach while he contemplated the future. Yet it was always there. Never ceasing, never ending.

“When, Uncle?” He raged as much as one could in a whisper. The three others were chatting amiably across the hollow where they had stopped. The hillside was awash with green grass and thickets. It was spring for certain here in the forest. “When will we fight a fight that matters? When will we strike a blow at their hearts? Either the humans or the Departed, I care not, so long as we do something important,” Ell continued as his uncle sat in silence listening. “We waste our strength and spill our blood,” Ell motioned to Dahranian as an example, “all for the sake of a few wagons of timber.”

His quiet tirade had almost run its course. He finished his thought. “This land is ours, Uncle, we are the Highest. It belongs to us.” Ell said the last words fiercely, possessively.

Now it was his uncle’s turn, and his generally calm exterior was now tinged with frustration. “You know little, boy.” His uncle punctuated that remark with a sigh of scarcely veiled contempt. “There are Ghouls spreading throughout *Legendwood*, when they hardly used to be found further south than the Broken Tree Range."

The wolves ravage with greater avarice and boldness than ever. There are even rumors of Icari flying by night and making their nests in the crags!” He shook his head at Ell, pain on his face and in his voice. “Darkness is spreading, such as I fear has not been seen since the First Days when the Highest initially began to win control of the land," Dacunda paused then stared straight at Ell. "This land is no longer under our dominion."

The words shook Ell to his core. The land had to be theirs. It had been for time immemorial. They, the Highest, had ruled the land. His people were fit to take dominion over it. They had ruled it, but always as a part of it, as one people joined to the land. They were part of the land, but the highest race, the *highest* in the land. Their history said they had tamed it, broken the unruly wild, and cast the darkness out to the furthest reaches and corners of the world.

Dacunda's gaze penetrated his eyes. Ell could see the look on his uncle's face. It was not a look of surrender. His uncle was not saying that the fight was over. He was simply trying to force a glimpse of reality upon Ell. Finally, Ell saw it, the truth. His people, the Highest, who were a once great race, had now been brought low. The land belonged to them only in their memories and hearts now. In reality, it was returning to the wild.

"You see it now, don't you Ell?" His uncle watched reality strike him. Pity flashed across Dacunda's face as he saw what he was taking away from Ell. A bleaker reality than ever before was now laid bare to his nephew.

Ell nodded. He did see. The land had grown unruly. The dominion his people had once possessed over the land was gone now, perhaps forever. A century of conflict would cause that to happen. The ruined and abandoned cities of his people had slowly been overtaken by the vines, creepers, and sprouts of an untamed wilderness until there was little left of their civilization but a memory.

"All is not lost, Elliyar," Dacunda spoke softly but purposefully. "You must never lose hope. Yet, one must see a situation from the view of reality before a true solution can be set in motion." His uncle forced him to meet his eyes. "You understand? This does not mean the battle is over, it just means that finally you see the war we are fighting in truth. You see it now."

Ell did see it, and in a way, he almost felt more hope now that he understood the depths of their struggle. It would be a long fight, but fight he would until his dying breath. The anger inside had not loosened its hold on him, yet he at least could look at life with a clearer head. For that, he was grateful.

The rest of his family was making their way over to them and Dacunda helped Ell to his feet with a firm, callused hand. His uncle's strength was surprising at times.

"Well," Ryder asked with a quirk of his mouth, "will we rest all night until Brother here bleeds out or shall we make our way onward, towards the East Mayn?" He was such a contradiction to his immediate family. Loud, where his father and brother were quiet, talkative and full of jests, where it was at times hard to pry a single word from either the laconic Dacunda or Dahranian.

"Onward," his father answered, with a hand on his son's shoulder in response. "North. Towards healing, and peace, and rest. I feel Verdantihya calling me deep within my soul." He placed a hand figuratively on his heart.

It was true, Ell thought. They had been long months away from the north and it was time to set their course homewards.

Chapter Three

They ran through the night and the morning of the next day, reaching the river East Mayn by midday. It was a good thing too because Dahranian was lagging. His wound had not been given time to heal in the push to get clear of the battle zone and gain some distance between themselves and any pursuit that might be following.

Dahranian emitted a groan of relief as he saw the river flowing ahead of them. Fortunately, for him, they had come upon a wide river bend with a large eddy created on the near shore of the river, the rapidly moving water sticking to the center and the far bank. The eddy sucked water in slowly, swirling sluggishly as it touched the near bank of the East Mayn, and Dahranian didn't even strip his clothes before toppling into the pool of water created by the eddy.

Even Rihya had begun to worry over the course of the morning as they had made their way north. Ell's sister was notorious for her lack of caution and her expectation that all would simply work itself out on her behalf. However, even her positively expectant outlook had wavered as they had pushed Dahranian to the point of exhaustion. The rest of them were tired. They had run slowly but steadily through the night and morning, with short breaks here and there, but never a real rest to sleep or rejuvenate their muscles. Ell's cousin, however, was on the brink of collapse. The wound was not mortal if treated right. It was deep, but they had stopped the initial bleeding and would tend to it again as soon as they were able. Yet, the bandage had grown red with blood, and the injury had begun to seep red tracks down his leg, staining his hose from the inside out, as they grew soaked with his blood.

Ell's cousin surfaced in the pool near the riverbank, and just floated face towards the heavens, letting the water minister to his wound as best it could. This far from the Source, it would not be able to do much beyond quench the flow of blood, and perhaps initiate the healing process, but that would likely be enough to turn the tide of the injury. The addition of a half-day's rest here might be enough to fix his cousin up properly until they made the push towards Verdantihya and the Source.

"Can you feel it, Son?" Dacunda queried Dahranian. "Is the pain ebbing?"

"Ever so slightly, Father," Dahranian responded letting out a sigh of relief. That was the beauty of being one of the Highest, of keeping to the oldest traditions of elves. They were bonded to the land, bonded to the Source. The Source was the heart of the land and it lay at the ancestral fortress of Verdantihya. Verdantihya was ruined now, but the Source still flowed pure and steady, strong enough to pump its ancient, healing power throughout the continent. Rivers in the north, in Andalaya, all had one common and powerful spring. The Source. The Mayn River which flowed strongest out of Verdantihya coursed its way due south, while the East Mayn, second in might, flowed east until it met the great sea called the Fracture. The Westrill and the Northrill, smaller in size, flowed in their respective directions, while the Skullit snuck off to the northeast, slow and small, creeping its way through the mossy barrows and moors until it met the far north coast of the Fracture just south of Hope's End. But they all began at Verdantihya; they all started at the Source.

The Source's ability to help heal those of the Highest was most powerful at its place of origin, and water carried directly from the Source in gourds or water skins lost none of its potency no matter how far you bore the water. Even the rivers could provide a slight healing touch if they flowed with enough volume. Not enough to cure a sickness, or completely heal a wound as deep as the one Dahranian had suffered, but enough to sustain a person until they could heal on their own or until one could make the journey to the Source itself. Even sending someone with a water skin to fill with the liquid and bring back to you was not uncommon if the injury made it difficult to walk. The Source could not heal all, no, nor did it give one everlasting life, but it could take care of the minor to moderate injuries one accumulated in life, let alone war. It would also give you a fighting chance to survive those few wounds that were severe, even mortal in nature.

Dahranian continued soaking, and they left him to his rest. The day was growing warm with springtime sunlight, and they sat on rocks to eat their midday meal.

"We will rest here, until nightfall," Ell's uncle proclaimed, "then we'll push on through the night again. With Dahranian soaking up what he can in order to heal, and an afternoon of rest, he should be able to be re-bandaged and ready to move more quickly by the time night comes. The trace amounts of Source diluted through the river should be enough to quicken his mending process, even this far from the Source."

They all nodded their agreement. It was still not ideal. The wound would not be healed and Dahranian would surely not be at full health, but the edge would be taken off the injury. Hopefully. There were no guarantees. Yet,

Dahranian was strong—he could endure. Besides, they could not afford to rest forever. They had no way of knowing whether the enemy had decided to follow them. They had left a trail clear enough for any of the Departed to be able to track. Unlike the Highest, the southern elves were not at home in the woods and the wild. The dark elves were more accustomed to their city and the surrounding ports. They were more at home on the deck of a ship than on a mountain slope. Yet, they could be counted on to track better than the humans. It would not be wise to assume they were not following. *A cautious elf was a live elf*, Dacunda always said.

They stripped off their long-sleeved, hooded tunics, of dark browns, greens, and blacks, revealing only their under-tunics. It felt amazing to let the warm sun bathe their pale skin after a long winter of fighting and raiding throughout the Lower Forest and the eastern shore. Ell hadn't realized how tired he was. He lay on his back with his eyes closed, and let his mind wander. The war was always the focus of his mind; his desire for revenge on the invaders was always forefront. The anger inside of him, of which his uncle had spoken the previous night, never left. He supposed it never would so long as there was a battle to be fought. The matters of the war occupied most of his thoughts. Yet in a tiny portion of his mind, he allowed himself to dream. On occasion, he would imagine what it would be like if the war was over and Andalaya was restored to her former state of peace and glory. Ell was glad to be moving north, towards the heart of his homeland, yet a tiny voice inside of him cried out to explore the world. He dreamed idly of what the south might be like. He would enjoy seeing it, although that did not seem likely to happen. He had never left the north. Sure, he had raided clear to the coastal waters of the Fracture, and been as far south as the North Tributary in the Lower Forest, but that was it.

It must be a sight to see the ruined walls of Akan Deraiya on the south east coast, broken and crumbling now during the conflict of the last few centuries between his people and the Departed. It had been a city fabled for its gleaming walls of white marble and polished white shells embedded in the rock of its citadels and palaces. A city of knowledge, his uncle had called it, before the Conflicts had swallowed it whole. *That would be a sight to see*. Or perhaps the remains of Riora along the Mayn River south of the forest, a tower it was said had reached the heavens before war and a decaying civilization had caused its downfall. Ell pondered the history of his people and the Departed. Theirs was truly a story of a race splintered by differences. Torn asunder by the departure of half of their people centuries ago, they had never recovered, and it appeared as if they never would. Conflict after conflict, skirmishes and wars, until the protectors of the land, those who held dominion over it, had lost and destroyed nearly all of their glorious achievements.

There had remained only two of the last, great, elven strongholds when the human invaders had arrived two decades ago, the rest were sacked and destroyed, ravaged by war between the two races of elves. Only Verdantihya and Dor Khabor in the south had stood. *Now even Verdantihya is gone*, Ell thought bitterly and not for the first time. It had been left to defend itself against an invading army of supremely superior numbers and sophisticated weaponry. It had fallen, abandoned, betrayed by the south in its moment of greatest need, while its southern counterpart had struck a deal with the darkness. The south had plunged itself into perversion and shadow to such a degree that it was arguably darker now than the invaders. Dor Khabor, or Dark Harbor as many called it now, had built itself an extremely unsavory reputation in recent decades. Darkness had been embodied there, and the great port city of the elves had adopted the darkness into its name.

A voice snapped Ell out of his historical musings. "Nephew. We need to talk."

Ell sat up and looked at his uncle's lean face, weathered by war, and wind, and age. He nodded to Dacunda. So the questions would now come. He was surprised his uncle had waited so long, all things considered. Well, his uncle had always been a patient person, so Ell supposed it might not be so surprising after all.

"Why did you burn the body of the Departed, Elliyar?" Straight and to the point. Dacunda was nothing if not blunt.

Ell looked at him and responded. "He was a strange one, Uncle. Not like many we have seen before. Oh, in appearance he was similar," Ell said in response to his uncle's narrowing eyes and tilted head in question. "But it was his eyes, there was a madness there I cannot describe, a..." Ell paused searching for the right word, "vacantness, which was then replaced by a delight in battle I have never seen before."

Dacunda nodded slowly as if trying to understand pieces of a puzzle. "I see." It was clear from his uncle's voice that in actuality he did not see and was still confused.

Ell went on. "There was also a look of sickness upon him, I believe." He shook his head at the memory. "I was not certain it was a plague but I burned the body just in case." Ell made no mention of the brief instant in which the diseased body had appeared normal again. He was not even convinced it had happened, and he would not burden his uncle with the worry that his nephew might be confused and not thinking clearly.

"What kind of sickness? If he was ill, shouldn't he have been easy to defeat in his weakness?" Dacunda had a strange look on his face now, as if his lack of understanding had been replaced by the idea of something else—something of which Ell had no knowledge or understanding. The information about the disease had shifted something in his uncle's thoughts. *What was his uncle not telling him?*

Ell answered the question. "No, in fact he was stronger than many of the Departed I have faced. He fought differently, but well. He was almost more than I could handle." That was a meaningful statement since Ell had been raised in battle. He had grown up with a knife at his side and a bow in his hands. He could fight and kill with the best of them, even at his young age, hardly past his eighteenth name day.

His uncle was now squatting down beside Ell. "It couldn't be, could it? But those winds… maybe." Dacunda appeared to be talking to himself now, engaging in some sort of inner debate.

"The Bonewinds." Ell spoke softly.

Dacunda turned his head in surprise; almost as if he was unaware he had spoken aloud to himself. He eyed Ell sideways, as if appraising Ell in a different light. Ell had always been quick of thought and had a good memory. His uncle should know that he was not flighty like his sister or his cousin Ryder. Ell paid attention to details, to sounds in the air, and scents on the wind. It was not that they didn't, simply that Ell took it a step further. His uncle should know that about him. It was a measure of his worry that he was caught off guard by Ell's understanding of what he was talking about to himself.

Dacunda didn't answer Ell. Instead, he simply put on his normal, impassive face, thanked Ell for the information, stood up, and walked over to sit on a rock nearby to think in quiet.

Ell was frustrated. Clearly, something was happening. Something deeper than a dead Departed, but Dacunda was withholding information. Ell hated being kept in the dark.

Ell shoved aside his frustration. When his uncle didn't want to talk, nothing could get him to speak. Ell would be getting no information until Dacunda was good and ready to share. Instead, he rolled over and dragged himself lazily to the riverbank. His cousin was still floating and drifting slightly in the pool, willing his body and wound to soak up as much healing powers and refreshment as possible. He would know when his body was ready to leave the water.

The wind rippled the grass where Ell lay and he gazed into the pool at his own reflection. Pale, thin, fine features looked back up at him. Pointed ears decorated the sides of his head, while golden-blond hair framed his face. His hair was lighter in color than the hair of his cousins and uncle. It was also shorter. Their hair was light brown and braided down their backs, while Ell's hair fell loosely to just about his shoulders. It hung forward now, however, as he leaned over the edge of the bank, looking at himself in nature's rippling mirror. Sometimes he would fasten his hair loosely with a rawhide tie, near the nape of his neck, but often as not, even in the heat of battle his hair would hang free and wild. His hair was not nearly so straight and fine as the hair of most elves either. Both he and his sister's hair had just the slightest ripple of wave in it. Blues eyes stared back at him.

A splash made Ell shift his gaze from his reflection to see Dahranian slogging his way through the shallow water towards the riverbank. As he stepped out of the water and onto the shore, he already looked stronger. The color had returned to his face and he smiled a small smile at Ell, to which Ell nodded back. He was glad that his cousin was feeling better. His wound would still need to be redressed but any one of his family members could see to it. They were all versed in battle medicine. You had to be if you lived in a state of constant war.

"Good as new," Dahranian said to Ell. "Well, almost," he amended. They all knew that a soak in the East Mayn wasn't going to be enough to heal his wound, but it would take the edge off of it, and allow him to bandage it up properly and push onwards with pace.

"Glad to see that," Ell responded amiably. "I was beginning to wonder if a little nick like that was going to be the end of you." Ell said it with a straight face, but his cousin knew he was jesting. Dahranian gave a little laugh, more of an exhalation than anything else and then walked back towards the others. He was still grimacing slightly as he walked, the pain had obviously not left completely, but it had lessened. Ell could tell the pain had reduced in intensity because his cousin was able to move more freely.

Ryder, Ell's other cousin, whistled softly and pointed to the horizon. Tendrils of wispy smoke were trailing above the top of the tree line to the south. Fire. Ell was instantly on guard as were the rest of his family. The Departed he had killed and then set on fire would not be able to give off enough smoke to be seen from here. Ell doubted it was even still burning by this point. This was something else.

"Departed?" Ryder asked his father.

Dacunda shook his head for lack of information. "No way to tell from here. A fire's a fire, whoever made it." However, Ell could see the strain of worry etched onto his face. The wisps of smoke could indicate that they were being pursued. A company of Departed following them would be no laughing matter. The Departed usually travelled in bands of ten to twenty, easily double the size of Ell and his family, if not even more. The odds would be far from in their favor should a confrontation arise. Besides, Departed were much harder to lose in the wild than the human soldiers. Even though they could not match the skills of the Highest, they were still elves, and elves could track. It was in their blood.

Dahranian approached his father. "Do we leave now?" he asked seriously.

"No." Dacunda answered after pausing a moment to think. "You still need rest. We can't push that injury of yours too far. Even with whatever healing you may have been able to extract from the river, your wound is still not even close to fully healed. If we push you too hard it may grow rank and give you a fever. Then we would be worse off than we are now."

Rihya nodded her agreement. She thought of herself as the designated medic in the family, even though her knowledge of medicine was really no greater than the rest of them. Less than Dacunda's understanding, actually, if Ell were being completely honest.

"Yes," she said, "besides, for all we know it could be another party of cutters or human soldiers. They'd be nothing for us to fear." Her statement tinged slightly on the side of bravado, but Ell was forced to agree, it would be much less worrisome if humans were following rather than Departed.

Dacunda held up a hand for quiet. "We rest the afternoon as planned, then push on at dark." Darkness would cover their trail if they truly were being followed.

Everyone sat back down to make the most of the time of rest after it had been established that rest they would, and Ryder began jesting and telling stories that were much too wild to be true. He was a joker if nothing else. The whole time he sat, he spun and twirled his hand-axe about in a careless manner. To the untrained eye, it would look foolhardy, spinning the weapon about his fingers with such reckless abandon. But the bystander would not know that Ryder had some of the quickest hands of anybody Ell had ever seen. His fingers were as safe from that axe as a babe in its mother's arms.

The rest of them listened or ignored him. However, they talked and ate some of the berries and nuts they had gathered. It would have been a rare moment of peace in the midst of war, if Ell could have shaken that smoke from his mind. If they were being followed, he itched to go. It would not do to be attacked on ground not of their own choosing. Yet he understood. Dahranian still needed the rest. As much as his cousin was strong and hid the pain well, Ell could see that his soak in the river had not done enough for him should they be forced into a fight. He needed the Source.

As the afternoon light dwindled, they readied themselves to leave. Hooded tunics were donned, and packs shouldered once again. Finally, with everyone gathered and ready, Dacunda spoke. "We head back towards Verdantihya. Dahranian needs the Source, that much is clear," he shared a look with his son who agreed.

"And after?" Rihya was always the inquisitive one.

Dacunda glanced briefly at Ell before he answered, as if his response had something to do with him. "After? Well, we shall see. I believe there is someone with whom I must speak." Again, his eyes flicked to Ell's face and back. The look was so quick it could be missed, but Ell was observant. Something in Ell's story earlier had shaken his uncle. "He can be… hard to find." The way he spoke of this mysterious person made Ell want to find out just exactly who it was, and why he needed to speak with him, but Ell waited. The questions would be asked for him.

Sure enough, Rihya obliged. "What are you talking about, Uncle?" she asked in exasperation. She had no patience and little tolerance for secrets and mysteries.

His uncle dodged being forced to divulge whatever it was he was hiding yet again. "Enough talk. We move. That smoke is gone, which means whoever made the fire is moving. Whether in our direction, I know not. But I do not care to find out. We are not all fit to fight."

Dacunda gave a quick glance at everyone, checking to make sure they were all prepared, and then he set off northwest. Rihya huffed in frustration but followed along, trailed by Ryder, then Dahranian with Ell bringing up the rear. Their trek continued.

They ran steadily for days, entering Legendwood not long after choosing a more westerly course rather than north, after their stop by the river. Legendwood was a forest that started at the base of the mountains but the heart of it was in the mountains themselves. The Lower Forest stretched for leagues south of the mountains and was comprised mostly of oak trees with their spreading, low-lying limbs, as well as birch and beech trees, elms and hawthorns. Legendwood was made up mostly of higher altitude trees. Of course, there was a blend of both where the two forests met, or in the deep valleys within the heart of Andalaya. But on the mountain slopes of Legendwood, one found all types of pine, fir, cedar, and aspen trees.

The part of Legendwood in which they traveled at the moment was a mixture. The lowland trees blended nicely into the foothills of the mountains. Cedar sat next to oaks and aspens. It was a pleasant mix, and the sunlight dappled the ground at their feet as it shone through the leaves above them.

One could almost forget that the world was at war, a violent place in the clear, spring air. However, Dacunda pushed them with an urgency that Ell was beginning to suspect had to do with more than just his son's need for the Source. There was definitely something else afoot that Dacunda did not wish to share. The others seemed to sense it as well. Everyone's manner was sharp and tense. Eyes watched all sides of the path for any sign of danger. They followed the East Mayn toward its source at Verdantihya, their path running low along the bank then climbing high onto cliffs at times. In forgotten times, elves would have used those cliffs for pleasure, jumping to the river below simply for the exhilaration of the fall. Today elves fought and died on a regular basis. They got enough of a blood rush from battle, and they did not need those types of activities to fulfill a need for excitement. Besides, the Highest lived nomadically now that Verdantihya had fallen almost nineteen years ago. Small bands of the Highest roved the land, and few lived in this southeast region of Andalaya, so close to the watchful eye of the enemy camps.

One day they paused for a quick midday meal next to the river. It was a spot not unlike where Dahranian had soaked a few days earlier. The only difference was that the river raged fast and strong here with no eddy to create a pool. If you went into the river here, you needed to be a strong swimmer else the current could sweep you away.

Ell stood near a cluster of trees particularly close together, grabbing a moment alone away from his family who sat across a small opening in the forest. He studied the water and frothing surface as it rushed down from the mountains and to the plains below. They were in the foothills here. Every so often, they came upon an opening in the trees and the view would stretch out over eastern plains behind them. If the day was particularly clear, one could sometimes see the human Camps. Places of pain and slavery, where his race and the human slaves, were forced to toil for cruel masters.

A prickling sensation grew on the back of his neck. He could not place the feeling. Suddenly, and without fully realizing why, he spun and drew his long dueling dagger in one fluid motion. His instincts did not betray him, as not a few inches from where his face now looked, a spindly, bony-fingered hand reached toward him from behind the tree next to which he had been standing. The hand had sticky pads on it and small suction cups to grasp its prey tightly, and many tiny stingers along its palm and the insides of its fingers. *Ghoul*! In the motion of his turn and draw, he also slashed at the hand stretching towards him, heard a satisfying screech of pain, and saw black ooze decorating his blade. Black blood. Evil blood. In a flash, the creature leaped from behind the tree. It was tall and skinny, skeletal almost. Its skin seemed to changed colors in whatever light in which it stood. First light green against the bushes, then brown for the tree trunk, then as it plunged rapidly into the water; it became a bluish grey and vanished downstream into the rapids.

Opportunistic hunters, Ghouls rarely stayed to fight if they could help it. They could be cowardly but they were also deadly. The stingers on their fingers released a fatal toxin. The poison leaked into your blood rather quickly it was said, and death followed soon after, either by the poison or by the Ghouls teeth as it attacked its prey. Once they grasped you with their cold fingers, all hope of survival was lost unless you had a large amount of Source Water with you, which at the moment Ell did not. Ghouls were a solitary race, not often wandering south of the northern marches. Stories said that for centuries you could hardly find them even there. But his uncle was correct, darkness and evil were spreading once again across the land. Ghouls in Legendwood had been unheard of not long ago. Apparently, that was no longer true. Dark creatures and shadowy swathes of terrain were returning like they had in the First Days. They punctuated the land, like the blemishes of youth resurfacing as pockmarks on a once beautiful, but now aged face.

Rihya, Dacunda, and his cousins heard the screech of pain from the Ghoul just before it bounded agilely into the river and disappeared. They came over quickly, weapons in hand, ready to defend themselves against whatever danger might be present.

"Ghoul," Ell said to answer their unspoken question.

"Here in Legendwood?" Rihya responded incredulously. Ell shared a look with his uncle. Their conversation the night after the raid was ringing true. The land no longer belonged fully to the Highest.

Ell didn't say anything. Rihya wasn't questioning him; she was simply voicing her surprise. He bent down and wiped his dueling dagger clean. Black blood could pit steel if left upon it without being cleaned after its use. He would not have one of his father's old dueling daggers ruined by the blood of a cursed Ghoul, that much was certain. He had inherited the dagger and he intended to keep it in good condition. It was his most prized possession.

Ell seethed with fury. He hated Ghouls. They fed on anything, even each other, glorifying in the pain and suffering of others. He wished he had managed to kill it. The crafty thing had been quick, leaping away to its escape before anyone could follow.

It seemed a plague of things evoked Ell's anger these days, such as the Departed in their southern cities, sending their slaver parties north into Andalaya to capture his people. The humans also, their sweat and death camps to the east; they came to his land for no other reason than to enslave. Now this incident—dark creatures inhabiting his fair Legendwood. It felt like almost too much to bear.

"Channel your anger, Elliyar," Dacunda said softly, seeming to read his thoughts as the others walked back to their packs. His uncle's reminder seemed to help. This time. Sometimes it infuriated Ell, but this time it helped to stem the flow of hot emotions welling up within him. *Channel it. Focus on what is at hand.* He finished cleaning his blade and then placed it back in the sheath strapped to the outside of his right thigh. The dueling dagger was longer than his forearm so it fit perfectly on his thigh. He would channel his emotions. He would shove them aside for now so that they did not swallow him, but he would bring them with him to the next fight. Of that much he was certain. He even found himself looking forward to it more than usual. It would be good to focus his anger on something useful, like killing his enemies, rather than letting it smother him.

Chapter Four

Verdantihya was a tapestry of nature and architecture woven together. It was abandoned and ruined, but it was fabulous. If Ell knew of any structure that could be referred to as art, Verdantihya was it. Ell and his family approached the most ancient stronghold of the elves from the narrow valley leading up to its shattered, front gate. Not that long ago, those massive doors had stood strong and firm, letting all beware of attacking its beautiful walls. The passage of two decades could change much.

They covered the remaining ground to Verdantihya rather quickly, pushing as hard as Dahranian's slowly recovering leg would allow. The tension was palpable. Between the escaped cutter, the smoke to the south at the start of their journey, and the most recent attack on Ell by a Ghoul three days prior, everyone was on edge. They ran hard without ever really acknowledging the reason why. They all just felt the need to cover ground and cover it quickly. Now that their journey appeared to be at an end, some of the tightness began to seep from Ell's shoulders and he imagined the same thing was happening with the others. He saw his uncle and Dahranian share a quiet laugh for the first time in days, while his sister giggled slightly when a butterfly lit upon her hand. Rihya had always had a soft spot for animals, but she took it even a step farther than most elves.

The Highest were born of the land and they treated the land with respect. There was no questioning that in comparison to their southern cousins or the human invaders, they might seem to have a kinship with nature. Animals seemed to fear them less and this contributed to that appearance. Also, the elves possessed an ability to move swiftly and silently where others could not, almost as if the land itself shifted around their feet to provide safe and silent passage. Ell did not know whether it was myth or legend, but he knew it was true; he could move quietly in the woods like no Departed ever could. His sister took things to the extreme however, as she often did. She would cut him quickly enough with a knife if he irked her without thinking twice, yet if you stepped on even an insect by accident, she would give you the rough side of her tongue. You were lucky if that was indeed all she gave you. Ell rolled his shoulders at the thought of all the pokes and prods he had received at the point of her knives. She loved him, loved them all, but it was her way. She solved conflict as quickly with her weapons as with words.

The valley was long and narrow, a perfect funnel to defend oneself from an attacking army. Hails of arrows would fall upon the foe before they could ever even reach the gates of Verdantihya. And if they finally did, they would already have been too bloodied and spent to breach the iron-enforced, oak door. *A pity one moment of betrayal could counter all of those defenses* Ell thought painfully. If there was one elf that could be held responsible for the fall of Verdantihya, it was the Traitor. That was how Ell thought of him; it was the only name he could bring himself to give to such a despicable person.

The lush, green valley began to rise and slope upward as they walked closer to their destination. A river flowed slowly yet steadily. It cut through the center of the valley before disappearing around a bend and out of sight. It would diverge into five separate flows, surging out of the high mountains with surety and grace, as they became the five major rivers of the north. Verdantihya sprung forth from the sheer cliff at its back and was aptly named for the mountainside upon which it perched. It was a monolith of a stronghold, a blend of rock, stone, and mountain.

It was a mosaic of perfectly fitted stones, moss, and ivy combining to form what looked like nature incarnate. A fortress pulled forth from the land itself, almost as if it had grown upwards like a living organism. It was hard to see where the back of the city became the mountain, and where the walls truly met the ground. Verdantihya was the place of origin for all elves, and as such, it held a mystical quality, a special presence. It was where creation had given birth to the Highest. As such, the lines where creation ended and elf-made structure began were blurry.

Ell breathed in deeply and filled his lungs with pure mountain air. This was what he had been missing in the south and east. There was nothing like the crispness of the air as it swirled from the snow-tipped mountaintops and blew down and out in all directions.

"The eager traveler enjoys his homecoming, I see," Ryder commented with a wink and a grin as he watched Ell kiss the tips of his fingers on both hands together then show them palm outwards in a sweeping motion to the land around him. It was the traditional greeting of one of the Highest to his homeland when an elf returned from afar.

Ell finished the tiny ceremony then curved his lips into a small smile in response to his cousin's jest. "Yes," he responded simply. Ell did not tell many jokes, therefore he was never entirely sure of what kind of response to give one. So he just smiled so as not to offend his witty cousin. It was true. As much as he longed to see the world, and often shared that desire with his family around the fire at night, there was something about Andalaya and the area surrounding Verdantihya, in particular, which always set his pulse racing and his blood singing. He couldn't explain it.

Ryder nodded his agreement, and said rather seriously for him, "Me too, Ell, me too. It has been long months in the Lower Forest for us." He rubbed his hand through his abnormally unbraided hair. He must have taken out the braids last night after Ell fell asleep. "Too long away."

They were almost at the walls now, walking steadily in a restful, refreshing way after so many days running. The river flowed outward through the broken gates of Verdantihya. It had always done so. Once the river had flowed carefully from underneath the great wooden doors, regulated by the reservoir that had contained the Source. Now the stout gates lay many feet from the grandly arched entryway as if flung by a giant hand to fall wherever they may. It was a sad sight. It pained Ell to see such a great city brought so low, even though he had not even been born yet when it had fallen. He had been born a year or so later.

Ell and his family were close enough now to see what was difficult to make out from far away. There were pits and chunks gouged from the walls, made by the war machines of the humans. Some of the destruction had been done to the city after the people had fled. After the city had fallen. But much of it had come during battle, as the man-made contraptions cast boulders in high arcs to crash into the fabled walls of the last, great city of the northern elves. Fires and explosions had singed and pocked the wall from end to end. Ultimately, it had taken cunning and deception from within to bring Verdantihya low, not brute strength. But the walls were a ready reminder of what the humans could do when they moved en masse. They were strong in the strength of their numbers, like a horde of locusts or a hive of some terrible insect.

"I sometimes wonder if your parents knew the future, Ell." Ell looked at his uncle in confusion. What was he talking about?

His uncle elaborated. "Centuries of conflict and struggle with our southern neighbors, the Departed, had led to a general lessening of both our lands. Civilization was waning. Historical records, knowledge, and understanding were lost, as centers of learning such as Riora and Castan Yol were crushed by battle, sacked like the Water Palaces of our western shore." He looked at Ell. "Yet nothing foretold the end of Verdantihya."

"What are you trying to say, Uncle?"

"You know the meaning of your name, Elliyar? It means Dusk Runner in the old tongue. Somehow you were born and your parents knew to give you the name that spoke of the twilight of our people." Dacunda shook his head as if he still didn't understand why or how they had known to name their son such an ominous name. Ell rolled his shoulders uncomfortably. He knew the meaning of his name; he just preferred not to think of it in regards to the Highest. *Couldn't it be something else linked to dusk*, he thought wistfully. Why did Dacunda have to reference the symbolism of his name as the end of hope for his people? They were not necessarily connected after all. If only he could ask his parents why they had named him Elliyar.

His uncle saw that he did not wish to speak more of it and let the matter drop. They all prepared to cross the threshold into Verdantihya proper but instead they paused. Dacunda held up for a moment as he gazed upwards towards the parapet of the monolithic, ruined walls.

"I remember loosing shaft after shaft of golden, silver, and pure white arrows from my quiver as we defended ourselves." The voice of Ell's uncle dropped low until it almost carried a storytelling quality. "Though I was only a few years beyond my day of Re-naming, I was still called upon to defend my home." There was a pride in Dacunda's voice that Ell did not often hear. His uncle was a humble man, confident yes, but never one to bring attention to his feats. Yet Ell could understand the pride he must feel at telling how he had fought the enemy from the greatest walls that had ever existed. Ell would never be able to say the same. Andalaya was no more. Her people scattered to the four winds, enslaved and hounded. Broken. The familiar bitterness rose up in Ell's throat, so real he could almost taste its bile.

Dacunda raised his arm and drew back an imaginary bowstring. They were all silent as they watched him relive his memories. Respect showed on Dahranian's face as he listened to his father. Ryder showed a glee at the tale, as if wishing he had been there. Ell's sister just looked thoughtful. He wondered what she thought of it all, what she thought of the reality in which they lived.

"I drew and loosed, drew and loosed, alongside the rain of arrows coming from around me from atop our walls. They cut the enemy in great swathes, felling them like a scythe to wheat during the harvest moon, yet it had no discernible effect. They threw an endless sea of humanity upon the stones of Verdantihya and eventually it crumbled." Dacunda continued, lost in a faraway time. "Your father, Ell, Rihya, was my commander at the time." He paused to remember.

"So you've told us before, Uncle," Rihya said as she leaned forward unconsciously, waiting for more of the story. Their uncle did have a way with words when he so desired.

Dacunda nodded, "Yes, I have." He made no apology for the repetition. This was a story he was not ashamed to tell, time and again. "The sun glinted off our burnished breastplates." Dacunda sighed. He directed a regretful look at them, the younger generation. "There was a time when we didn't fight from the shadows. A time when our mail and armor was white, gold, and shining silver in the light. We fought in the sun—in the light—and the light reflected the brilliance of our weapons. Our enemies feared us."

Ell tried to imagine what that would be like. He had fought from the shadows all his life. They used their Dreampine and black yew for arrows and bows now, wood that had once only been reserved for assassins who needed the cover of the dark. They fought with black shafts for arrows and dark hafts on their spears and axes now. *Dark arrows*. The thought flew involuntarily across Ell's mind. But it was true. Dark arrows indeed were theirs now, and it was time he began to own that reality. While listening to his uncle, he realized that there had been a time for brightness and the brilliance of his people's warriors. That time was not now.

His uncle began to wrap up his tale of how the city had stood strong and tall, proud in the face of their valley being awash with enemies. He spoke of Ell's father and how they had fought side-by-side, repelling attack after attack until it seemed for certain that their foes would never break the walls of Verdantihya. Then came the betrayal. That viper of an elf, no longer fit to call himself one of the Highest. It pained Ell to hear this part of the story told.

"He had been discovered as a traitor and chained in a dungeon with one hand manacled to the wall," Dacunda retold the fateful tale, a story that all throughout Andalaya knew only too well. "The battle raged outside, yet with cunning and trickery he lured a guard near, bested him with his free hand and took his weapon. However, the guard had no key, and so the Traitor lopped of his own hand in order to escape."

Ell seethed inside, his anger bubbling up hot as the history of his people's demise could be traced back to one traitor of an elf. *Silverfist, that snake*!

If there ever was one to hate it was he. Ell clenched his teeth as he thought of the elf who was responsible for the capture of so many of his own people. Ell tasted a coppery flavor, and realized he had bitten down on his cheek as he had clenched his teeth. He spit the tiny flow of blood and saliva from his mouth, a fitting end to that train of thought, he supposed.

His uncle finished the story. "Silverfist, the traitor, the great betrayer, made his way silently to the heart of our castle. He reached the Source, and plunged his wounded stump of a hand directly into its pure, life-giving water."

"It healed him," Dahranian grunted the obvious, possibly thinking of his own wound that was soon to be taken care of in the same manner.

"Yes," Dacunda nodded as if that had been a valid question or statement, Ell was not sure which one it was. "Yes, it healed him as the Source will do, so potent and powerful at its concentrated place of origin. The spring now flows into a river and floods out of the broken gates of Verdantihya, right at our very feet," Ell's uncle looked down at the water rushing past them.

"Silverfist opened the reservoir that we had built to stem and control the steady flow of water from the spring of life, the Source. We regulated it carefully as it rushed down from the highest point of our city." Dacunda grimaced in pain now—emotional agony at the difficulty of finishing his recounting of the tragedy of their people. "The Source raged forward, all the dammed water rushing through its canal and met the inside of our strong gates with a force that I have never seen matched. It burst the gates from within and the doors lay now exactly as they did then. Untouched, a memorial to our final battle."

Dacunda paused to gather his emotions. "It was all an effort to gain time from that point on wasn't it, Uncle?" Rihya looked shaken, even though she must have heard the story countless times. Ell supposed it had that effect on a person.

His uncle nodded in affirmation. "Once the gates were breached, we knew the battle was lost. There were too many foes outside our walls. It was a losing effort and we knew it, yet we fought on as long as possible to buy as much time as we could for the civilians to flee." He passed a hand over his eyes in sorrow. "I cannot say how many of the Highest died that day, all I can say is that I have never seen a slaughter of its like. Our people have never recovered from it. The number of dead was simply too great for us to rebound." Then it was done. Dacunda's mouth closed and Ell could see he would say no more at this moment.

It was all due to Silverfist. First, the traitor had brought false tidings of an alliance against the humans, a treaty with the Departed. Silverfist had been the elected ambassador for the Highest. It had been the first time in centuries that there had been hope of a true peace and alliance between the two races of elves. It had all been a ruse. No help from the south was coming. Silverfist had carried his false tidings and the defenders of Verdantihya had prepared to meet the human assault confident that aid was arriving from their cousins to the south. They had discovered the truth of Silverfist's lies too late to evacuate the city. It had been too late to do anything but imprison the traitor for a later trial and prepare to fight. And pray. Such a painful tale. It was a terrible story to have to remember. Yet each and every elf of the Highest, who wandered nomadically throughout Andalaya, carried it always close to his heart and mind. They carried the bitter truth that the humans had invaded simply to conquer. They had come to claim land, wealth, resources, and most of all, to secure more slaves to fuel the insatiable need of their society for forced laborers.

Ell and his family walked into the wounded fortress, its gate open like a maw of some giant animal gaping in the pain of torture. His uncle's story was sobering. There was no easy way to recover one's joy from a recounting of such death and destruction. They strode inwards and upwards as the abandoned city thrust out from where the land met the mountain. The backside of the city was actually built against the mountainside, using the mountain as an enormous wall that overshadowed everything. The city itself was a blend of nature and civilization. It was as if the forest had half grown into the city. This was not a product of its abandonment. No, it had always been like that, such was the bond between the Highest and the land—forest and city, nature and people, overlapping in a way unlike any other place on earth. Trees grew out of walls, and bushes from between stones. Ferns dotted the banks of the Source as it flowed in its canal from its place of origin. But buildings still stood upright and strong, some clean as the day they were built, others fractured and fragmented. Ivy and vines curled around corners and over whatever rooftops were still in place. It was gorgeous in a heart wrenching way, a melancholy beauty, the way a familiar gravesite is a painful reminder yet important memory to the living.

Up to the top of the city they walked. The cobblestones of the street were still intact and climbing the path was easy. They made their way through the ruins, stopping to look around here and there. They had all seen this before, but there was a draw, a *rightness* about Verdantihya, and it felt good to return. Even Dahranian seemed to grow invigorated as they neared the summit of the hill at the height of the city. His body seemed to know that the ordeal of the past week was at an end. His pain was near to ceasing and the hitch in his step, the limp with which he had moved over the past few days was beginning to fade, almost as if his body and mind were loosening subconsciously in anticipation of the coming relief from the pain.

Verdantihya was a large city, and the roads were not straight and orderly. Instead, they zigzagged in different directions, a rabbit's warren of fern-lined streets and ivy-covered squares. Trees often grew out of the stones and a passerby who knew nothing of the history of Verdantihya might have thought that the city was being overrun by nature. But it wasn't. It had always been that way. It was the strange blending of land and city that Ell had only ever seen here in Verdantihya. Even the other great elven cities of old had never had the same naturalized aesthetics. The Source flowed constantly by them and occasionally branched off into tiny streams. In turn, those streams often created small pools or miniature cascading waterfalls over roofs of lower, squatter buildings or over stairs before finding their way back toward the main flow again and out of the shattered gates.

Ell and his family finally reached the end of their climb. A huge domed building lay in front of them. From a water gateway in the wall, half the distance beneath its large, arched doorway to the street below, the Source water flowed. There was a drop of about one hundred feet from the mouth of the door, where the dome began, all the way down the face of the building to the street upon which they stood. Stairs led from the street, where Ell and his family were, to the mouth of the dome. Halfway up the side of the wall the large water gateway opened its maw. The Source Water poured through the gateway in a mossy waterfall sparkling in the sunlight as it rushed down to the canal that did its best to corral the water on its way down through the city.

They climbed the steps to reach the mouth of the raised dome and Ell turned to look out over Verdantihya and the valley surrounding. It was stunning. Even to the eyes of one who had seen it all before. Snowy peaks herded valleys to and fro like shepherds with their flocks. The valley stretched in front of the city, narrow and full of life. Nearly nineteen years after the fall of Verdantihya, it was difficult to tell that a battle had been fought here. Dirt and wind and rain had worn the valley into a new look. Grass had grown and nature had taken its due course of covering up the carnage of almost two decades hence. Life covering death. Growth over destruction. Ell preferred it that way.

"Ready?" Dacunda asked his son as they prepared to enter the grand chamber where the Source originated.

"Long past ready!" Dahranian quipped with a tight grin and pulled his mending body over the last step and through the large, arched doorway.

Ell took one last look at the waterfall rushing out from the wall nearly fifty feet below him then walked inside the building. The rest of the company followed him. They entered a vast chamber, circular like the dome that covered it. It was the largest single building that Ell had ever seen.

Rihya closed her eyes and sighed with delight. There was definitely a presence in the room. Peace flowed from the life-blood of the land, the Source, which lay below them. They stood on a great sill that ran around the circle of what now appeared to be a giant, man-made crater. An enormous stone bowl created to hold a huge reservoir of the precious Source that bubbled up from the bottom. There was an exit point down low, the gateway through which it now flowed. But in days gone, they had stoppered the water gateway to allow the bowl to fill, creating a massive indoor pool. A lake was really more like it. It had been completely full, regulated stringently by elves who knew exactly how much flow to release from the mouth of the building to cascade down the steps leading up to the dome, then through the city, and finally under the oaken gates of Verdantihya and into the valley beyond. Not so anymore. Silverfist had changed all of that when on that fateful day he opened the large gateway completely, allowing all of the reservoir to release in one fell swoop, bursting

Verdantihya's defenses from within its own walls. Ell did not wish to dwell on that story again as his uncle had retold it not long ago. It was a story to remember, but not one to tell too often lest one fall to the grips of depression and sorrow.

Dahranian stumbled down the steps leading to the heart of the giant bowl, towards the smaller bowl within a bowl that lay at the bottom. It was a small pool now. The Source was a spring that bubbled up pure, and powerful, flowing steadily out of the water gate and into the city. This was the heart of the land. This was the heart of Andalaya, perhaps not geographically, but in spirit, it definitely was. Dahranian splashed into the pool. The water bubbling up buoyed him, buffeting him in a massaging, comfortable manner. He sighed with relief. They followed in his footsteps and reached the center of the giant bowl.

"Fill all of the water skins to the brim and drink more than your fill," Dacunda ordered. "I know not when we shall again return here once we depart."

Rihya rolled her eyes sarcastically and jibed back, "As if we didn't already know what to do, Uncle." He frowned at her response. "I mean really, sometimes I believe you think us still the children you took under your wing once our parents died, rather than the bloodied, seasoned, battle-veterans into which we have become. Under your tutelage, of course." Rihya added the last comment almost as an afterthought.

"Peace, Valerihya," Dacunda shifted his weight as he leaned forward to fill one of his gourds full of the crystal clear water. "I meant no disrespect. I know you are a woman grown now, three years past your day of renaming."

Rihya tossed her short, dyed-green hair, "Just so long as that is clear." But she quickly flashed their uncle a smile to take the sting from the encounter. She was quicksilver that way, angry one moment and then offering you forgiveness the next.

Ryder, Rihya, and Ell followed suit, filling skins and gourds to their fullest capacity as Dahranian finally pulled himself out of the billowing water upon which he floated. When he left the pool, he stripped off his hose revealing his loincloth and muscled legs. Ell's cousin unwound the soaking bandage. The wound, which had been a deep gash only one week prior, was now a freshly healed, pink scar. That was the power of the Source and it never failed to astound Ell.

"A miracle, is it not?" Dahranian motioned to his leg in wonder. It appeared he too had never outgrown his awe at how their elven bond with the land functioned. It was a bond that Ell was thankful for indeed. Elves were united with the world around them. They were in a covenant with the land, bonded to it. It gave them speed and endurance, an ability to move through the wilds freely and swiftly, and most importantly, the water that flowed from the Source had the power to heal them. Farther from here, from its point of origination, it grew diluted and its power waned, sometimes completely. However, the closer an elf of the Highest came to the Source, the more concentrated its power became. Rivers in the valley beneath them for instance, this close to their origin, were miraculously more powerful than at the base of the mountains or in the plains beyond. It was the reason why the East Mayn flowing a day north of the raid had only slightly stemmed the worst effects of Dahranian's injury, where here, the Source could erase them almost completely.

The Source couldn't reverse death or quell the most fatal of wounds, but nearly any other injury could be mended. Dahranian's scar was tight and fresh. It would still require rest, yet it was weeks farther than where it would have been without any Source Water available. It was the reason they carried the precious life-water in their skins and rationed its use for only emergencies. Drinking a mouthful of the Source from a gourd and bathing a wound with some of the precious liquid could do wonders to stave off infection, and mend up gashes received in the skirmishes in which they often found themselves. The beauty of the Source was that its properties belonged solely to the Highest. They were bonded to the land, like no one else. It was their connection to the world in which they lived that gave them access to this wondrous boon. The humans spat upon the land, and gave no heed to its protection. They carved out mines and cut down forests. They ravaged the plains with their never-ending camps. The Departed had once been linked to the world as the Highest still were. In fact, they had once been the same race. But the great split had occurred. Out of arrogance and pride, half their race had left and gained the name of the *Departed.* They had thought themselves above the land. They no longer wished to be bonded to it. The schism had led to two civilizations where there had once been one. In truth, it made no sense to Ell. *How could they have turned their back on the bond? How could they forget the covenant we made with the land?* It was like rejecting the core of who they were. Ell supposed he would never understand.

He finished filling his water skins as he watched Dahranian redress in his soaking wet clothing. Good thing it was pleasant weather, otherwise wet clothes would be bothersome indeed. Although, Ell had to admit there was something soothing about Source water. He supposed it would not be terrible to be covered in the fine liquid.

Rihya and Ryder began sparring as they also finished filling their owns skins. Their uncle watched them.

"Haven't had enough combat in the last few months?" Dacunda asked incredulously.

"Just staying sharp, Father," Ryder answered lightly as he thrust with a dagger and Rihya sidestepped smoothly. They fought quickly but each was skilled enough to avoid whatever maneuver the other threw at them and they both knew it. This was just sport. Oh, one or both might get a nick or two—Ell's wager was on Rihya ending up with a little bit of Ryder's blood on her blades—but either way, the Source was nearby and they could patch themselves up with a quick dip in the spring.

Ell sat on the rim of the pool, trailing his hand in the water behind him as he watched. Dacunda and Dahranian were deep in a quiet conversation, and the other two were sparring. All of a sudden, he felt strange. It was as if the entire pool of water in which his lean-fingered hand dangled had transported itself within his chest. Ell felt cold all over; however, it was not uncomfortable. Rather it was the cold of a long, deep, drink of spring water on a hot day, the way the water ran down ones throat and chilled the entire chest and stomach in a refreshing way. Ell felt that sensation multiplied infinitely. It was as if all the water in the ceaselessly springing well was transported inside of him and was ready for his use. His head felt almost fuzzy from the feeling of pure, raw power. The dizziness grew from the sudden slew of power and he lost his balance and fell backward from the unfamiliarity of it all. With a splash, he was in the pool, over his head in water, and then bobbing back to the surface. He quickly pulled himself out of the spring and over the cobbled lip of the pool in embarrassment.

His four companions turned to stare at him in amazement, then shared an uproarious laugh together. Although his uncle shook his head in disbelief, it was Ryder, of course, who was the one to comment. "Why cousin, you've never been one to lack coordination! Why now? What's has your balance in a bind?"

Ell shrugged uncomfortably. He hated being the center of attention. He especially despised being the focus of everyone's laughter. "Just a minor mishap. I must be more tired than I realized," he lied in response.

Until he knew what was going on he wasn't going to share anything with them. He was already the laughing stock today just by falling in the pool, and he wasn't about to tell them that he felt like the spring had mystically transported itself inside of him, while actually it had remained exactly where it was physically.

Dacunda seemed to see through his façade however, and his eyes narrowed in thought. He had always been shrewd. As long as he asked no questions though, Ell would be forced to give no more answers. It was time to shift the subject.

"Leg all better, Dahranian?" Ell immediately regretted the question. It was obvious. They had already spoken of it earlier. Indeed his cousin made a face of confusion.

"The same as it was five minutes ago when we discussed it. Still good and healed as far as I know." Ell nodded. What else was there to say? He just hoped they moved on quickly enough. His wish was granted, as Ryder seemed to decide that now was the time to tell a joke he had once heard, and the topic of conversation plowed forward until his mishap with the pool was lost in the history of the day to all but Ell. He would not forget. He had also felt something similar after the last raid as he touched the dead dark elf's diseased face. That flicker of change and then it was gone when he blinked. It had not felt the same as this, but there had been a similarity in the feeling, a sense of power to which he was completely unaccustomed.

He dwelled on the strange occurrence for the rest of the day. The afternoon was spent on a moss-covered veranda of a slightly dilapidated keep. The keep rose from the high hillside on the uppermost portion of Verdantihya, the old royal district. It lay just beneath the dome with the Source and they had chosen it for its comfort and its unspeakably beautiful view of the valley. The afternoon passed with food and stories, laughter and the tending of tasks that had long been ignored. Strings and pouches were mended, blades sharpened on whetstones, and clothes darned. The tension from the past week of travel and running seeped out of them. It felt more peaceful than Ell could remember. They had been fighting, raiding, and running for so many months in a row now that he almost couldn't remember what it was like to have fun and relax.

They rested in the fading light. It was cool as evening fell, and Ell pulled up the deep hood of his long-sleeved tunic over his face to ward off the chill of night falling. His hair flowed freely out from under the hood and spread just over the front of his shoulders, slightly wavy, a dirty blond wave of locks.

He took an apple from his sack. Apples were good. They transported well and could withstand a dropping or two, where as other fruit could not without spoiling. He bit into the crisp fruit and enjoyed the sweet and tangy mixture of the juice as he chewed it.

Rihya came to sit beside him and they stared out over the land together. "Spectacular, isn't it?" She murmured after a time, indicating the view before them.

Ell simply nodded in response. It seemed he did that often these days. Words seemed rather less of a necessity after one had fought and bled and braved death beside somebody. You could communicate more with the blink of an eye or the twitch of a limb than most people could with an entire conversation. That was the way of it. It was one of the few beneficial side effects of war, the bond between comrades. And this was his older sister—older by three years—their bond went even deeper.

Eventually she leaned into him and they shared warmth as they watched the sun drop and then finally sink below the western horizon. Night came fully, and they unrolled their blankets and wrapped themselves in them, curling around the fire. Many nights on the run, they slept in the cold, a fire too dangerous to make since it might give their position away to their enemies. But Dacunda had given in this time, perhaps feeling safe, as they had seen no sign of pursuit ever since that first sighting of smoke. Besides, they had been running hard for days. The only thing that could even have come close to catching them was a band of Departed. It was not unheard of, that, but his uncle seemed hopeful that the escaped cutter had not brought a chase upon them as they had initially thought. Either way however, they kept the fire small. It was just big enough for cooking and for curling near it for a little bit of warmth. The rest of the heat they needed was provided by close proximity to each other. That was another bond they shared. On the cold nights traveling in dangerous territory, you slept close together and shared heat. It created a familiarity of contact, which Ell appreciated. He might not always speak of it, but the emotions ran deep. This was his family. They were all he had left in the world and they meant everything to him.

Sleep took him and he ended his wakefulness on that thought. *Family*. He slept the night through and it wasn't until the morning dew misted his forehead and hair that he awoke. Rihya had rolled away from him during the night and looked cold. She shivered and hugged her knees to her chest beneath the blanket. The fire had long since died out. Ell pulled his own blanket over his sister as he rose and watched the sun begin to rise.

Dacunda returned from around the corner after most likely answering nature's call. He had probably stayed up most of the night keeping watch. Usually they shared that duty, but he had deemed them all in need of rest and had taken the task solely upon himself. Their eyes met in the stillness of the morning, neither one speaking. Their lack of words was not just for fear of waking the others; Dacunda simply understood already, what Ell was only just coming to realize. Words were not always required.

The moment did not last long. His sister and cousins began to stir and before long, all were awake and preparing a cold breakfast of dried meat and bread. "Shall we stay another day and rest, Father?" Dahranian queried sincerely. He did everything with sincerity.

His father shook his head and answered between mouthfuls. "No. I have business with a friend farther north." Dacunda so clearly avoided looking at Ell as he spoke those words that something was triggered in Ell's mind. His uncle had been acting strangely all week when asked about his plans for the coming days. Ever since Ell had relayed to them the incident with the sickly Departed that he had killed in combat, Dacunda had been a touch more secretive than usual. It was a burr in Ell's tunic that he could not figure out what his uncle was planning.

Ryder seemed just as curious as Ell, if not realizing quite so much of the reasons. "Who, Father?" he asked.

"A friend," is all that Dacunda would reveal after many attempts to pry more information from him. They asked and asked, yet he would divulge no more than a friend of his to the north, and that they would move out after the morning meal.

As they sat and ate, not for the first time that week, a strange occurrence began to happen. The dueling dagger strapped to Ell's thigh on the outside of his hose, began to vibrate ever so slightly. At first, it was almost indiscernible, but over time, the sensation grew. He slapped it at first, without looking, thinking it to be a bug or bee flitting around his leg. After a time, his uncle witnessed him paying heed to the dagger and questioned him while the others continued packing up and readying themselves to leave.

"What has you so preoccupied, Nephew?" Dacunda asked from not far away, as he tied the laces on his pack.

Ell hated not knowing the why of things before he communicated them to others, but he responded nonetheless. "It's this dagger, Uncle, my dueling dagger." Dacunda grew very still.

"Yes, Elliyar. What about it?" Something in his uncle's tone of voice made Ell grow cold inside. This was his serious voice, the way he sounded when hearing their scouting reports before a raid.

At his uncle's tone, Ell immediately snapped into a serious demeanor, as if it was reconnaissance information. It was an instinctual reflex to do so. He began relaying facts. "It's vibrating, Uncle. Softly at first but now with more force. It feels like it is just buzzing with energy."

"Has it ever done this before, Elliyar?"

Ell pondered the question for a moment. "Possibly," he responded with a bit of hesitancy. "I seem to remember it doing so for a brief time in one of our raids far to the south some months ago. But as soon as we left the skirmish, it lessened. I just assumed that I had imagined it, seeing as how it made no sense." He finished with a slight shake of his head at his own lack of understanding.

Ell's uncle gazed out from their vantage point over the valley for a long moment, watching the mists of dawn swirl lazily between the trees lining the sides of the meadows. "Do not be so quick to assume that something which you cannot explain or understand is simply your imagination, Nephew. There is much in this world that would shock you if you knew the truth of it. There are mysteries about which we know nothing." Ell stayed silent, not knowing how to respond.

Dacunda shook himself from the moment of reflection, and his face snapped into its command posture. "Let's be on our way! Now, quickly!" He clapped his hands at the group in an effort to get them moving faster. "We must be gone within the hour."

"What is it, Uncle?" Ell asked as he watched the rest of his family ready themselves more rapidly and in some confusion as to the sudden urgency.

"I fear I may have made a grave mistake," Dacunda responded. Ell cocked his head sideways in question. "I underestimated our enemies. We have been tracked." Dacunda said firmly and with a slight bitterness at his own complacency from the day before, when allowing time to rest and refresh themselves on the veranda of the keep.

Ell's eyes narrowed as he watched the valley for movement. *How did his uncle know that?*

Dacunda seemed to hear Ell's unspoken question. "That dagger you carry," he began.

"My father's old, dueling dagger," Ell patted it for comfort. It was his prized possession, a relic from a family he did not remember and a father he would never meet.

Dacunda nodded in affirmation. "You are correct. He would be glad you have it. However, you are aware that traditionally two dueling daggers are made in a set. One, longer blade is forged at first, until far into the process when the blade is split into two. Quenched in Source Water, the two blades retain a kinship. They are a pair like no other two types of weapons of which I have ever heard. They can oft retain an energy when in the same location. Not enough to disrupt the warrior, but just a hint of the greater power with which they were forged."

Ell knew all of this. The process for making dueling daggers was not new to him. Perhaps the daggers were not quite in fashion anymore with the fall of Verdantihya and the use of forges being limited, but he was still proud to bear at least one of his father's weapons.

"Yes, Uncle, I know about the process of forging the daggers." Dacunda looked at him, a soul-piercing gaze. Ell spoke further. "I have one blade and the other was lost. You said so yourself."

Dacunda's shoulders seemed to wilt a bit at Ell's statement. "Lost," he trailed off, then began to speak again. "Yes, you could call it that. Although, it would be more accurate to say it was *taken*." He emphasized the last word bitterly. Ell realized he was not the only one who mourned the loss of his father. It had been Dacunda's older brother, someone with whom he had spent half his life. Ell had never even known his father, yet he still felt the loss keenly. Ell realized he had a deeper insight now into how much Dacunda must miss him.

Yet a fire welled up inside of him. If he understood what Dacunda was implying, then that would mean his uncle had an idea of who had killed his father and had never told him. "What are you not telling me, Uncle?" *Had he been hiding this truth all along?* "Do you know who has the other dagger?" His uncle didn't respond; he just stared moodily out into the distance.

"All this time you told me my father fell in combat, that you didn't know who ended his life!" Ell had heard the story time and time again. There had been an attack; his father had led the party of warriors, which had been defending one of the villages where they had fled to hide after Verdantihya had fallen. By the time his uncle, Dacunda, had reached the scene, it had been all over and his father had been slain.

Dacunda sighed again. "Yes, I did tell you that," was all he said.

"You know who it is, don't you? You know who's out there!" Ell was angry that his uncle had kept this from him for so long. A way to know how to recognize his father's killer and he had never spoken of it.

Ell spoke forcefully again. "You know who killed my father, don't you?"

His uncle's pained silence was all the confirmation he needed. Somewhere, not far away, was the person who had stolen any chance Ell and Rihya might've had at anything akin to a normal life. Somewhere in the dancing mist and swirling fog of the valley beyond, was the person who had killed his father. He was following them. And Ell couldn't wait to meet him.

Chapter Five

They were running. Again. Ell had wanted to stay and fight but he had been overruled by the others in his family. It galled him to no end that his father's murderer roamed free, following, with them as his quarry, but Dacunda had been adamant that they should not fight. Not yet at least. And so they ran. It felt like Ell had spent his entire life fighting from the shadows and then running. Just once, he longed to stand and meet his foes in the open, in the light. However, his uncle seemed nervous about whoever was chasing them. It was as if his uncle was afraid of the person behind them for some reason. It had to be a company of Departed. *Slavers*. Humans could not have made such good time while tracking them. The tanned brown, southern elves would fight to capture first, and to kill second. Ell could not recall a time when he had seen Dacunda frightened. So they stuck to familiar tactics. The shadows it was. For now.

The argument on whether to stay and fight or attempt to flee had been heated. Ell's passionate claims that they should engage the enemy in combat had been deemed reckless. They had said his judgment was clouded by the circumstances and a desire for vengeance. Even his sister had said so. Maybe they were correct. There were likely anywhere from fifteen to twenty of the dark elves following, since that was the typical size of slaver parties traveling and catching captives throughout these parts. Instead of fighting, they had made their way to the northwestern corner of the city and left by an old sally port opening onto the mountainside. They could not afford to exit the city by the main, southern entrance, as that was the direction in which their pursuers awaited. Also, Dacunda was still determined to go north and eventually find that mysterious acquaintance of his, whoever it was. Therefore, it was, with the mountain to the north, they headed west along the slopes on an ancient and nearly overgrown game trail.

It was always difficult to leave Verdantihya, even when it was necessary to do so. The instinctual pull it held over the Highest was undeniable. It was said that even the traitors, those rare few of the Highest who betrayed their race and followed in the steps of Silverfist to serve the enemy, would sometimes return here just to feel that link with creation so ever-present and potent in Verdantihya near the Source. They didn't deserve the right to return here, not ever, in Ell's opinion, but there were certain issues beyond one's control, particularly when you were on the losing end of a war.

Ell ran last in the column as he so often did, watching the lean, lithe frames of his family go before him. His sister skated through the forest with more ease than a person would imagine possible. She was a deer on the high paths, surefooted and light of weight and stature. His cousins were larger, and more powerfully built, yet still slender. They were like mountain cats on the prowl. An observer could be forgiven if they mistook his family as the predators instead of the prey, for at the moment their strong, measured gate and focused stares made them look more like the aggressors than the quarry. Then there was his uncle. His long, light-brown braid slapped up and down and side-to-side upon his back as he ran smoothly at the front. Gracefully, he led them through the wilderness. The brush and trees hid them, yet often left hints of their passage to a watchful eye. The unavoidable twig snapped here, a partial footprint there. Their goal at the moment was to quickly create distance between themselves and their enemies and to worry about giving them the slip later.

Conversation from the front drifted back towards Ell. "Slavers, do you think, Father?" Ryder was asking his sire. Dacunda grunted in assent. Of course they were slavers. Human troops would never have been able to keep pace only a day or so behind them for the past week before reaching Verdantihya. That meant elves, dark elves. And dark elves meant slavers.

Ryder spat in disgust. "Bastards."

Ell agreed. There was little he hated more than slavers. Hostilities had arisen centuries ago between north and south. It had begun when the Departed had chosen to separate from tradition and sever their covenant with the land, with creation, and by doing so had created a void between them and the Highest, earning them the name 'Departed'. The continent had divided and battle lines had been drawn. Skirmishes of all sorts and full-scale war had ebbed and flowed over the decades until only Dor Khabor, otherwise known as Dark Harbor, and Verdantihya had stood. Then had come the humans. They had arrived at the perfect moment in history to take advantage of the splintered elven society, and their invasion had enticed the dark, southern cousins of the Highest into forming an alliance of sorts, forever driving a wedge between what were now two separate races of elves.

Silverfist had been the betrayer, but he had not been the only one. A number of the Highest, often younger elves, fearful of fighting on behalf of a losing effort, had defected. They sold their services to the Departed who had struck a deal with the invading humans.

Ell was breathing hard as they ran. The swift pace was necessary if they were to gain back any of the time that they had lost while resting in the city. It had been needed. Dahranian had required the healing of the Source and the time for recovery. Source Water wasn't a cure all. It was mystical and powerful certainly, but it was no substitute for time and rest. Yet, Ell couldn't help but feel that if they were to outrun their pursuers, it would have been better to continue on last night. Ell couldn't really complain, however, as he was after all, the one who wanted to turn and confront whoever it was behind them. However, logic dictated that if their goal was to escape, then resting all of the prior day might have been a poor decision. Dacunda seemed to share that opinion because he pushed them at a hard, fast pace all morning long. They drank on the run from a few water skins containing normal water and did not stop to eat.

Step, breathe, step, breathe. Jump a fallen log, sidestep an overgrown bush, turn around the bend in the path. Step, breathe, step. It was the rhythm of the run and it was as familiar to Ell as living. He had been doing it his entire life.

More snatches of conversation drifted to Ell at the back of the pack. This time it was his sister talking to their uncle and it appeared as if it was Rihya's turn to dig for answers. Apparently, she wasn't nearly as satisfied with being kept in the dark as Ell had assumed she was when they had made their escape this morning without a single complaint from her.

"Who is he?" She was asking forcefully, venom in her voice. "Is he very dangerous?"

"Yes." Dacunda was responding in his typical short answers. Grunts as often as words. However, it appeared that he felt he owed his niece more of an explanation. "You know who your father was, Valerihya," he said, "whether you remember him or not, you have heard of his reputation. Do you think any minor warrior would have been able to best him, Adan the Green?"

Rain had begun to fall on this overcast day, and it spattered gently off the leaves above and around them. Ell's senses were sharp, the same as the rest of the Highest. The senses of his brethren were keen and bright in connection with the land around them. Hearing was strong; their nose could scent a smell from far away. But the noise of the rain, and the occasional swell of wind through the branches rustling the leaves, made overhearing every word of their conversation difficult. And this was not a conversation he cared to miss. Ell spurred himself forward, running as closely as he could to his cousin in front of him and straining his pale, pointed, slender ears to catch what they were saying.

He had missed a portion of the conversation but he picked up the rest.

"Does Ell know?" His sister was asking his uncle.

"No," Dacunda answered. "You know his rash decision making at times. I have not thought it wise to tell him." He paused and glanced at her. "Or you for that matter. You are headstrong, and your emotions move as quickly as your blades at times." He smiled to take the sting from his words and it appeared Rihya took no offense as her knives stayed exactly where they were.

She nodded to herself as if in thought. "Do you think he would have pursued him if you had told him sooner?"

Dacunda answered his niece with a question. "Do you not? You know him." He shook his head ruefully, describing Ell in a low voice. "Like you, your brother is headstrong and over confident in his own abilities."

"Ell is talented, you must concede that," Rihya said quietly. Ell silently thanked his sister for her defense. "Perhaps he could stand a chance against the traitor. After all, I have not seen many as good as my brother in a battle. And he is young, so imagine where he will be in a few years."

Traitor. Did that mean his father's killer was not one of the Departed but a traitorous deserter from the north, a despicable slaver with the red, Traitor's Tears tattooed on his cheeks? Ell's mind was spinning with that new evidence and the possibilities of who it might be. He was salivating over every new piece of information and he almost forgot to pay attention to the rest of the discussion that was supposed to be kept from him.

"In a few years indeed. Maybe then. But now, I fear the traitor would kill him and kill him quickly. I would not care to stand across from him myself on the field of battle." Dacunda shivered slightly. So, his uncle was slightly afraid of this man. He must be dangerous indeed. "He is renowned in the land not only for his prowess but for his cunning as well. The number of tricks he has up his sleeve I cannot guess."

They grew silent then and Ell dropped back to run so his presence while eavesdropping would not be noticed. He was glad to have acquired the new information and frustrated to have missed the divulgence of the traitor's name earlier in the conversation. However, that last bit of knowledge would be revealed sooner or later. He knew it was only a matter of time.

The rest of the day passed in silence. Only the heavy breathing of his family rivaled the rain for sound. Even elves of the mountains grew tired when they had to run all day. The wet ground and forest around Ell sent his senses tingling. Moist earth smelled rich and full to his nose and the scent mingled with the wetness of the air and sky overhead. A bird trilled from afar answered by another and another. They were in the wild true now. It felt good.

Mist glided among the trees and dropped in from the canopy above them. Spring rain was good for the land, but it made their footprints easy to follow. It was not going to be easy to fool their enemies into going a different direction. They crisscrossed streams, running in the water for times, and doubled back occasionally, changing course every so often. Their general direction continued west and north but the exact trajectory of it was subject to variation.

Night approached and the rain tapered off. They were fatigued from their day of running. Only time would tell whether or not they had put enough distance between themselves and their followers.

They camped for the night on a hillside overlooking a gorge. The Westrill flowed through it, deep at the bottom of the narrow chasm. It churned and frothed as it ran over rocks and boulders and coursed around bends. There would be fish a plenty in the river if they had time to stop and fish. But they did not. They were too far up the cliff for it to be worthwhile to make the treacherous climb down at night. Besides, a fire was out of the question and raw fish was distinctly unappetizing. Left over bread and berries would have to suffice.

They reclined against the earth, damp from the day's rain. They would not be able to avoid the wetness so why fight it. Tonight would be cold and chill, but that was not unusual. Ell and his family had spent many fireless nights in the cold, as tonight would be, to lessen the possibility of detection.

Dacunda looked at Dahranian, the oldest of them. "I am going to scout back behind us, cover any traces I find, and see whether we have gained any ground."

"I'll set up a watch rotation, Father," Dahranian responded. He was serious as ever, and was used to assuming command when his father was not there.

Dacunda nodded solemnly back at him. Then he looked at Ell, the youngest. "I expect nothing rash to be done while I am gone."

Ell met his gaze defiantly. However, his uncle's gaze did not waver and finally Ell was forced to submit himself. It wasn't like he had planned on anything stupid such as going alone to meet the enemy tonight, after all. He wasn't *that* rash.

Satisfied with his nephew's acquiescence, Dacunda vanished into the night, silently, stealthily. He was like them, born of the mountains. A shadow among shadows as he moved. It was not likely anybody would see him if he did not wish it.

They sat in silence for a time until Ell cozied up next to his sister. He gave her what he assumed was a pleasant, winning smile.

"No." She said immediately. Ell put on his most innocent face and spread his hands wide as if he did not know what she meant.

"Uncle will tell you when he feels you are ready." And with that comment, she rolled over in her blankets to sleep while Ryder took the first watch.

There was nothing to do but to sleep or stay awake half the night until his watch came around. That was foolhardy. A seasoned fighter knew to grab sleep and rest whenever the chance provided itself. Ell rolled over, albeit a bit grumpily, back-to-back with his sister. She may frustrate him, but she loved him, and he her. They kept each other warm, fighting the chill with the close proximity of their bodies to one another. Sleep came slowly to Ell as his thoughts raced. He examined every aspect of the conversation he had overheard earlier that day between his uncle and Rihya. Several possible answers emerged and it wasn't until he had thought his way through it all that his mind finally allowed him to fall asleep. He slept fitfully, however, until his turn to watch arrived.

He awoke to Dahranian finishing the second watch after Ryder had taken the first. Ell took the third and watched the gloom as the rest of his family slept. He took the fourth, as well, for his sister—why should she have to wake when he knew he would not sleep again that night?

The grey of morning was just beginning to peek through the trees when his uncle's shadowy form slipped back into camp through the stillness. He wasn't sure how his uncle could function on such little rest. He supposed it must be a quality of age.

Dacunda walked up to him quietly so as not to disturb the others. His shoulders were still upright and his stance firm, even after expending so much extra energy gathering reconnaissance.

"And?" Ell quirked his head in question to the fruit of his uncle's night spent scouting.

Dacunda grimaced in annoyance. "We have not lost them. And likely we will not be able to lose them. They have a traitor guiding them. It is time to think of other options."

A traitor. *The traitor* from the earlier conversation. Bands of Departed guided by elves who used to be the Highest were the most dangerous because they were able to navigate the terrain better than most slavers. Those bands of slavers were usually the most successful. Perhaps he would get his chance to face the killer after all. Satisfaction settled in Ell's chest as he gripped his dagger and planned how he might avenge his father's death.

Chapter Six

The weather had reverted back to winter. Spring had arrived but it had not well and truly decided to remain yet. For this time of year that was normal, the seasons danced back and forth in a duel to see who would survive. Spring always won. Eventually.

Today, however, the wind whipped Ell's hair in front of him and a spattering of cold rain dampened it just enough so that a few locks clung to his face. It didn't seriously obscure his view from the tree in which he lurked, but it was an annoyance. For some reason, however, he chose not to tie it back in the loose mane he usually did before a fight. Today just seemed like a day for freedom and if his hair got in his way slightly as it proved that symbolic point, then so be it. It wasn't very warrior-like of him at all. In fact, it was fairly childish, but there were moments when disregarding common sense just felt right. His uncle had always taught him that any extra distraction could be fatal in combat. *There are always distractions* Dacunda would say, *but a good warrior minimizes them*. Hence, the sleeveless shirt his uncle often wore when the weather permitted. It did not permit today. Ell shivered in his hooded tunic, the dark colors of his clothing helping him blend into his surroundings. The hood fell unused behind his head, allowing his windswept hair the freedom he so desired of it. He could not put his finger on exactly why he felt the need to rebel against wise counsel, but perhaps it was the way his entire family seemed to think that he would do something foolish when the ambush began.

Nothing unwise Elliyar, nothing we have not planned. His uncle's last words to him rang out in the stillness of his mind, an annoyance. How was someone supposed to have the necessary confidence before a battle when his comrades clearly did not have faith in him?

He could see them in their respective locations. His sister sat crouched in a tree like his own, watching him from across the small ravine through which the game trail ran. *What was she thinking as she watched him? Was she worried about her little brother doing something stupid?* People often branded him as rash. His uncle, his cousins. But this was far from the truth. *Usually*. Almost everything he did was a calculated risk. Dangerous? Yes, often. Foolhardy? Possibly at times, especially in the eyes of a bystander. But rash? Never. The word rash implied that a person acted without thinking. Ell thought things through as meticulously as each situation allowed. Once again, the tiny voice in his mind reminded him, *usually. Not always*. He would be the first to admit that he was bold. There was not much fear inside of him. However, his uncle didn't see it that way. In fact, his sister, Rihya, was probably the only one who never labeled him as rash. Most likely it was because in reality, she was the fieriest of them all, and to brand him in such a way would be to admit that she was rash herself. That was something she would never do. Or perhaps, it was because she understood him. She had always known him better than anybody else. Maybe it was because of both those reasons, he conceded, the wry smile a rarity on his normally solemn and serious countenance.

The others were in similar positions. Dacunda was closest to the mouth of the ravine, the direction from which their enemies would be approaching. He stood behind a tree; only the toes of his worn leather boots could be seen poking from his hiding spot. Ell could only see him because he knew where to look. His uncle was in charge of beginning the ambush. Nobody would fire until he did. He always led their coordinated assaults.

Ryder and Dahranian were on Ell's side of the ravine, to his left, further toward the middle of the ravine. They were also hidden, and Ell could not even catch a glimpse of them, only knowing their locations from previous discussion. His emotions boiled within him. Excitement, energy. A touch of fear even wormed its way into his senses. That was an uncommon emotion—he was rarely afraid. Death had no hold on him. After all, his life was just one extended battle. It was a war without an end. In truth, his death would probably be the most pleasant part of his existence since his parents and the sister he had never known would be waiting for him in the Third Reality.

There are three realities, Dacunda's voice echoed back to him from many years ago when Ell had been very young. *The First Reality. This is where you and I eat and sleep, live and fight. The Second Reality,* his uncle had waved a hand mystically toward the heavens around him. *That is the reality overlaying this one. We struggle in the flesh, but there are other forces. Good. Evil. Chaos. Fortune. These truths collide in the Second Reality, a reality most will never see.*

Ell drew a deep breath of the rain-clogged air and let his mind keep remembering. *Then there is the Third Reality, the place all will go when they depart this land. That reality is like many reflections of this one. It is as if the First Reality is reflected a million times over, creating a ripple of possibilities, pleasures, and emotions*. His uncle had placed a hand on Ell's young shoulder in comfort. *Fear not nephew, you will go there one day. The Third Reality is reserved for those who oppose evil and uphold creation.*

In death there was freedom—something every good warrior knew. If they didn't, then they would never reach their full potential. It did not mean he was completely fearless. There were things to fear. Pain, the loss of loved ones, failure. But death was not something to fear. It was a release. If a soldier feared death, then who knew when even the most courageous of souls would falter. No, fear of death was not a concern for Ell.

He smiled another smile. The action was as uncharacteristic on his face as was his silent philosophizing. He felt eagerness, a bundle of anticipation in his gut at the possibility of what was to come. Today might be the day where his father finally was avenged. *Nothing foolish.* His uncle's cautions prior to their placements restrained his eagerness just enough. It sobered him enough to focus.

The forest parted above the ravine over which Ell surveyed. It was a rent in the green, a gash in the canopy, revealing a grey, dismal sky. The wind whipped again and he tossed his head back glorying in the feel of the cool mountain air and the cold wet drops that fell upon his face. He had missed Andalaya more than he had realized.

Suddenly, he felt the buzzing in his dueling dagger, the strange, energized connection it had with its counterpart, increase sharply. Their enemies must be close, very close. Dahranian had questioned whether fighting was the correct option. Ever the thinker, he like his father, was cautious in all things. Surprisingly though, Dacunda had overridden his objections. Ell's dueling daggers had given them, his family, the edge by allowing them to realize they were being tracked. Their enemies did not know that their prey, Ell's family, were aware of their pursuit and had become the hunters. The element of surprise had switched hands. That was their advantage and Dacunda planned to make use of it.

And so they waited. It would not be long now, Ell realized, as his dagger fairly pulsed with energy. He looked at it. It was long for a knife in the manner of dueling daggers, longer than his forearm. It was narrow and straight until the last few inches, where the tip of the blade curved slightly. The point wasn't curved enough to make stabbing with it unnatural, but it was just enough to make slashing slightly more effective. The handle was wrapped in brown leather, softened from use, and the pommel was simple, just a small, rounded end of steel. It had only a small crossguard. It was not meant to catch a bigger blade in defense. It was not a defensive weapon. It was built for attack and attack alone. It suited Ell well.

Ell waited until he felt the dagger might surely jump from its sheath from the sheer vibration of its energy before making the Crestwell call. It was a bird common to these parts, and one that Ell could mimic perfectly. It was the signal so that his family would know to expect the arrival of their enemies shortly. They all knew that his dagger was the best way to detect the approach of the enemy and therefore, Ell had been dubbed the lookout, of sorts.

The first Departed ran lightly into the ravine, slowly but not fearfully. They were in enemy territory and they knew it. Whoever carried the opposing dagger must also know they were drawing near and was having them exercise caution, yet it was clear they were not frightened, not expecting to come under an attack. They thought themselves the predators, not the prey. How wrong they were. Numbers didn't mean everything. Even if they had twenty elves instead of only five, they had forfeited the element of surprise, and that was going to make all the difference.

As if in preparation for the imminent ambush, the heavens drizzled, tears for the bloodshed and deaths of those who should have been allies. *In another lifetime, another era*, Ell though grimly as he knocked a dark, black Dreampine arrow and sighted one of the Departed who was in the middle of the pack. Whatever ties there had once been between the two races, they were long lost now.

The twenty or so Departed finally entered the ravine fully, and ran lightly some ten paces lower than the lip of the ravine upon which his uncle stood. A traitor ran with them. Ell marked him immediately by his pale hair and blue eyes. He was fair of skin like all northern elves, yet slightly more tanned for having spent such a long time in the south. His head was shaved on the sides and his hair pulled back in numerous clasps as it ran down his back. It was not braided, but the clasps would make it so the hair would not impede his fighting. A dagger, the twin of Ell's, hung at his hip and rage enflamed Ell's senses as he saw for the first time the man who had stolen his father from him. Anger was all he could feel and then…

Suddenly, shock added itself to his emotions. This was no simple traitor. The red, tattooed tears that streaked down his cheeks, marking him as a betrayer of Andalaya, were not the most distinguishing feature upon him. No, it was his left hand. Or lack thereof. Where a normal hand of flesh should be there was only a metal fist. The elf who had killed Ell's father, the one who carried Ell's birthright, his father's dagger, and who was responsible for not only the death of Ell's father, but for the death of his mother and sister as well, was none other than the most hated elf in the realm. His father's murderer was the first betrayer, the catalyst for Andalaya's downfall. It was Silverfist himself.

Arrows plummeted from the ridgeline as Dacunda led the ambush. Ell fired instinctively, first one, then two black, Dreampine arrows and the first of his shots found its way into the chest of one of the Departed. The dark elf let out a scream of pain as it fell. It was not the only death to take place that quickly. In a matter of seconds, six Departed were down and two more wounded. Ell's family kept firing as everything was going according to plan. Everything except for the sheer and utter fury that was welling up in Ell's chest and threatening to consume him. He wanted to do more than shoot arrows. Five more Departed fell, dead or mortally wounded, and there were only seven dark elves standing below now, holding the small, lightweight leather shields in front of them, hoping to protect themselves from further arrows. It was not going to be very effective. Then there was Silverfist. He was standing and directing his men, a general in their midst. Ell could see the aura of power and command he radiated. He was an elf to be feared. He was also an elf to be hated.

Ell could tolerate it no longer. The rage of seventeen years without his family finally boiled over. All the nameless faces and human soldiers against whom he had fought. All of the Departed he had killed. Nothing would bring him satisfaction like killing this one elf. He screamed in anger and defiance, and pulled his two blades, showing himself as he leapt from the tree. He was going to do something foolish after all. A small voice in the back of his mind cautioned him to stop, but he shoved the voice aside easily.

With his small belt knife held with the point down and his dueling dagger tip up, he flung himself from the lip of the ravine into the midst of his enemies. Two Departed immediately confronted him, snarls of battle written on their faces, revealing the pointed, upper row of teeth each possessed. Vaguely, Ell heard voices. It might have been his family following him into battle, after all they could not allow him to fight and die alone, even if he had ruined their ambush, but Ell wasn't sure. It was difficult to concentrate on anything other than his anger.

Nothing mattered but reaching Silverfist. It was as if something snapped within him. He drew upon a strange wealth of power from within, from the land itself. It must be the rage from which he gained such strength, a small part of his mind thought, as it observed him slice through the two Departed like a blade through water. It didn't matter. He was strong.

Another Departed approached him, the dark elf's face curled into a rictus of a snarl. Ell's vision grew slightly cloudy as if he was seeing through a fog. He fought quickly. His goal was to reach Silverfist, not to waste his time on this worthless life. The dark elf swung his sword high at Ell's head and he ducked easily, coiling and then springing upward with an over hand strike of his own. His dueling dagger felt alive in his hands like he had never before felt. Was it a side effect of its proximity to its twin? As the blade arced down toward the

Departed, the dark elf threw up its shield in a last ditch defense and Ell's momentum carried his blade and his fist into it. The shield shattered like a tree in the Broken Tree Range during one of the ice storms of the far north, and the Departed's arm shattered also from the force of Ell's blade. The limb hung limply from his shoulder. The dark elf was no danger now and he let Ell past in fright as he scrambled to get away. Ell completely disregarded it now. His family would dispose of the injured Departed.

The fog in his eyes was still there. The experience was new and strange. It made it difficult to see, yet easier at the same time, as if he was made for it. He couldn't explain the strange sensation.

Finally, he was there. Silverfist awaited Ell with a smirk on his face. The confrontation had arrived. The traitor dropped his shield and freed up his metal fist while holding his sword in his good right hand.

"The son of Adan the Green, I presume?" Silverfist questioned with a turn of his head as if waiting for a response. He got none. Ell saw no reason to waste his breath on this filth. He just wanted him dead.

"Yes? No?" Silverfist waited for an answer as Ell advanced in a crouch, blades at the ready. "I'll take your silence and extreme focus as an affirmative," the pale elf smirked again. "Adan always was overly serious for my taste. Apparently, his son is no different."

Ell lurched forward in anger. His father was long gone, that could not be changed, but hearing somebody speak so disparagingly of him turned his blaze of anger into a bonfire. Ell pulled. He called deeply upon the strength within himself and it almost felt as if he could feel a sense of power grow as he focused. Good. Let him be strong for this fight. Engaging in combat was what he had been born to do.

The clouds in his eyes did not lessen as the distance between them closed. Blade met blade in a clash of blue sparks and Ell spun away deftly as Silverfist swung his silver fist in a thunderous blow towards Ell's face. The hammer blow missed, but Ell could feel the wind of it whistling past his face as the metal fist just rustled the hairs of his head. Ell saw a flicker of disappointment in Silverfist's eyes as the fist missed connection. As soon as Ell saw it, the look disappeared, lost in the mask of focus on the face of his enemy. But Ell filed the information away. *Avoid the fist*. There was something sinister about it; Ell had a feeling.

They danced in the rhythm of battle. Engage, slash, peel away. Over and again. The traitor dealt a vicious slash to Ell's shoulder and his arm ached painfully from the wound, but Ell drew deeply on the source of power within him. He focused himself on the fight.

Cut, dodge, duck, coil, and spring. The dance went on and on, it felt like forever, yet as Ell knew from previous battle experience, this duel was most likely only a minute or so in length. Time passed differently in combat.

The weather swirled and mists grew thick around them, adding to fog in Ell's eyes—the strange fog that made it harder and yet easier to see. Droplets of mist water flicked off Ell's blades as he slashed and swung. He cut a shallow gash in Silverfist's forearm, just above his metal hand. A flash of annoyance and pain crossed the traitor's face. Silverfist attacked in earnest now as he sought to finish the duel quickly. He lunged with his sword, slipping as it missed Ell. When Ell leapt in to take advantage of his foe's mistake, Silverfist recovered much too rapidly for it to have been a real slip. A feint. Silverfist was trying to bait Ell. He truly was as crafty as the stories said. Silverfist swung another powerful blow with his fist. Ell was too close. He would never be able to avoid it. Yet he felt the strength in his limbs, more strength than he normally possessed. With an uncanny speed, he swung up a knife to block the blow and deflected the metal fist before it could collide with his head. Once again, a look of frustration crossed his opponent's face. Then it was gone. Instead, Silverfist cut deeply into Ell's leg with his sword and Ell could feel even the extra strength with which he had fought begin to ebb. This was it. The traitor would finish him now. Ell stumbled a bit as he tried to recover, but in a flash, Silverfist turned and bolted up one edge of the ravine into the undergrowth, and off into the forest.

Ell was exhausted but he watched the man run, feeling anger at his escape and confusion as to why he was still alive. He looked behind him to see that the ambush had ended. The Departed were dead and his family was coming up behind him, eyeing him strangely. *Silverfist was cutting his losses, just waiting for his chance to escape*. Ell thought groggily, wounds and an unnatural fatigue overcoming his mind. *The traitor never fought me truly* he thought in frustration, *if he had, I'd be dead. He was just stalling, waiting for the first opportunity to run.*

Ell crumpled to his knees as his cousins reached him, lifting him back up to be hoisted by the arms, one over each of their shoulders.

"The fog, the clouds are gone," Ell mumbled to himself, trying to process the fact that his eyes perceived things normally once again. Again, his family looked at him strangely.

Finally, Dacunda spoke as they sat him down, with his back leaning against an embankment. "What fog, Elliyar? We saw no fog or clouds, save the ones far above your head." His uncle looked to the sky.

Ell blinked in confusion. Why was it so hard to think? Dacunda ordered Ryder to retrieve a flask of Source Water. Apparently, Ell's wounds were serious.

"Did the rain finally stop also?" Ell questioned in half delirium from the strange exhaustion. "It was misting so much as we fought," he muttered half to himself.

Again, his family exchanged worried looks. Dahranian spoke this time. "It was only misting… around you Ell." And on that note of complete confusion Ell passed out, hardly feeling the Source Water poured down his throat and in his wounds as the blackness took him.

* * * *

Silverfist was troubled. He moved quickly through the forest of his birth, though it was his homeland no longer. He didn't have a home. It was better that way. No bonds of loyalty or emotion to weaken you. He had forsaken all emotions except for the pursuit of pleasure and success long ago.

He moved swiftly. His time in the south had not lessened his ability to move stealthily and quickly through the woods. The band of slavers he had taken with him, to pursue the handful of the Highest who had ended up ambushing them, moved well enough for the dark, southern elves. But they could not quite match the grace and ease with which one born of Andalaya could proceed through its wilderness.

Dead. He gritted his teeth in frustration. That had been a good crew. One of his best, if he was to be completely honest. He had chosen them for the latest mission given to him by Half-Mask because of their efficiency. Yet they hadn't lasted minutes against the ambush. *What did that say of his ability to recruit? To lead? What did that say of those Highest he had just faced? Were they really that competent?*

He ran south and east, angling his course in the direction of the closest camps and safety. It was far from safe for a Traitor alone in the mountains of Andalaya. He had come north following raiders, trailing them for the havoc they had been wreaking on the plains and in the Lower Forest. Only recently had he noticed the buzzing in the dagger at his hip. *He should have paid more attention to it. He should have known they might recognize what it meant.* Not all the ancient lore and knowledge had been lost. That had been a grievous oversight on his part. It had almost cost him his life.

Yet that was not what troubled him most. No, it was the boy. He should have expected to see Adan's son when he felt the dagger buzzing. The Highest did like to keep dueling daggers within the family, after all. The art of forging them was long lost, and those who possessed them kept them as priceless heirlooms, a family inheritance.

The boy had so resembled his father, even down to his unkempt hair blowing wildly in the wind, just the way his father had preferred. Silverfist had almost felt like he was back at that day, eighteen years ago, when he had won the dagger at his hip in combat. However, it was not just the family resemblance to an old enemy that had shaken the traitor to his core. No, it was more. It was the boy's *strength and speed.* He was young and still green, even for all the raiding he had done. There was no way he should have been able to match Silverfist blow for blow. The boy had uncanny power and strength, albeit power the boy had clearly yet to learn to control. True, Silverfist would have finished the lad if he hadn't had to flee from the other four elves advancing over the corpses of his slavers, yet it had been a hard fought duel. And the *mist!* What had that been? Its swirling around their duel alone was beyond unnatural. The strangeness of it all troubled him.

He ran on to the south and east, pondering whether or not to inform Half-Mask of these developments. *Would it strengthen the Prince's trust to hear him report on such things or would his failure at the hands of a few of the Highest, one no more than a boy, weaken his standing with Half-Mask?* One could not afford to show weakness when dealing with the Prince of Darkness. Subservience and reverence, yes. Weakness, no. And so it was that Silverfist made up his mind not to tell. *Perhaps our paths will cross again*, he speculated idly as the buzzing in his dagger lessened the farther he went from the boy. Yes, he firmed that thought in his mind. He would take care of this irregularity somehow. He had been too long from the north. It was time to step up slaving and see if he could crush Andalaya once and for all. That would no doubt bring the boy across his path again. Silverfist had a feeling the boy was more patriotic than most and would not be able to bear the subjugation of his people. He ran on easily, content to brew his plans for the final collapse of Andalaya.

Chapter Seven

Ell awoke to the sound of water dripping off the leaves above his head and plinking gently against the blade of his cousin Ryder's long axe that lay next to him on the ground. Some people felt the need to keep their weapons pristine and clean, but many of the Highest preferred to let them absorb as much of the land around them as possible. They were bonded to Andalaya for a reason, a purpose, and as such, many of the pale, northern elves felt it was good and right that their weapons should reflect the connection between elf and creation. That wasn't to say that blades were left to rust. By no means was that so. Yet, a smudge of dirt on the shiny steel was not looked upon amiss. Moss and lichen often adorned the wooden hafts of spears and axes almost as if the blades had been forged and then the metal grown into the wood of a straight tree branch before being separated and used for war. Andalayan blades were a blend of construction and nature much akin to what one saw on the streets of Verdantihya where land and elf, nature and architecture, converged. Ell kept his own blades fairly clean, but it was not a matter of dislike for the tradition, it was simply that his dueling dagger and belt knife, his most common hand-to-hand weapons, did not allow much room for the wild to make its mark upon them. His bow, however, had a splash or two of moss and lichen akin to Ryder's axe. It camouflaged their weapons in times of need, such as during an ambush or raid. Such was his people's way now. Fight from the shadows; fight from the sides and from the rear. The ambush they had executed earlier had been a perfect example of that type of warfare.

"So you have finally decided to end your napping and join us in the waking world?" Ryder sat with a typical smile a few feet from where Ell was just opening his eyes.

His brain slightly muddled still, Ell took a moment to organize his thoughts. "What… happened?" He finally managed to ask. The question felt flimsy as it left his lips. Something strange had indeed taken place during the fight, and asking Ryder what had happened was not likely to lead to answers. His cousin had never been one for the study of knowledge or Highest lore, let alone anything at all really. No, Dacunda was the only one to ask about what had happened.

His mind clearing, Ell amended his previous question before his cousin could respond. "How long have I been unconscious?" Ell looked at the sky as he propped himself up on an elbow. The sky was still overcast and grey, but presently no rain fell. The droplets of water on the axe beside him were the residue of a previous rainfall. Ell noticed his clothes were wet. *They could have bothered to at least cover me instead of leaving me in the rain,* he thought a bit sullenly.

Ryder bit off a chunk of the venison he had in his hand. The wild stags of the mountains were difficult to bring down, even for a skilled hunter, but when one managed to do so they provided meat for many days. Ell and his family dried much of their kills and packed it with them, as a lightweight, energy-rich food source.

Between mouthfuls his cousin spoke. "About half a day, give or take, I suppose." It was difficult to understand him, since he made no effort to cease his eating to converse. Food was a priority to Ryder. He went out of his way to eat whenever it was possible.

His cousin continued. "Father and Dahranian have scouted behind us to make sure that the most recent company of slavers was all that we needed to fear. You know how sometimes the slave bands will coordinate at times?" Ell nodded in agreement. He did know. The slavers would often come through in small bands of ten or twenty, but they were also known to coordinate their efforts at times. Occasionally they would form a giant net to sweep up and force from hiding any of the Highest that might be caught in their way. The familiar burn of anger pulsed in his gut at the thought. Sometimes it felt like his anger was the only constant thing in his life. That and the fray. Scars dotted his young body as a testament to the fact that he had spent his whole life fighting.

His head still fuzzy, Ell reached out to his cousin for a handful of venison, thinking that perhaps some sustenance would clear the fog from his mind. Ryder, half made as if to horde his wealth of meat, then rolled his eyes and winked at Ell as he extended some food. Ryder played the part of the scoundrel and jokester, and he played it well. But when you got down to his core, he was as sincere as his father and Dahranian were. They simply showed it more.

Ell forced a laugh at his cousin's fooling around and tried to think positively. They had killed an entire band of slavers. That was good. Silverfist had left with his tail between his legs, which was even more priceless. But he *had* left, and therein lay Ell's frustration. That coupled with the fact that there were too many unanswered questions about the fight. *Why had he blacked out?* His wounds did not appear to have been as serious as he had previously thought. Ell checked his body and found new pink scars, the skin pulled tight as it did when freshly healed. If the Source Water had been able to heal him so quickly, then the wounds could not have been deep. *Could they? And what of his cloudy mind?* He hadn't felt such a blinding headache in all his years, let alone this inability to think straight. He needed Dacunda. He wanted some answers.

He shoved himself to his feet roughly and found that at least his body was working properly even though he was much sorer than he normally would have been after a fight, even allowing for the injuries. Something was definitely out of the ordinary.

"Where's my sister?" Ell queried, still trying to get his bearings, as a ray of light pierced the gray above him, shining down and illuminating the ravine with a wet luminescence. The light shone and sparkled in every dewdrop and puddle that remained from the last rainfall. Judging by the looks of things, that had been not longer than an hour or so past.

Ryder jerked his head backwards as he continued to chew his way through the meat, indicating that apparently Ell's sister was somewhere to the south. Ell widened his eyes in expectation and cocked his head forward and to the side, waiting for a vocal response.

His cousin managed to respond in a voice muffled by the food in his mouth. "Hunting. Need to replenish supplies," Ryder smirked good-naturedly and shrugged, holding up handfuls of food that he would no doubt eat, as if to say he understood that he was to blame for the shortage and felt no shame about it. Ell shook his head silently.

"Well, I could do to stretch my legs. I'll go see if I can find her." Ell turned to make his way up the embankment and into the forest to the south.

In a heartbeat, Ryder was up and on his feet. All jesting had left his face and in its place was a serious expression. "Look, Ell, I don't know if that's a good idea." The sun passed behind a cloud again and the shadows fell on his cousin's face as he spoke. "Father said after everything that… happened, that maybe you should just rest. If you were to wake up before he returned, I was to keep you here. Resting." He said the word, *resting*, differently, as if it was to replace something else. It didn't feel like Ryder was telling him he should rest. It felt like Ryder was trying to politely tell him that he was being babysat. Guarded.

In frustration, Ell acquiesced. It was true that his legs felt a bit wobbly still. Traipsing through the forest and trying to track his sister, did feel like a lot of effort at the moment. But he wanted somebody to talk to about recent events. His sister was usually the one to whom he went for discussions such as these. If he went to anybody at all that is.

Perhaps Ryder might know something, he supposed. "Ry, be straight with me. What happened? What's got you all so spooked?"

"Spooked maybe isn't the right word, Ell," he said after swallowing. "Uncertain, confused, or even astonished might be more apt descriptions to use."

Ell rolled his eyes. "Never can get a straight answer out of you."

His cousin looked at him with a more serious expression again. "I know you're confused Ell, so are we." He shook his head, and his two long braids wiggled back and forth on either side of his chest where they hung forward over each shoulder. Ryder's skin was as pale as Ell's, but his hair was just the lightest shade of brown, not the blond locks that Ell possessed.

His cousin continued. "I just don't really know what to say. Don't think any of us do really." He paused and then finished his thought, grabbing another hunk of meat almost as if his hand did it subconsciously. Ryder was nothing if not a hungry elf. "I've never seen anything like it." His cousin's voice dropped as if telling a tale. In a way he was, because even though Ell had occupied the main role in the tale, he was also the one seeking answers. "It was like you were twice, three times the warrior you are normally."

Ell cocked his head in confusion. That didn't make sense. *Did it?* He had felt a sense of power within him during the ambush, but he had chalked it up to the intense fury he had let loose as he fought. "What do you mean?"

Now it was Ryder's turn to look confused. "What do you mean, what do I mean? Ell, you cut through the first three Departed who confronted you like they were children learning their first sword forms. Those were slavers in a battle rage, and you killed them in a matter of heartbeats." He looked piercingly at Ell. "Cousin, you *shattered* one of their shields with just a knife, not to mention the arm beneath. And that's not even getting to the strangest part."

"It's not?" Ell was beginning to feel bewildered now. Why was his cousin looking at him like he was some kind of unnatural thing? He searched his memory. What *had* happened in the ambush? There had been killing for sure. He had felt stronger, but had assumed it was the torrent of emotions pouring through him. *What else?* The mist!

Ryder spoke as if telling a story to someone who had not witnessed the event, realizing that Ell must be having a hard time putting the pieces together.

"You fought Silverfist. He's known to be one of the deadliest warriors in the whole land. Yet you stood toe to toe with him and gave as good as you got, if not better. He wounded you, sure, but from where I was standing, the traitor looked to be doing his best just to stay alive."

"He was holding back, waiting for his chance to escape," Ell argued, not willing to accept whatever it was his cousin was trying to impress upon him.

Ryder shook his head almost angrily, "No Ell, you *bled* him! I don't think even Father could have done that, the speed with which Silverfist fought. You should have died, yet you were equal to him, his match. And I haven't even gotten to the mist yet!"

"Alright, alright," Ell placated his cousin, hands up in front of himself. "I get it. I had a lucky day and fought well, even for me."

His cousin was again shaking his head in a frustrated manner, and opened his mouth to argue just as his brother and father arrived from the east. "You aren't listening, Ell. Even if we put the duel aside it was still strange. The mist *followed* you. I've never seen anything like it, nor heard of it… except in myths."

At that, his cousin shut up and allowed his returning father to speak, almost as if his father had cautioned him to keep quiet and he had broken that vow. Ryder often wore a guilty expression from one prank or another, like when stealing food, and he wore that same look now as he gazed upon Dacunda.

Ell's uncle looked none the worse for wear after a battle and a half day spent scouting. Come to think of it, Dacunda rarely looked anything but strong and able.

"Ah, awake now." It was a statement not a question. "Glad you are up. We need to get moving as soon as you're able, Elliyar." Dacunda spoke in his matter of fact tone of voice. He would never push one of his family members beyond their limitations, yet neither would he coddle them. If they could move then they would. Ell and his family lived in a constant state of movement. They were nomads, whether it was traveling from one raid to another or simply place-to-place in the mountains of Andalaya. Either way protected them from falling prey to random slaver bands. The nomadic life had been adopted by nearly all of the Highest since the fall of Verdantihya. Villages had been abandoned and the people moved from place to place, staying low, until it was time to strike from the shadows and retreat yet again.

"Uncle," he began hesitantly, and then paused. How did one make sense of what had happened?

Dacunda seemed to sense what he was thinking and stalled further questions with an upraised hand. There was a glimmer of understanding in his eyes, a spark of knowledge that he was not prepared to share just yet. "There will be time for questions later. After scouting back along his trail, I believe Silverfist was alone with this band, yet it would be good to move and put distance between us and this place." His uncle glanced at the dead Departed left lying in the wet earth of the ravine. A stench had arisen from the bodies. They deserved no burial and would receive none. Ell felt a surge of savage satisfaction at that.

Ell allowed himself to be persuaded to set his questions aside. In a way, he was glad. He wasn't sure if he was ready to face whatever answers his uncle possessed. Sometimes knowing was worse than not knowing—ignorance could be bliss. There were things in life that could just confuse a person. Right now, his life was simple. Fight. Bleed. Kill. Defend Andalaya and exact vengeance. *Did he want to muddy that world up?*

Rihya arrived as they were beginning to break the small camp they had made while Ell was unconscious, and she readied her things with the rest of them. Ell expected a quip from her about sleeping the day away, just as Ryder had done earlier, but surprisingly she said nothing other than that it was good to see him up and about. Perhaps the lack of answers had her on edge also. It was not always easy to forget her fiery, passionate nature and see that, when all was said and done, she was still a big sister and he her little brother. She was probably worried. He put on his best show of being recovered, not complaining as they began to run, even though his body fairly screamed with aches and pains that never should have been there from a simple ambush.

"Where to?" Dahranian asked his father. Short and to the point.

"Let us follow the river west a ways," Dacunda headed their course back towards the Westrill. "I still seek my…acquaintance. Though I am not certain where he is, I feel in my gut west is the way we should go. And if that fails, then we'll turn north."

Dacunda often lead from his instincts. His *gut* he called it. Whatever it was, it was usually worth listening to. Whether it was a manifestation of his bond with the land or just keen instincts, Ell was not sure. Yet, he knew that on more than one occasion his uncle's gut decision making had saved their lives. This time their lives might not be on the line, but the way his uncle kept going on about finding this acquaintance of his, made Ell fairly certain that Dacunda felt it was very important. Ell wondered idly who this mysterious person might be.

They ran hard but did not push themselves to exhaustion, for which Ell was thankful. He was hard pressed to keep up as it was. He hid his fatigue from the others, not wishing to show weakness or be faced with a discussion about why he was so exhausted from a few, simple wounds. The questions lurked in the back of his mind, however, taking up space with their unwanted whispers of confusion, hinting at things that were just beyond his reach of understanding.

The following days passed quietly. No more slavers were encountered. Winter was a season of fewer raids and spring had only just spread its green fingers across the land. Their path along the Westrill led them gradually northwest and snow still lay on the ground in patches as they went farther north into the mountains. It was not everywhere, but a light dusting here and patch of white there, and the reminders of a winter not long past were evident. Ell didn't mind. The cold didn't bother him the way it did some, and he found the snow beautiful, the way each flake seemed to glow, a shiny crystal of cold in the weak, spring sunlight.

Rugged, steep-peeked mountains made up the western region of Andalaya, reaching almost the entire way to the high-cliffed, western coast. Day blended into night, blended into day, as they ran lightly through their surroundings. They hunted or fished at resting spots along the trail or wherever they decided to make camp for the night. Sometimes they set snares for whatever animals might be around, to be checked at the morning's first light.

At one campsite, their path had run high along the cliffs of a gorge overlooking the Westrill, the river a small, fast moving, water snake beneath them. Their camp overlooked the land from a vantage point. A never-ending sea of forest stretched in all directions, punctuated by peak after peak of white-tipped mountains. At dusk, the sun set beyond the horizon and the stars shone brightly. They were a silver dusting across the night sky. Ell couldn't help but imagine that whatever Creator had made the world, had done a fine job at painting the Andalayan nightscape. Here, Ell felt the land and the wild. Where Verdantihya had been a connection to his people's origins, this far out into the wild simply reminded him of how big the world was and how small one elf really was in comparison to all the rest.

The path continued west and north, day after day, and yet they saw no sign of Dacunda's acquaintance. Or rather, Dacunda saw no sign of him as he had volunteered hardly any more information as they traveled. Only Rihya in her vibrant frustration, green hair flaring in the wind at a resting point, could manage to pry even the tiniest clue from their uncle.

She stamped her foot and fondled a knife at her belt as if considering using it. "Where are we going, Uncle?" She demanded an answer. "We have been moving for days. Why, we might soon reach the cliffs of Anover. They can't be more than a few days on from here." The western cliffs were renowned for their views and sunsets. It was said that watching the sun set from the cliffs of Anover was as close as one got to experiencing the beauty and peace that had been won by the Highest during the First Days when the land had been subdued and the darkness pressed to the farthest corners of the world. But those days were gone, lost in myth and mystery. Even the lore of the Highest, that surrounded the First Days, was little more than legend. Much of it was hard to believe, even for members of its own race.

Dacunda shrugged his shoulders, stretching the muscles as he rolled them. He was powerfully built. Long, long ago he must have had an ancestor that was from the south, back when the two races had been on more pleasant terms. Ell supposed he had the same ancestor as Dacunda since he was the brother of Ell's father, Adan, yet the characteristics had not manifested in Ell or his sister. They were both typically fair-haired and lean, like the majority of the northern elves. At least his sister would have been fair-haired were it not for her desire for flair and flash. Her green hair, the color of spring grass, was distinctive if nothing else. He was not entirely sure how she dyed it either. But now did not seem the time to interrupt and ask.

"It is likely I will not be able to find him," Dacunda finally responded and Rihya's mouth dropped open in incredulous vexation.

"What?" she cried. "We run for days and now you admit you will likely not even be able to find this friend of yours?" Ell was forced to admit he agreed with his sister on this one. What were they doing if they were not going to be able to locate this elf?

His uncle put up a hand for silence. His presence was commanding and silence he got. "I said that I would not be able to find him. I rarely can. However, if we get close enough, *he* will most likely find *me*." His uncle's description of this friend was making him sound more mysterious by the moment.

Apparently, that was enough of an answer, even for Rihya. She knew how to pick and choose her battles and the look on Dacunda's face brooked no further argument.

They ran the rest of the day in silence, each person lost in their own thoughts. The day waned and the sun began to drop from its crest, sinking towards the west. It sank lazily, in no hurry, and although the day waned, it seemed to do so without rush, as if it had its own mind and knew that one did not force the day to turn to night, nor the night to day.

As they followed the path along the river through a mountain pass, they crossed the summit and saw something Ell never thought to see in his lifetime. It was a village. All the towns of Andalaya had long since been abandoned, a sitting population was one that was quickly found and picked off by slavers. Yet there they were. It was not a city by any means, but it was a group of people. There was a hustle and bustle of activity in what could only be called a village square in the center of a cluster of perhaps a dozen or so houses, which had been built from logs, dirt, and plants, or dug into the green hillsides. There were even a couple of elf homes cradled in the branches of a large tree. All in all, there could not have been much more than seventy of the Highest living there, yet even that amount was beyond a shock to Ell. Most of the Highest traveled in bands of five to ten, twenty at the most. Families grouped together and lived nomadically, sharing what they had with other families when they crossed their paths, yet moving on when it was time to go.

Dacunda's face darkened as he watched the scene far below. He set his course down the mountain path and into the small valley with a determined step. Ell could tell there was almost an angry cast to his eyes, uncommon for Dacunda except when he looked upon his enemies. And these surely were not his enemies. Yet the look on his face remained as they ran towards the village.

The path cut sharply into the downward slope of the land, zigzagging back and forth to dull the steepness. Next to it, the Westrill poured forth in a foaming waterfall and cascaded down to the pool far beneath it, before gathering its torrents and moving on a touch more lazily into the valley.

They finally reached the valley floor after a dizzying descent and set their course for the village. What was to come, Ell didn't know. But he knew that his uncle had a set to his gait that suggested conflict of some kind. Ell almost felt the way he had as a child when his uncle had scolded him for doing something wrong. He glanced left and right at his cousins running beside him and he could see from the resigned looks on their faces that they had recognized it also and were determined to stay in their father's good graces by not questioning him.

Ell looked back at his sister, just as she was about to open her mouth and clearly ask something of Dacunda. Ell shook his head at his sister in an attempt to silence her. Their uncle did not grow angry often, but when he did, it was best to not provoke his wrath further. Rihya seemed to catch the meaning of his shaken head in her direction and her mouth snapped shut before she voiced whatever she had been on the verge of saying.

He felt relief that she controlled herself. Sometimes his sister would push and prod until she got what she wanted. In this case, he wasn't sure what it was that she wanted, but at other times, her prodding could lead to an explosion of emotion from any of the males with whom she accompanied. She had that effect at times. With a toss of her hair, she pursed her lips and stayed silent.

And so on they ran, the silence stretching more loudly than their footfalls. The distance from the head of the valley to the village on its opposite western side was not far. It was a small valley, cut from the mountains by the Westrill as it flowed, and a few meadows and trees dotted its face and then the mountains rose up again, masking it from the outside.

Ell wasn't sure what they would find exactly when they reached the village, but from the way his uncle ran, almost with the intensity he carried as he ran towards battle, Ell began preparing himself for whatever might come. Whatever they were to find in this village, it was clear that Dacunda disapproved of something, and that put Ell on his guard. One didn't survive long in Andalaya without staying on guard. The wind was cool and crisp across their faces as they breezed through the tiny valley, their bodies moving powerfully and lithely as they always did. With the sun near to setting, they finally reached the village in the hazy light of dusk. It was like nothing Ell had ever experienced.

Chapter Eight

She stood as part of the ring of people surrounding Ell and his family. Her hair was the typical blonde of the northern race, with just a hint more wave to it, like Ell's own. The wings of her hair were braided and pulled behind her head, then fastened into a crown-like appearance. There were wildflowers speckled here and there throughout her crown of braids, as if she were the princess of the land around her. Something about her separated her from the rest. Perhaps it was the way she looked. She was beautiful in an earthy, natural way, with a nose that was just slightly too wide to ever be referred to as elegant or refined. The Highest, as a whole, tended to carry an air of immaculateness to them. The northern race was nothing if not dignified. But she was different, beautifully imbalanced. Imperfect. And for some reason Ell could not take his eyes off her.

Dacunda spoke with the leaders of this village, while the rest of Ell's family waited uncomfortably at the center of attention, as the number of spectators grew. His uncle wore an impassive, stern face, a face that cowed resistance and usually got him his way. That was not the case here.

"This is beyond folly. Madness," Dacunda said with a sweeping gesture of his arm to indicate the village and its surroundings. "You are inviting destruction." He punctuated the sentence with his firmest look.

Two elderly elves stood across from him, maintaining a mask of calm that seemed a bit strained to Ell. They wore faces that said they had heard this all before and were not inclined to listen again.

"That may be," one of them said, his voice strong despite being nearly twice the age of Dacunda, "but we are willing to take that chance." Elves of any race did not normally live much longer than humans, but there were a few exceptions. Ell had heard stories, legends, and whispers around the fire of some of the Highest who had lived far beyond the typical length of a lifespan. However, it was not common. In general, the difference between humans and elves was that elves simply wore time better. They remained more capable, more competent, up until their passing from this reality into the next. Humans withered gradually, but from a younger age. Elves did not. Even the elderly of the Highest were sometimes seen to pick up a bow or spear and lend an arm to combat when necessary. However, even though the aging process happened later in life for an elf, they were not immortal. Far from it. The time took its toll on them as well, but more suddenly. Whereas humans eased into old age, the Highest were thrust into it. When the end came for an elf it came rapidly, the way a plant shrivels in the summer sun when it is uprooted. No time to think much on the matter before it was over and done.

Dacunda was growing frustrated and it was showing as anger. “Chance?” He said in a low, dangerous voice. “Certainty is more like it.”

The female elf blinked her eyes slowly, as if carrying an exhaustion that she did not show. “We know the risks.” She said simply to Ell’s uncle. The crowd around them grew restless, and there were mutterings from them in response to what Dacunda had said. Ell wondered how they felt about his uncle’s proclamation of impending doom for their establishment.

Dacunda shook his head forcefully now, not bothering to hide his anger or word his response tactfully. “We fight to slow the enemy’s advance. We spend our lives, pay a price in blood that you cannot imagine, and here you sit as if the world were spinning as normal. Where is the honor in that? Where is the wisdom?” Dacunda was breathing harder than Ell had seen him do even when they were running. His uncle was angrier than Ell had realized.

Ell understood the emotion. What right had these elves to leave the battle for others? Did they not care about paying the enemy back, life for life, vengeance for a dead realm? He felt his own heart hardening as he mentally supported his uncle’s words. He glanced around and saw his cousins and sister with similar hard expressions on their faces. The scars they wore on their bodies no longer felt trivial or part of everyday life when compared to the blissful apathy of this settlement.

Ell stared hard at the crowd of onlookers and not a few pulled back from his angry gaze. Then she was there again. She had moved from the outskirts of the circle, coming closer. To hear more clearly, he assumed. She moved with an exaggerated limp. It must have been a hideous wound to cause such a limp. Source Water could prevent lasting damage from all but the worst of injuries. That or perhaps they hadn’t had Source Water available when it happened. Ell knew well how true that could be, since many of his own scars could bear testament to the fact that what you needed in life was not always available.

Ell made to shift his focus back to the conversation at hand, determined to interject his own harsh opinion into the matter, but as he was about to speak their eyes caught. They held the gaze for a moment. Then she smiled. When she did, her average mouth opened into the most perfect smile upon which he had ever laid eyes. Her smile said that even though he was a stranger, and potentially dangerous, she welcomed him nonetheless.

Their eyes broke contact and she turned and whispered something to a friend beside her. They laughed together, genuine delight as if the angry conversation in front of her could do nothing to stem her enjoyment of life.

Ell turned back to the conversation. Dacunda was still telling the elders, and everyone else listening, why their decisions were poor.

"Do you think that the slavers will not pass by here, that this is too remote a location for them to discover?" His uncle clenched his fists tightly.

The female elf spoke again and her age was even more apparent. Weariness crept into her voice. "Again, I say, we are aware of the risk. But is it not right to hope for the slimmest of chances that we might be able to live in peace here?"

"What right have you to peace?" Dacunda questioned with a sincerity he had lacked in the conversation previously, as if he was trying to soothe his own anger. His voice softened slightly. "What right? When the rest of the world, your own people, are at war?"

"As much right as any," the male leader interjected sharply as if he had heard enough. His stiff response sparked Dacunda's anger again and his uncle let it show.

"Fools! You blindly wish for what is not possible." He shook his head in disgust. "If you are so eager to be taken captive and enslaved, then come with us on a raid. I assure you there is chance enough of capture whenever we fight. This," He gestured again to the village around him, "is a trap waiting to close." His words carried finality and brought a clear end to the discussion.

The two elders bowed their heads in understanding that he was finished.

"That as may be, you are welcome to Indiria's Emerald—or as we tend to call it, Little Vale. Can we offer you some refreshment, a place to rest your head? It is the least we could do for those of you brave enough to fight." The lady elf was honest in her offer of hospitality and she seemed well able to overcome or put aside the differences from their discussion.

Dacunda snorted in response and stared off in frustration into the shifting clouds above the cliffs that overlooked the valley—Indiria's Emerald, named for the tiny, green gem worn by one of Andalaya's most famous queens. Dahranian spoke up in his father's place.

"We would appreciate that very much, Elder. Thank you." But even his tone was stiff and clipped as if Dacunda's viewpoints were too deeply ingrained in him, as well, to be able to shed the emotions of the argument.

Ell felt similarly. He couldn't imagine trying to wait out the conflict on the sidelines, in an out of the way corner of the world. He understood the need for rest. Indeed, he and his family would likely not plan any attacks on the enemy to the south for some time, yet that did not mean they were ignoring their duty to resist. It was the cycle. Fight, rest. Fight, rest. Fight. In his mind, the cycle always began and ended with fight because he had been fighting for as long as he could remember. It was all he had known. It was where his memories began. And his life would end with fighting he had no doubt. One day, he would fall in battle and not get up. That was the reality of life as a warrior and he was at peace with the idea.

He looked around as the crowd began to disperse, hoping to catch a glimpse of the girl, that strange girl, who had shaken something loose in his head. She was standing still, watching him as well. There was an odd look in her eyes, something he had never encountered before. *Was nothing about this girl recognizable? Was nothing normal?* Everything about her hinted at mysteries of life he did not know or could not yet understand.

He strode over to her, purposeful and confident, prepared to ask her what she was thinking, why she stared at him so blatantly for so long. But as he approached, his mind seemed to empty. All he could remember was the public argument from moments before. She smiled as he approached and made no move to leave.

Ell wracked his brain for what he had been going to say. The silence stretched awkwardly as he couldn't remember anything he had planned to say. She cocked her head slightly to the side as if trying to figure out why he had come over to her. Finally, giving up on whatever the reason for which he had approached in the first place, Ell regurgitated the previous discussion.

"Why will you not fight?" He asked rather lamely. After listening to nearly twenty minutes of arguing between his uncle and the elders, how necessary was it to repeat the question? Ell swore silently in his head. This was foreign ground to him. Give his hands a weapon to hold, a hood to pull low over his face, and an enemy to stalk. Those were the actions to which he was accustomed. Not this. Talking to pretty girls was not something he had experience doing. *Why was he focusing on the fact that she was pretty?* Ell frantically tried to clear his mind, since she had just answered his question and he had heard none of her response.

"What?" Ell was forced to ask dumbly, berating himself for his lack of attention. Inattentiveness got you killed on the battlefield. *But this isn't the battlefield, is it?* A corner of his mind whispered.

She giggled. "I answered your question with a question," She said, "before your eyes went blank from staring, that is." She smiled again at him humorously.

Ell blushed slightly. "Well, would you care to repeat yourself?"

The elf laughed again. She did that a lot. "If I must. I said, is fighting the only thing worth doing?" Her face grew mysterious as she said it. "Answer me that and I will tell you why I do not fight." Then she spun on her heel and limped off towards one of the shelters dug into the hillside.

It was probably just as well that she left; it spared Ell the shame of not having been able to come up with a quick response to her question. He watched her walk away. It was amazing how graceful she managed to look even with such a pronounced limp. Her right leg was the leg she favored. She wore typical, tight-fitting, green hose, a small, light brown tunic that she filled out nicely. She was slender like all northern elves, and he found himself filled with regret at seeing the back of her. She disappeared into a shelter that was dug into the hillside; the grass growing all over what was now walls and a roof, with only a simple, carved hole in the wall for a door and one more for a window. The moment had passed. Ell sighed and looked to return to his family.

His uncle, Dahranian, and Rihya were conversing in low voices, unaware of his momentary excursion to speak with the girl. He hadn't even asked her name, he realized. However, Ryder was not so oblivious. His keen eye had sighted Ell's movement and he smirked good-naturedly.

"Girlfriend, eh?" He asked with a grin. "About time, I say."

"What are you talking about, Ry?" Ell jabbed back verbally, "I've never seen you with a girl either."

Ryder laughed and responded amiably. "That you haven't. Too much fighting to be done." He winked and added, "Plus, I already have my favorite company right here," he pulled out a pouch full of dried meat and started nibbling. "Girly elf, would find herself in stiff competition for my attention. Wouldn't be fair to her," he mumbled between mouthfuls. Ell didn't know how he could eat so much! He was a never-ending meal, a feast waiting to happen. Ell couldn't help but smile at his cousin's quips. If anyone could make him laugh, it was Ryder.

His uncle broke off his discussion as he heard their laughing. He was still in no mood for nonsense and his look, sobered them both up quickly.

"Dahranian has made his point well," he paused and inclined his head in respect to his eldest son, "I was against the idea of staying here for any more time than to simply wrap up that idiotic discussion from earlier," Dacunda breathed deeply to calm himself. "However, my son has pointed out that we have covered much ground in the last few weeks. Too much perhaps. I feel it in my bones, and I assume the rest of you do also." He rubbed one hand wearily over his eyes as if to accentuate the statement. It shaded his face a moment from the fading light.

Dacunda continued. “We will rest the night here,” he looked up at the twilight sky. “Perhaps even a day longer. Then we will keep to our course. So rest up, there is no life of peace, no quiet existence for you all, I am afraid.” He clenched his fist and tapped his chest, “For we have honor and duty, and we do not neglect it.” He said the last words slowly, pointedly, for emphasis. When he saw that his words had the desired impact on his family, he nodded, satisfied.

They made camp on the outskirts of the village, next to the river. A young boy, no more than six or seven years of age, brought them a basketful of food and Ryder accepted it with delight. Rihya rolled her eyes expressively at their cousin and yanked it away from him.

“So you don’t gobble it all up,” she explained as she set it next to her hip on the far side of her body away from Ryder. “It’s a wonder you aren’t as fat as a human, the way you eat.” Ell watched his cousin Ryder act emotionally wounded, but they all knew that Rihya was kidding.

The rest of the night passed uneventfully. With the sun gone, they unrolled their bedrolls and tried to get some sleep. Dacunda kept the first watch, even though Rihya had protested that it wasn’t necessary with the village right next to them. However, Ell’s uncle was nothing if not cautious. Ell fell asleep to a night sky filled with sparkles and swirls of the many stars and their various patterns.

Chapter Nine

Ell awoke in the morning feeling more refreshed than he could remember. He must have missed his shift on watch or somebody had failed to wake him. He was supposed to have taken the last shift, but Ryder, who was the one who should have awakened him, sat slumped against a log. It appeared as if he had fallen asleep on his own shift and had therefore, been unable to wake Ell for his. His cousin's mistake would have been unacceptable in nearly any other circumstance, but Ell felt like they would be fairly safe here in this tiny valley. There was always the chance of a slaver band making its way through here, but a couple hours of missed surveillance surely wouldn't end up killing them. Likely Ryder was as tired as Ell had found himself when he had lay down to sleep last night. Weeks of running without much rest could wear down even the hardiest of elves.

He rose and folded his bedroll neatly, tucking it into a corner of his pack. They traveled lightly, but a small pack was still necessary for survival in the mountains, especially in the winter. A bedroll, tinder and flint, some food, Source Water, and weapons were all among the necessities they carried with them. However, they of course, used the most lightweight items they could find.

The morning light was just peeking into Little Vale, over the eastern pass through which they had arrived yesterday. The sun shone brightly and it was just cresting the pass, which allowed for the light to shine directly through the river running into a waterfall on this side. The result was what appeared to be golden water cascading over the mountainside to the valley far below its peak. It was a glorious sight. One of the most incredible sunrises he had ever seen. He felt slightly jealous that these elves, who had settled this small valley, were able to look at the sight each morning if they desired.

He filled his hand with water from the flowing river in front of him, kneeling low on the lip of the grassy bank to drink. The water was cool and refreshing to his dry mouth. Somehow, he always ended up with a dry mouth in the morning. It didn't matter if he was here in the west of Andalaya, in the north, or far to the south, it was habitual. His morning routine was to grab a drink first thing, and without it, he felt it hard to concentrate on anything but the dry, itchy sensation in his throat. Ell gulped down a few more mouthfuls of water and rose off his knee to return to camp, when he froze.

A few feet to the side of him was a long-eared roebuck, daring the morning light and an unprotected, open meadow for a drink of water itself. Ell's hand went to his belt; he had a knife there, attached at all times. With one quick motion, he would probably be able to draw, throw, and bring down the buck. He was good at a knife toss. Not quite so talented as Rihya perhaps, but adept nonetheless. Yet something restrained him. Maybe it was the stillness of the dawn, which he felt loathe to interrupt, or the eagerness of the creature as it had its own morning drink, just as Ell had been doing only moments earlier. Whatever the reason, Ell's hand was stayed, and he did not draw the blade. He just watched. *Not everything had to be life and death, did it?* Perhaps there were moments like this that one could grab even in the midst of war where instincts and weapons could be set aside. Ell didn't believe for a second that he or any others of the Highest could escape the growing turmoil of their world completely the way these elves were trying to do here in the village in Indiria's Emerald—or Little Vale as they called it—yet perhaps moments of tranquility were still possible.

The buck raised its head as it finished drinking and then stared Ell in the eyes as if recognizing that the hunter had stayed his instincts. It inclined its head fractionally—it was such a minimal motion Ell wasn't even sure that he had seen it correctly—then it bounded off, back into Legendwood. Andalaya had always been a magical land, a place where even interactions with the beasts of the forest were possible. Ell smiled slightly at the encounter and then stepped lightly back to camp.

The others had awakened and were unhappy with Ryder for falling asleep on his watch. They were badgering Ryder for his lack of attention in their own separate ways. Rihya was half scolding, half teasing her cousin, making verbal jabs at his dignity. It was the sort of thing they often did together and he was doing his best to ignore. The reason he was trying to ignore Rihya was because Dacunda was giving his youngest son an earful about proper conduct as a watchman. Ell's uncle was never one to relax. He, like them, lived in a state of war. The only difference was that he was the leader, therefore a weight of responsibility rested upon his shoulders. He took that responsibility seriously, and any who failed to meet his expectations could anticipate a similar set of responsibilities placed upon them as well in his eyes. Dahranian simply looked at his brother quietly, a frown of disapproval on his face.

Ell made his good mornings and grabbed a mouthful of nuts and berries before slinging his bow over his shoulder and making his way towards the village.

"And where are you going, Elliyar?" Dacunda sounded ready to transfer some of his annoyance with Ryder upon his nephew. Ryder saw the interaction begin and ducked away quickly, mumbling something about a drink from the river before his father could rein him in again with further chastisement. Dacunda grimaced slightly at his departing son and then focused on Ell.

"To the village." The sun was shining directly in Ell's eyes and he was forced to squint as he attempted to make out his uncle's face.

Dacunda grunted noncommittally to that answer then spoke. "Just don't get too comfortable here. I doubt we shall spend longer than one more night before moving on." Ell felt a slight tug of disappointment at that statement. That was odd. *Why did he feel disappointed?* He had never felt disappointment at leaving anywhere other than perhaps, Verdantihya.

He agreed that he would not and then turned to walk the short distance to the village. He reached it in a matter of minutes, and in typical Highest fashion, the village was awake and already moving with the morning light. Dawn was the time when most of his people rose and began their day.

He saw one elf from the village stride off with a companion towards the woods that abutted the north edge of the village. The small settlement nestled just on the northern bank of the Westrill, with one side of the village near the river and tree-studded mountain slopes on the other. The elf had his bow slung over his shoulder and was obviously off to do some hunting. A female elf was patching the roof of a shelter, while another elf taught a group of children who were gathered around his feet. It was all what Ell had seen before in the nomadic bands of the Highest that roamed Andalaya, yet it was different. This place was set, it was fixed in one spot, and the pattern and rhythm of life was clearly established. It would not be changing and neither would their setting. It was a foreign concept to Ell who had spent his entire existence moving from place to place, whether it was running away from slavers or running towards battle.

Conflicting feelings clashed within him. He felt the draw, the pull of this place, a village where peace seemed to thrive. Yet his uncle's words about the folly of such a location as this echoed in his mind. He felt the eerie sensation that what he looked upon at this moment, although it may seem like fixed circumstances, would not last long.

Ell wandered idly for a time, just soaking up the presence of the place. He was greeted with friendly smiles and the occasional waved hand. They were one people. Everybody in the village was one of the Highest, and even the frustrated argument from the night before couldn't change the fact that Ell was their kin.

It wasn't until he saw her that Ell realized he had been looking for her. She was walking with a child on her back, beside a youth. She was tickling the child as best as she could while it was behind her and the child was squirming with delight and giggling, nearly falling off her back. The youth beside her was tall. He was as tall as Ell, and he could not have been much more than a year younger, and must almost be reaching his renaming also. Ell had just recently passed his own day of renaming, the eighteenth year, where a father renamed his son with the name he would carry for the rest of his life. Dacunda had offered to do it, but Ell had respectfully declined. His name, Elliyar, meant dusk runner. And while that name might be slightly foreboding, a dark foreshadowing of the future of the Highest and the nightfall of their civilization, it was his name all the same. Something in him rejected the idea of taking any name other than the one given to him by his real father. And so Elliyar he remained.

This youth would soon be approaching his own renaming, yet he seemed green, springtime to Ell's wintered experience with life and danger. Ell watched them walk.

"I have an answer for you." Ell called out without thinking. His voice caught the little party's attention and they all turned to watch him approach.

The girl cocked her head to the side as if waiting for him to continue. "You do? And what is it?" Her voice was friendly, even curious.

"Yes," Ell responded firmly, resolutely. "Yes, fighting is the only thing worth doing."

She gave a disappointed look and made as if to respond, but Ell raised his hand to forestall her. He then elaborated, "In the state of our world, that is, in this state of war, fighting is all that is worth doing. However," he paused and inclined his head as if to concede an imaginary point, "in a different reality, a different setting, it would not necessarily be so."

The girl seemed to be thinking deeply on his answer. The boy beside her seemed to be as well. He was a young man really, yet Ell could not seem to think of him that way. There was just a freshness, an inexperienced look to him that made one estimate him younger than his true number of years.

Finally, the girl responded. She no longer looked disappointed. It was as if Ell's answer had challenged her in an unexpected way. "I see your point and understand your opinion." The girl was cloaked in sunlight now, her face illuminated by the morning ambiance. She continued, "But I cannot agree." Then she smiled at him. "And in fairness to our deal, I will now tell you why I do not fight."

Ell waited expectantly.

"Not all of us were created to be warriors," she said. She watched his face as if anticipating his lack of satisfaction at her answer. Her answer left him feeling slightly underwhelmed.

"That's it? That's all you have to say?" Ell asked incredulously. "That's not much of an answer."

She tilted her head back and let forth a silvery laugh, not at all offended by his dissatisfaction. "Well, neither was yours, when you think about it." And with that, she turned and continued to walk in the direction in which she had been going. The youth beside her had a faintly smug look on his face, though Ell could not see a reason for his attitude.

Panic hit Ell. She was leaving. *Why was he panicking? It was the most ludicrous of emotions.* "Wait!" He cried out. She turned back expectantly. "What's your name?"

"Miriyah. But my friends call me Miri." Then she was gone around the corner of a log building before he could get in another word. *Miriyah.*

He sighed to himself. It was time to explore the rest of the village, he supposed. As long as he was here, he might as well get a feel for what "peace" felt like even if it wouldn't last.

The village was small, compact, but not crowded. There were log shelters erected throughout the village, big enough to house a family and no more. Some of the shelters were not built of wood but instead were dug out of the hillside at the bottom of the mountain. Their walls were made of earth and grass, and the walls grew straight into the roof in a curved, continuous slope. The last types of homes were a few shelters built in the trees. The tree shelters were beautifully crafted, the homes erected from wood that appeared to be more like a part of the tree itself than any created structure. It was as if the elves here had somehow managed to grow houses in the trees rather than build them. Braced on some of the spreading limbs, the houses in the trees were large enough for a family.

It was strange for Ell to look at these shelters. It wasn't that he hadn't seen their like before. In fact, many times he had seen the homes and villages of his people spread far and wide across Andalaya. However, previously they had always been abandoned. He had never seen a village that wasn't cold and deserted. This place of warmth and hope and life was something altogether foreign. It wasn't that he thought it wise or disagreed with his uncle. No, he was just as firm in his speculations that the end would come swiftly and painfully for this little out of the way and sedentary corner of the map. But a small part of him wished it weren't so. A part wished that he could stay here longer than a day or two, long enough to experience what it might be like to have a life other than just the struggle in which he now lived.

Ell sighed. It was simply not meant to be. Wishing that Andalaya wasn't ruined and its people not at the mercy of their enemies did not make it so. He could wish until the summer came and it would not change a thing. It was better to accept the world for the way it was.

He finished wandering through the small village in a short amount of time and found his way back to camp. The others were still there, having broken their fast with the usual fare of berries, nuts, light bread, and dried venison.

Upon his arrival, Dahranian stood up and grabbed his pitch-black quiver of arrows and bow, and gave Ell a wave in greeting as he strode off into the woods. Ell raised his eyebrows at Ryder and then jerked his head towards the disappearing shadow of his oldest cousin. Ryder answered his unspoken question.

"Off to hunt. Ever the practical one, my brother. He can never just enjoy a moment of rest." Ryder swallowed a mouthful of food and bit off another piece of venison.

"You rest enough for the both of you," Ell quipped.

Ryder threw his head back and laughed. "Is that supposed to offend me, Cousin? I do indeed know when it's time to grab a spear and when it's time to grab a spoon." Ell smiled at his cousin's response. Ryder was almost impossible to offend. He was completely at home in his skin.

Rest. True rest. It had been so long since he had experienced rest and relaxation that he wasn't even sure what it was like. Rest so he could run again. That was the routine. It would be nice to simply lie down beneath the warm, spring skies and maybe even close his eyes.

The late morning light shone brightly through his eyelids as he did just that, making the shadows of his closed eyes, much less dark. He breathed regularly, in and out, until sleep took him. It was not the deep sleep of recovery from a wound or exhaustion, the kind of sleep that isn't truly refreshing because the body was already too worn down to be fully refreshed. No, this was the sleep of idle times at his own convenience rather than out of any real necessity. The kind of rest that one took when there was nothing to do but rest. In truth, it was nearly as foreign a concept to him as the village itself was. Yet, Ell took the rest all the same.

He awoke from his light slumber and, judging by the sky, it had been some hours. Perhaps he had been more tired than he thought. Dahranian had recently returned and was skinning a roebuck beside the camp. It was possible that it was the same buck which Ell had spared this morning by the river, and for some strange reason, Ell felt a twinge of regret that it might be so. He was a hunter, a fighter, and these qualms of mercy were a weakness he could not afford to have, yet for some reason, it would have been nice to think that for once his blade had been stayed from taking blood, and that as a result the creature had run free. He supposed he wouldn't really know whether or not it was the same buck or a different one, and he would eat it and enjoy it all the same. However, a small part of him was beginning to wonder at the strange desire to do more than swing a blade or fire an arrow.

Dahranian was conversing quietly with his father as he cut the meat into manageable portions to then strip and dry. Dacunda often chatted so with his eldest son, since Dahranian was, in effect, second in command to his father. Dacunda greatly valued Dahranian's opinions and perspectives. They finished their conference and Dacunda approached Ell, Rihya, and Ryder, while Dahranian continued his work with the carcass.

"Dahranian has made a good point," Dacunda began, "this valley is fat and fertile. It is relatively safe," his uncle paused then finished his sentence grimly, "for now." His voice carried undertones of the conversation from last night. He clearly did not believe it would stay safe for long.

Dacunda kept speaking quietly to his family, conveying directives. "Dahranian believes that we should stay longer than just one more day."

Ryder's face brightened up a bit. He was never one to complain when less work and more rest was suggested.

Dacunda continued, the early afternoon light causing shadows to dance across his face as it shown through the limbs of the trees overhead. "While I am loathe to halt our journey, the search for my friend, I recognize that you are all much more tired than I have admitted. This will be a good place to replenish our food stores and to regain our health and strength before we forge onward." Ell's uncle cracked a small smile at his family. He was their leader and he carried the role well, but leading was more than just battle tactics and strategies. It was about knowing when to encourage and when to make a follower smile. In this case, it was also about understanding when to create determination and to enforce courage for what was to come.

Dacunda finished up. "Make no mistake; the road ahead is long and arduous. It will not become easier. But we have our honor and we have each other." He tapped a fist to his heart for emphasis. "So enjoy the time we spend here. Learn to refocus and rest. It may be that we will stay longer than a day or two."

He stood up from his squatting position and stepped back beside Dahranian. The two continued setting plans for the future for when they finally did decide to leave Little Vale.

They were staying. Ell felt a strange elation at that knowledge. He couldn't quite figure out why, but for some reason the prospect of not leaving immediately, of staying in one place for a time, was immensely exciting. It was a new experience. He shoved the image of Miri from his mind. Miri wasn't why he was excited, he told himself, although he could not quite convince himself of the fact.

The next few days were a blur of laziness. It was an aspect of life to which Ell was completely unaccustomed. He lay by the river on many occasions, dangling his fingers in the swift current, the water a brisk contrast to the sunny days. He met various elves in the village, and at times helped them with some of their tasks, and at other times, he simply watched, soaking up the ambiance of the place. At nights, he danced with the rest of the Highest by the communal fires in the center of the town. The people here danced with a pure joy for life that was new to Ell. He enjoyed the singing and dancing, especially when his path crossed with Miri's.

And cross it did. He spoke with her on many instances. He often conjured up a reason to be nearby wherever she happened to be, whether it was fixing a shelter, watching a child, or helping clean a fresh kill. Miri was different from anyone he had met. She held a vibrancy for life that was unmatched. Dancing along with the best of them, with or without a limp, singing at the top of her lungs and laughing more than most.

They talked and laughed, and argued often, but Ell always left her company looking forward to the next time when he would be able to share it. Her young friend, Borian, as Ell soon learned was his name, was not as welcoming. He frequently wore a tight expression when Ell was around and was clearly relieved, even pleased, when their company parted. Ell shrugged it off and supposed he simply didn't like strangers. After all not everyone could be as open to new people as Miri was. She always had a smile for whoever was in front of her.

Ell was not the only one who appeared to be enjoying himself during their respite in the village. Ryder had no shortage of food to eat as all was shared in the community. Dahranian fell in with a few of the local hunters and spent a number of days out in the surrounding woods, helping to bring in game or as he liked to refer to it, "earning their keep." He was ever the responsible one just like his father.

Even Dacunda seemed to relax. Ell actually saw him speaking on a number of occasions with the two elders who he had confronted on the afternoon of their arrival. The conversations looked courteous, even containing genuine enjoyment. Ell was surprised and pleased to see his uncle taking his own advice and doing his best to relax.

Riyha was the only one who did not appear to think much of their surroundings. She frequently said to anyone who would listen that she was bored with this place. It didn't seem to hold much interest for her. In truth, Ell understood. The hold the little valley had on his mind might have waned considerably after a day or two the way it had for his sister were it not for Miri. She was what made the experience exciting.

On the morning of their third full day in the village, Ell sat on a rock watching the village bustle into action. He chewed an apple as he saw hunters gather their bows and head to the forest, elves singing as they patched roofs preparing for the spring rains to come, and fixing up what winter's snow, cold, and ice had left in disarray. Children were wandering from lesson to lesson. Their lessons were basically observing the different adults at their tasks, and when they were old enough, participating. Tales and legends laced with the history of the Highest punctuated instruction. The stories brought life and enjoyment to the lessons, providing a break from the mundane, yet they also were important. They carried hidden instruction, teaching the children about their past, their ancestors and the way their people thought, and what they believed. Ell had experienced some of this, he supposed, from his uncle, Dacunda, but it had not been so organized and scheduled. His uncle had simply taught them whatever was needed for the moment. How to string a bow before it was time to hunt, how to sharpen an axe or sword on the eve of battle, the stories around the fire at night to help them forget the fear of running and fighting all the time. Of course, Ell hadn't actually engaged in battle as a child, but as soon as his body had even hinted at reaching manhood, his uncle had put a weapon in his hands and reminded him of duty and honor. Duty and honor were important to Dacunda. Ell could understand. In many ways that was all that remained from the vestiges of a past life in the service of the great kingdom of Andalaya—the land that was no more.

He finished his apple and threw it as hard as he could toward the river. It caught the lip of the bank, tumbled, and spun into the swift flow, carried away by the current.

"And what do you think of it all?" Miri came out of nowhere and sat on the rock beside him. Borian trailed behind her with a slightly sour expression on his face. He was clearly unhappy, as usual, to be in Ell's company.

"Of all what?" Ell asked, not completely sure about what she was speaking.

Miri extended an arm toward the village and the elves going about their business, and basked in the morning light that shone over the eastern pass. "The village, the people, our way of life." She trailed off as if she might have had more to add to that list but chose not to continue.

Ell considered it for a long moment. It was hard to understand his emotions about this tranquil valley, mixed as they were. On the one hand, it held a peace he had not encountered before; it was almost like a flashback to what life must have been like before the fall of Verdantihya. On the other hand, he had seen the war to the south, he had experienced slaver bands raiding farther north and west than this location, so he knew that Little Vale was no more off limits to war than anywhere else.

Finally, he answered. “I find myself wishing that such a place like this could exist yet again.” It was hard to formulate his thoughts into words and he wasn’t sure the meaning came through to Miri.

Miri quirked an eyebrow, “But it does. You are looking at it.”

Ell shook his head regretfully. “I do not mean to offend, Miriyah, but I fear this place will not long survive.”

Borian’s face darkened as he heard Ell’s comment. Ell would have to tread lightly with that one, if he desired to avoid an altercation.

The young hunter spoke. He was lean and tall like all of the Highest, and his skin was paler than most, as if the sun’s kisses slid off and could not stick upon his face. “That is a dark prediction to speak over those who have shown you nothing but hospitality.”

“Not a prediction,” Ell rebutted calmly. Keeping composure with someone who clearly disliked you was key to avoiding a fight. “Simply a fear, a hunch you might say.” He paused, wondering if he should continue. Miri gazed at him as did Borian, and they stayed silent. “I have long learned to listen to my hunches, instincts if you will, and doing so has saved my life more times than I care to remember.”

Borian clenched his hands tightly. “If you are so attuned to your instincts,” he spat sarcastically, “perhaps you would care to prove them on the hunt today. I leave momentarily for my turn to seek game.” He smirked, “A little, shall we say, competition, would not be amiss.”

Ell considered it for a brief instant. It would be fun to test his skill with a bow against this unseasoned, upstart of an elf. A reminder in humility would do him well. Then the thought left his head, and he looked at Miri. No, he would rather converse with this girl, than humble Borian ten times over.

“Thank you, Borian, but I must respectfully decline.” He spread his hands peacefully, “Best of luck on your venture.”

The elf’s face soured again. He really had wanted Ell to come. Perhaps he was better with a bow than Ell gave him credit. Or, perhaps he was simply arrogant. Either way, Ell was glad to have sidestepped the invitation. Borian bid farewell to Miri politely and amiably, then stalked away ignoring Ell. Borian’s exit left Ell alone with Miri, for which he was glad.

“He really doesn’t care for me, does he?” Ell said once Borian was out of earshot.

Miri giggled, “Indeed he does not, although I must admit, I cannot say why that is." She looked at him from the corner of her eye as if to see whether her compliment had gone unnoticed. It had not. Ell smiled faintly in response. *So, perhaps he wasn't the only one quite taken with the other*. For some reason that comforted him. His interest did not seem to be completely unfounded.

She continued, "Give him a chance, however, for we have been friends a long time and he is not always so ornery towards others." She laughed again, that silvery laugh that reminded Ell of nothing so much as a vocal waterfall. "Or, perhaps his dislike of you is founded on something quite real. Your unwashed hair or maybe the smell of someone who has been weeks on the road. You know, there is a river right there," she indicated with her hand, "perfect for bathing." She nudged him with a shoulder as they sat, clarifying the joke for him if he had not already known that she was jesting, lightening the moment. Ell smiled again. She managed to get him to smile more than most people he knew.

Then the moment of levity was past and she circled back to the serious topic that had spurred the entire interaction. "So, you truly believe that all this," she swept her arm lazily towards the village and the valley beyond; "cannot last?"

Ell sighed. He did not wish to burst the bubble of serenity that these villagers seemed to have achieved. Indeed, they must have had outrageous fortune to avoid attack by roving slave bands already. It could not, would not last.

He looked at her seriously. "I have seen war. I have fought the enemy and witnessed its depravity first hand, suffered the consequences of their reign of terror upon the land." He thought painfully of his own dead family. Ell went on, the rock suddenly feeling hard and uncomfortable beneath his body, seeming to reflect the difficult nature of their conversation. "I have seen even the most cautious and capable of the Highest, ambushed, even as they lived nomadically, sticking to the shadows and hidden trails of our fair Andalaya." He paused with remorse before finishing. "No, I am sorry Miriyah, but if that can happen to the best of our people, it will most certainly happen to those who flaunt the freedom they no longer truly possess, those who sit in the open and invite attack."

Miri smiled faintly, as if glad to have finally evoked more of a response from him than a few short phrases. "So, there is a depth to you after all." She had a mysterious look to her face before responding again. "Well, perhaps we will be the lucky few." Ell nodded. One could always hope, but it was not likely.

The girl changed the subject slightly. "Do you do anything other than fight?" She asked curiously. "Have you ever really seen the world you work so hard to defend?"

Ell shifted uncomfortably. He had seen some, the areas of battle. He'd seen the plains where his family raided the camps, the Lower Forest where they often attacked the Departed as they encroached north. But no, he had never really traveled simply for the enjoyment of it. He had crisscrossed Andalaya, setting ambushes and fighting evil enemies and dark creatures, but he had never really *seen* the land just to see it.

He was not ready to fully admit that to her though. "I've seen some."

She saw through his lie immediately. "Right. That's it. We are going on an adventure." She leapt up, staggered a second as her weak right leg gave slightly, and then balanced herself.

"Where?" Ell asked cautiously. Dacunda might not approve of his leaving while they were supposed to be resting.

"The Cliffs of Anover." She smiled and grabbed his hand playfully. "You have heard the stories of the ancient Water Palaces and the legendary Floating Gardens. Well, at least now you can see the ruins and leave the rest up to imagination."

Ell still hesitated. "I'm not sure."

Miri let go of his hand and took a step to the west. Ell wished she had not let go. "Come. It's only a half-day's journey west. We'll be back by nightfall." She shook her head in disbelief at his hesitancy. "Come on! You spend your life fighting and facing death. It's time you lived a little bit."

He gave in and followed her. He picked up his bow from the ground and slung it over his shoulder. He ran beside her lightly, as they cleared the village and headed toward the western pass of the valley. Ell couldn't help but wonder whether or not it would be difficult for her to keep pace with her injured leg.

She managed. It was much slower going than Ell would have done by himself or with his family, yet it was steady. The old wound was something she had learned to tolerate, something to which she had adjusted. It did not prevent her from doing much, only slowing her slightly. She would not be much good in a fight, however. Suddenly, Ell realized what she had meant when she spoke of how not everyone was created to fight. Her opinions made a little more sense now.

They chatted as they ran. Her limp had not lessened the capacity of her lungs whatsoever and she was able to talk and run as easily as any of the Highest, if at a slightly slower pace. They talked of life in the valley, hunting, and their favorite things to do. Ell even found himself talking of his family.

Miri was keeping stride beside him as he spoke, telling her of his personal history. "My father was Adan, Adan the Green to some, a captain in the forces at Verdantihya before the fall." Ell felt strange speaking of his family, yet at the same time, it felt right to do so.

He continued as they moved beneath the shadow of the mountains, sheer peaks that rose from the ground to gouge the sky. The western part of Andalaya was rugged and beautiful.

"Both my father and mother survived the fall of the city, along with my uncle and his wife. Yet that survival did not last long."

"What happened?" Miri asked. She was polite but always inquisitive.

"Slaver band." Ell said simply. "It hit their camp while my uncle was out hunting with my father." Miri made a sympathetic sound in her throat, but Ell was used to the pain of this story. He had desensitized himself to the agony long ago. He told it in a simple, matter-of-fact way now.

"The camp resisted, and my mother and an older sister were killed along with my uncle's wife. Luckily, my sister, Rihya, my cousins, and I were just babies, and for some reason we weren't worth the slavers time. They took those who they managed to capture and headed south."

Ell ran on, his face impassive. "Dacunda says that my father chased after them, to avenge their deaths, but was slain." Dacunda had been left to raise four young elves, fresh with the grief from his family's passing. Miri was quiet for a while, as if sensing that there were no more questions needed to be asked of that history.

The land passed around them. It was green. Simply put, spring had well and truly arrived. Flowers were in blossom. Lilies of white and lavender dotted the hillsides and trees sprigged a lighter shade of green than many of their current leaves and needles. Birdcalls were heard often and even the insects seemed to join in their songs with a chorus of their own chirping. It felt peaceful. Of course, that didn't mean that Ell let down his guard. A semblance of peace did not mean that calamity could not strike. He had experienced before the transition from rest to battle in the space of a heartbeat. He would not be caught unaware.

Miri seemed to sense his inability to fully let down his guard but she appeared to understand. He was a creature of war, an elf of battle. That would never leave his blood.

They followed the path through a dense portion of woods. Overhanging limbs from small crooked trees and tall over grown bushes created a tunnel of green and brown through which to make their way. For once, Ell's dark hooded tunic stood out just slightly, whereas Miri's fitted, light green hose and sleeveless tunic seemed to blend in to the bright spring growth perfectly.

They made their way through the densest part of the trail. Thickets with hardly room for the game trail finally yielded, and opened up to brilliant blue skies and scudding clouds overhead.

A sharp peak rose higher than the rest and then an arm of narrow rock jutted out from the top, overhanging the trail. It was so far above that it could not be made out clearly.

Miri noticed him looking at it. "Mantiriol's Blade. Named for the legendary warrior, Mantiriol, one of the first warriors to grace this land during the days of the birthing of our race." Ell nodded. He knew the story well. Mantiriol had been a famed warrior, so the myths said. He had been crucial to helping banish the darkness from the land during the First Days. Ell wondered how much of the ancient myths were true. The darkness that had inhabited the lands, the Bonewinds, it seemed almost fantastical. Yet weeks ago, he had scented the air and it had reminded him of the stories, the day of the raid before leaving the plains for Verdantihya with Silverfist on their tail. Perhaps there was truth in the old stories, more truth than Ell gave them credit.

The landscape passed and just after midday, they had reached the cliffs. Ell's breath caught in his chest as they slowed to a walk and then approached the Cliffs of Anover. Beyond the cliffs, ocean stretched out into the horizon endlessly. Rugged mountain peaks approached the cliffs and the land fell away sharply and deeply to the distant shoreline that preceded them. The cliffs were almost the height of a small mountain themselves and sheer. The drop was straight down and there were almost no passes leading up from the shoreline to the top. They formed an impregnable wall that ran an incredible length of the western coast. They were a primary reason why the Departed's famed warships didn't strike up the coast from the south and ravage the west of Andalaya with slave raids. There was nowhere to land a ship and only the Highest knew of the few, secret trails that led from the bottom of the cliffs to the top. The Cliffs of Anover were a powerful, natural protection. If only the rest of Andalaya was so well defended.

"Astounding, isn't it?" Miri said softly, staring out into the distance. They sat on the grassy ground and reclined against the mountainside behind them, gazing out at the epic scenery in front of their eyes.

Ell nodded his response. The water beyond was a deep, bluish grey. This was not the crystalline blue water of which he had heard of in the warm, southern oceans. This was the dark of deep ocean, colder waters, and greener swirling currents. It was a sight to see.

Miri pointed an arm towards the water and leaned close so he could see where she pointed. "There, see the ruins?" Ell did. He saw the shattered walls rising up out of the ocean surrounding them. They were leagues off shore, but the cliffs were high enough and their elven eyes keen enough to decipher them. "The Water Palaces," Miri breathed regretfully. "If only they hadn't been destroyed. They must truly have been spectacular."

Ell agreed. They had been one of the wonders of the ancient realm before the race of elves had split asunder into two distinct factions. Akan Deraiya in the south, its fabled walls, Riora, the center of learning, and of course, Verdantihya and Dor Khabor, or Dark Harbor as it was now called, had dominated the elven civilization. But the Water Palaces of the northern shore had been accounted one of the greatest architectural feats in the history of their people.

Miri spoke as if reading his thoughts. "It's said the ocean off the Cliffs of Anover is countless fathoms deep. Yet our ancestors somehow managed to build foundations deep enough to erect palaces that rose up from the sea around them." Her voice held wonder.

Ell closed his eyes and imagined for a moment. *What would they have looked like?* His mind's eye could see them the way the stories spoke of them. There were dark stonewalls, worn and weathered by countless sea storms, breaking their primal teeth against the walls of the Water Palaces. Bastions of elven advancement, they had stood, defying nature around them, fortresses built from the depths of the water itself. The stories said the walls had risen, high and thick, to protect the palaces from the giant waves that arose during the tempests that ravaged in the winter. Never falling, never failing, they had stood for countless years.

Ell sighed. *They had stood, that is, until they were sacked by the Departed's swift and violent ships many centuries later.* He opened his eyes and saw the ruins for what they really were, yet another reminder of the brokenness of his civilization. The split between the north and south had been the beginning of the end for the elves. The humans had just placed the last rock on top of the pile that made their entire world collapse.

He spoke to Miri, the afternoon sun sliding slowly overhead on its daily course towards the western horizon, the sea. "The Floating Gardens would have been something to see also." He sighed again as she nodded. "Enough food grown right on the ocean swells to feed thousands upon thousands of the Highest living in the palaces and the shores around."

"It would have been amazing to see the flowers and plants. Sea Dragonpods, Floating Roses, Half Sunken Trees." She named a few of the legendary plant species long gone from the world without the deft cultivating hand of the ancient Highest to guide their growth.

"I hate them," Ell shattered the reverent musing about the past, with a vehement exclamation.

"Who?" Miri asked. "The Departed?"

"All of them! The Departed, the humans," he paused and then spoke with even more emphasis, "the traitors."

Ell looked at Miri beside him and watched her nod complacently at his comments. *Didn't she ever get angry too?*

"Don't you feel sad, angry, bitter or anything about the state of the world?" He exclaimed.

Miri gazed at him for a long moment. "Yes, at times," she answered simply. "But there is more to life than bitterness and hatred." Ell didn't know how she managed to look at the world in such a positive light, with such a calm acceptance. He wasn't sure it was entirely healthy, the acceptance of evil, yet he also couldn't shake the fact that she seemed to live and retain a measure of peace in her life that he had never been able to grasp.

Ell shook his head at her. "I don't know how you do that."

"Do what?"

"Look at life and the world as if everything's alright." He wasn't frustrated with her, just frustrated with not being able to understand her.

Miri continued to look at him, but she smiled to show she wasn't offended by his comment. "I don't honestly know, Ell. I just feel like if I spent my whole life angry, then I would be missing out on so much of the good that life has to offer."

Ell shook his head again. "I cannot grasp it. I want them dead. All of our enemies, the ones who caused the world to be the way it is. I want their blood spilled."

"If all you seek is blood, are you any different than them?" Miri's question cut softly through the afternoon air. It stilled Ell's tongue. He didn't know what to say in answer. Battle was a part of who he was, but was it truly the only way? He didn't know.

They passed the rest of their time at the cliffs in silence. Ell stared south, imagining he could see far enough to make out the Enclaves of the Departed. The Enclaves were a cluster of island ports and harbors off the mainland to the south. The Departed's center of power was Dark Harbor, but they had maintained their own autonomy in the great city and their island strongholds as part of the deal with the humans. Partly this was due to the fact that they had ceded most of their mainland holdings in the alliance, the other part was that they were strong, a force on the water with which to be reckoned. Their Longships and naval centers would inflict a depth of harm to an attacking enemy, not to mention the fact that Dark Harbor was protected by the fleet on its western, ocean side, and a ring of mountains with hill forts at every pass on its opposite border. The humans knew that to take the southern harbors would cost them too dearly at this point in time. So instead, they had struck a deal to form an alliance, which was all at the expense of the Highest and Andalaya. The Departed had agreed to not come to the aid of their northern neighbors when Verdantihya had fallen, and had also agreed to raid and send their slavers to the north to capture and bring as many of the Highest as they could to the auction block. According to the deal, three quarters of the slaves went directly to the humans, but the Departed kept one quarter. As a result, the Departed need not fear an attack by the humans. The southern elves were in a slightly subservient role to the humans, but Ell had no doubt that it was just a matter of circumstance. His interactions with the dark elves had shown to him that they bowed only when it was necessary. Even now, they were likely plotting a betrayal of their new allies just as they had betrayed Ell's people when Verdantihya fell.

Ell's eyes stretched, trying to see far enough south to make out the Enclaves but they couldn't. He imagined the Outer Rim islands as well, the farthest range of islands reaching into the heart of the Western Ocean. The Outer Rim islands were hardly populated and still being explored.

The Highest were not a seafaring folk like their southern, darker cousins with their Longships and fleets. The Departed were more at home in their harbors and on their war ships than they were in the forest. Being linked to nature was the only advantage the Highest had at this point in time. Ell's people had the ability to out maneuver the Departed in the wilds of their Andalayan homeland.

Finally, Miri interrupted their quiet contemplation. "We should head back now. After all, I cannot move quite as quickly as most elves." She smiled, making light of her old limp.

"If I may ask, what did happen to your leg?" Ell had shared a lot today; perhaps it would be all right to ask a more probing question of his own.

Miri smiled as if it was no problem that he had asked. She always seemed to be smiling. "Slaver attack on our camp when I was a child. We had run out of Source Water, so the wound was forced to heal naturally."

So she also had experienced the enemy. Ell supposed it was foolish to have assumed that her positive outlook on life simply stemmed from a lack of difficult experiences. It just wasn't possible. There was nobody in broken Andalaya that was without the pain of losing someone or something to the enemy. The realm was well and truly shattered. No, her attitude was birthed from something inside of her, something good and pure. And all of life's hardships had not been able to take it from her. Ell hoped that they never would.

Chapter Ten

The light faded quickly as they made their way back towards Indiria's Emerald. Soft and sure, their light footfalls hardly disturbed the world around them. The Highest were adept at traversing their homeland quickly and quietly, and Ell and Miri were no exception. On a number of occasions, they moved so swiftly and silently through the woods that they would startle a flock of birds or a lone hare as they came upon them suddenly. The animals always started and then bolted, but if he had been hunting, Ell was certain he could have brought down a few of them. He even considered unlimbering his bow once or twice so that he could bring back some game to the village, but Miri's presence at his side stilled his hand. She already viewed him as a warrior and killer, and a part of him wanted to make sure that wasn't the only thing she saw in him. However, Dahranian had spent most of his resting time working, and Ell felt slightly guilty that he hadn't done similarly, choosing instead to gallivant across the countryside seeing sights. He forced that thought down. *No, he deserved to see a little of the world, more than just the trees and game trails of his homeland.* So they ran on, letting startled animals flee from their path as the sun sank, casting lengthening shadows across the forest floor.

Night finally came and they traveled beneath the pale light of the moon. It was nearly full, so their vision was not limited, especially when they ran by the Westrill or a pond, which would catch the moon's luminescence and reflect it to brighten the surrounding area even more.

They stopped for a brief rest by a small pond surrounded by trees growing right up to the edge of the water. The forest grew so thick around this little body of water that if a game trail had not passed directly by its side then hardly a soul would have been able to find it. They breathed in the night air, crisp and cold, as it filled their lungs. Spring had arrived, but the temperature at night still fell drastically here in the mountains until summer was just around the corner. Their breath began to form just a hint of mist in the air in front of them. The chill was nice after their blood had been heated by almost an entire day spent on the move. Ell dipped his hand into the pond beside him and cupped a mouthful of water to drink. He stirred the water as he did so, sending ripples across the shining reflection of the moon on the surface of the pond.

Night was a beautiful time in the mountains of his homeland. It was like a different world altogether. Dark trees framed by the moon and stars cast brooding silhouettes across the land. Plants that looked bright and green in the daylight took on a gloomy cast. It was shadowy and beautiful. It reminded him of his life as a warrior, his life as a fighter and raider. He was pale and fair in the sunlight, but he fought with dark arrows and a black bow. He fought from the shadows, a dark form terrorizing his enemies. Lost in contemplation, he didn't see the large hare creep from the brush a short stone's throw to his side, hoping for an undisturbed drink of pond water. Miri did, however, and as she called it to his attention, Ell's hand started to move involuntarily towards his knife before he had the chance to still it.

"I've seen you twitch for your bow like a paranoid soldier every time we have come across a flock of birds or a group of animals," she laughed silently to herself. "I don't know why you haven't tried to bring any of them down. By all means, don't let me stop you." She indicated the hare drinking from the pool.

So, she wanted Ell to be himself, did she? Well, he could do that. In a way, it would be nice to show off a little bit. Most of their interactions had centered on issues Ell was still figuring out, emotions and deep subjects on which he wasn't sure of his opinion yet. It would be nice to finally do something with her at which he was excellent.

In one smooth motion he drew and threw his belt knife with a side arm cast. The blade flew, twirling circularly in a whirlwind of death, toward the unsuspecting animal. It lodged itself deep in the hare's chest, killing it upon impact. One thing Ell strove for when hunting, was to make his initial strike his killing strike. He didn't mind at all, if his enemies suffered a little bit when they faced him on the battlefield, but the beasts of the forest were something different. All of creation was connected. The elves of the north called themselves the Highest, which meant exactly what it said. They were still part of the land, part of creation—the highest part—yet still a part. It was a fundamental difference that separated them from their brethren to the south. The Departed, as their name dictated, had rejected their bond, their covenant with creation, and viewed themselves as separate. The dark elves of the south viewed themselves as different, above and better than creation, rather than simply the highest life form. It might seem like a small difference, but it was a fundamentally important one nonetheless.

Ell walked over, removed his knife, and cleaned it on the grass. He then rinsed it in the water. He didn't always wash his blades after use, but if water was available, he rarely said no to the opportunity.

Miri was watching him with a strange, small smile on her face. "You know, we are not as different as you think," she murmured under her breath, so quietly Ell was not certain he was supposed to have heard, so he elected not to answer. What did one say to a comment like that anyways? However, he supposed he understood what she was implying. There had been no reason to fear revealing his true self around her. His hunting instincts had put food in his stomach for his entire life, and there was no need to change or apologize for that skill. She knew that. She ate the meat hunters brought to the village. Ell felt silly for pretending to be something he was not. He placed his belt knife in its sheath and sat back down on the fallen log beside her, where she was sitting. He placed the dead hare on the ground by his side. He would bring it back to camp and do the majority of the cleaning there.

Ell watched Miri look at him in the dark light of the night. Their eyes held for a long moment and then acting upon the very instincts that he had been ignoring all afternoon and evening long, Ell leaned in and kissed her.

Miri's mouth was moist and it tasted of lily water, liquid gathered from the petals of the flowers after a rainfall or from the morning's dew. She had been drinking it from a small flask all afternoon as they ran. Her tongue touched his and sent a chill of excitement trembling down his spine. They pressed their lips together gently, but passionately for a time, losing track of all other things of seeming importance. Each kiss was like a brush stroke made by a masterful artist as he formed a beautiful painting. There was only the moment, their lips, and their hearts pounding. Ell wrapped his arms around her tightly, firmly pressing her close to him. Then it ended as naturally at it had begun.

As Miri's lips pressed against his, Ell felt her lips curl up into a smile as they finished their last kiss. Her smile at that moment was the best thing Ell could ever have imagined. They pulled apart slightly, just leaving their foreheads touching. It was an intimate moment and Ell knew that something had just shifted inside of him. For better or worse, from this instant forward, he knew he would not be the same person.

"Well," Miri said a bit breathlessly, "that was… delightfully unexpected." She had a way with words, Ell thought amused, as he listened to her musical voice. She seemed to be at a loss for what to say next, as was he. *What was one supposed to say after such a moment?*

"I suppose we should continue on back to the valley, so that the others do not worry." Ell ventured after a time of comfortable silence had elapsed.

Miri nodded in agreement, her head pressed against his chest as he hugged her. So they rather regretfully grabbed their belongings and made their way further along the game trail in a generally eastward direction.

The hare hung from a thong tied around its feet and fastened to Ell's hip. It banged annoyingly against him as they ran. Lugging the killed game back to camp was the one part of hunting that Ell did not enjoy. They ran side by side, their shoulders brushing each other's occasionally, but after the kiss they had shared by the moonlit pond, the accidental touches now brought a sense of closeness rather than an awkward apology. Ell wondered at the newfound intimacy one kiss had created between himself and this wonderful creature that moved beside him. Her limp did not diminish the fact that she was still able to move with a subtlety and grace. It was not the traditional lithe movement with which the Highest were born, but it was graceful nonetheless. An acquired grace. Ell found it more impressive for that very reason. Everything about her was amazing Ell marveled as they continued to run, losing himself in his thoughts of Miri.

His usual attentiveness was lacking drastically as they went. Dacunda and even Dahranian would have been looking at him in disgust. Ell couldn't help it. His mind was consumed with thoughts other than caution.

A dark shape blotted out the stars above them. "Mantiriol's Blade," Miri murmured beside him, pointing upwards to the giant shadow cutting a swathe of darkness through the starlit night sky overhead. He nodded at her comment, not thinking it particularly important to point out. Apparently, she was more observant than he was at the moment.

They ran on lightly, not breathing very hard. Ell was impressed at how Miri was keeping pace. She had not faltered the entire day. Maybe her lame leg wasn't quite the debilitation he had deemed it to be. Night passed immeasurably as they traveled, as it is nearly impossible to measure how long a journey takes when there is no sun in the sky rising or sinking to take your bearing.

They must have been close, within an hour or two of the village, when the tiny hairs on the back of Ell's neck began to prickle. Something tugged on his senses. He had let them go too long unchecked. Ell peered into the darkness around him, but his keen eyesight could make out nothing amiss. His ears strained valiantly to find a hint of something wrong but could not. Whatever had Ell's instincts in a knot was not presenting itself.

He now ran at high alert, not telling Miri what he was thinking lest she become frightened. She was not a fighter, and he did not know how she would respond to danger. And danger it was, although he could not have said from what even if his life depended on it.

They broke from the trees overhead as the game path lead them along the side of a small clearing. The trail hugged the brush on the side of the meadow, but the hole in the sky gave a clear glimpse of the thousands of tiny stars far above them speckling the heavens. Miri ran straight on, head forward as Ell glanced upwards at the night sky. Then suddenly, the sky above them went completely dark, the stars vanishing for a brief instant only to reappear a moment later. Ell tensed and grabbed Miri, tackling her to the ground and rolling beneath a bush as once again the night sky was blotted out by a silently swooping immensity. How had something that big moved that quietly? It did not seem possible. There was only one thing that could possibly match what Ell had just seen, and if that was the case, then they were in serious danger.

They lay squished under the thicket, obscured from view, or at least Ell fervently hoped they were. Miri's body was half on top of his, her leg overlapping his, her chest pressed tightly against his side so as to fit beneath their covering. Her face couldn't have been more than a finger's width from his and he could feel her warm breath caressing his face, a contradiction to the chill night air. In the midst of all that was going on, Ell found himself wanting to kiss her again. It was ridiculous. Their lives were at stake here and yet he couldn't seem to quell his desire to kiss her even at a time like this. *Focus, Ell. You may not survive if you don't use your head.* He told himself that over and over again as he glanced up and out through the thin branches of their hiding place at the sky. The stars were gone and then they were there again, and this time Ell heard the faintest whoosh of wind beneath wings. *So, they aren't infallible hunters, are they? They can be heard, sensed.* It was strange how just the realization that he, in fact, could sense this creature gave him the confidence to believe in their ability to escape it.

"What is it?" Miri whispered to him, her lips barely moving as they strove for quiet. At least she had the wisdom to realize that silence was their friend right now. "I think you would have kissed me by now if this was a ploy to get me close again." She finished with a hint of a smile and Ell couldn't help but smile in return. However, his face regained a serious look as he was reminded of their dire predicament.

"No," he whispered back. "No ploy, though I wish it were." And then the moment of levity was gone. "Icari." He breathed solemnly, resolutely.

"What!" Miri jerked in his arms in surprise. She tried to get up. "We have to warn the village. They don't know about the Icari. It could be there in a matter of minutes and they wouldn't be prepared!" She was frantic, but he held her tightly, to prevent her from shaking the bush and attracting attention, not letting her get up. The beast was terrifying in legend, no doubt. Ell had never actually seen one, but had heard of them from his uncle. Part man, part eagle, with a distinctly predatory nature, and of all the dark creatures of myth and tale, it was by far one of the most fearsome and frightening. It was said they were twice, even three times the size of the largest warrior.

"We can't move. It's got our scent now, so it's not worried about the village. If we move now we are dead," Ell said. Miri might know how to embrace life, and find joy anywhere, something with which Ell struggled, but she had a lot to learn about keeping her head and composure during danger.

Miri shivered in his arms, apparently accepting what he said. "I didn't believe those creatures actually existed," she mumbled fearfully.

"They do," Ell responded grimly, "Uncle told me. He's seen a nest before, though not an actual Icari." The creatures of legend, the darkness of the First Days into which the Highest had been birthed by creation were indeed returning, if the Icari once again flew by night and nested in the high peaks. There was no other explanation for a flying creature able to block so much of the sky above or to hunt with such stealth for a beast so large. No, it matched the description from myth perfectly and wishing it were not so would not change the fact. Ell and Miri would be lucky to survive the night. The Icari had their trail. It must, otherwise it would not have swooped over the clearing again and again as if searching for a hint of movement from a prey that had given the predator the slip. Ell found he was shivering as well, as he thought of becoming a meal for the giant, fanged creature.

He heard the measured wing beat of enormous wings pass overhead once again. It was said that the Icari had impeccable sight at night, and a sharp sense of smell. He wasn't sure how they were going to be able to give it the slip.

They lay in quiet for an indeterminable amount of minutes and the shape obscured the sky, time and again, like a watchful sentinel, monitoring the scene for a sign of its prey. It came and went, came and went. Ell noticed that nearly every time it passed, it came again, half a minute or a minute later. A plan began to form in his mind.

Ell untied the hare at his belt quietly and waited for the thing to pass overhead. Once it did, he slid out quickly and silently from under the bush, just slightly, so that he lay still as a stone on the forest trail as the giant shape was just skimming past the far edge of the clearing and away. He had a minute to wait before it came back and he set his plan in motion.

"What are you doing?" Miri questioned, looking at him as if he was insane to have left the safety of their meager covering of leaves.

"We have to distract it. It has our scent," Ell murmured his urgent plan. "We have to confuse its scent, give it something else to focus on for an instant." He looked at the sky; he still had a few seconds before it came back. Then he looked back at Miriyah, "As soon as I throw this hare, you need to shuffle out the other side, the forest side of the thicket and into the dense woods beyond. I'll be right behind you." He tried to sound more confident and assuring than he felt. How did Dacunda and Dahranian manage such an air of ease and control and leadership in the midst of danger?

Miri looked at him as if she was about to argue. He cut her off before she could voice the unspoken argument he knew was coming. They simply didn't have time for questions. "I'll be right behind you," he promised forcefully, determination in his eyes. Finally, she nodded and acquiesced.

The shape flew into sight, blocking the sky, and from his back on the dirt of the forest floor Ell heaved and threw the hare as best he could from a supine position. It did not carry far through the air but it did the trick. The shape overhead made a grunting, keening combination sound, as if a bird of prey had mixed with the ogres of ancient tales, and the flying predator darted so quickly after the hare that Ell lay almost frozen in fear. It was fast. Nothing should be able to move that fast. He now saw why the Icari were the creatures of old, about which people only whispered on dark nights around the fire, not wishing to speak of such a deadly creature.

Miri rolled out of the bushes on the opposite side of the thicket and into the woods. Ell could hear her moving. If he could hear her then so could the Icari. Indeed, it plummeted to the ground, falling upon the dead hare in a heap as Ell managed to force his body up from the dirt, but as the two elves made noise to move into the forest, it whipped its head around to look in their direction. As the head swiveled, Ell could see its fiery, reddish-orange eyes, flames in the night that would definitely frighten an already fearful person. It screamed in rage as it saw its quarry disappearing from the meadow and into the thick undergrowth of the woods where it could not follow. All of its scenting and hunting, waiting for an opening was ruined.

It dropped the hare, and in a flash, launched itself, flying low towards Ell as he stood on the edge of the forest. No time to run or even think, Ell resorted to muscle memory. His bow came off his shoulder automatically and before he knew it, he had a Dreampine arrow knocked and sighted. He loosed the arrow as the flying predator drew near. The whole event was slow motion for him. Ell realized that his life was in the hands of that one arrow. If it flew true, he might survive. If not, well, he had lived a good life.

The arrow sprung from the bow as Miri screamed his name, watching helplessly from the shelter of the trees where the beast could not follow. Its wingspan too big, nearly twenty arm lengths from tip to tip. The arrow didn't strike anything vital, but it did bury itself in the shoulder of the Icari and threw it off course just enough that the creature collided with Ell slightly off center, its fanged mouth ripping into Ell's arm instead of his throat.

The whole encounter had taken only moments from the toss of the hare to the shot arrow and now the collision. The force of the impact of their two bodies knocked Ell to the ground and the wind from his lungs. The creature was huge! Its momentum carried it into the trees next to Miri, and it crashed its way through branches.

Ell lay on the ground stunned, bleeding from his arm and trying to clear the fog from his mind, as he tried to scramble to his feet. Vaguely he heard Miri shout his name again urgently, and then when it was clear that he was still unable to function with a clear head, she limped quickly to his side and helped him regain his legs beneath him. The Icari thrashed and screamed as it tried to free itself from the tangle of limbs and trunks in which it was enmeshed from the force and momentum of its flight toward Ell.

"Ell. Ell! Elliyar!" Miri was shaking him trying to get his attention. Finally, it seemed his head was clearing just a bit. Fortune was on his side tonight for him to have survived such an attack. "We have to go. Now!" She was saying.

Ell nodded a little less fuzzily. He grabbed his bow and quiver from the ground where it had fallen and then ran off beside her into the deep woods, where the creature would not be able to follow or track them once it finally freed itself from its natural cage of trees, branches, and bushes. It screamed in rage at a kill escaped, as Ell and Miri ran. Ell pressed his hand against his torn arm to stem the flow of blood and wished he had thought to carry at least a tiny vial of Source Water with him. He vowed never to go without it again, if it was at all possible. Ell prayed a prayer of thanks that he and Miri had somehow both managed to survive an attack by one of the most fabled predators and feared creatures of legend. If this was what Andalaya was coming to, Ghouls in Legendwood, Icari once again roosting in the high peaks, then he must do something about it. He would not let his land succumb to darkness. The Highest had rescued the land from the depths of shadow during the First Days, cutting their empire and safety from their foes surrounding them. They had held the land for a millennium, or more, and Ell was not willing to see that come to an end during his lifetime.

They staggered back towards the village, only a short hour's run away. He was bleeding badly and would need the Source Water they had at camp. He hoped he would not have to use too much, as he did not relish a return journey to Verdantihya to refill their gourds so soon after they had left there.

The night air was crisp and it kept Ell's mind, which was woozy from loss of blood, awake. Miri murmured in his ear. What she said he wasn't sure, due to the delirium of pain and loss of blood, but it was still a comfort. Her presence gave him strength and it kept him going as they made their way back to the village and to safety.

Chapter Eleven

"I would leave. Now." Ell's uncle spoke to the village elders, his voice resolute. "I warned you, it is no longer safe to simply make a home in one single location any longer." Dacunda passed a hand over his forehead and eyes, perhaps wearily, or maybe in regret. "The days when we could do that are long gone. Staying on the move is your best source of safety now."

Ell sat on an elaborately carved wooden bench, holding Miri's hand lightly. As they sat, they listened to his uncle attempt yet again to persuade the elves to leave the village behind them and adopt the nomadic lifestyle that had marked the Highest for the last two decades.

It was amazing how quickly it had become normal to hold her hand in the day and a half since they had returned to Little Vale from the Cliffs of Anover. Ell marveled that this was happening to him. He had never figured himself for the romantic type. The more strings you had attached to your heart, the more difficult it was to charge into battle fearlessly, so he had never allowed himself to become attached to anyone outside of his family unit until now. However, Miri had changed all of that. With one kiss and more than a few heartfelt conversations, she had wormed her way into his affections more deeply than he cared to admit.

"That will not be possible," one elder said, his long golden hair swaying slightly in the breeze as he shook his head. "We shall be staying here." The lady elder beside him looked a touch less determined, yet she nodded her head in affirmation of what her partner had said. They would stay, their looks said. Fair weather or foul, good idea or bad, they would stay.

Dacunda huffed in frustration. He cared. They were his people after all. He did not wish to see harm come to them, so he counseled them to follow what he believed to be the safest course.

"Thick headed," he muttered at the two elders. "An Icari nests not a half day's journey from here, and considerably less time by the flight of its gigantic wings I might add, yet you stubbornly refuse to move." He sighed. "It is beyond foolhardy."

"And is it not foolish to attack an enemy many times your number?" The lady elder queried sharply.

Dacunda's eyes narrowed at her question. "That's different," he said, his hand unconsciously reaching up over his shoulder to loosen his sword in its sheath as it was strapped to his back. A long sword, it was a powerful weapon, with a double-edged blade and a beautifully engraved sheath. It was a relic of the ancient days, passed down in his family for countless generations. It was quite possibly Dacunda's most prized possession.

The lady seemed to feel she had gained an advantage in the conversation and she pressed him further. "How is it different? Tell me how rushing into battle is different than protecting one's home."

Ell's uncle sighed again before answering. He held up his two hands in front of him, as if in a gesture of peace. "I mean no disrespect, Elders, honestly I have only the best wishes for you in my heart." Both of the elders' eyes softened as they heard the truth of Dacunda's words. Ell's uncle pushed on forcefully, however. "Yet you fail to see reality! This is not a 'home' you will be able to keep. The Icari to the west at Mantiriol's Blade is not the only threat. Wolves ravage the wilds in greater abundance, Ghouls are being seen in Legendwood, not to mention their usual northern habitats, in much greater numbers, and of course, there is the greatest threat of all, the slavers to the south. You are a beacon of light attracting the darkness all around you. If it is not one of those evils it will be another that brings about your demise." Dacunda paused for breath and saw that his latest words had erased whatever previous goodwill he had won. The elders wore frowns of disapproval on their faces. He plowed on to his finish. "You must move on. It is your best chance of survival. How is it different from battle you ask? I'll tell you." His voice swelled with more passion than Ell normally heard from him. "When we fight the enemy, we show them that they cannot take our land lightly. We do not wait and let them slaughter us heedlessly without a plan or protection. We take the war to them and bleed for Andalaya. You," he shook his head, "you in this valley are simply sheep waiting for the slaughter, not warriors in a war."

The lady elder's eyes took on an ancient air. Ell could see that for all her disagreement with what Ell considered to be sound logic from his uncle, there was still great wisdom and knowledge in the elf before them. She replied. "Is it not a strike as well at the heart of the enemy when we show them they cannot push us from our homes, whoever they may be?"

Dacunda shook his head silently and gave up the argument, seeing it would end fruitlessly as it had so many times before. Ell pondered the conversation. *What was it that made a people dig in their heels to protect a location? It was just a place after all.* He supposed that was what having a home did to a person. It made you fight to keep it, rather than listen to the logic and battle tactics that had helped his family and many others of the Highest raid the enemy, then evade and survive for so many years.

"At least let me counsel you on fortifying your location should the need arise." Dacunda conceded his first point and sought a secondary goal in the argument. "We will not be able to stay and rest forever, and I would leave knowing I had done everything within my means to see to the safety of this valley."

The two elders nodded their assent in unison, almost as if they were one person. Dacunda finally smiled and the tension of the conversation waned as Ell's uncle surrendered the battle he now realized he could not win and set about planning defense for the location. The elders and Dacunda began to walk as they talked, leaving Ell and Miri alone on the bench.

Across the way, Borian cleaned a recent kill, a buck. He frequently cast sullen glares in their direction, mainly directed at Ell. Ell was beginning to believe that the young hunter's dislike of him was less to do with his being a stranger and much more to do with the fact that he kept company with Miri. Since their return two nights prior, after the Icari's attack, Miri and Ell had spent a considerable amount of time together, and if possible, Borian's attitude towards Ell had only soured even further than it had been initially.

"I believe he is quite jealous of me." Ell commented as he watched Borian clean the animal carcass.

Miri responded, leaning into his body as she held his hand. "Why?" Her tone was so naïve, so innocent. "He is quite a good hunter after all, what cause has he to be jealous of you?" Ell snorted but did not respond. If she could not see that to which he was alluding then he would not voice the belief. Miri had the tendency to see the best in others and in the world around her. It was what he loved about her, but she could be a bit blind at times. Either way he did not quite feel like bursting her cloud of innocence surrounding how she viewed Borian. At least not today.

Instead of answering her question, he reached up and adjusted the bandage to his shoulder. It ached painfully whenever he moved, and often even when he didn't.

"Does it hurt badly?" Miri switched subjects, her compassionate side coming out. Her fingers traced the bandage gently as she looked at it. The wound was to his upper arm and the linen bandage was wrapped rather tightly around it. He wore a sleeveless vest to prevent the bandage catching on his clothes.

He nodded his response to Miri. It did hurt. A lot. Dacunda had deemed the injury serious enough to merit a small allocation of Source Water on that first night of their arrival, but not serious enough to require much of it. Therefore, a small sip to stimulate his body's health, and a quick, tiny pour from the flask directly into the open wound was all that had been allotted to Ell. The result was a wound that would gradually heal just fine with time, without the worry of infection and festering that accompanied many battle injuries. However, he had not been given anywhere near enough of the Source Water to heal the wound completely or to dull the pain.

Ell rolled his shoulder subconsciously in an attempt to lessen the pain. He was left with a slowly healing wound that would take time and yet more rest to finish its natural process. He began to feel admiration for his eldest cousin, Dahranian, who had managed to run from their last raid on the plains all the way to Verdantihya with a grievous injury. He had done so with only trace amounts of Source Water to aid his wounded thigh, which they had found in a much-diluted form, washing downstream from Verdantihya in the flow of the East Mayn. Ell had to admit that his cousin's strength and ability to endure pain was impressive. He would have found it difficult to do much of anything important with his body feeling the way it did now.

Miri made a compassionate sound in the back of her throat at his nodded admission of pain and then kissed his cheek. Ell couldn't help but feel that her solitary kiss on the side of his face did more to give him strength than a day and a half of rest. Miri had that effect on him.

They sat and watched the village bustle into greater activity as the elders allowed Dacunda to lend his wisdom on how to better defend their village, should the need arise. Dacunda strode about, pointing to things here, then there, and giving directions to the elves all around him.

Over the next few days, much changed in Little Vale. Sentries were posted on the passes and scouts sent out even further to patrol the surrounding area on a regular basis. Campfires were limited to only the smallest size necessary and defensive archers were posted around the village in case the Icari decided to make its way east. Ell wasn't sure a few archers were going to do much good should that creature appear. His own arrow had hardly done a thing to slow its progress toward him during the attack, but he supposed some action was better than none. At least the village looked a little less like the cozy, lazy home of a peaceful people, and a little more like a cautious and guarded village of the Highest. Ell mourned slightly the loss of innocence that his family had brought to the valley, yet he was glad. It would be safer for them. Safer for her.

The biggest project that Dacunda was overseeing before they left was a real fortification. The village was on the valley floor next to the river and it was without a wall or even a large building in which to retreat should the need arise. Dacunda had instead settled upon a small series of caves high on the mountain slope above the village. The caves were an ideal place to hold off the enemy. One entrance allowed for easier defense, and a small spring bubbled forth, trickling down the mountainside until it met the swiftly flowing Westrill on the valley below. It was not much of a spring, but it would be enough to provide water for the elves of the village should they need to retreat and hold the caves for an extended period of time. Dacunda had instructed that gradually they should build up food stores and place them inside the cave, allowing them to retreat there and survive for a time if danger ever came.

Ell and Miri lay side by side on the grass outside the village, watching as Dacunda organized the erecting of fortifications in front of the cave mouth. Elves were digging barricades and shoving sharpened stakes into the ground facing outwards as a palisade. Taking the hill and the cave beyond would not be an easy task. Even an enemy of greater number would be forced to wade their way uphill through a sea of sharpened stakes and a hail of arrows raining down upon them.

Ell had been expressly forbidden to help. Dacunda had said they would move on as soon as Ell was recovered enough to travel. Ell's uncle wished that to be as soon as possible and so Ell was forced to wait on the side and watch as everyone else did all the hard work. Dacunda had been especially antsy to leave after hearing about the Icari to the west. He kept muttering to himself about getting answers from "Arendahl," though where or what Arendahl was, was beyond Ell. He had never heard of that place before hearing his uncle's mutterings. Perhaps it could be an ancient library in Verdantihya full of old scrolls and hidden knowledge, but his uncle had never spoken of it before now, so Ell was not certain. Besides, they had left Verdantihya behind them so it did not make sense that what his uncle sought would be there.

He didn't even know exactly what it was about which his uncle so badly wanted answers. But if Ell was sure of one thing, it was that Dacunda had been acting strangely ever since their last raid, ever since Ell had killed the Departed who had looked to be carrying the plague and the Ghoul in Legendwood on the way to Verdantihya, and now the Icari. Dacunda was agitated and Ell had adopted some of his uncle's tension. One couldn't spend such a long time around a person who was leading them, without picking up on their emotions and anxieties. Ell wanted to do something, wanted to relieve the stress and tension by helping, by being productive in some way. But he couldn't. He was ordered to rest and to be practically immobile until he was completely healed. Dacunda was determined to leave as soon as he was better.

And so it was that Ell found himself laying in the grass beside Miri, watching restlessly as everyone around him worked and sweated in the warm sunlight. Admittedly, it was pleasant to spend time alone with Miri, trading quick kisses, and allowing their bodies to lean against one another in the warming, spring air. Especially, he enjoyed it because he knew that he was leaving soon and so he grasped every last moment with her, taking them captive and savoring each one. Oh, he hoped he would return, and sooner rather than later. Miri had, after all, intimated that if he didn't do so, she would hunt him down and give him a limp to match her own. He smiled at that thought as she snuggled in closer to his body, content to simply share his embrace without talking. Yet Ell knew that where he and his family went there was no guarantee they would be back within weeks or months. *Or at all.* He shoved that thought down forcefully, not allowing his mind to go there. No, he would be back. He said it over and over again to himself. He had to. The prospect of dying before he ever saw this beautiful elf again was too bleak a prospect to even consider. However, he did admit that the road ahead would be dangerous. He had been raiding his whole life, killing the humans who hounded his people, and the dark elves who betrayed their own race. Yet there was a look to Dacunda's eyes recently, a hint that what was ahead in the coming times would be even worse. Ell had begun preparing himself for the war again. This respite in Little Vale had been a joy beyond what he had even known he wanted, yet the battle beckoned. The world was darkening. Whether these few of the Highest who dwelt in the valley chose to admit or deny it, it didn't make it as they wished. It was true. He pushed the gloomy thoughts from the forefront of his mind and wedged them in a crevice in the back of his head, ready to be pulled out again and sorted through at another time, when he would not rather be spending it with a person he cared for deeply.

A few days stretched into a few weeks and Ell's shoulder wound slowly mended. Dacunda chafed at the delay to his search for whatever answers he required, but Ell was close to better now. He was nearly ready to begin using his arm and taxing his body again. He was looking forward to testing his muscles, perhaps sparring with Ryder a time or two, to get his speed and reflexes back to the ready. Ryder always did have a fondness for sparring. However, Ell couldn't shake the feeling that as his body healed, his heart began to grow more and more pained as he realized it would soon be time to bid farewell to Miri. They were nearly inseparable these days and Ell's cousin, Ryder, was not the only one to jest and smirk, asking when the Joining would occur. Many others in and around the village began to smile slyly as they saw the two of them stroll by hand in hand. Ell shrugged off most remarks and comments and tried not to focus too much on questions about his future with Miri. Life was serious enough without complicating things further. He had no doubt that he would return as soon as possible to the village after he left, Miri was that important to him, but he felt no need to voice those thoughts to other people. Miri and he had said enough to one another in private. They knew how they felt about one another. While voicing their emotions to others might seem unnecessary, he did give her a bracelet one day, a small thing that she twined about her wrist delicately, for all to see. It looked pretty against her fair skin.

Ell's time in the village culminated on a hot day. The spring air was beginning to drift more towards summer, even here in the heart of the mountains, and Ell enjoyed bathing in the sun's heat. He stood with Miri in the village common area, chatting about what was to come. The common area abutted a lazy, sweeping eddy of the Westrill as it detached from the main force of the river and flowed circuitously toward the village green before swooping back slowly to rejoin the main body of the river.

"It will not be long now before I leave," he said, moving his mending arm in a circle. The freedom of movement had increased greatly and the pain was almost gone.

Miri smiled at his being nearly healed but he could see the pain in her eyes at his imminent departure. "You could stay," she whispered into his chest as she hugged him close, burying her face into his hooded tunic, warm from its dark colors soaking in the sun's rays.

He sighed. "We've talked about this. I cannot abandon my family just now. Something is… wrong." Ell struggled to communicate his growing apprehension at the world around him.

It was difficult to convey to Miri the way he had noticed Dacunda's growing tension, even nervousness, as he anxiously waited for Ell's body to mend. Dacunda was eager to move on and accomplish whatever goal he had set for them on their journey.

"I cannot place my finger on it exactly," he went on, "but it's the Icari, and the Ghoul, and the war in the south, the way the wind smells." Ell remembered the scented breeze that had reminded him so much of the tales of the Bonewinds of myth and legend. "The world is darkening around us and we cannot turn our backs on that danger." Unbidden, Ell's thoughts flashed to the sickly dark elf he had killed and then burned. He didn't know what part, if any, it had to play in what he was sensing in the world around him, but he couldn't seem to shake the memory.

Miri nodded in disappointment. She said she understood when they had spoken of it earlier, yet he could tell it didn't fully make sense to her. She had a different attitude about life, a distinct view of the world. Ell saw things black and white the way he had been raised by Dacunda. Duty and honor. Right and wrong. Good and evil. Miri saw things through a different lens. She looked at life through her emotions, her desires, and joys. Her perspective was of the pain that their separation would cause both of them and how much easier it would be if he stayed. He didn't ask her to come with them because he knew she couldn't keep up with his family on the move. She managed with her limp. But there was no way she could keep the quick pace set by Dacunda. Ell and his family moved fast and traveled light.

"I will miss you," she murmured, her face still in his chest. He lifted her chin and kissed her soundly.

Their lips parted. "I will be back," he promised.

A scornful laugh sounded to the side of them and Ell turned his gaze from Miri's face to see Borian walking past. "Sure you will," the elf sneered sarcastically.

"And what do you mean by that?" Ell asked stiffly. His dislike for the young hunter had increased greatly over the time they had spent near one another in the village. The elf shook his head and made as if to move on.

"I said, what did you mean by that?" Ell said again a little more forcefully.

Borian was baited enough to respond. "What I mean," he sneered, "is that you and your family speak of your precious honor and duty. Fight! Raid!" He did a poor impression of Ell's uncle as he tried to mimic him. "But the odds are you'll be dead before you have the chance to return."

Miri wore a hurt expression on her face as he continued. She viewed him as a friend, and maybe they were Ell admitted to himself, but Borian was definitely no friend to Ell.

"That may be true," Ell responded, "But if that is the case, at least I will have died with honor."

"There you go again," Borian spat, "always spouting your drivel about your precious honor." The elf had a venomous look to his face. "But where's the honor in enticing the emotions of our village people and then leaving the first chance you get?" His eyes flicked towards Miri and then back to Ell's face. *So. She was what this was really about.* They were finally going to speak about it. Ell tried to keep his emotions calm.

Ell stepped away from Miri and towards Borian. "I have not 'enticed' anyone, Borian." He looked long and hard at the hunter before he continued. "The way Miri and I feel about one another is mutual. I would have a care with what you say from this point onward. You are treading on treacherous ground." His eyes conveyed menace and his voice carried a chill. He was not doing well at containing his emotions. Miri placed a hand on his arm trying to pull him back. He ignored it.

"Or what, Outsider?" Borian sneered yet again. "What will you do if I speak my mind? She should be mine," the elf whispered fiercely. "Apparently she has not the wit at this moment in time to choose well." He eyed Ell's bandaged arm derisively, clearly not thinking him a threat while wounded.

All of a sudden, Ell could stand it no more. It was as if all the sullen glares, sneers, and snide comments from Borian had compounded to make him furious in this one moment. He was too angry to contain it. A small voice in the back of his head told him to regain his composure but he didn't listen.

Ell swung his fist solidly into the elf's face. The force of the blow knocked Borian to the ground. The hunter was up in a flash and his eyes were alight at the opportunity to attack the injured Ell. When explanations were asked of this incident later, Borian would have the excuse of being struck first in answer to questions that Ell knew would come.

Borian practically flew at Ell as he tackled him to the ground. The collision sent them both sprawling and they rolled to their knees a few feet from one another where they had landed in the dirt and the grass. They popped to their feet in unison and circled each other warily. Borian was the aggressor. Ell immediately began to feel the fatigue from his wound and from the lack of movement over the past weeks as he had allowed his body to heal. He was rested but weak. Borian was a hunter, fit and ready for action. The elf smirked as he saw Ell eye him warily. He knew he had the advantage and he meant to press it.

The hunter worked his way in close, landing blows on Ell's body and face as Ell attempted to move his arms fast enough to block. Borian was only a year or so younger than Ell and he was strong. He danced in lightly, landed a kick to Ell's side that was too quick to block, then moved to strike another side of Ell's body. Ell fell for the feint and Borian slithered back the other direction and swung a vicious blow that connected with Ell's wounded arm.

A film of white-hot agony was all Ell could see and the strike drove him to his knees in pain. He heard a satisfied laugh from Borian and the hunter kicked him in the face, sending Ell flying onto his back. Ell rolled on his stomach and pushed himself to his feet unsteadily. Normally he would be a match for the elf, more than a match really, but not now, not in his weakened state. The most he could hope for would be to survive the encounter without growing too much the worse for wear.

He staggered as he tried to block and Borian drove another swift blow into his injured arm. This one didn't send him to his knees like the last one had, but it did force him backward a step or two. The hunter advanced, smiling with a nasty satisfaction.

"Lifelong fighter, honorable warrior," he mocked Ell. "And me just the simple village hunter. Who says we can't defend our valley?" He lashed a fist across Ell's face and Ell staggered backward another step toward the lazy shallows of the river behind.

"Who says you know what's best for us?" Borian said as he punched again. "Who says you should be chosen by her instead of me?" He punctuated each question with a blow and Ell's strength was draining within him. He stepped unsteadily backwards and his right foot entered the water.

Miri was crying out about him being injured, telling Borian to stop, but the hunter was paying no attention. On the outer edges of his senses, Ell thought he could hear people beginning to arrive. The fight would probably be over soon, whether people arrived quickly or not, he thought raggedly as he struggled for breath and strength to his limbs.

However, as the river swirled around his right foot something shifted. Borian cocked his arm back to land another strike and Ell felt something inside of him, some part of his consciousness, reach out instinctively into water around his foot and ankle. Power and vigor swelled within him, like it had the time at the Source in Verdantihya, when he had dipped his hand in the Source and then fallen into the spring with surprise at the sensation it had stirred within him. Once again he couldn't explain the sensation, couldn't describe how it happened. It made no sense, yet suddenly he was invigorated and felt as strong as if he had never been injured. He thrust his hand up to meet the blow and braced his forearm against the collision.

The impact didn't hurt Ell as Ell's forearm stopped the blow forcefully, causing pain for Borian who made a noise of agony as his fist recoiled. Ell stepped out of the river swiftly, agilely, with his rejuvenated body. A part of his mind was still in shock at what was happening, unable to explain why his body felt so good and strong. The other part of his brain was listening to battle instincts, and those instincts told him to press his unforeseen advantage.

The look of surprise on Borian's face as Ell unexpectedly and quickly closed the distance between the two of them and then swung his own blow toward the hunter, was almost as satisfying as the powerful connection of Ell's fist as it struck the youth's face. A few of Borian's teeth sprayed from the contact of Ell's blow and Borian's eyes glazed over instantly in his head. He dropped in a heap, unconscious. Ell looked at his hand. He didn't think he had swung that hard. The unexplainable swell of strength inside of him scared him. He was not sure he could argue it away as rage or coincidence like he had after the incidents in Verdantihya or during the ambush on Silverfist's band of slavers.

What was it about Ell that was different? What enabled him to fight with sudden and added strength? By all rights, he should have been the one knocked out in a pile in the dirt. Granted, as the power drained from him he returned to his former state of pain and fatigue. Actually, he was even more exhausted than he had been during the fight, but at least he was still standing. A splitting headache was forming in his skull, making it difficult to even think or be able to ponder what had happened. Miri rushed over to see to him, sparing a pitying glance at Borian, who was in a heap on the ground before Ell.

Apparently, the fight had garnered much attention and the village elders were looking on as well as many of the villagers themselves. Dacunda had a disapproving look on his face as he approached.

"You didn't have to hurt the lad so," an elf who was seeing to the unconscious Borian said to Ell in an accusatory voice. "He's not even a seasoned fighter like you. Spent your whole life raiding. Hardly a fair fight, I'd say, even injured as you are."

How could Ell go about trying to explain something he didn't understand himself? How did he say that in reality, it should be him in a heap on the ground, not Borian? He opted for silence and walked away from the scene. People began to scatter as soon as Borian regained consciousness, even if he was a little woozy, and they assured themselves that he was all right.

Dacunda walked up stiffly, even angrily. He shook his head in disgust. He clearly had the same thing in mind as the villager who thought Ell had taken advantage of Borian. *Had he? He had started the fight after all.*

"If you can fight, you can run. We leave on the morrow." That was all Dacunda said in his gruff, disapproving voice before striding resolutely out of the village towards their camp to begin readying their belongings to leave.

So. Their time in Little Vale was at an end. Ell's time with Miri was over.

He bitterly wished he had held his temper. Miri held his hand tightly. She clearly didn't want their time together to draw to a close either. *He would be back, wouldn't he?* He fought the fear inside of him that this was his last night with the girl he was beginning to realize he loved. He had never felt afraid of dying before, yet all of a sudden, the fear was there. It wasn't a giant hulking fear in the front of his mind. He knew he would be able to press through it for now. However, it was the type of worry that festered insidiously in the back of a warrior's mind, sapping their strength and their will to fight, slowly until the fear itself finally cost them their life. He prayed that would not be so for him. Fear was a strange emotion. For some it withered them inside, yet for others they grew so fearful it drove them to anger. Fear could do that to a person. It could do extraordinary things. To some the fear built until it sent them cowering to hide. To others, well, if you heaped enough fear on a person, it was like heaping burning coals on a lump of metal until something had to give. Eventually they snapped and the fear drove them to become something else entirely, a weapon desperate to fight back. Ell hoped that his newfound fear would drive him to become a better weapon. He wasn't sure how that would happen, but he prayed it was possible. The consequences alternatively were grim.

Ell hugged Miri closely beside him, breathing in the soft, lavender scent of her body from the plants she used while bathing. The braided wings of her hair as they fastened behind in a coronet of golden strands pressed into his cheek. He hugged her fiercely and she him. They clung to one another not speaking, just enjoying the presence of each other.

Tomorrow everything would change. Ell knew it from the bottom of his soul.

Chapter Twelve

Ell and Miri spent their last night together on the eastern edge of the valley. The Westrill poured over the pass and cascaded to the valley floor below in a huge sparkling waterfall. However, although the main bulk of the river flowed into the large waterfall, a series of small streams split from the Westrill at the top of the pass, forming their own set of smaller, terraced waterfalls. Whereas the main fall was huge, blasting over the edge of the mountain and then straight down in a rush of force, the smaller falls fell more gently. They bounced from rock to rock, some stronger as two streams merged, some weaker as the streams divided again into various little cascades. The arm of the mountain jutted out, a rocky promenade forming a natural wall between the giant falls and the trail on one side, and the array of miniature falls leading one to another on the other side of the rock formation. The path on which Ell and his family had entered the valley—formally known as Indiria's Emerald and referred to fondly as Little Vale by its inhabitants—switch backed beside the main falls.

Ell stood next to Miri among the small cascades of water on the opposite side of the rock formation from the main path. The evening had come and they sought privacy. Time had run out but Ell was determined to make the most of the precious few hours remaining. They gazed at the water plinking here and there, as it meandered its way down the rocky slope of the mountain before finally meeting the valley floor and rejoining the main flow of water known as the Westrill.

The smaller falls ran over mossy stones and through stands of trees that clung to the mountainside, bursting forth from cracks in the rock that hardly appeared to be able to support a full tree, roots and all. It was symbolic in a way. Life sprang forth even where it looked to be near impossible, halfway up the face of the mountain. It was just like his relationship with Miri. Times ahead would be challenging, he had no doubt, but they would survive. They would manage to rejoin each other and their relationship would grow in the face of the odds, just as the courageous trees survived, growing out from a steep, rocky face.

They hiked their way up, no longer walking on any sort of footpath, just grasping tree trunks hanging out of the rock face at strange angles that provided perfect hand holds, and stepping carefully yet surely on the slick, wet stones of the mountainside. A human would have fallen long since, but that was the beauty of the Highest. Elves were agile, surefooted, and lithe of grace. Their impeccable balance allowed them to traverse where others would fear to do so.

Ell and Miri stepped along the stony mountainside, leaping lightly from one boulder to the next, until they reached a suitable vantage point. It was private, the arm of the mountain jutting out to provide them with their own special view of the valley and the lightly forested hillside below. The tinkling of water falling, then trickling, then cascading again, was a comforting background noise. Ell sighed with pleasure at the beauty of it all, doing his best not to allow the urgency of his departure in the morning to ruin the moment.

Miri picked a water lily of pure white, sipped the lily water from the petals, as it was her favorite drink, and then placed the flower in her hair. She was stunning.

They watched the sun finally set and the shadows lengthen along the valley floor, creeping their way slowly towards them on the eastern pass. It was like a small haven of perfection. Ell imagined that this must be what living in Andalaya had been like before the invasion and subsequent fall of Verdantihya. Peace. Tranquility. Those were emotions to which he was not well accustomed. But deep down he longed for them. Yet the longing never surpassed his regretful belief that a few stolen moments of solitude with his love in the midst of this beauty were all that the harsh reality facing his shattered realm would ever allow him. The war. That was real. This simply was not, however much he wished it were. This was a dream, a fantasy that could not last.

Ell settled himself on a rock, his back to the mountainside, Miri beside him. "I will return you know," he said finally, after a period of comfortable silence. Talking was always a bonus with Miri. He loved their conversations, but he was just as pleased with the way they could sit for hours, simply holding hands or leaning against one another with their shoulders touching. It was a depth of connection he had never felt before, not even with his sister.

Miri turned and looked straight into his eyes. "Will you?" she whispered.

"You cannot think I would forget about you," Ell said back softly yet vehemently. "I would never do so."

Miri sighed, "You are not hearing the meaning behind my words, Ell. I do not fear your forgetfulness but for your survival." Her words rang out into the stillness. Death. It waited behind every tree, and rode the tip of every blade he faced in battle. Ell was aware of that reality. But he couldn't change that fact, and neither could he change his duty. His duty to Andalaya. His duty to support his family. His duty to Miri and the future he wanted for them. There was an evil afoot in the land right now, and its fell darkness lay brooding, awaiting its chance to swallow up even the remnants of their fair people. Ell had a responsibility to Miri, to do what he could to make their future together a better future.

"I cannot abandon my family," he said sorrowfully as he knew it would pain her to hear him commit himself yet again to the fray. "But I will return. I swear it."

Miri leaned closer to him. She smiled, as if giving up hope that he would simply remain. She now meant to just enjoy the time they had together. "You had better then, Elliyar Wintermoon. You see, I mean for us to be Joined before this is all over and I would be most disappointed with you if you died before I could accomplish that goal." She kissed him thoroughly, twining a hand in his wavy, blond hair as it hung loosely over the shoulders of his hooded tunic.

So, it was out in the open. Joining. The bonding of one elf to another for the rest of their lives. It didn't feel quite so strange to be considering the idea as it once had. For so long he had never had anything but the bitterness and rage inside his chest to drive him forward. But a new emotion was growing. Love. He imagined what it would be like to Join with Miri, have children, and raise a family. It would not be bad at all. In fact, it would be wonderful. He smiled at the thought.

"And I also mean for that to become our reality," he murmured back to her intimately. They shared a smile as the moon's silvery light replaced the sun as the source of brilliance in the sky. They kissed again, long and passionately, as if to seal their promise and commitment to each other.

Almost in punctuation of their promised covenant, a sheen of bluish-purple sparkling lights swirled around them, dotting each other's faces, hands, and clothes before winking out and allowing other sparks to take their place. Ell sat stunned as Miri gasped. They watched the shimmering mist, first lavender, then blue, then a turquoise, now back to purple, as it blinked alight. Each misty spark of light was like a million shapes all at once. Each one was a glimmer of the most beautiful fire, the shape of a droplet of the purest water, a Candlebug, a star, or a tiny butterfly. Their form shifted and changed with every moment that passed, blinking alight then darkening then reappearing again in another place. The swarm of dots lit the night around them, like a wind given starry form and flowed in flashing, twinkling circles as it danced in the pale moonlight and swirled around them. It was beyond spectacular. It was perfectly imperfect just as the world was with its beautiful imbalances exemplified in the flickering colors first here then there, ever changing. It was the single most amazing thing Ell had ever seen.

"The Wandering Mist," Ell's amazement was simultaneous with Miri's.

She spoke aloud in the same moment. "The Spirit of the Land," Miri breathed in wonder, mouth open as a few of the sparks twisted down and touched her tongue before winking out, making her giggle with delight.

It was known as both. The Wandering Mist or The Spirit of the Land was a legend, which so few had ever seen that even among the eldest of the Highest, barely a soul had ever witnessed it in their long lifetime. It was said that it was the spirit of creation incarnate, only appearing in moments of absolute alignment between the Three Realities. It was the best of all omens. Creation was painting its delight over their love in incredible fashion. The joy he felt at watching the mystical wind rush soundlessly around them was go great that all he could do was pull Miri, his love, to her feet and dance an elven jig. Dancing on a steep mountainside, bounding from stone to stone, boulder to rock with the precipice of a fall always beneath them might have seemed dangerous, even ludicrous, but Ell could feel peace that they would be protected. The Spirit of the Land was watching over them.

They celebrated creation by dancing for as long as the moment lasted, letting the world play its natural melody as their music. Ell had no clear perception of time. It might have been a minute or hours. He would not have been surprised if either were true. Miri threw her head back and danced wildly, never fearing that her lame leg might buckle, betraying her on the heights. No, for just this moment, she was as whole as any other of the Highest, the power of the Wandering Mist made it so. He didn't know how it did, but it did. He watched as her limp evaporated like dew on a hot morning. Her dancing was exuberant, beyond joyous. He laughed at the perfection of it.

Then it was gone. In a moment, the Wandering Mist swirled in a final whirlwind of blues and purples then vanished into the night as quickly as it had appeared. His breath caught as he watched it disappear and he prayed a prayer of thanks that he had been privileged to witness such an event.

Miri clutched his hand as they sat back against the rocky face of the mountain, resting from their exertions before making their way carefully back down to the valley floor by the light of the moon and the stars. They didn't speak of the event. No words were necessary. Yet both their spirits were lifted. For some reason he knew everything would be all right. Miri must have felt the same because she did not speak again of his leaving for the rest of the night as they made their way back to the village. Instead, they spoke only about their glorious plans for a future without war, destruction, and violence. A future in which they were always together. Ell listened intently, determined to seal those dreams of hers in his heart and not forget them. They were a reason to fight. For once, he had a reason to fight other than for revenge. At last, he could race into battle with hope for something greater than the blood and chaos that always followed the first clash of blades. Perhaps this was how he would silence the newfound fear he found of dying, of the possibility of leaving her behind. He forged them into his mind as he prepared his heart to leave. Their dreams for a future together would sustain him, as he pressed onward into whatever challenges lay ahead.

Chapter Thirteen

North. It was astounding how after a short week of travel to the north, spring had been effectively left behind them. Winter lingered in the far northern reaches of Andalaya. Legendwood's trees stood tall and firm resisting the harsh winds that blew from the northern marches, their tips still frosted, the occasional patch of snow still clinging to the ground around the base of one or another as if hoping to hide in their shade for yet a day longer.

Leaving Little Vale, leaving Miri behind seven days ago, had been difficult. Actually, it had been the hardest thing Ell had ever had to do in his life. However, it had been necessary. His family needed him, especially his uncle. Dacunda was on edge. It was as if the time spent in the valley had weighed upon him in a way it had not the others in his family. He often mentioned the urgency of their task, their search for his unknown friend. It was infuriatingly mysterious, and every time one of them asked Dacunda about what they were doing, he closed his mouth and refused to talk. Nevertheless, this was about family. This was about duty and honor, as Dacunda had always taught his family, and Ell had to continue the war. His conscience would allow nothing less. If this was where his uncle thought they would be the most effective, then even if Ell did not understand, he still trusted his uncle, his leader. It was enough. For now.

Ell pulled his cloak tighter around him as he walked next to his cousin, Ryder, their footfalls crunching slightly in the still-crisp, newly fallen pine needles. The pine needles were Dreampine, black like the midnight trees that surrounded them. The infrequent fir or spruce tree dotted the hillsides as they strode through the high elevation of the northern mountains, but for the most part, an eerie, black forest spread before them. This was the far north, the last stretch of Legendwood before the Broken Tree Range began, and they entered the part of the land, which could not be said to truly belong to the Highest any longer. Once his people's reign had stretched all the way to edges of the northern marches that abutted the frozen waste of ocean far to the north. That day was no more. The Broken Tree Range was now only a shade safer than the raiding and war torn south. An older, more primal war raged here in the north. Darkness, filthy and hungry to claim more domain encroached on Andalaya, as Ghouls edged their way further south in greater and greater numbers. To stay long in the far north was to surely risk your life to one of those opportunistic and clever hunters.

Ghouls would feed on anything with their mismatched teeth, some sharp and some flat or rounded. They would even eat each other if their bellies felt starved enough. And it did not take much for a Ghoul to feel the clutches of hunger pangs in their stomachs, for in truth, they fed as often as they could. Their sole purpose in life was to eat. Find more food. Eat more prey. It was amazing that they remained so slender. Ell thought back to the near death encounter he'd had on the way to Verdantihya more than a month ago and shuddered. It was almost the worst fate imaginable to wind up as the meal for a Ghoul. He had almost been taken. Those fingers, with their suctions and stingers that were filled with deadly toxin, had nearly touched his face. Had they reached his flesh and injected their poison he would have surely died, and quickly. Only his instincts sharpened by years of battle had allowed him to react fast enough to evade the opportunistic predator. If Ghouls had spread south of Verdantihya then they would surely be found here. It would pay to stay alert.

Ell marched on grimly in the cold weather. A light drizzle was sprinkling down from the grey sky above, and in truth, it felt more like frigid snow. Too much time in the south and then in Little Vale had made him soft he thought. This weather wouldn't have bothered him in the slightest not too long ago. Now, he found himself wishing for a blanket and a warm fire. He threw his hood back in disgust, freeing his wavy locks to the wind that danced around his family as they walked, its invisible feet springing lightly from hillside to hillside, peak to peak, as it ripped at cloaks and bit at noses. Ell shrugged it aside as best he could, silently daring the wintry weather to do its worst. It was time he hardened himself for the fight again. The war was far from over. He would start here with the weather as his foe and the rain as his enemy's weapon of choice. He welcomed the icy spatter of rain as it fell, lifting his face defiantly to the sky and allowing it to fall in cold drops upon his fair skin.

"Rain, this weather, cuts deep into your soul, does it not?" A voice, hard and old spoke beside Ell, shocking him out of his ponderings. "Reminds you that *this* is the fight you were born for, not that ill begotten drain of life to the south. Oh, I don't deny it is necessary that we fight there too, no way around the facts. However, here," Ell heard a deep breath inhale a lungful of cold, wet, mountain air before continuing, "here is where we were *born* to fight!"

Ell swore in surprise as he tried to find the source of the words. There. A shape moved in the rocky slope beside the mountain path on which they walked. Ell brought up the rear and his family had not yet noticed that he had paused.

"Show yourself!" Ell demanded, his belt knife already drawn in one hand and his other hand at the ready to unsheathe his dueling dagger, as well.

Again, he saw a flicker of shadow move on the hillside near him and then an elf wearing dull, ash colored clothes to match the grey, rocky surroundings materialized as if from nowhere. *How had he hidden himself so absolutely?*

"Easy lad, I am a friend not a foe." The elf was one of the Highest and the oldest elf upon which Ell had ever laid eyes. He was ancient, his grey hair shimmering in a color mix of silver and dull iron. However, there remained a spryness to his step as if despite his vast weight of years, he could still move with the dexterity of one many years his junior. Ell relaxed slightly. He had hardly ever met one of the Highest who was not his friend, yet recent encounters with the Traitor, Silverfist, and Ell's fight with the jealous Borian, stayed him from dropping his guard completely and sheathing his belt knife. These days caution was the best practice. He simply narrowed his eyes and watched. Besides, Ell trusted his instincts, and his instincts were screaming at him that a person would underestimate this old elf at their own risk. This elf was extremely dangerous despite his age.

The old elf took a step towards him and spoke again, "Cautious. Good." He stopped a foot from Ell and appraised him the way a herdsman appraised livestock. "Adan's boy, eh? Shame about your father. He was one of the good ones." The old elf spoke in the choppy language only acquired by those of extreme age, those elves who lived so long that they sometimes lost track of whether they were speaking or thinking and therefore ended up mixing and matching the both.

"How do you know my father?" Ell asked perhaps a bit harshly. He did not like the idea of this stranger speaking so familiarly of his father. Besides, Ell was still just a bit put off that he had been startled so by the elder. It galled him to think that this ancient elf would have gotten the jump on him if it had come to a fight or ambush of some kind.

The old elf ignored his question, picking up the topic with which he had started his conversation with Ell. "Yes, this," he motioned to the landscape around them, "this is the battle you were born for." He tapped Ell's chest with a finger. "The darkness breeds in the east and south, but it is a new darkness, the darkness of man. Here," he spread his arm again, "the far north is where our people's most ancient of wars resides. And most of our people have forgotten that, blinded by a desire for revenge." His face took on a disgruntled look as he mentioned what had been forgotten.

Ell wasn't quite sure what to make of this elf. He was so old and sounded so brittle. Yet his body was hard, well beyond what it should have been at his years. He was a mountain stone whittled down by wind and rain over the course of time but still strong enough upon which to break yourself. A boulder.

He didn't even wear a cloak, just a loose fitting tunic, allowing the wind to rattle at his clothing and whip it to and fro. The rain speckled his clothes that were as grey as his hair.

Out of nowhere, he whisked out a dagger from a hiding spot on his back, and held it to Ell's throat. Ell froze, mentally cursing himself for allowing the old elf to bring his guard down through his chatter.

"First lesson," the old elf began in an instructor's voice, "never allow appearance," he indicated his obviously aging body, "or someone claiming to be a friend as I have just done, to get close enough within your guard to get a knife to your throat. Make sure you take the time to verify that what they claim to be is indeed the truth." His mouth parted in a toothy grin.

"Arendahl!" a voice shouted from up the path, the wind doing its best to impede the cry and carry the words away. Ell's uncle and the rest of his family strode quickly back down the path, having seen what was happening.

Rihya and Dahranian looked extremely wary as they approached, hands on weapons, as they noticed the dagger to Ell's throat. Ryder looked a mix between wary and mirth, at his appraisal of Ell's predicament.

"Father," Dahranian asked quietly, "is this a friend of yours?"

Dacunda didn't answer his eldest son, but simply directed his voice towards the old elf again. "Arendahl, by the First Days, it is good to see you. Come now, give the lad a break, we have been traveling for days and he is probably pining over the girl he left behind, not paying the attention he should to his surroundings. You've proven your point, but is a knife at his throat really a great introduction?"

"Why, it's the best introduction," Arendahl responded spritely as he whipped the blade back to its furtive location on his body. He was quick! "No better way to get a feel for the mettle of an elf than to see what he's like with a knife at his neck." He paused eyeing Ell up and down, not revealing whether he found Ell sufficient or lacking.

He continued. "It is good to see you too, Dac my boy." Apparently, he figured himself old enough to refer to even Ell's uncle as a youth.

Dacunda crossed the remaining distance between them and grasped the old elf's forearm tightly, affectionately.

"Is this the 'friend' we've been searching for?" Rihya asked sourly. "The reason we've wasted these three days trekking through the north, cold and wet."

"I told you, he would most likely find us," Dacunda reminded them of previous conversations.

The old elf, Arendahl, turned his appraisal to Rihya and while she tried to withstand it for a time, even her fiery nature quelled slightly under his heavy gaze. Arendahl stared then spoke. "Fiery, just like your mother. But she was a sight more polite than you were. Didn't have your odd color of hair either," the old elf commented on the fashion of Rihya's dyed green hair. "You've been spoiling them Dac, you're too soft. Give them to me for a month or a year and I'll have them back to you iron hard and mountain firm." *Dacunda soft?* Ell began to wonder how well this old elf really knew his uncle. Dacunda was not one to be referred to as soft.

Yet his uncle only smiled slightly, not taking offense at the comment. In fact, he nodded his agreement. "That's probably true, Arendahl. I'll not likely forget my own time under your tutelage, yet I need them still. They cannot be spared."

"Why, boy? Why must you persist this fight to the south?" Arendahl muttered in frustration. "Leave it to the others. Come here. Fight alongside me once again. This is the fight that truly matters." He clenched his fists in front of him with the excitement only a warrior could muster when they spoke of battle, and his arms knotted up like gnarled, ancient oak. Suddenly Ell did not feel quite so embarrassed for allowing Arendahl to get the jump on him. There was a primal passion to the old elf, a battle savvy and strength he carried that was fearsome to behold.

Dacunda's face tightened, the contentment fading. He glanced quickly at Ell, and then spoke obliquely. "I have... information that might make you think otherwise. There is possibly more to the war in the south than we had previously realized." He paused again, obviously wishing to say more, yet not wanting to do so in front of the younger elves. "There is much we should discuss, Elder. Much."

Arendahl's eyes narrowed as he studied Dacunda. "Very well. It's not far to my camp. Follow me." And with that, he was striding away, off the trail and through the rocky slopes, weaving his way through the Dreampines all around.

To what was Dacunda referring? Ell wondered suspiciously. *Why had he looked at Ell and what was he hiding?* Ell hated not knowing.

The fog was rolling in from the north, grey, smoke-like wisps of cloud, weaving their way through valleys and between trees. It would not be long before the sky could no longer be seen and visibility in general all but disappeared. It felt strange. Ell was used to the blue skies and scattered fluffy clouds of southern Legendwood and the Lower Forest these days. Even the plains and their gentle rolling hills leading into the human camps felt more familiar right now than these hard, northern mountains. Granite boulders met jagged, black Ashrock to form an alien landscape. Here and there, chunks of black bark were ripped off the Dreampine trees that filled the slopes, leaving the white underwood beneath open to the elements. They resembled fleshy, open sores on a wounded beast, more than skinless trees.

"Ghouls," Arendahl grunted as Rihya asked him what had done that to the small sections of bark on the Dreampines. "They'll eat anything—elves, animals, plants, even each other. Opportunistic bastards." Ell shuddered inwardly to think of a species so vile that it ate its own kind.

It was not long before Arendahl's determined stride led them to the smallest of camps. In fact, if the old elf hadn't stopped where he did, Ell would have passed it by, considering it to be just an old burned out campfire spot with a rock or two left beside it for sitting, the remnants of passersby long gone.

Dacunda, laughed quietly to himself as they arrived, as if finding something humorous to which only he was privy. "Still living as simply as can be, I see," he commented in his old mentor's direction.

"Heh, it's just me out here. Nobody to impress, no soft skinned elves that I'm needing to coddle." He peered at the four elves of the younger generation, as he answered Ell's uncle. He was interesting, Ell realized. More intriguing than almost anyone he had ever met. There was an unrefined quality to him, to the way he thought and spoke, and it did not reflect the way most of the Highest conducted themselves. However, if Dacunda trusted him, and had traveled all this way to try to find him, then Ell supposed he might as well do the same. They sat on a few stones surrounding the burnt out fire pit.

"Shall we start a fire then and get dinner going?" Rihya asked, as she rubbed her hands together to ward off the chill.

Arendahl shook his head, "Not yet. We'll wait until the fog rolls in completely. Ghouls can see keenly and smelly sharply. They often scent a campfire from leagues off. The fog will hide the smoke, and the dampness in the air will cover the smell like a blanket and keep it from drifting."

"Do you find many of them around here?" Ryder inquired, pulling a hidden stash of dried meat from somewhere on his person and beginning to chew as he waited for a response.

The old elf eyed him balefully. "Find? What sort of nonsense is that? As if I was collecting them or something! I don't *find* many. I kill them. Them and whatever else comes across my path as shouldn't be here." Ryder looked at him doubtfully as if not sure of the truth of his words.

The old elf snorted in disdain. "You think I am too old to be speaking truthfully. Well, I would wager the last of my supplies on myself if we were to cross blades boy." Ell found himself agreeing silently, a bit unexpectedly. Ryder was strong and fast with his axes, but there had been something crafty about the old man. A clever warrior was often more dangerous than a powerful one. And that speed! He'd had a dagger to Ell's throat before he had even a chance to blink.

Ryder raised his eyebrows in surprise and held up his hands showing that he had meant no offense, placating Arendahl for the moment. The fog continued to roll in, blanketing the already dim landscape in a cloak of grey. The mountains were black and grey rock, black trees, and now a hovering cloud of grey obscured all but the closest of objects from sight.

Dacunda spoke up, "Don't be so touchy, Arendahl. They don't know anything about you. Once they see you fight, they'll come around."

"Ah, so you will be joining me in a scuffle or two?" Arendahl asked, brightening at the thought.

Dacunda inclined his head, "If the occasion arises we will certainly not back down from a fight. Though I must say, I would prefer we not go looking for one. I have a matter of some urgency that I wish to discuss with you." He paused, clearly searching for the words with which to speak and not allow Ell and his family to understand the full meaning. "It is a topic on which you might be the most knowledgeable person I know. I need your counsel, Elder."

The ancient member of the Highest considered Dacunda carefully. He spent a lot of time staring at people, appraising, weighing them. Then he snorted. "What you really mean, Dac, is that I'm the oldest elf you know, and therefore, likely the most knowledgeable."

Dacunda acknowledged that with another nod, "Yes, I suppose that might be the truth, yet you know that you have a wealth of… information about certain topics." He gave the old elf a meaningful look.

Ryder interjected, lacking tact as always, "Excuse me, but how old are you, Arendahl. Sir?"

"That's none of your concern, boy!" the old elf snapped back. "Suffice to say that I am old enough to merit the respect that none of you need ask that again." He was touchy indeed. Ell supposed enough time spent this far north by yourself, with only the Ghouls and other ghastly beasts he encountered for company would do that to a person. What was it that Dacunda was so eager to discuss with the old elf in private? Ell couldn't help but think it had something to do with himself, the way his uncle kept flicking his gaze towards Ell any time he mentioned it.

"Is it foggy enough yet?" Rihya questioned, clearly ready for some warmth and a hot meal.

Quick as lightning, Arendahl whipped a knife from his belt and flung it end over end toward Rihya. She didn't even have time to scream or startle before it had whisked by her head and pinned a small creature to the trunk of a tree a few yards behind her.

"Now we are ready for that fire." Arendahl muttered as he stood to finish off the squealing, squirming creature. It was quite pitiful really. "Curious bastards," he muttered again, "always poking their noses where they shouldn't."

Ell looked closely and could now make out what the thing was. It was a Ghoul; skin the color of ash to blend well against the dark Dreampines and grey fog. It was much smaller than the one that had attacked Ell in Legendwood along the banks of the East Mayn. This was probably a juvenile.

Arendahl yanked out the knife that had pinned the Ghoul to the black, Dreampine tree trunk and then casually slit its throat before it had a chance to inject any of its deadly venom into the elf.

"Young one," he said, "looking for a meal. Should've known better than to approach a full camp of travelers. They are growing bolder." He said the last part under his breath, almost to himself.

Ell's uncle spoke up as Rihya had her hands on her knives ready to draw. That creature had been sneaking her way, most likely judging her the easiest kill since she was the smallest.

"Now we should be able to make a fire." Dacunda began the prep work to start a small blaze. "Ghouls always live and hunt alone. There will not be another in the area for leagues," he spoke with confidence, surety.

Arendahl grunted as he peered off into the swirling fog, searching for some unknown shape or movement as he wiped his dagger clean. "Maybe. Things aren't the way they always used to be these days. There's information I could tell you too, Dac, not just the other way around."

Ell's uncle cocked his head inquisitively. Arendahl responded to his unspoken query and continued.

"Saw a pack of four young Ghouls pull down an adult the other day," he punctuated the remark by kicking the dead ghoul at his feet. It was slender, but with a queer looking frame that implied a deceptive strength and limberness. Ell could just see the tiny suctions and stingers on one hand as it rolled palm up in death. The lips were peeled back in a rictus of a snarl, mismatching teeth of all types in the mouth, depicting the manner of its violent death. The Ghoul's ashen skin began to shift just slightly to adjust to the browner earth beneath it. Even in death, apparently, its nerves still functioned enough to try to camouflage it.

"A pack?" Dacunda exclaimed, startled.

The old elf nodded grimly. "A pack. Although, once the big one was down and they had eaten their fill, they all turned on one another, fighting to the death." He shook his head in disbelief. "Yet the fact still remains, four of them *worked together*. I've never seen such a thing in my life. They've always been solitary monsters, going back as far as the First Days. It does not bode well."

Dacunda had gotten the fire started as they spoke and Rihya was warming her hands by the flames, roasting a few nuts from her pack that she had jammed on the end of a sharpened stick. Ryder was doing the same with some dried meat, heating and softening it up as much as possible before eating it. Dahranian was like Ell, listening intently to the conversation between Dacunda and Arendahl.

They settled in for the evening as the shadows grew. It was already dim and gloomy with the fog enshrouding them, and with night falling it became even more so. Ell shivered as he imagined other Ghouls sneaking up on them in the night, their cold fingers of death clasping his neck, strangling him even as they released their toxin into his veins. He shook the thought from his head. Even so, Ell determined that he would volunteer to take the first watch when the time came to seek their blankets. He knew sleep would not come easily for him this night.

They ate in relative silence, a more somber group than normal. Finally, the old elf broke the stillness.

"Care to hear the story?" Arendahl asked.

Dahranian, responded respectfully, "We are a bit old for stories, Elder. Don't you think?"

Arendahl snorted. "I didn't say a story. I said *the* story. Would you care to hear the story?" He repeated his question.

"Which story might that be?" Dahranian responded, still respectful. He had ignored the jab at his listening skills. Dahranian would be polite if it killed him.

"The story of us, obviously. Of how our people came to be." Arendahl's face lit up as he spoke. Apparently, he liked that story.

"We have already heard it," Ryder chimed in.

Arendahl snorted again. He did that often. "You have heard bits and pieces. A snatch told here, a story there. But not all together, and not by one who has studied our roots."

Dacunda answered, "We would be honored to hear you speak, Arendahl. By all means please begin." There was the hint of something strange in the voice of Ell's uncle, an eagerness. *What answers did he think to find in the history of their race? Could the matter about which he wished to speak with the old elf have something to do with it?* Ell resolved to pay close attention as the ancient one spoke.

They listened to Arendahl speak as the darkness crept in closer with the waning light of their campfire. The fire had shrunk down to embers that were just hot enough to provide a little warmth if one stretched their hands towards it. Ell opted to clutch his cloak tightly around him instead, rather than scooting closer to the fire. He pulled up his hood and listened, watching his uncle's face all the while for a clue as to what he was thinking.

Arendahl's voice carried an unrefined, rugged quality that most of the Highest did not possess. However, now as he spoke the history of the elves, his voice changed slightly. It was still rough at the edges, granite scraped against the side of the mountain from which it was chiseled, yet there was a depth, a mesmerizing sound to it now. Ell found himself getting lost rather quickly in the story and had to force his mind to stay sharp as he paid close attention to the details of it and to his uncle as well.

"The dusk of our people is upon the land. Darkness swells like a rising tide, a storm blown in off the Fracture to ravage the rocky coastline." The coals of the campfire gleamed in the ancient elf's eyes as he spoke. "Your father named you aptly, Elliyar. Dusk Runner. You have certainly witnessed the twilight of our race. It was not always so. We, the Highest, love to remember the golden ages before the split, before our cousins to the south were just that, cousins. Yet, our people often forget that our lives in this land did not begin in ease and comfort. In some ways, we have only just come full circle. The present evil facing us is but a return to our beginnings."

The night seemed to grow darker as he spoke. Ell had heard different stories, and versions of their history, but something drew him into the tale more than the previous times. It was as if Arendahl spoke about something he understood, something familiar.

"I speak of the beginnings," he intoned, "the First Days." Arendahl's voice would rise and fall as he spoke, first drawing you in with a whisper then sending your senses recoiling slightly as his voice grew in force and stature.

"Our people are called the Highest and we were birthed into a land buried in shadow. All the evil of creation had spread like a plague of destruction, threatening to swallow the land. We were fate's balance, a race created to right a world gone wrong. And we did so. Through blood and sweat, through toil and tears, the darkness was nearly banished. At least for a time.

"When we came into this world, the land was a den of madness, diseased with evil, ridden with the decay and rot of a land twisted to insanity by the darkness dwelling among it. Fate spun us out, birthing us from the very mountains we now roam to subdue the darkness, to restore peace and justice, and to heal the land of evil."

Ell imagined what it would have been like running to battle in the first days, the wind at his back, a blade in his hand, and a horde of darkness awaiting.

Arendahl spoke of the shadow creatures that had inhabited the land;

Ghouls, Ogres, hulking wolf-like beasts with spotted coats and jaws capable of snapping bone in two. He spoke of the Icari and their eyries in the mountain peaks. Ell shivered as he spoke. Arendahl painted a grim picture.

The old elf continued, "The Bonewinds blew in from the north daily in the First Days, heralding the waves of darkness that abounded. Strongholds in the northern marches and the Broken Tree Range of the enemies had to be taken and broken, shattered by the Highest.

"We were the armies of light, born to destroy the works of darkness." The old elf was impassioned as he spoke, his fists clenched tightly as if he longed to have been there himself holding a spear or loosing an arrow.

Ell glanced around the fire and saw that his entire family was lost in the story, mouths slightly agape as they heard their people's history told as never before. Even Dacunda had the look of a young boy listening to his elder as he focused on Arendahl. Ell supposed that was exactly what it was. After all, Arendahl must be old enough for Dacunda to have known him as a child.

Arendahl went on with his tale of danger and battle, of conquering the forces of evil. Ell's family members hung on every word.

"Ogres brought clubs to battle that were made from the leg bones of the ancient mammoths of the north, long dead now in their frigid wastes. They beat the ground until it shook, their bellows echoing in the mountain valleys and passes." The old elf paused and looked around at his mesmerized audience. "Ghouls, preyed on anything and everything, their cold, spindly fingers grasping and stealing the life from whatever they touched. Icari flew in flocks the sizes of which are unheard, feasting on the flesh of elf and dark creature alike, their talons snatching whatever was careless enough to be caught.

"They were a fearsome host of darkness. Their unruly combat lines stretched across the horizon as they met the forces of light, the Highest, on the field of battle." Arendahl raised up his fist in emphasis. "But we elves were made of stern stuff. Our souls forged like steel in the winds of destiny, we stood our ground."

A bird called in the darkness from afar, the muffled sound carrying through the fog of the night like a strange, distant creature. Even the familiar seemed odd in this untamed wilderness in the north. Ell felt like an intruding outsider. This was his homeland; it was a part of Andalaya, yet he had never truly felt to claim it as his own. It was harsh and wild.

Arendahl continued to share his story as the coals all faded except one solitary ember, burning resolutely in the night. The sight seemed a symbolic testament to the Highest in the First Days as they stood as a similarly solitary force of light against the darkness of their time.

"The host of darkness that faced those first, valiant warriors in the beginnings of our time in this land was enough to make even the most courageous lose hope as their hearts crumbled beneath a weight of fear. Yet, as if that wasn't already enough, an even more terrible foe awaited them." Arendahl's voice dropped to a whisper and Ell strained his ears to hear. "We were born of the land, birthed at the Source at Verdantihya, spun out by fate for a purpose. The Highest are nothing, if not in a covenant with creation, to protect it, govern it, uphold, and defend it. But covenants with the light are not the only type of bonds that one can make." His eyes and face grew sly as he spoke of evil unimaginable.

He paused for as long as possible, forcing Ell and his family to wonder at what could possibly be worse than Icari and Ghouls and everything else. Ell glanced at Dacunda's face and saw an intensity in his gaze. Ell perked up. Perhaps this was something to pay attention to in particular. Indeed, this tale did have new information. Ell had heard murmurs before of an ancient foe, the marshals of darkness during the First Days. Most of the people with whom he talked knew nothing of them or did not actually believe they existed. Ghouls, ogres, and Icari, there was proof to back up their existence, but the darker foe, one had to believe the myths of old on faith alone.

Ell paid close attention as Arendahl began his story anew.

"Yes," the old elf drew out the word, knowing he had his audience well and truly hooked, that they hung on his every word. Ell realized he was the best storyteller he had ever witnessed. "Indeed, a darker evil existed. The Lords of Darkness, captains of the enemy forces." He paused again for dramatic effect. "I tell you all, that the humans who now abound on our shores are not the first to dwell here. No, indeed. The Unsired were here before them. Men twisted by darkness, mad from hate and anger and bloodlust." He whispered his words but they sounded a shout in the still darkness of the night.

Ell craved to know more of the story as he lost himself in it.

"No longer of the land, they had entered into a covenant with the darkness, gaining dark powers, and the strength to control and bind all the unruly shadow creatures to their evil will. Indeed, it is even said that the Unsired could inspire speech in their dark creatures, their beastly followers. Although, that fact has never been verified since." It felt right hearing this history in the wild north with its black landscape and dim stones, its grey fog and cold, misty air. The myth fit, and Ell felt himself realizing that it was no false tale, no legend told to scare children. He could see the belief in Arendahl's eyes as he spoke and feel the weight of his words.

The old elf shifted his position on his rocky seat. "Other creatures of darkness did their bidding. The Lords of Darkness, or Unsired as their fate was no longer tied to the creation in which they lived, marshaled the dark forces and led the battle for earth against the Highest. The Unsired were a plague against creation, both in intent and form. Their shapes had been twisted by the evil to which they had attached themselves, their bodies strong yet resembling the sickly. As strange a paradox as there ever was, symbolic of their merging of dark powers and the most evil of plans for creation.

"Elf steel bit deeply into creatures and black blood spurted forth to rain across their faces in the midst of battle." Ell listened as Arendahl painted a gruesome picture of the battle for life and health and love, the fight against destruction. The old elf relayed how the Highest had fought the Unsired and their host of dark creatures until they had pushed them back to their strongholds in the north.

"It took time," Arendahl said, "much time and much effort, but at last the strongholds were crushed." He let out a sigh of ecstasy. He reveled in the victory though it had occurred over a millennia past. Here was an elf who truly preserved and cherished the history of his people. "The Unsired were destroyed. Their minions of Ghouls, Icari, and more scattered, scarcely to show their faces again until this present age when evil has returned again. Returned in many forms." He muttered.

He grew silent and the quiet stretched until they realized he was done speaking. The abrupt ending left Ell feeling empty, as if the story wasn't over. But, then again, perhaps it wasn't, he realized. The story of the fight of good versus evil was ongoing and they were the current crop of warriors upon which the future depended. It was a bleak idea as he thought of how few warriors there were left to fight. Honor. Duty. Those words carried a greater weight than ever after hearing the history of his people told so eloquently.

Dahranian wore a confused expression. "Elder, how did the Highest manage to defeat the Unsired and their manipulated hosts if they were so powerful? Didn't you call them the Lords of Darkness? It must not have been that easy."

The old elf smiled slyly. "Clever boy. Clever boy." He was back to speaking in his rough, stilted speech, no longer the flowery storytelling voice from a few moments past. "Yes. No easy task it was to defeat them. In fact, we would have failed were it not for the Water Callers."

"Water Callers?" Rihya said. "I don't think I've heard that term before." Dacunda leaned forward intently as she spoke and Ell perked up.

"Nor would you," Arendahl answered. "It is a rather closely guarded secret, not spoken of outside our elders. But I tell you now as a privilege. Besides, our people are waning, the history in its entirety must be preserved and remembered. Even if it is by the youth." He continued as he picked up a branch gathered for kindling and idly began snapping off pieces of twig and black bark.

"Water Callers were our balance to the Unsired. They drew upon the strength of the earth, the water around them, and channeled its use for many different purposes." His voice grew quiet in a thoughtful way, as if this was a very revered topic for him. "Strength, endurance, healing, even the manipulation of the element in its natural form. They were capable of much. We, the Highest, were born from the Source, the pure water that is the life-blood of the land. It was only fitting that our most skilled and important warriors drew upon that very connection to enhance their abilities to defeat the enemy we had been created to destroy."

It all sounded a little vague to Ell and he thirsted for more information. A deep part of his being cried out for more knowledge, more understanding of that of which Arendahl spoke. However, suddenly the old elf was done talking. He was tired he said. It was past time they were asleep, as one would die in this rugged portion of Andalaya if one didn't make sure they got enough rest to keep their wits about them.

"Thank you for the story, Elder. It was particularly relevant. Especially the latter part, I believe." Dacunda concluded the night's discussion, his eyes speaking volumes to his old friend. Something passed between them. It was as if they communicated silently, mind to mind, and then the old elf's eyes widened and his eyebrows rose. A small smile played at the corners of his mouth.

"Yes, well it's about time. The old blood is needed at a time like this." It was an oblique response. It was meant to be. Dacunda nodded solemnly in agreement. With their shared moment of understanding over, they went about setting up their bedrolls like the rest of the company.

Ell took the first watch as he had promised earlier. His mind was still racing, filled with thoughts of the distant past, thoughts of the future, of the battles that still lay ahead. Yet most of all, his thoughts dwelled on Miri. He prayed she was safe and happy at the moment in her valley along the Westrill. He imagined himself holding her, kissing her. It was nowhere near as satisfying as reality, yet his thoughts of her kept him going.

He stared into the damp, dark fog, hardly able to see a thing. He relied on his hearing and even his sense of smell to discern whether danger approached. Nothing stirred around them in the silence of the night. Occasionally an owl hooted in the distance but that was it. He was left with his thoughts and the ponderous weight of silence of the night, until his shift was over and he went to wake Dahranian. He rolled into his bedroll as his cousin replaced him on the watch and huddled deep into his hood and cloak as well. It was cold here in the north. His last thoughts before drifting off to sleep were Arendahl's words at the beginning of the story. *Your father named you aptly, Elliyar. Dusk Runner. You have certainly witnessed the twilight of our race.* It was a grim thought to which he fell asleep, yet it was not that uncommon. His life had been full of grim thoughts until recently. The wind rose and shook the Dreampines, breaking the silence and singing a wild lullaby to Ell as his mind clouded with sleep and the night took him.

Chapter Fourteen

Ell awoke before his eyes opened. His ears registered the sounds of his sleeping family around him. Ryder's heavy breathing rose and fell directly to his left. Beyond Ryder, Ell could hear the slow and steady, measured breathing of Dahranian as he slept—in and out, in and out. Lastly, there was Rihya. Her breathing was so quiet that he almost could not hear it. It fit her tiny frame.

That left the elders. Ell stretched his ears and strained to hear around him, cracking one eye open just slightly to begin surveying the campsite. There. Off to the side of the camp, sitting against a tree was his uncle, deep in conversation with Arendahl as he finished the morning watch.

"...Change in the wind," Dacunda was saying. "I tell you, there is something afoot to the south. All I have told you lends credence to the possibility of it being true."

The old elf nodded silently to his, now adult, pupil. "Yes. If your conjectures are correct, then it would explain much, here in the north. The odd behavior of the Ghouls and other creatures." Arendahl ran a hand through his lanky, grey hair. It looked as if it had gone too long without a washing. Ell supposed that here in the north, where every moment required watchfulness lest you become the meal of a predator, bathing was a low priority.

"What shall we do then?" Ell's uncle queried. It was strange to see him so dependent upon another for direction. All of Ell's life his uncle had been the leader, the protector, the battle commander. This was a different glimpse inside his mind. Perhaps Dacunda wasn't so sure and calm as he always seemed to be. Maybe deep down he too longed for somebody to step in and tell him where to go and what to do. Everyone needed a leader. In a way, it made Ell feel closer to his uncle. It made him seem just a bit more reachable, more normal, where for so long his uncle had appeared to have supernatural resolve, determination, and grit. His uncle fought so hard, and refused to give up on what he had decided was the duty and honor of the Highest, to resist their enemies. It was easy to forget at times, that perhaps, he felt fear too. Perhaps, there were times when he didn't know what was the right course of action.

Arendahl took it in stride that Dacunda would submit to his authority on whatever matter they were discussing. Ell desperately wished he had awoken earlier to hear the beginning of their conversation.

"We carry on. Head south. You keep raiding." He spoke in that stilted, abrupt way of communicating. "You will continue your duty. I will investigate the matters of which we have spoken. Bonewinds, Ghouls gathering, it is certainly a matter I must look into." Ell didn't understand. *Why would he be looking into those matters in the south? The Ghouls were here in the north, at least for the most part, in the Broken Tree Range and the northern marches*. It didn't make sense.

The old elf continued. "But first," he paused and scratched his face, "I will take the son of Adan Wintermoon and remain here in the north to attend to a small matter. It will only be a few days before we will follow you to Verdantihya to replenish our Source Water before raiding begins again." Ell and his family had shared much of their Source Water in Little Vale with Miri's village and they would need to refill their water skins before heading into the war zone again.

Arendahl smirked slightly as he finished his thought, "After all," he murmured slyly, "the boy has been listening to our conversation for the last few minutes, and we might as well get better acquainted than just by means of my knife at his throat and his ill-mannered eavesdropping." He turned his head and peered at Ell. His gaze was hard, but Ell could just see a hint of mirth dancing behind the wall of granite in his eyes.

Ell sighed. He hated when he felt like someone had gotten the best of him in regards to anything. It irked him that Arendahl had somehow known he was listening. He opened his eyes fully and met the stone gaze of the ancient elf. Everything about this elf was strange. Even his eyes were more of a greyish color with only very tiny flecks of the traditional blue and green of the Highest. He was an anomaly.

"Well, boy?" The old elf asked an undefined question. It was open-ended and Ell could feel its latent meanings. *Can you match me? Can you keep up? Are you worthy of the name Wintermoon? Will a few days alone with me in the north break you down or make you stronger?* Ell firmed his own gaze and nodded his assent to Arendahl. He would stay with the old elf.

"Good," Arendahl responded to Ell's nod. "Pack up your things quietly then and we'll remove ourselves from the camp. If we slip away without waking the others, then there are a few less bothersome questions we shall have to answer." Ell looked questioningly at his uncle. Dacunda nodded once and Ell began stowing his things away in his small pack. It only took him a moment to get ready. They all traveled light. One had to do so when they ran from battle to battle, from southern skirmish to northern wasteland.

He threw the pack over his shoulder and followed the old elf out of the camp, heading north. However, just as he passed Dacunda, his uncle laid a hand on his arm and motioned for him to pause a moment.

"Listen closely to him, Elliyar," Dacunda said seriously. "Try to move beyond what can, at times, be his abrasive nature. Arendahl is the person I trust most in the world to lead me. I would ask that you place your confidence in him also."

It was a strange comment from Dacunda. *What did he expect Ell to be doing with Arendahl that required so much trust?* Ell decided to allay his uncle's worries.

"I will, Uncle." Dacunda nodded approvingly.

"We shall see you soon enough. I don't doubt that you will be back with us long before we reach Verdantihya." Ell nodded to his uncle in affirmation and then quietly followed the quickly receding form of the old elf out into the damp, dim, morning fog.

It was an odd feeling to be setting out for an unknown destination without his family by his side. Ell knew that he would be reunited with them shortly, but for now, he was in unfamiliar territory, with an unfamiliar elf.

Arendahl strode lithely, resolutely through the stony landscape, weaving his way through black Dreampines and stepping over and sometimes into the nearly endless supply of tiny streams and creeks that bubbled up from springs. This was a wet and cold place. This northern territory was damp, both on the ground and in the air, as water often flowed at their feet and swirled about in a damp mist at their head.

The old elf offered no explanation as to where they were heading, and Ell decided not to ask. His present company was the type not to suffer fools lightly. Besides, Ell did not want to risk vexing Arendahl with, as the old elf had put it earlier while sneaking quietly from the camp, *bothersome questions*.

Arendahl seemed agreeable to silence at the moment and they made their way for a few hours, through the morning mist, north and east, away from the camp. They walked for what seemed like forever and finally Ell could stand it no longer.

"Where are we going?" he exclaimed in exasperation. "We have been walking for half the day and you have said barely two words to me about what we are doing, let alone anything!" His frustration had mounted so much that he didn't even care that he was being disrespectful to an elder.

Arendahl laughed, it was the sound of rock being mined out of the mountains, the song of iron, steel, and stone. "So he speaks. Heh, about time. I was wondering when you would finally give in and ask." He appraised Ell with a sideways glance, still not stopping despite Ell's question. "Glad to see you have spirit, boy. Wouldn't want you to be a weakling, where we are going."

"And where is that?" Ell asked again, keeping stride with the old elf. His frustration was starting to ebb since Arendahl was at least speaking to him, yet he still felt slightly vexed at not actually receiving any real answers.

Arendahl grinned wolfishly at him. "Why, we are going to pick a fight." He said it simply, as a matter of fact. He actually seemed excited about it.

"A fight?" Ell said flatly. "With whom, might I ask? And were you even going to consider talking to me about it before we engaged in combat?" he added as an afterthought.

"Yes," Arendahl answered the first question, and then proceeded to the second. "With whomever we come across that deserves a scuffle," the old elf said with a vicious smile. He still lived for the battle even at his age. "And no. I was not going to consult with you, boy. Didn't your uncle tell you to do what I say?"

Ell narrowed his eyes, his frustration turning to a seed of rebellion. He didn't even know this elf and he was supposed to take orders from him. Elder or not, that wasn't going to happen. Ell didn't take orders from people he didn't know.

"No." Ell answered just as abruptly as the old elf spoke, "He didn't. He told me to trust you. I will consider doing so, but he said nothing about taking orders."

"Heh," Arendahl laughed again, seeming genuinely amused by the interaction. "Headstrong. I like that. Reminds me of your father, boy." Then he turned his face forward to the path ahead, as if the conversation was over.

The conversation was not over. Ell pressed on determinedly. "So, where will we pick this fight?"

The old elf sighed as if realizing Ell had the bit between his teeth and was not about to let go. He made a sour looking twist with his lips and responded. "Fine. You want answers? I'll give them. We are heading towards the Barren Maze. Heard of it?" Ell cocked his head as he tried to think. It did sound familiar.

"I think so. Remind me again what it is."

"It's a series of hundreds of interconnecting canyons, tunnels, and gullies. Soil's too rocky and hard for much to grow, hence the word barren. Bit of a maze also, obviously, as it can be easy to become lost in a warren of trails and paths leading through all of the ravines." As Arendahl spoke, Ell realized that he was already beginning to grow accustomed to the old elf's stilted, rough way of speaking. Only the facts mattered to Arendahl. Ell wondered if it was a personality trait or if being old simply meant you didn't have time for wastes of energy, even if those wastes were only the common niceties of normal speech.

Ell did remember now. The Barren Maze was spoken of in legends. Some of the stories of the First Days told of battles that had been fought and won, and also many lost in that catacomb of dry earth and rock.

"Isn't the Barren Maze supposed to be dangerous?" he asked carefully. He didn't want to appear afraid but Dacunda had taught him to use caution. Measured risks, carefully thought out plans and strategies whenever possible.

The old elf snorted. "Of course, it is. Why would I go there to pick a fight if it weren't?" He turned to look at Ell. "Really boy, I thought you were cleverer than that. Don't ask me silly questions." He shook his head and kept walking. "Not long now."

And so they continued. They followed the paths down towards a valley floor and the dense fog didn't make it easy to see ahead of them. Suddenly there it was. A swift drop in the trail and their path sloped, entering a narrow ravine. Walls of grey Ashrock and tan Lionstone surged upwards around them and before Ell knew it, the looming walls of the Barren Maze were all around them. Fine pebbles, almost sand-like in quality, scattered across the hard soil of the path, making a strange footing beneath their soft, leather boots. The hard stone, covered by only a small amount of sand made for a slippery surface.

Ell had faced down charging ranks of human cavalry on their strange riding beasts from the other side of the Fracture, he had fought and killed the Departed with the best of them, but something about this place made him feel apprehensive. Perhaps it was the unknown factor. He had never spent as much time in the north as some of the Highest had, and this land, so close to the dangerous Broken Tree Range was unfamiliar, and rather foreign at times.

"So," Ell dragged out the word, filling the imposing silence, "what type of," he searched for the right word, "...thing are we going to fight?"

"Nervous?" The old elf seemed to see right through Ell's emotions. Ell wasn't sure if he liked Arendahl's perceptiveness. "Good," Arendahl continued, "you should be. This place is dangerous."

"Do you ever just answer questions?" Ell asked peevishly.

"Yes, I do. See, I just answered this last one about whether or not I answer questions." His predatory grin flashed white teeth in the gloom of the canyons. The fog didn't drop down into the gullies and caverns of the canyons. Instead, it hovered above like a trap door locking them into a nasty prison of cold and dismal rock.

Ell sighed. Maybe he would have to content himself with not knowing. Arendahl didn't appear to be forthcoming with information.

"Oh fine, boy. Stop it. You look like you're just shy of your sixth name day when you're pouting." He shook his head the way older people do when they disapprove of the behavior of someone younger, and Ell clenched his teeth in frustration. *Pouting?*

Arendahl elaborated. "I'll tell you alright. Barren Maze is usually home to all sorts of creatures, but most likely, we'll come upon some Ghouls. There are always any number of them that inhabit this rocky terrain. They don't like to share space with each other, but it's big enough to support more than a few of them. This place stretches for leagues in all directions." He paused then spoke further. "Might even encounter a Stone Ogre that's woken up from the long sleep. Though you better hope we don't. Those big, burly bastards are downright nasty, especially if they've just arisen. They are a fair size bigger than their woodsy brethren."

Ell narrowed his eyes. "You speak as if you've seen them." It was not a question. "All I have ever seen is Ghouls and now an Icari. I don't question that the Ogres of all types were real once, yet how is it that they have remained hidden for so long without being uncovered? I know the legends of the First Days speak of them, but there has been no real evidence in support of their continued existence."

"And my word isn't proof enough?" Arendahl's eyes hardened dangerously. "Most of the Highest avoid the far north, even with all the ruckus that is taking over the southlands. I've spent the majority of my life up here. Nobody knows these parts the way I do, and nobody knows the old lore like I do either." That seemed to be answer enough in his mind.

They continued to walk deeper into the canyons, Ell's body tense, and eyes searching for any slight movement that might betray a camouflaged Ghoul waiting to spring its trap. He was determined to be ready for whatever fight it was that Arendahl was trying to pick.

"Well, how have they remained hidden all these years?" Ell decided to change course of action. Instead of questioning the existence of Ogres, he just asked their methods of concealment.

"Better question. You're learning." Arendahl grunted before answering, his thin, grey hair swirling slightly in the air as his head swiveled all around searching for danger. He might be looking for a fight, the wisdom of which was debatable, yet he was also determined not to be caught unawares.

Arendahl went on. "When the First Days came to an end and the Unsired were finally defeated, their powerful hold over the land vanished and the dark creatures lost their ability to work together. They reverted to their usual solitary, violent ways, killing elves, but also killing each other and animals, in equal measure. Many were simply bent on destruction of any kind and they were much easier to dispose of without their cohesive front." The old elf eyed Ell. "A wall of Ogres advancing in battle is an entirely different situation than a solitary Ogre. Even if it is a Stone Ogre, the biggest of the batch."

Ell listened carefully, waiting for more information.

"We, the Highest, went about disposing of the creatures we could, ridding the land of the darkness that had seeped deeply into its pores. Some of the evil creatures we killed, some we drove out. Others hid.

"Ghouls, masters of camouflage, fled to hiding first. We thinned their numbers greatly but could never find every last one of them in order to finish the task. And so some few remained, and gradually as our civilization split and declined," he spat to emphasize his disgust at what he thought of the great schism, "they have slowly repopulated."

They ducked through a natural archway made of Lionstone, light brown, layered rock. It would have been beautiful if Ell hadn't been equally focused on the recounting of history and watching his surroundings.

"And, well, the Ogres were hunted too." Arendahl spoke, "They had their own way of hiding, a hibernation of sorts. The Stone Ogres hid away in the rock clefts of the mountains, the crevices big enough in which to squeeze. Then they hardened."

"What?" Ell asked in confusion.

"I said they *hardened*. Are you deaf, boy?" The old elf shook his head. "They aren't called Stone Ogres for their habitats. They can harden their bodies into a rocky slumber, sometimes for centuries or even longer. Impossible to find when they do that since they look exactly like the rocks for which they are named."

"So why have they begun to awaken?" Ell asked curiously. Against his common sense, he found himself taking Arendahl at his word. After all, what reason did he have for giving false information? He did not seem the type to conjure a tale for a sense of self-importance.

"They sense the change." The old elf whispered grimly. "Your uncle told me that you recognized the Bonewinds blowing, even far to the south as they were. Not easy to do that, without experience. I'm impressed, boy. All that's to say, there has been a shift. The land is no longer under dominion of the Highest. You've felt it, I know. The darkness is stretching forth its inky tendrils from its hiding places in the holes and tunnels of our land. The Ogres, among others, can feel it. They can feel it deep down in their stony bones that it's time for them to awaken. And so they do."

Ell shivered at the prospect of what Arendahl was saying. "Are you saying it's the First Days come again?"

"I'm not saying anything, boy. Enough to say that it's not the golden age and leave it at that. Who really needs a label? Give the darkness too much attention, too much credit, and it has already won half the battle." He tapped his chest, then his head. "The battle begins here, and here, before it ever transfers onto the battlefield."

They were silent for a time as Ell pondered their discussion. Finally, a random thought popped into his mind. "What about the Icari? How did they hide?"

The old elf shrugged, "Nobody really knows. We actually thought they had been exterminated. Filthy, flying devils. They'll eat you before you can blink if they get a chance." He spat again. He liked to spit. "One day they just began reappearing. Don't really have any idea how or to where they disappeared for all those centuries. All that matters is they are back again and need to be dealt with." His voice carried a grim resolution. He was one who was determined to fight the fight whatever the cost.

"That's why you stay in the north, isn't it?" Ell asked, suddenly realizing. "You said when we first met that this was the battle for which we were born."

Arendahl looked at him appraisingly. "Yes. The fight to the south is important. Dire even. But this, this fight against the purest of evil, still exists in our land. It has existed since we began as a species and it is our true battle. We were born from the land a millennia past in order to counteract the rottenness that abounded."

Ell thought about what he was saying. He understood the elf's opinions. It was important to fight here. But the south was important too. Ell was unwilling to believe that he had risked his life countless times in a war of secondary importance. Until the threat of the human alliance with the Departed had been resolved, the war on both fronts would suffer.

They wandered aimlessly, or at least it seemed so to Ell, for nearly an hour. Taking turns left, then right, then left again. He began to hope that Arendahl could remember the course that they had taken, because he now saw why the place had been named a maze. It was a warren of canyons, caverns, gullies, and ravines. Small trails and tunnels crisscrossed the entire area and it was difficult to keep direction straight. By the end of the hour, Ell had to admit he was hopelessly lost. Dacunda had said to trust Arendahl, so Ell supposed that was all he could do. Just trust that the old elf knew what he was doing and where he was going.

The attack came suddenly. A slight movement on the rock wall about ten feet above Ell's head warned him to the imminent threat. He reacted instinctively by immediately shifting his position and shouting to alert Arendahl as he drew his long, dueling dagger in a fluid, sweeping motion. The old elf heard his warning cry and dove instantly into a somersault roll, ending up in a crouch with his hands and feet balancing him lightly on the sandy stone floor of the path.

A Ghoul, its body a mix of different shades of brown, mostly on the lighter side to match the tan Lionstone wall upon which it clung, recognized that it had been detected and leapt into action. It bounded lithely from the wall on one side, ten feet above Ell's head, to the wall five feet opposite it on the narrow ravine trail. These were close quarters and the Ghoul obviously knew the territory well, as it transferred walls with an agile leap. Ell focused. He didn't like the way the Ghoul had moved with such precision and grace. For some reason he liked to think that the grace and beauty of movement should be reserved for more pure beings, such as his own elfish kin.

But he had to admit that was not the case. This Ghoul moved with a dark beauty, a lithe, catlike accuracy to its every movement as it stalked headfirst down the wall towards him. Ell had never seen Ghouls do such a thing. Of course, he was only accustomed to seeing them in the Dreampine forest outside this maze, where they had neither the need nor the opportunity to showcase this clever, wall-walking ability. Apparently, the suctions on their hands and feet were good for more than just a death grasp on their unfortunate prey.

It opened its mouth in a ghastly grin. Its teeth were putrid looking, some dripping with saliva and ugly brown mucus. Each tooth was different. Some were white, some grey, black even, some round and wide, others sharp and canine in form. There were even some that looked to have been twisted sideways and loosened in its mouth as if a particularly feisty meal had thrashed a bit too much as it died. The entire interaction since he had noticed the motion on the wall above him had taken only moments and Arendahl still crouched looking his way.

The old elf glanced over his shoulder and laughed. "Well boy, we've found the fight we were looking for." Ell watched him draw his short sword, perfectly suited for close quarter fighting such as this, and turn away from Ell.

Ell didn't have time to think about why he was moving in the opposite direction before the Ghoul above him jumped down off the wall and launched straight at Ell's face. It was fast, but he was just as quick. Lightning reflexes of the Highest kicked in and his dueling dagger scored a gash on the creatures face as he spun and slashed then ducked as it streaked by him to land on the ground next to him. It was up in a flash, screaming in an insentient way, the sound of rage from a wounded beast. It pressed a spindly hand to its face in an attempt to stem the flow of dark, black blood that streamed from its cut.

Ell felt the satisfaction of having wounded it, but that lasted only a heartbeat as the battle raged afresh. The thing bounded at him again, so fast this time that it was all he could do to avoid its deadly fingers with their stingers full of poison. *Don't let it grab hold of you. That is certain death.* The thought pounded in his head over and over again, as it lashed out again and again. He fended it off and was able to draw his second belt knife. Now he had two blades at the ready between him and the creature. They circled for a moment and Ell was able to glance quickly down the trail to see Arendahl engaged in his own combat. *So that was it. So much for Ghouls never working in tandem.* Two Ghouls weaved in and out between each other, fighting for an opening around the tip of Arendahl's sword with which he kept them at bay.

"Gets the blood pumping, doesn't it, boy!" he exclaimed with a wild glee, without turning to look at Ell. He maintained his gaze steadily on the two vicious beasts in front of him. "Finish yours quickly. A Ghoul isn't like an elf or a human. The longer you let it persist living, the more likely it will manage to get its deadly fingers wrapped around some part of your body. You will surely perish if that happens." He spoke as if he didn't fear death, and perhaps he did not.

As if to punctuate his last piece of advice to finish the Ghoul off quickly, Arendahl threw himself forward into the fray. Ell's breath caught for a moment. If he, young and vigorous, were having trouble with one Ghoul, how would Arendahl manage two? There was not time to think, as the Ghoul in front of him launched itself at him once more. Startled, Ell swung wildly, and was fortunate as his swing of the long, dueling dagger lashed the creature across its face and it fell in a heap in front of him twitching. His blow may have been wild, but it had been swung with force. It had cleaved the Ghoul's face almost in two. The beast whined and whimpered pitifully but Ell felt not a hint of remorse. He didn't even feel merciful enough to put it out of its misery. Some things deserved the end they got, and if a Ghoul was not one of those things, then Ell wasn't sure what was.

Arendahl, was striding back towards him, wiping his blade on a tiny piece of cloth he had cut from his cloak. It was never good to allow black blood to pit and corrode metal. *How had he disposed of those two Ghouls so effortlessly?* Ell was beyond surprised. He had expected the old elf to meet his death at the hands of the two Ghouls and that Ell would have been forced to run. Instead, the elf smiled fiercely. Clearly, he enjoyed this sort of thing.

"How did you do that?" Ell asked incredulously. "Two of those things might have overwhelmed me, especially in these tight quarters with no ability to create any space for myself."

The old elf winked at him. "I have my tricks," was all he said. Indeed, he must. Ell was impressed.

Arendahl continued. "How did you manage? Anything… out of the ordinary happen?"

"You mean apart from the fact that three Ghouls attacked simultaneously when they haven't done that since the First Days?" Ell responded sarcastically.

"Yes, apart from that, boy. I told you I saw them do that the other day." The elf paused, his pointed ears quivering with some unsaid emotions. "I admit it bodes ill for the future but it is not an entirely new piece of information."

Ell's eyes narrowed suspiciously. "No," he said slowly, "nothing else out of the ordinary, I don't think. It felt rather the same as most battles in which I have fought. Chaos, confusion, and lightning fast decisions driven by instinct." The separation between life and death in a fight was usually one's ability to react correctly without having to think all the way through the motion before doing it. Instincts prevailed over wit in close quarter fighting more often than not.

Arendahl wore a look of slight disappointment on his face. *What had he expected Ell to say?*

"Ahh, of course," the old elf said more politely than normal as he turned away.

They walked back the way they had come, on guard after the skirmish with the Ghouls. Apparently, Arendahl had fought enough to suit him for the day. The barren stonewalls passed by peacefully this time, yet despite the calm surrounding them, Ell couldn't shake the feeling of danger. Maybe it was just this foreign landscape, or the brush with death from the Ghouls earlier, but to him the stillness in the air felt latent with hidden threat. His eyes searched in a paranoid manner for any hint of movement or motion in the rocks ahead of them or on the stonewalls that rose up on either side like endless pillars of Ashrock and Lionstone.

Their path led them out of the maze, gradually rising up from the dangerous pit of ravines in which they had wandered for much of the day. However, Ell couldn't recognize any of the markings on the wall. It appeared that Arendahl was taking them out by a different and unknown route.

"Do you come in here often?" Ell asked making conversation. If he had to spend time with this elf then he might as well get to know him. After all, Dacunda must have sent him along for a reason.

The old elf grunted. "Only when I feel particularly in need of a good battle rush. This place is a death trap to any who meander into its confines unaware of the pitfalls it contains."

So, he had walked them into certain danger, all to satisfy a craving for adventure. Ell would have thought that age might have curbed the elf's reckless side, but apparently, it had only enhanced it.

"You've seen Ghouls fight together before this?" he asked, already knowing the answer, just hoping to prod Arendahl into further discussion.

The old elf nodded. "Saw it the other day. Watched some juveniles take down an older one. But this," he jabbed a thumb back over his shoulder indicating the battle they had left behind them, "was the first time I have faced it myself." He grinned that aged, wolfish grin again, and said, "Glad to have stood up to the challenge of two at once." He raised his eyebrows remembering the excitement of the clash. "I would've hated to have gone down and become a meal for the likes of those wily bastards." He spat as he had a tendency of doing when he mentioned the creatures.

Ell listened and then questioned him again. "What do you think it means that they attacked together? I must confess, I don't understand. All of the old lore says they are solitary."

"What does it mean, boy?" Arendahl rubbed his finger and his thumb across his eyes wearily, suddenly appearing his age for the first time all day. "Nothing good. That's what," he finished darkly, grimly. He kept walking, not saying anything more on the subject.

As they reached the edge of their path and the final slope leading up from the Barren Maze and out onto the northern slopes ahead of them, Ell breathed a sigh of relief. Not often did he feel so out of sorts in a place, but this warren of earth, devoid of abundant vegetation and animal life, felt alien. It was not an environment to which he was accustomed.

They walked out, and as they reached what could only be referred to as the gateway out of the Barren Maze, they were forced to pass by two huge boulders, three times the height of an elf, standing sentinels of their rocky abode. The Dreampines in the distance had never looked so appealing in all of their gloomy, dim glory.

"Finally," Ell exclaimed as they crossed the threshold out of the death trap behind them, not caring if the old elf heard the relief in his voice. He breathed deeply of the chill, damp air. What had before felt like oppressive fog and dreary sky had never looked so beautiful in his entire life after the stale air of the natural catacombs behind him. He closed his eyes and simply reveled in being out of there.

"Open your eyes, boy," the old elf's voice snapped quietly, commandingly.

"In a moment, Arendahl," he murmured in response, not yet willing to end his tranquil respite before going on.

He heard a frustrated sound. "I said," the old elf's voice commanded firmly and clearly, "Open. Your. Eyes." Something in his voice told Ell this wasn't a light matter. *What was going on?*

Just as he opened his eyes, he heard a groaning sound. He turned to the side and watched as the giant boulder beside him creaked and moaned as it rumbled apart. The pit of his stomach sank. Something wasn't right.

"Run, boy!" Arendahl's voice came urgently from behind him. But Ell couldn't listen; instead, he stood transfixed as a hulking shape appeared out of the converted boulder. The monolith of stone had become something else entirely, as body parts freed themselves from their statuesque structure. *Was it still stone?* Ell wasn't sure. What he was sure of was that it was enormous. Easily five times his side, at least twice the size of the Icari that had attacked him near Little Vale. The thing shifted its weight ponderously on one foot as it moved towards Ell. It had arms, legs, and a head as well as a huge torso, all looking as if they were made of the same boulder out of which the thing had morphed. The face was rough, its features rugged as if hewn from a mountain, but the hands and fingers of the beast resembled that of an elf or human in shape, if not in size or substance.

Arendahl's urgings to run continued but Ell could only back up slowly as the beast took another step towards him. It was a nightmare become reality. This was the stuff with which to frighten young children around a fire.

"Stone Ogre," he breathed and he didn't need to hear the old elf's assent to know it for true. The legends were true. If Ogres were real then the Unsired must have been also. That was a thought too frightening to even consider. *At least the Unsired were all destroyed*, he thought frantically, as his mind bounced nervously from idea to idea without laying hold of any of them truly.

The Stone Ogre was enormous as it stood in front of him. It let out a roar that shook the canyon walls, reverberating off the mountainsides in the distance. There was a reason these were among the most feared of all the dark creatures of legend. It was said that during the First Days, Stone Ogres had sometimes pounded castle walls to rubble, boring a hole for the enemy to breach in order to lay waste to the inhabitants. Ell had always assumed that to be an exaggeration. Now he knew it for true.

Before Ell's mind could register what was happening, one massive stone arm cocked back, the body groaning like a landslide under the strain of bearing that weight and then swung forward, ponderously towards Ell. It gained momentum as it swung, and by the time Ell had the presence of mind to roll to the side, landing in a crouch, the fist had crashed into the ground where he had stood, pulverizing smaller stones and leaving a tiny crater in its wake. The other arm was already swinging forward in a giant blow. Apparently, it could move faster than it appeared. Ell supposed it just needed time to loosen its joints by moving, after having spent centuries locked up and confined in the shape of an enormous boulder.

He rolled to the side again, narrowly avoiding another furious stone fist. This time there was no time to think or react as the first fist careened towards him at a frightening speed. Arendahl cried something unintelligible over the sound of the wind as the fist plummeted in Ell's prone position of liability.

He wouldn't be able to move fast enough to avoid it. This was the end. He put his hands palm down on the rocky soil, feeling the earth as he braced for the blow that would send him into oblivion.

Then suddenly something shifted inside of him. Like before during the ambush of the slave party that was led by Silverfist, some deeply hidden instinct kicked in. His eyes clouded up and he saw differently. Time froze and it was as if all of the fog and mist from the dreary, rainy day was contained within his eyes. He saw through the mist in front of him in a personal way. Strength filled his body in a way he had never before felt, not even during the ambush, and he felt it absorbed into his body from the damp air around him, and especially through his palms that were touching the rocky, moist soil.

His reflexes sharpened, in a heartbeat he had raised his arms instinctively, forearms crossed above his head as if a shield, although no shield was present. Ell watched the massive fist swing vengefully down towards him through his misty, watery vision. It was like seeing through a dense fog, at once difficult, yet at the same time it felt natural, as if he had been born to see this way all of his life.

Ell leaned his body slightly to one side, acting upon instinct again and the giant Stone Ogre's fist collided with enough force to destroy a boulder. Yet, instead of crushing him, it glanced off his strange, forearm shield and pounded into the ground beside him, creating a third tiny crater to go with the first two. The force of the blow still sent him flying back a few feet, but he was alive, blessedly alive.

"Elliyar!" Arendahl screamed at him and then tackled him out of the way of a fourth punch thrown by the Ogre. It wouldn't be long before the beast managed to connect fully and put an end to this farce of a fight. Ell didn't stand a chance.

The old elf tackling him out of the way seemed to knock his senses back to normal. The cloudy vision vanished, and the strange strength sapped from his limbs, leaving him feeling weak, his arms and legs a quivering mess. Arendahl hauled him to his feet and pulled him in the direction of the mountains, the opposite direction of the Stone Ogre who was taking a crashing step in their direction.

"Run, boy! And this time do as I tell you." Then the old elf turned and ran as well, sprinting as fast as he could away from the creature. Ell took one glance at the Stone Ogre's huge, malevolently featured face, its piercing reddish-orange eyes, rocky-formed nose and lips raging for his destruction, and complied with Arendahl's instructions.

He turned and ran, pushing his tired legs as fast as they would go. The Stone Ogre behind them bellowed a gravelly roar in anger as they outdistanced it quickly. It was giant and powerful, but they had the speed and agility of elves and they used it to their advantage, putting distance between them and the beast for a good half hour before Arendahl finally slowed to a stop in a copse of Dreampines. Ell collapsed beside him on the ground, unusually exhausted. Whatever he had done back there had sapped him of nearly all of his strength.

Arendahl knelt beside him, staring seriously at him in the eyes, yet with a touch of hope, as well. "So," was all the old elf said at first. He just stared, placing his hand on the side of Ell's head. "So, after all this time, I finally meet another of the Highest like me." He breathed the sentence with an almost reverent sound to it. There was vulnerability in his eyes, an aloneness that he saw coming to an end.

Ell knew that what the old elf was speaking about must have something to do with his brush with death and the way he had somehow managed to deflect the powerful blow of the Stone Ogre. He did not think that, this time, he would be able to explain the situation away to anyone, let alone to himself, as simply an increased strength from rage and battle lust.

"What are you? We?" Ell corrected himself, admitting finally aloud, that he was somehow different than most of the Highest.

"An ancient bloodline," Arendahl murmured. "The remnants of warriors from the First Days risen again." It didn't really make any sense to Ell what he was saying. "Your uncle was right. You really are one."

"One what?" Ell asked again.

Arendahl ignored the question and grasped the hair on the side of Ell's head, yanking it painfully. "Don't you ever disobey me like that again. I'll pull you out from the grave myself just to put you back in it if you make me return to your uncle Dac alone, having to explain to him how I got his idiot nephew killed. When I tell you to run, run!"

Ell pursed his lips in frustration and then retorted, "Fine. But would you answer my question?"

The old elf shook his head. "There'll be plenty of time for talk and questions when we've made camp for the night. It's still not safe here. We need to keep moving." He peered around them into the growing gloom. "That Stone Ogre's roar is bound to alert a few Ghouls in the area, hoping to clean up the mess of its after kill. Best we keep moving." And with that, he rose, hauled Ell to his feet, and set off into the late afternoon light, moving south and east away from the Barren Maze.

Ell followed, his exasperation on a knife's edge. But he settled his anger and weary frustration. *Tonight. He would finally get some long awaited answers at the camp tonight.* He would hold Arendahl to his promise, he thought determinedly as he set off following the old elf yet again. Tonight he would finally gain some understanding of the strange events from the past months. It felt good to realize that, and it spurred his exhausted limbs forward, as he strained to keep up with the uncharacteristically spritely Arendahl. Before long, Ell found himself hoping that camp wouldn't be too far off as he could do with some rest. As they made their way through the forest of Dreampines, his weariness increased. By the time they found a spot to camp that Arendahl deemed far enough from the scene of their last fight, Ell was almost looking forward to sleep as much as his long awaited answers.

Chapter Fifteen

Mist curled over the mountaintops and down into the small valley in which Ell and Arendahl stood. The early morning fog flowed down over the northern pass like a slow moving, grey flood, inexorably descending towards them on the valley floor far below it. The chill of dawn had hardly left yet Arendahl stood in a short sleeve tunic, his forearms bare. Ell wore his typical, long sleeved, hooded tunic. He saw no reason to be cold if it was not necessary.

"Focus, boy," the old elf barked the command. He had a rough tongue and apparently no use for tact or courtesy. Results were all that mattered with him, and so far this morning, Ell had been failing woefully.

Ell dutifully attempted to do so, waiting for further instructions that he knew would come. Indeed, Arendahl's voice swiftly followed his first command with another.

"Send your senses out. Listen, look, touch the world around you." Ell did so the best he knew how, as he heard Arendahl breathe deeply of the chill mountain air. They were two day's journey southeast of the camp they had made on the night after leaving the Barren Maze. This valley had seemed a good location to stop and rest. And learn.

The old elf's voice spoke on, course and rough like sand rubbing against stone. "Feel the land. There is power in the land. Can you feel it?" He asked as if he expected Ell to have a positive answer. Well, perhaps he did. After all, this was the second session of practice that Ell had been forced to endure with Arendahl as a teacher and the elf's abrasive nature expected that his pupil understand and be able to implement everything he taught him immediately.

Ell remained silent not wanting to answer negatively. He felt nothing. Ell bent down to touch the ground. Maybe that would help. The earth was moist beneath his hands, the morning dew on the grass a cool reminder that winter had not fully left the far north quite yet. He crouched waiting for the old elf's next instructions, as an eagle called from far and high above the peaks, piercing the silence with its lonely cry.

Arendahl grunted. "Should have figured you wouldn't yet, I suppose," he said in a more agreeable tone than he normally possessed. During the last two days on the trail together, he had pushed Ell for answers, answers Ell didn't possess. Arendahl was the one who was supposed to tell Ell all about this strange power inside of him, inside them both, but instead the old elf had been his usual frustrating self. Arendahl had asked more questions than he had answered, volunteering information only grudgingly. It drove Ell insane but he had finally accepted the fact that Arendahl gave information on his own terms. Ell decided to follow his directions implicitly. As long as he did what the old elf required of him, eventually he would get his answers. So far, however, all Arendahl had told him was that his abilities stemmed from an ancient bloodline of the Highest, dating back to the First Days. He said it was a balance of life, to counteract the evil running rampant during those times. Other than that measly bit of information, all he had done was ask questions about how Ell had felt every time he had experienced the ability working within him. How had he felt physically, emotionally? What had the world looked like in those moments? How had his normal limitations changed? On and on, until Ell was numb from the endless questions. He had also forced Ell to train, to attempt to use these abilities that Ell had never heard of before this, and didn't understand, let alone the fact that he didn't know how to even access them on purpose. It was annoying to say the least, but Ell pushed through, hoping to eventually secure the answers that he sought.

"Try again, boy." Arendahl attempted to encourage Ell, yet only succeeded in sounding demanding. Ell felt like he had been trying endlessly to 'learn' these abilities with no information and no breakthroughs whatsoever. It was mentally exhausting to continually push for something you had no idea how to achieve. Yet he did so anyways, such was his desire to succeed and understand the way he was different than most of the Highest.

Dutifully Ell tried. He stayed crouched and pressed his hands against the soil. Arendahl had not told him to bend down, but the old elf wasn't particularly forth coming with detailed instructions at the moment. Ell was left to flounder on his own, while trying to obey the few commands Arendahl gave him.

The moisture of the earth, soft from last night's rainfall, caressed his tired hands. He felt a bit refreshed just by touching it for a few moments. Push. He stretched his mind and tensed his muscles, pushing his cognizance and his body in any way he could imagine in order to try to gain the desired breakthrough. Nothing.

Arendahl was pleased, however. "Good, lad, good. Try harder." And Ell did. To no avail. Yet the old elf was content as long as he could tell that his pupil was at least attempting to do *something*, even if he didn't volunteer much in the way of new information.

"What am I even doing?" Ell asked in exasperation. "I don't even know what you want me to try and do." His frustrations were finally beginning to win out over his patience. He stood and wiped the thin layer of mulch from the palms of his hands, dirtying his hose. It mattered not; his garb was brown and dark green, mottled with greys and blacks. A bit of dirt would not be amiss, rather it would simply add to the ability of his clothing to camouflage.

"Your abilities are connected to the land," Arendahl responded gruffly. "I am trying to teach you to become in tune with creation. Once you can do that, your abilities will manifest more easily." The old elf inclined his head as if that was enough of an answer and now he expected Ell to continue. Ell wasn't satisfied—he wanted more.

Ell shook his head, still frustrated. "What are my abilities? You've said not a word about what they are, or why I, we, have them!" He stared the old elf down, youth challenging age, impatience crossing knowledge.

Arendahl stared right back, his piercing gray eyes laced with traces of blue around the edges. He did not back down. Finally, Ell glanced away, uncomfortable as the moment drew onward, yet it appeared he had made his point, as Arendahl finally responded.

"Oh, fine. I guess the impatience of youth was bound to win eventually. It had to happen at some point." Even while giving him what he wanted, the old elf made Ell feel petulant in his victory. Ell rolled his eyes and waited for what was coming.

"Water Caller." That was all Arendahl said. Ell opened his eyes and leaned his head forward in exasperated anticipation. His body language showed that he expected more from the old elf.

"Well, what does that mean?" he asked, as Arendahl remained silent. It was clear that Ell was going to have to tug every bit of information out of him, piece by piece.

The old elf harrumphed. After he had cleared his throat, he sat down cross-legged on the grass of the meadow, hands on knees. He was in full blown instructor mode now, Ell could see, and Ell took it as a good sign that at long last he was about to get some of those much desired answers. He sat down on the grass across from Arendahl, waiting expectantly.

"That doesn't *mean* anything in the sense of a word meaning one thing or another. It is simply what you *are*," the old elf began. Ell was confused already. Arendahl continued, "You are a Water Caller." He pointed at Ell, then at himself. "And so am I."

Ell narrowed his eyes, thinking. There were so many questions to ask. How to make sure he asked the right ones? Arendahl was just getting started however, and saved Ell the need to ask, as he simply continued speaking.

"The Unsired dominated the First Days before our people were born. We were birthed as a direct response of the land," he paused searching for the right words, "creation's natural correction to a diseased portion of existence. The way a blazing summer fire purges the weeds and underbrush from the forest floor clearing out the choking vines and creepers, making way for new life and fresh and healthy growth." Ell thought he understood what the elf meant. It was a bit confusing, but from what he understood, it was almost like the Highest had been medicine for the wild and unruly land.

Ell stayed silent, waiting for more. Arendahl obliged and continued speaking. "The greatest of our people's weapons against the darkness of that time were the Water Callers. When they discovered their abilities, a few of the Highest were able to greatly aid in turning the tide against the evil infesting our world. It was creation's gift to us, a balance of life for the evil already at work in the land." The old elf was quiet for a moment, a far off look in his eyes as if he was seeing something from long past, a glimpse of history. Ell tried to imagine what it would have looked like to have many of these Water Callers, fighting the darkness. It made him feel good knowing his gift was meant for fighting the evil at work in the world, both then and now. He still felt frightened, nervous about being different from others of his kind, but now he knew what his abilities were meant for in regards to the world. If he ever mastered them, he could use them for a worthy cause.

The moment stretched long before Arendahl continued his train of thought. The morning air around them matched the sudden stillness in their conversation. Finally, the old elf spoke.

"Much has been lost," he said wearily in one of those rare moments when his age showed. "The Departed broke away centuries ago and the conflicts between our two civilizations began shortly after." He sighed as if an old grief was wearing down upon him, a loss that was still tangible even after so many long years. He snapped tiny blades of grass from the earth beneath his hands and broke them apart idly in each hand, using his fingers dexterously to make short work of the plants. It looked to be a subconscious habit that Arendahl had picked up somewhere.

The old elf spoke as his fingers crumbled the grass. "Our two civilizations collided. Again and again, we struck blows. We feinted and attacked, fought and drew up peace treaties only to have them broken again. Entire cities were swallowed up in the wars. Riora, Akan Deraiya, the Water Palaces to name a few." His face carried a sad expression. "Our centers of learning, our libraries full of history, were sacked or burned. They were torn to rubble and the knowledge they possessed was lost." He opened his hand and let the crumpled pieces of grass scatter lightly on the air as they fell to the meadow a few feet below. “They were lost forever.”

“So how do you know so much about the First Days and the old lore?” Ell queried curiously.

Arendahl snorted disdainfully. “I don’t, boy.” He shook his head in disgust at his own understanding. “I may know more than anyone else alive today, but what secrets and mysteries I know of the past is but a flyspeck compared to what was once considered common knowledge.” He exhaled a frustrated sigh, his lanky gray hair drifting casually in a light breeze. “I know next to nothing compared to our forefathers. What I have learned I have had to discover through experience and by piecing together the different myths and legends surrounding that time.”

Ell had a newfound respect for the old elf. It must have taken a lifetime spent in the north, and studying what was left of the old lore, to even begin to gather any knowledge whatsoever. What Ell knew of the old lore, the tales of the First Days, he had thought to be much. But as he began to hear of things like the Water Callers and Unsired, and the habits and characteristics of the dark creatures, he began to realize how minimal his understanding truly was. All he really knew about the history of his people was that there had been a great war, a war the Highest had been born to fight and win. Apart from that, his knowledge of history was rather murky. He knew of Icari, and Ogres, and Ghouls, yes. But before recent times, his knowledge had gone no farther than to admit they had once existed, nothing more. Now he had faced them, and their mystique frightened him. What memory of the ancient war had been forgotten? What crucial piece of information would his people be missing when the time came to fight that battle again? It was becoming more and more apparent to Ell, after speaking with his uncle and with Arendahl, that the war was returning. The land was indeed regressing to darkness.

The old elf watched him quietly as Ell processed what had been said. “You begin to see now.” Arendahl finally broke the silence. “It is not over. The war is returning. And you,” he indicated Ell, “are the first person other than myself who has manifested the ability to call the water in so long that there are no records to say who the last of our kind was.” He stared at Ell solemnly. “You are a Water Caller. The world will need you.”

Ell knew it was true. “So, what do I need to do?”

“Do? Practice, boy!” Arendahl said forcefully, but not unkindly. “What little we do know from the ancient lore hints at the fact that many who manifested the ability never learned to control it. They were of minimal use to our people. You must not let that happen.” His gaze was penetrating, the way an old person passing on important knowledge can manage.

Ell nodded slowly, understanding. A small part of him shrunk inside at the responsibility he felt. What if he couldn't do it, master it? He asked the question.

"And if I cannot master it?"

"You will. You must," Arendahl retorted, his face pinched in frustration at just the thought of his new pupil failing to do so. He was a harsh taskmaster, but Ell had the feeling the old elf usually managed to squeeze every drop of potential out of his students. Ell didn't relish the idea of being squeezed, yet the alternative of never understanding his ability, never being able to control it, seemed an infinitely worse scenario.

"Now, back to training." The old elf motioned with his hands for Ell to continue their previous exercises. Ell complied.

He stretched his senses, his willpower, and whatever else he could possibly think to stretch out to the land beneath him and around him. His mind felt like it would explode.

"Open your eyes, boy." The rough voice of his teacher interrupted his attempts to grasp at something of which he knew not how to lay hold. His eyes snapped open by reflex. It was amazing to see how rapidly he was falling into the pattern of complete obedience to Arendahl. The old elf's commanding presence and vastly superior knowledge made it a simple case of follow the leader. Yet it bothered Ell. He didn't know why exactly, but it felt wrong to do everything he said so soon after meeting him. As if in reaction to the thought, he found himself arguing with Arendahl.

"How am I supposed to concentrate without closing my eyes? I don't even know what it is I am reaching to do and it helps me focus." He frowned at the old elf.

The old elf shook his head, muttering something under his breath about youth and willfulness. "Quit complaining, boy, you sound like a whelp fresh from the teat." He grinned wolfishly as Ell's eyes narrowed at the insult. "And don't take everything I say so personally, either. Now," he said, getting down to business, "I want your eyes open because if you are in the midst of battle you will not be able to close your eyes as you strive to access your abilities as a Water Caller. We must ingrain the correct instincts in you." It made perfect sense, and Ell hated that he had to admit it to himself. It made him feel childish for arguing. Well, he supposed he had been.

He forced his eyes to stay open as he attempted yet again to no avail. "Help me, Arendahl. I cannot keep reaching out on instincts alone. It's not working. I need more information. What is it you want me to try and *feel* in the land?"

The old elf nodded slowly. "Perhaps you do need more information. I had hoped to have you do it on your own, discover it for yourself first, thereby making it easier time and again after you practice it, but maybe that will not suffice with you." He thought for a moment. "I led you into the Barren Maze to fight, hoping for you to manifest your ability under the strain of battle again. You did so at the end when you defended yourself from the Stone Ogre, confirming your uncle's suspicions to be true. You were, are, a Water Caller. But perchance you need more understanding of the ability if you are to access it again under less stringent circumstances."

Ell agreed. He liked the sound of what Arendahl had said. Answers. Understanding. It sounded good to him. "Okay, what else do I need to know?"

"Feel the land," Arendahl began again, but this time he continued. "What is it you feel?"

Ell put his hands on the grass of the meadow. Thinking. Waiting. He searched for what it was he felt. The wind tickled his hair into his ears gently as it fluttered by on a small breeze. The grass beneath his hands was moist as it plunged roots into the still wet soil from the rainfall last night. He smelled the air, also carrying a dampness from the spring showers, which had been spouting intermittently for the last few days.

"Wetness. All around me," Ell finally responded to Arendahl.

The old elf smiled. "Good. Water. Yes, it is the essence of life, is it not?" Ell nodded. Not sure how else to react to the rhetorical questions. The old elf bulled on, not even acknowledging Ell's agreement.

"Water, is life. It is in everything. It is evident everywhere if you know what to look for. Even in a desert, water is not far below the ground if you just know where to dig." Arendahl motioned around them with a sweeping gesture of one hand. "It gives sustenance, quenches thirst. There is nothing alive that can survive without it. Evil dominated the land in the First Days. Death reigned. Creation gave us the boon of the ability to *call* life, to *call* water, to our fingertips. The land spun us into existence and granted us the ability to wield the very thing that gives life to all, in order to help us defeat the darkness. Life to balance death. Water is the key to what you need to feel in the land."

Ell furrowed his brow as he thought. It was beginning to make sense. The few times his ability had manifested, there had been indications that water was involved somehow. The time he had dipped his hand in the Source and the strange feeling of immense power had filled him, the odd mist that had accompanied him during their ambush of Silverfist weeks ago. Even the strange cloudiness fogging his eyes when it happened, making it harder yet somehow easier to see all at once. They all traced roots back to water of some kind. Yes, it was beginning to make some sense.

Arendahl saw he was beginning to catch on. Ell focused, making it clear he was ready for the old elf to continue. All of a sudden a thought popped into his mind and he interrupted the old elf as Arendahl was about to speak.

"You said Water Callers were made by creation as a balance to the evil. But the Highest themselves should have been enough of a balance, shouldn't they have been? What exactly were the Water Callers a balance *for*?" Ell questioned.

Arendahl pursed his lips grimly before speaking, hinting at dark truths behind his stony mask of a face. "Better not to think on such things now." It was not much of an answer. But Ell was becoming used to the fact that his ancient teacher seemed to enjoy, or at least feel obligated, to dodge any question he wasn't completely ready to answer. "Ready to continue?"

Ell nodded. If Arendahl didn't feel like being forthcoming with all of his information, then Ell knew his badgering would make no difference. When the old elf desired, he could beat a stone at unyielding silence and stubbornness.

"Good," Arendahl responded and then continued. "As I was saying, water is the key. There is power in water." He motioned to the peaks surrounding their tiny valley. "The power of mist to help the wind and weather wear down the mountains." He spoke further. "The lash of rain in a thunderstorm, the surge of a wave as it breaks the rocky shoreline and bends it to its will over time. There is the power of a flood raging through the canyon or the latent power of water in the earth and sky, to grow and create. Water is power. It gives life to the land, and forms it, fashions it. You must learn to feel the water around you and draw it into you, bend it to your will." He finished the short speech with a passionately clenched fist.

In one sense it all made sense to Ell in how it had reflected many of his past experiences with his ability, yet in many ways it felt farther away than ever. How was he supposed to harness the power of water? How did one bend a part of creation to their will? Insecurities welled up within him. He did his best to shove them down but they lingered insidiously in the back of his mind. What if he never was able to manifest his ability again? That particular thought almost scared him the most, since it would be the cruelest of misfortunes to discover a new power only to realize it had become unattainable. It would be like a treasure being shown to someone who had previously been unaware, only to tell the person it was not available for their use.

Ell gritted his teeth and set his mind to the task of searching for the water, within the land, within himself, since he was part of the land. The Highest were, after all, just the highest form of creation, not separate but part of the whole. He reached his mind out into his surroundings, stretched his will out from his own being. Yet anything of merit, any measure of success eluded him. His brow was covered in a sheen of perspiration at the efforts

He tried and tried, until it was past midday and the entire morning had disappeared. Finally, he collapsed onto his back from the sitting position, which he had previously occupied. Ell groaned in frustration just as simultaneously Arendahl let out a sigh of disappointment as well.

"Aren't you supposed to gain patience with age?" Ell asked wryly, somehow managing to find the humor in the situation even through the exhaustion and vexation.

"Not all the rumors are true, boy," the old elf snapped peevishly. "There isn't time for failure, and I find my patience wearing thin." Arendahl sighed again but this time it was a sigh of regret not frustration. "Although I admit, it is not entirely fair to expect this much of you on our first training session together. It took me years to gain even a minimal amount of control over my ability."

"See, now doesn't it feel good to be gracious for a change," Ell quipped with a weary smile, attempting to extend the moment of levity. He felt the need for some laughter due to the frustrations of the morning and the raw emotions of the past few days after discovering and accepting the truth of his uniqueness.

Arendahl snorted. "Don't tempt me, boy! I had no teacher to help me. I had to flounder through the entire experience on my own. You on the other hand, have me, a teacher to guide you. I don't want to hear any excuses from you." Ell should have known his moment of understanding would pass quickly and Arendahl would return to his normal, rough-tongued, high-demanding self.

Ell ignored the last comment although he realized there was certainly truth to it, and shoved himself to his feet. It would have been a terrible experience to try to sift through all of the emotions, sensations, and consequences of this powerful ability on his own.

He trudged slowly towards their makeshift camp. Arendahl would, no doubt, want to move soon and Ell wanted a few minutes to rest before they did so. He slumped back down to the earth as soon as he reached his pack, using the bulky, uncomfortable object as a pillow of sorts. It did the job required of it, and he closed his eyes for some peace and quiet.

He must have drifted off because he was startled awake with a soft-toed leather boot nudging his ribs. "Tired you out, did I?" Arendahl grinned, taking some sadistic satisfaction in Ell's exhaustion. Well, perhaps sadistic was a touch extreme, but the old elf definitely enjoyed seeing Ell's fatigue from straining to water call all morning.

"How long have I been asleep?" Ell asked quickly. A warrior always needed to keep his bearings, which included knowing the elapse of time as well as many other details of life. Paying attention to details kept you alive, both in battle and in the wilds.

"Not even an hour. I couldn't let you sleep forever for we have much ground to cover today." *Of course*, Ell thought. They always had ground to cover, always somewhere they needed to be. It felt like his whole life, apart from the time spent in the valley with Miri, had been spent rushing from one engagement to another. One raid to the next, back to Verdantihya, then on to the next camp. He was tired. It wasn't just the exhaustion from the activities of the morning dictating his thoughts either. He wanted a rest.

He ignored his thoughts. Rest was needed but laziness benefited no one. He couldn't allow himself to grow weak. The war was far from over. He pushed himself up off the dry, bumpy soil at the base of the great Evergrow Trees at which they had made their camp and grabbed his pack. He glanced upwards. The Evergrow Trees surrounding them were gorgeous and ancient. They reached to the skies far above any other tree and they were large enough in circumference that it would take many of his people clasping hands just to reach around them. The tops of the Evergrows jutted above the forest canopy, and in the springtime such as it was now, small seedlings drifted off from its highest branches. They were so high that the wind caught the seedlings and spread them far and wide over the land. Because the wind caught the seedlings so high in the air, Evergrow Trees tended to not be clumped together like many other species. The wind dispersed them, and there would be one or two or three in an area and then a few hundred feet further another, and so on and so forth throughout this northern stretch of Andalaya.

"This is what you fight for." Arendahl put his hand on the trunk of the massive tree. "Not just our people, not just our survival, but the beauty of existence. The First Days were marked by a rotted corpse of a world. Trees and plants were sick with the darkness dominating the land. We purged it, and the land slowly healed, but the danger is returning." He finished seriously then turned and loped off across the meadow and southward.

Ell knew it was true. He wanted to preserve his beautiful homeland, whether from the human cutters and their machines and modernizations, or from the terrible evil of the First Days returning.

He followed from the camp at a slow run. Arendahl knew Ell was tired, so he kept a slow but steady pace. They would likely catch his family soon. At least Ell hoped they would. He was beginning to grow accustomed to the old elf's rough mannerisms, but he wouldn't quite go as far as to say he enjoyed the elf's company. It would be good to return to people who knew him, and with whom he could be comfortable, with whom he could be himself. Or could he? *Will I ever again truly be the same Elliyar they knew?* The discovery of his abilities changed everything. That much was certain.

Chapter Sixteen

The next three days were a blur of running, futile attempts at training with his water calling ability, and exhaustion. They moved south, angling their course slightly towards Verdantihya. The weather warmed as they left the north behind them where winter's chill grasp was still clinging tenaciously, unwilling to let go.

Ell took a drink from his water skin as they stopped for a rest on the crest of a mountain. Up passes and down the other side, they ran. He loved his mountainous homeland, but there was no denying it could push even an elf to become fatigued when one was forced to cover large amounts of ground quickly. Andalaya was gorgeous beyond compare with its rugged, rough-hewn peaks surging upwards towards the sky. It was a land of uncompromising beauty and freedom. It felt wrong that its people should be subjected to so precarious a situation as the Highest faced at this moment in time. Scattered and drifting in the winds, or running for their lives, his people faced death and enslavement at every turn. Something had to shift. Ell felt his determination swell as he thought of the need of his people. He didn't know what he alone could do; all he knew was that something had to shift.

"Ready?" Arendahl questioned, pulling Ell's gaze from the incomparable view of his land and back to the old elf's aged face. Arendahl's face was smooth and unwrinkled in the manner of the Highest, his face not marked by wear the way a human's face changed as time passed. Yet, there were the beginnings of wrinkles forming at the edges of his eyes and on his forehead. It wasn't much, but for an elf, it was the markings of age. His lank, silvery hair was the greatest indication, however, of his status as an elder. It marked him as much older than anyone Ell had ever encountered.

Ell sighed, feeling just a bit sorry for himself. It was the third time today they had taken a brief rest from running. Only instead of actually resting, Arendahl had determined they would make use of their rest period by practicing water calling.

"Don't give up on me now, boy, we've barely gotten started," the aged elf clapped Ell on the shoulder in an uncharacteristically friendly way. Usually all Ell received from Arendahl were instructions, demands, and exhortations to work harder. "You are improving. Each time we train you get better."

"What do you mean, I am improving?" Ell retorted. "I haven't even been able to touch my ability since the fight in the Barren Maze days ago.

"That's what you think," Arendahl smirked mysteriously.

Ell furrowed his brow, not understanding. He tilted his head in question at his instructor. The old elf responded.

"Sometimes when you disobey me and close your eyes, I have seen the air thicken ever so slightly with mist before it disappears again. Small victories yes, but a victory nonetheless. It means you are beginning to tap into your powers." Arendahl made an encouraging face to his pupil.

"It doesn't feel like much," Ell complained. "We have been practicing for days and I still cannot do anything at will." He was frustrated, more frustrated than he was willing to admit. What if he was one of those Water Callers, who Arendahl had mentioned, a Water Caller who never learned how to control their abilities? What a waste that would be. He couldn't bear the thought.

"Trust me, boy, you are learning. Slowly, I'll grant you, but learning all the same." The old elf shook out his hands as if to loosen them before speaking again. "Now, perhaps it would help if I gave you a small demonstration."

Ell nodded a thoughtful look upon his face. Yes, that might help. For some reason up to this point, Arendahl had been reluctant to show Ell how to utilize his water calling ability. The old elf claimed he wanted Ell to "discover it for himself," through trial and error, whatever that meant. Oh, Arendahl was willing to tell him all about the experience and describe it to Ell, but when it came to demonstrations he was loathe to do so. It didn't make sense to Ell.

The old elf bored holes in Ell's face with his eyes. "Pay close attention, boy, I won't be doing this for you all the time." Then he closed his eyes and knelt down, placing his palms on the ground.

He stayed there, kneeling for a moment, before Ell noticed the wind beginning to swirl slightly around his body, and with it, there seemed to be a very fine mist forming in the air, thickening it just a bit. Arendahl tilted his head up and his eyes snapped open as he stared hard at Ell. His eyes were a milky, whitish-grey, like the milk from a mother's breast mixed with muddy clay.

All of a sudden, Arendahl burst upwards in an incredible leap, leaving Ell staring at him, as the old elf landed atop a rock formation jutting out of the hillside directly behind him. The rock formation was easily twenty feet above him and was an impossible jump. Ell had never seen anything like it. The old elf leaped lightly back to the earth in front of Ell, landing quietly with all of the grace and ease of one of the Highest.

It took a moment for Ell to stop gaping. Finally he spoke. "That was incredible! I've never seen anything like it!"

Arendahl snorted a laugh. "Boy, you blocked a full swing from a maddened Stone Ogre with just your bare forearms. You've not only seen a feat as impressive as this, you have *done* one yourself." It took a moment for the truth to sink in. And it was truth, Ell knew it. Yet, he hadn't known what he was doing at the time, and he'd felt like it invalidated his efforts somehow. Not like this. Arendahl had jumped from a crouch up to the top of a boulder in an effortless bound. And, the crucial difference in Ell's mind was the old elf had done so on purpose.

"I guess," Ell admitted reluctantly. "But I cannot do it at will, the way you can."

"Yet." Arendahl held up a finger to emphasize his point. "You cannot do it at will yet. But that will change with time. Like I said, it took me years to gain any sort of control over my abilities." He motioned for Ell to ready himself to begin practicing.

However, Ell wasn't ready yet. He had a few more questions. "Why did you close your eyes? And why did you kneel down? You always tell me to do the exact opposite."

Arendahl sighed before answering. "That," he paused for dramatic effect, "is why I do not often demonstrate the ability to you." The old elf continued his discourse, the backdrop of empty sky and jagged peaks behind him, painting a rugged scene in the distance.

"I learned alone," the old elf explained, "with nobody to teach me. I developed bad…habits. Ways of doing things, which I have never been able to fully shake. Such as needing to close my eyes to activate my ability, or having to actually feel the earth beneath my hands before being able to draw the power of the water into me." He exhaled in frustration at his own shortcomings. "I have tried to fix it, but I have simply not been able to. In truth, I am not certain why it is. It's not because I lack the strength of will for it, that much is certain." He stopped for a moment, his hard eyes daring Ell to disagree with that statement.

No, Ell did not disagree. This elf lacked not for willpower. Arendahl continued. "No, I believe it to be connected to the way we learn the power, the way it first manifests in our bodies. I have seen you activate your abilities in the fight without ever needing to do any of the things I require, which means my personal habits are not universal. I want to allow you to practice with me, yet not acquire my own… limitations." He peered at Ell. "I want you to have the power of the land, of water at your fingertips during a fight. But if you are like me, then you will need to grab a moment in the midst of danger to touch the earth and close your eyes. This can be fatal in the middle of battle." The old elf paused. "Believe me, I know," he said, hinting at perhaps an old wound acquired in such a manner. He continued, driving home his point. "I want you to have full access to your ability, without limitations or bad habits. I don't want you to experience the drawbacks of the fatigue you feel after accessing your abilities instinctually. Understand?"

And Ell did understand now. It made perfect sense. Perhaps not the why of it all, but at least Arendahl's reasons for being obtuse. Ell had previously thought him simply a cantankerous, stubborn old elf, determined to make things as difficult as possible. Maybe he deserved a touch more credit. And more respect also. Ell nodded his response.

"Is that why I feel so tired after I used this… power?" Ell asked, still struggling for language to describe it all, "Because I've been using it accidentally?"

"I believe so," Arendahl replied. "I think by activating your abilities by instinct rather than conscious choice, you unawares put a greater strain on your body and mind." The old elf looked at him with honest eyes. "I am not entirely certain about the why of everything regarding water calling, as there is still much unknown even to me, but that would be my conjecture."

"Alright," Ell breathed, looking at Arendahl, "let's practice then."

"That's the spirit, boy!" The old elf grinned. "Now then, eyes open. Feel the land. Stretch your consciousness into creation all around you. Feel the water in everything, the life in everything. It is a power, a strength, a well from which to draw."

Ell did as he was told and tried not to close his eyes. He didn't kneel down. He just felt. He stretched and stretched his consciousness until his mind felt like it was about to burst.

Nothing.

Why does this have to be so unbearably vexing? He grabbed a stone and cast it off the mountainside, sending it careening through the windy, Andalayan air as it soared a long distance before finally landing in the forested slope far below. Hours of fruitless training and there was still nothing to show for it.

Arendahl concealed his frustration and impatience and instructed him to pack up his things. It was time to run again. The rest of the day was made up of three things. Run, rest, train. It all felt futile except for the running. They were gaining ground on his family, of course, pushing as hard as they were, but everything else did not feel productive. The training for the rest of the day felt just as useless as the days prior, and the scheduled breaks were spent trying to train.

The landscape slid by as they ran, afternoon fading to twilight. The sun dropped low onto the horizon and it shone golden across Andalaya. They ran on ridge tops and mountainsides, overlooking the land. The rivers churned through gorges and slid slowly through lazy meadows below them. The sun illuminated the rivers and the water reflected the golden light, almost as if they were shining from within on their own, liquid light.

The chase went on deep into the night. Arendahl pushed hard. He must suspect they were close behind Ell's family and was eager to catch up to them. Ell was also. It had only been about a week, but he missed them deeply. He felt the absence of Ryder's laugh, and his sister Rihya's quick temper and even quicker smile, and he wanted them back.

They finally made camp in a shallow hollow of a cave on the mountainside. The trail ran along the edge of the mountain, and not far from where they had made camp, a sheer cliff dropped away hundreds of feet to the forest below. The two of them were high up. They were high enough to have had a good view of the entire landscape if it had been light out. It wasn't. It was the depths of night and the stars shone overhead dimly, flickering weakly through a thin sheen of misty clouds. The night sky was just visible through those clouds as Ell gazed out over the cliffs through the darkness, his body aching for sleep, but his mind not ready. For some reason he felt the need to think. Why was this happening to him? The last month had been a crazier month than he could remember. It had been filled with good, bad, and everything in between. Meeting Miri and falling in love had been incredible and he could hardly imagine life without the warmth of emotions he felt in his chest every time he thought of her. Yet there had been sore moments recently, as well. Finally facing his father's killer, only to have him slip away unscathed. Ell had no idea whether he would ever have another chance at defeating Silverfist and the thought of not being able to avenge his father's death seared his mind with anger and hatred. And there were other events that had been difficult to handle. He was only just coming to terms with things spoken to him by his uncle and Arendahl, truths about the land around them. Icari flew. He had seen them himself, fought one. Ghouls in pairs attacked together. Even a Stone Ogre out of legend had nearly killed him. The world he knew was changing, shifting. It might not be the First Days come again, but it was definitely dark, and growing darker by the day. The evil in the land was spreading, his fair Andalaya was growing unruly and out from under the control of the Highest as his people's fortunes waned.

That wasn't all. The biggest issue to confront was the realization in the last weeks of how he was different. There had been hints all the way back before their last visit to Verdantihya, over a month ago, but Ell had not accepted it for truth until the Barren Maze. Reality was sinking its teeth into his life in many ways, his outlook on the world changing, and this realization of his water calling potential was the greatest change of all.

What would it mean for him, for his family, and his people? Ell feared being different and what people would think. Would his family look at him the same way as always? More than anything though, he feared failure. He feared not being able to ever gain control, not being able to call the power of water to him at will. Arendahl spoke often of the many warriors in the old lore who were said to have never activated their abilities beyond an instinctual level, only able to access their power in moments of extreme danger and desperation. Ell would not settle for a similar inefficiency. His determination grew simultaneously with his frustration at failing to tap into the land around him each time he trained with the old elf.

"Sleep, boy." Arendahl put a rough, callused hand on his shoulder. "There will be time enough for deep thoughts on the morrow. Tonight you must rest. We will make the final push to catch young Dac and the rest of your family tomorrow."

Ell nodded in agreement. It was true. He did need rest. His body, his mind, screamed at him for a good night's sleep, so he lay his head down on the pack and pulled his lightweight travel blanket over him. It was a cold night. High up in these rugged peaks of Andalaya spring had come by day, but the residue of winter still held the night. Ell pulled up the hood on his long sleeved tunic and tucked his arms close around himself for extra warmth. The blanket kept off the worst of the chill, but a little more comfort from hugging his body close would not be amiss. Sleep tried to avoid him, his thoughts still racing—love, anger, vengeance, and newfound power. They swirled a delicate dance through his thoughts, evading his mental grasp as he tried to quell them and allow the night to claim his mind. Finally, at long last, he was able to squash them to barely a murmur. He was not able to get rid of them completely, but it was enough to fall asleep.

The crisp morning air woke Ell, along with the sound of Arendahl packing his belongings and pulling out a bit of dried meat for breakfast.

"Good, you're awake," grunted the old elf, his mouth full of food as he broke his nightly fast. "Means I won't have to wake you from your slumber. Won't have to waste the time." He still spoke in his stilted speech. Half-formed thoughts put into sentences would sound strange coming from another, but from Arendahl it was normal. By now, Ell had grown accustomed to the short way he communicated.

Ell grunted in response. Perhaps he was picking up some of Arendahl's stilted mannerisms himself. He rose, rolled his lightweight blanket back up and secured it to the pack. It had served its purpose yet again and protected him from the cold, mountain night.

"Training?" Ell questioned Arendahl a bit sourly. Every morning the old elf had desired to train. He wanted to squeeze as much out of Ell as possible.

Arendahl nodded as if it was a matter of fact. Ell sighed wearily. He was tired still, even after a night's sleep, but he grabbed hold of the determination to succeed that he had felt last night. Determination and grit would help him accomplish his goals. He steeled himself for the practice, the frustration that was bound to follow.

They finished a quick meal and then stood face to face in the shallow indent of the cliff. The tiny cave to one side, the trail, and then the sheer cliff to the forest below on the other. They faced off and Ell stretched his consciousness outwards from himself. Towards the land, he pushed his mind, feeling for something, anything of which to mentally grab hold.

"Push your consciousness, boy." Arendahl spoke the familiar command. "Feel the land around you. Feel the water in everything." The old elf's voice was hardly more than a whisper, but it was loud to Ell's enhanced elf ears. It was one of the perks of his body in comparison to the human invaders. Ell once again thanked creation for gifting him with his sharp senses and his extremely agile reflexes.

Arendahl continued. "Feel the water seeping through the cracks in the rocky cliff. Feel the rain, which sank deep into it during the winter storms and is now gradually seeping back out. Feel the moisture in the air, the mist on your face, the tiny drops of water carried by the wind as they graze your bare hands."

Ell blanked his mind, ignored his thoughts, and focused on the old elf's voice. He just listened and stretched his mind outwards, attempting to do what Arendahl was saying. Sometimes he felt like he was so close to accomplishing the sense of *oneness* with the land of which Arendahl spoke when the old elf described his own experiences and feelings while using his water calling ability.

Arendahl often commented on how he felt a deeper connection, a oneness with creation in a way that even one of the Highest wouldn't normally feel, when he tapped into the vast power of the water in nature all around him. Ell stretched his mind further. He focused on feeling. He felt. He felt...

Ell felt something beginning to shift in his senses. It was like something was coming closer. He stretched his mind again and focused on the land, on creation all around him. Keeping his eyes open as Arendahl commanded, he focused all of his mental energy on the mountains and peaks of Andalaya, on the moist mountain air, and the verdant green firs, and pines clinging to the slopes. The black Dreampines had been left in the north, days of travel behind them.

Ell felt. He reached out his consciousness further and it was as if his fingertips were lightly brushing something, as if they were lightly dipping their tips into the deepest, pool of water he had ever felt. It was all in his consciousness, just a feeling, an emotion. But it was real. He knew it. He was finally making progress!

Then it was gone. All at once, it was gone as if he had never felt it. Yet there was excitement knowing that something productive had finally happened after days of endless, fruitless practice and training.

"What is it?" Arendahl asked sharply, his tone implying he sensed something had happened.

"I finally felt something!" Ell gushed with all the enthusiasm of youth. He felt just a bit silly to be acting so excited, but he couldn't help it. The first major step toward accessing his abilities had been taken.

"Explain," Arendahl said, his eyes narrowing. Ell did. Ell relayed the feelings. The sense of a deep, endless pool, a never-ending source of water at his fingertips.

Ell finished explaining and asked in his excitement, "Is that what you feel? That endless pool of liquid at your disposal?"

The old elf paused a moment and Ell thought this might be one of the times he would decline to answer as he sometimes did. Finally, he responded. "No." His words were hard, but not negative. "What you speak of is not what I experience. But, as I said, your ability has already manifested itself in a slightly different manner than mine so I would not spend my thoughts on such questions. If you felt it, then something must have happened. After all, we've been at this for enough hours over the past week with nothing to show that I believe you would know when a new experience finally did occur."

Ell nodded his agreement slowly. True, he would know, but a part of him wished he could share the experience with the old elf, just as a confirmation to himself that it had been real. *It was real*, he told himself, *it had to be. Please let it have been real.* Once the experience had passed, it would be easy to explain it away as the desperation of the mind grasping at whatever success it could, even if that meant fooling itself.

Arendahl seemed to read Ell's thoughts on the matter and clapped him on the shoulder. "Easy lad, it was real. I don't doubt you." He spoke gruffly, the morning sun illuminating his face. Dark grey and midnight thunderheads had built up while they trained. Spring squalls would soon wash the land, purifying it with copious amounts of water. Water. It all came back to water.

"Enough now," the old elf commented, "It's time we were off. There will be time to train again on the way or perhaps even after we have reached your family."

"What do you mean perhaps?" Ell questioned in confusion. "Why wouldn't there be time to train once we reach my family?"

The old elf sighed. "There is much to be done, boy. Your uncle will no doubt want to begin raiding again, he was always an impetuous one, never patient." Arendahl shook his head at his memories of Dacunda. *Impatient?* Ell thought incredulously. His uncle Dacunda was the perfect model of patience, resolve, and determination. He never let circumstances dictate his actions. Well, leastwise, not when it was avoidable. It was at times like these Ell wondered how well Arendahl really knew Dacunda. Or perhaps, Ell thought, maybe his uncle had been quite different as a youth. Either way it was something on which to ponder.

The old elf had not finished speaking, and he continued as he closed up his travel pack and laced the ties tightly, throwing it over one shoulder when he was done. "Besides," Arendahl added to his former comment on Dacunda's supposed impatience, "I have… matters to which I must attend. I will not be able to stay with you long once we reach your family."

He spoke with a mysterious glint in his eye, and not for the first time Ell wondered how many secrets he kept stored away in his mind, locked deep in the vault of his consciousness. Ell had noticed during the week they had spent in each other's company, that the old elf liked to keep his information close, even on matters of importance such as the ability to water call. It had taken Ell days to pry any information out of him about the topic. Of course, Ell understood the reason now. Arendahl had not wished to taint his perception of the ability or cloud his process of learning it for himself. Learning without succumbing to the limitations and restrictions, which Arendahl's own mind had placed upon his water calling ability, would be vital. Nevertheless, Ell couldn't help but feel it would have been helpful to receive just a bit more knowledge prior to training.

"What sort of matters?" Ell couldn't keep the slight note of suspicion or perhaps curiosity from his voice. What was more important than the war? Arendahl would be a huge asset while raiding. After all, he was the only one of the Highest who could control the ability to water call, let alone even had the ability, other than Ell—and Ell had not learned enough yet to make it work for him. It was strange to think of a power such as water calling, an ability out of the old lore, out of legend, and to think of it with such a nonchalant, cavalier mentality. It just showed what a person could grow used to when the circumstances dictated.

Arendahl evaded the answer as usual. "None of your concern, boy. Matters for me to worry on, not you." But his face was grim, a picture of real worry, and even uncertainty. It was not the type of expression Ell was accustomed to seeing on the old elf's face. Arendahl was nothing if not confident and sure of himself. What would put uncertainty on his face? And was that fear Ell saw flicker in the depths of the old elf's eyes? Ell revised his opinion. Mayhap whatever Arendahl was off to do after reaching Ell's family had more legitimacy than Ell realized. Ell decided to drop it and trust the old elf knew what was best. It was strange to see how trusting Arendahl was becoming easier and easier, as well as more natural. Events often did turn on their heads.

They traveled hard as usual, racing lithely down mountain slopes. Their pace would have looked haphazard to the eyes of a human as the human would see two elves bounding from boulder to boulder, sometimes on the trail but often as not off of it, like a couple of the giant mountain cats known to inhabit this area. The Highest could attain a measure of grace and lightness of foot enabling them to do things that would look incredible to a human, and even to one of the Departed, as their southern cousins were sturdier, stronger, and less graceful. The Departed were built for ships and dark cities. They had adapted to a lifestyle riding the waves and swells of the Great Ocean rather than the forested paths and trails of the mountains.

Ell leaped from one boulder to another five feet away and before pausing, he leaped again to another down the hillside just a few feet farther. They ran at a breakneck pace, but it was no more dangerous to them than traveling at any other speed. It allowed them to cover distances quickly, especially going downhill where jumping and leaping from location to location could cover more ground than by simply running. Ell became excited thinking of all the possibilities that might be available to him once he learned to control his ability. He always thought in terms of when it happened rather than if it did. His determination was rock hard to become a true Water Caller. Once he did, he imagined that even this effortless speed and grace he could attain now would feel dismal compared to what would be possible then. After all, seeing Arendahl jump directly upwards twenty feet without any effort had opened his mind to what might be possible. For all he knew, that leap had been easy for the old elf, and much greater things might be normal and simple to attain for a Water Caller in complete control of his abilities. It was thrilling to think of such possibilities.

They covered lots of ground and by midday, they could see the ancient peaks above their ancestral fortress of Verdantihya on the horizon. They might be able to reach it by nightfall and surely, they would find his family there. Dacunda would not have gone further without reuniting with Ell and Arendahl. Refill, replenish their supply of Source Water, and then form a plan for what to do next, where to continue raiding. Ell felt his excitement grow at the thought of seeing his family. It had been only a week in separation from them, but it was the longest he had ever been away from them in his lifetime. He realized the depth of feeling he had for them, ran much deeper than simply comrades in arms. It was a difficult love to even describe. He had missed them greatly.

They stopped for a quick rest before pushing on. The spot Arendahl chose to stop and regain the wind for their lungs was in the heart of the forest. Much of their travel over the last week had been on high mountain ridge trails and passes as they traversed their way out of rugged northern Andalaya. Now they were back in the heart of Legendwood. Ell smelled the pine, and the oak, and the black yew trees, all a mix of beautiful scents. His keen sense of smell separated them each, one from the other, and he enjoyed their unique fragrances, and then allowed them to blend back together in his nose as a medley of smells, until they became one smell. The scent of Legendwood. He loved it.

"Snap out of it, boy," Arendahl spoke harshly. He was not trying to be unkind; it was just his typical, hard way of speaking to everyone about everything. "How many times must I tell you to keep your eyes open?"

"We aren't training right now," Ell muttered a bit sullenly and then instantly regretted the tone in his voice as it sounded like nothing so much as a scolded child whining to a parent. It never paid to give Arendahl the upper hand in a disagreement. One had to respond to the old elf with force if one intended to retort at all.

Arendahl snorted, "Boy, we are always training. You are greener than you are willing to admit. A few humans slain, and a dead Departed or two and you think you have seen the world and conquered it." He shook his old head, the lanky, silver grey hair shaking with it. "You have much to learn still. And one of those things is learning to remain vigilant constantly."

Ell opted for silence and reached into his pack for some dried meat. He understood what the old elf meant. It was important to keep your senses sharp and your body ready for action. But constant vigilance, unceasing watchfulness, wore a person down. Sometimes you had to stop and feel the land for more reasons than just an attempt to use your water calling ability. Miri had taught him that you needed to grab hold of moments of joy, instances of beauty, because in a lifetime of war, chaos and struggle, those moments sustained you, they carried you through and allowed you to continue fighting. Arendahl was right, keeping your guard was important. But Miri was right also, grabbing hold of beauty and pleasure and admiring them were just as important. He kept it all to himself, though, and the old elf took his silence for acquiescence.

They swallowed their meager mouthfuls in comfortable silence. It was one thing they had in common. Neither of them felt the need to fill a quiet moment with unnecessary words. Ell was not like his cousin Ryder that way. Arendahl also valued stillness. They spoke when it was necessary.

Finally, eating was done and Arendahl called for another training session. "Ready?" Ell knew what he meant by that one word. It was time to practice, or at least attempt to practice, his ability.

Ell nodded. He was ready, determined. But it would be good to see some results. They stood face to face again. Ell stretching out his consciousness, in yet another futile attempt to reach the water lying all around him in creation. He pushed his mind out and tried to somehow pull the moisture from the land into him. No success. His eyes closed involuntarily as he strained his mind.

Out of nowhere, a hard, gnarled fist crashed into his face sending him sprawling to the ground a few yards away. Arendahl had a smirk on his face as he watched Ell pick himself up off the turf.

"What was that for?" Ell snarled angrily.

"Teaching you a lesson, boy. Keep your eyes open. Next time I won't be so gentle."

Ell shook his head in annoyance. Arendahl was insufferable at times. He felt his cheek as it began to swell just slightly. *Gentle? The old elf had almost broken his jaw. He had fists of stone!*

"Besides," Arendahl added, "I wanted to see if anger or pain would help activate your ability."

"And?" Ell asked sarcastically already knowing the answer.

The old elf grinned wolfishly and then laughed. "No luck. But it was fun to try." He winked mirthlessly at Ell.

Ell brushed some dirt from his hose and his long sleeved, mottled tunic. He shook his head in annoyance and then caught the twinkle in the old elf's eye. Ell was frustrated and annoyed, there was no doubt, but he had to admit something about the moment was funny. He let himself smile, and then they laughed together. If you couldn't laugh at the pain of a lesson well taught, then you had better not become Arendahl's pupil. He taught in a very strict, forceful style. Results mattered, not comfort. They shared a laugh and Ell forgave the old elf.

Training over for the moment, they set their course for Verdantihya. They would find his family soon, Ell knew. The rest of the day passed with nothing happening of any significance. Verdantihya had been their appointed rendezvous assuming Arendahl and Ell were not able to find Dacunda and the rest before then. Since it looked increasingly like this would be the case, they increased their speed even more. Arendahl and Ell pushed harder and faster, not spending as much time reading the signs of the forest for passage. The need to track and look for clues of his family's passing was not so necessary.

By nightfall, they had reached Verdantihya. Inside those ruined walls, beautiful, aged, overgrown by the wild yet retaining their sense of stark power and strength, he would see his family. It would be a happy reunion.

Arendahl pressed his fingers to his lips and spread his hands outwards in the traditional greeting of the Highest as they returned to their ancestral roots after time spent away. Ell did the same. Ceremony completed, they ran lightly, swiftly towards the side gate in the western wall from which Ell and his family had exited over a month ago now while being pursued by the company of Departed led by Silverfist. They reached the wall and entered the city through the doorway, a mixture of moss, lichen, and ancient stone. The stone of the city walls were huge blocks of rock, cut and fashioned to perfection in the age they had been made, and then fit together so precisely even the tip of a blade would not penetrate far into the cracks and seams. The wilderness had claimed the city, or reclaimed it, as it had always been partially wild to begin with. Verdantihya was a strange mix of natural beauty and astounding elven stonework and architecture. The feel of the great city was impressive. Ell knew that a place could not think or feel. Yet he couldn't shake the feeling that the birthplace of his people was almost sentient. Nearly.

He and Arendahl glided through the cobble stoned alleys and side streets, keeping a low profile. Shadows and darkness of the night hid them, and it was well to be hidden. This place was home, it was their roots, but the slavers were aware of it, and one had to keep a watchful eye when visiting Verdantihya, since slave bands often passed through or set traps to wait for captives.

This night there was none of that, however. They made their way, through the looming spiral towers of the city, barely illuminated by starlight and moonlight as the spring storm clouds covered much of the sky. As if on cue to Ell's thoughts, the sky ruptured and the squall hit. Soaked to the skin in moments they continued upward toward the city's center on the hill. Further on, Ell could see the far side of the city abutting the mountain slope behind it—the mountain that formed the city's natural northern wall.

Upward and onward, they went towards the Source. Ell's family would have made camp somewhere near there, high up as they had done the last time they were here.

Walking was a challenge, even for their dexterous and nimble feet, since rivers of rainwater were sluicing down the slanted streets. The water rushed around their feet making the footing slick, especially since many of the streets were covered in moss. This lent a slippery feel, the way a river bottom felt when mossy rocks were underfoot.

Finally, they reached the top of the hill and were among the mansions and palaces overlooking the rest of Verdantihya from their hilltop splendor. Once bright and full of majesty, they were shrouded in darkness now, shadowy and wet, spires and towers jutting into the storm. They wandered carefully, cautiously, Arendahl leading the way, until they came across his family's camp. They were tucked into the interior of a cliff top palace. Ancient stone architecture overhung the cliff below. A balcony swung out over gaping air. The palace was small, yet it had three levels; One at street level into which they had entered. One secondary story above, and also a level below, built into the cliff side. Ell and Arendahl stepped quietly as they could down the stairs, thankful for the shelter from the storm.

They came upon his family's camp. It was late in the night so Dacunda was the only one awake, on his watch. He nodded to them so as not to wake the others. He then exchanged a long look with Arendahl, to which the old elf finally gave a single serious nod. Dacunda's eyes widened and he glanced at Ell as if seeing him for the first time. Then he smiled proudly.

They shrugged out of their wet things and changed into the only change of clothes they packed with them. Dacunda decided a whisper was fine. "How did you find us? We are pretty well hidden, tucked away in here without a fire."

Arendahl smiled secretively. "I have my ways."

Dacunda quirked an eyebrow at the comment.

"Oh fine," Arendahl said, "I used my ability. All this rain and water makes it easy to tap into it. We were ankle deep in a river, and I was able to sense where you were in a general way."

Ell perked up at the conversation. Dacunda did as well. Arendahl wasn't usually so forthcoming with information about water calling.

The old elf continued. "It's almost like a sense of feel… a vibration. Even though you were not in that river of rainwater, sounds you make, even small ones transmit into the air, and are then caught up partially into river rainwater flowing down the streets outside. I could feel that there was a presence of someone in this vicinity. I didn't know it was you, but I suspected." He paused, looking at their two faces filled with interest and intrigue. "That ability isn't always an option, there has to be a large amount of water around to make it worthwhile."

Ell could see the truth of that statement. The times when the circumstances would allow for the sensing of vibrations to be helpful were few, because one was not often ankle deep in a river in the middle of a city. However, it was information he filed away for later.

He embraced his uncle and then collapsed onto the ground next to his slumbering sister, Rihya. Dacunda and Arendahl spoke for a time quietly, but Ell was too tired to care what they were saying. He closed his eyes and sleep took him immediately. Blissful, dreamless sleep.

Chapter Seventeen

"Why?" The Departed questioned, narrowing his eyes belligerently. This far from Dark Harbor one had to keep a tight rein on the soldiers. The Departed tended to grow restless when too much time was spent in the north. It wasn't that they didn't enjoy taking part in slave raids. No, they were all here because they wanted to squeeze Andalaya and crush its people. The problem was that the fear began to leave them, just slightly, the farther they went from the south. In Dark Harbor and on the Pillars, the evidence of royal control was very clear. People, slaves, soldiers, everyone had their place and if you put a toe out of line, it could carry fatal consequences. Silverfist had seen elves killed for looking at a slave captain the wrong way or speaking in the wrong tone of voice. Here in the north, as they traveled and collected slaves, those restrictions began to wane. Gradually the Departed he led grew more unruly, restless, and ready to make their own decisions rather than obey orders. A slave captain had to keep a tight rein on his slavers.

"Because I said so, Grimaldi," Silverfist answered the question in a fake, pleasant voice. "I said no fires. We don't know who is around to watch, and we don't want to give any of the Highest a warning that we are near."

The Departed slaver sneered with his upper lip, revealing the top row of his teeth, which had been filed into points. It was gruesome, and it looked ridiculous, but Silverfist had to admit the fashion was not without its ability to intimidate through its sheer vicious appearance. Grimaldi was the biggest of his soldiers. He was also the most belligerent, the most likely to cause trouble. It was not uncommon for fights to break out within the troops and even between captains and their slavers. After all, it was the way of the Departed. The strong kept their place and the weak, well the weak died and were replaced by those with enough strength to maintain their grip on power. Fortunately, Silverfist was strong. He had held his power and increased it a hundred fold over the years.

"What if I don't want to put out this fire?" The big dark elf asked, fondling a knife at his hip.

"Well, then you and I will have a serious problem," Silverfist spoke pleasantly again. He found it was always best to maintain a façade of courtesy. That way when you were forced to kill, and you would always be forced to do so eventually, those watching could say you had attempted to avoid it if necessary. It also served as a sort of distraction, lulling the enemy into a false sense of security around you. When you spoke calmly and courteously, your opponents were not often prepared for a lighting quick strike. If you were screaming and yelling in a person's face, however, it was clear a fight was imminent and that person kept up their guard. Silverfist liked to gain as much advantage as possible when a fight was brewing, ergo he kept calm, spoke plainly and pleasantly, and then stuck a knife in their throat just as quickly as he could if he didn't get what he wanted.

The Departed bared all of his teeth in what was clearly a snarl of anger. This fight was imminent indeed. "What if we have a problem?" The dark elf asked, trying to be clever. He wasn't very clever at all.

Silverfist adjusted the sleeves of his tunic in an excuse to be able to check the daggers up his sleeves. He shook his head. *Stupid oaf of an elf. Does he really think to defy me?* "What if you quit trying to be crafty in your speech, gave up this charade of a conversation, drew that knife and just got this over with already?" Silverfist asked in an overly bored tone of voice, glancing idly at his fingernails as if his personal hygiene were more important than the conversation at hand. Silverfist always found that goading his opponent into reckless action was a good idea. Any way of unbalancing your enemy was desirable. Fear, rage, anxiety, pleasure. Any of those emotions could do the trick. With this ox of an elf, Silverfist settled on anger as his most likely ally in this venture.

Sure enough, the Departed growled in rage and then screamed a war cry as he charged the few feet of intervening space between them, the knife in his hand and a short axe ripped from his belt. He looked formidable, but Silverfist was not concerned. He hadn't survived so long in the south and gained power, authority, and privilege without being dangerous, as well.

The dark elf covered the ground quickly and swung a massive sideswipe with the hand axe. The blade whistled through the air where Silverfist's head had been. Silverfist ducked the swing and flicked his wrist. His own dagger appeared from its hiding place up his sleeve and into his right hand as if by magic. He was more than adept with his daggers. The dark elf tried to recover his momentum and stance after losing his balance slightly after such a ferocious attack, but he wasn't fast enough. Silverfist was quick. He snaked in rapidly and easy as could be, used his metal fist to block the dark elf's desperate defense with the knife, and then planted his own dagger in the Departed's throat. Rust colored blood, darker than that of the Highest, poured from the southern elf's neck. Silverfist wiggled his dagger around in his enemy's throat painfully, just to inflict a bit more agony before the elf died.

"I. Am. Silverfist." He punctuated each word with a sideways movement of the dagger in his enemy's throat, each slash opened the wound wider and by the last twist of the knife, the dark elf was dead. "Did you really think you could defeat me?" he asked as he dropped the dead elf to the ground at his feet. His good hand was covered in the dark blood of his elven, southern cousin. He would have to wash it. He preferred to be clean whenever possible.

Silverfist turned to the rest of his slavers who were watching. "Anyone else questioning my decision to put out that fire?" He smiled pleasantly again. Nobody answered. Instead, one of his minions walked over and kicked some loose dirt over top of the flame, suffocating it. The fire died just as quickly as the Departed who Silverfist had just slain. He nodded decisively. They knew who was in control. He was glad the fight had happened. It had given him a chance to remind the Departed around him why he was the one that led the slaver band. He was the captain, not them.

A scout appeared from out of the bushes to the side of the camp and absently kicked one of the slaves who the band had already captured as he walked towards Silverfist to report. The slave girl whimpered and tried to huddle closer to her fellow prisoners who were bound hand and foot, lying on the ground next to her. Their feet would be unbound when it was time to move again. It was a trip to the Pillars for these captives. They would have their will broken at the Pillars, the way posts for slavers, and then afterwards would be shipped out for their destination. It was onward to the camps and then the human lands beyond the Fracture or else deep into the south to Dark Harbor and the Enclaves beyond.

The Departed scout strode up to Silverfist and saluted in their manner by tapping his fist to his chest. "Another sighting. Small group not far to the north of us. Mostly youth. Ripe fruit fresh for the plucking," he leered as he delivered his report. He spoke in a sharp voice, without full sentences. Many of the Departed lacked communicative prowess. It was the result of being a warrior in a society with a war-heavy cultural emphasis. Learning and education of any kind was not encouraged in the south. As a result, more and more of their warriors were bestial in nature, lacking refinement or even proper speech. However, they still served their purpose, and that purpose was to fight, bleed, and do what their captain and king told them to do.

"Good," Silverfist answered. One more batch of slaves and they would turn back south and towards the Lower Forest and the Pillars beyond. Right now they were a day or so west of Verdantihya.

"Orders?" the scout asked.

"Attack and capture, obviously." Silverfist responded. "How far away are they?"

"Not far. Hour's run maybe." Not only was the scout's speech partially broken, not able to form full sentences and proper structure, but the upper row of teeth filed to points also managed to effect a slur of sorts in many of the Departed's speech. It was yet another reason Silverfist found the tradition of filing one's teeth displeasing. He preferred to look cultured and to be understood when he spoke. Intimidation and fear were good, but one could accomplish the aim with demeanor and actions better than a few sharp teeth.

Silverfist nodded at the scout then turned to his slavers. "Four stay to guard the captives, the other twenty with me. Let's round up this latest batch of cherries to be plucked for the Prince of Darkness! We wouldn't want him or the humans to grow short of warm bodies to perform their many tasks." He joked grotesquely and the rest of his soldiers chuckled. It was an evil sound, the sound of torturers and captors enjoying their work. Silverfist felt right at home among the sound. He was a slave captain. It was his job.

He smiled to himself as they set out north at a fast run. The sooner they caught these youths, the sooner they could take them south to the Pillars. The quicker they were taken to the Pillars, then the more rapidly Silverfist could return north with his band of slavers and raid the carcass of Andalaya again. He had told himself he would crush his former homeland. Half-Mask had given him permission to step up slave raids, to increase the pressure upon the domain of the Highest. He had done so over the last month, both with his own slave band and by delegating others to do so, as well. Ever since the boy and his companions had slaughtered his last slave party, he had planned and strategized on how to make them pay. Silverfist's hand fondled his dueling dagger won so long ago now. Adan's son would eventually come to him. He knew it to be true somehow. If he tightened his fist and squeezed Andalaya for all the proverbial juice that was in it, then eventually the boy would come and face him. He felt in his gut that it was true.

Silverfist opened his good hand and looked at the clump of berries he had subconsciously grabbed from the bushes beside him. They were flattened to a pulp in his palm; the red juice of the berries trickling down his hands like the blood of Andalaya would be, as he continued to crush this once fair, northern land.

Chapter Eighteen

The small, cliff side palace in which they had set up camp was a comfortable place for them to rest. Ell's family had been there less than a day before he and Arendahl had caught up with them. The lower level where they had made their camp was built into the cliff. It was created to perfection with wide-open rooms and columns holding up the ceilings. For a palace, it was small and cozy, but in comparison to normal housing throughout the city, it was still large. Time spent without inhabitants had worn it down, of course. Cobwebs filled the corners where walls met ceilings, and dust and debris had accumulated along with them. But it still carried remnants of its former glory. One could look around and imagine what it would have been like to reside in a place of such luxury. Come to think of it, Arendahl and Dacunda could probably *remember* what it had been like, since Verdantihya had been abandoned over nineteen years ago now. Nineteen years was a long time when a person had only been alive for eighteen, but for the elder elves in this company, Ell didn't doubt the memory of their time here was still vivid in their minds. He imagined it would be hard to forget a place such as this city in full splendor.

Ell strode through dilapidated doors onto the small balcony that wrapped around the outside of the bottom story of the palace. The building was modest in comparison to many of the palaces he could see to the other sides of this one. The other elven palaces were also built into or onto the cliff. They gazed out over the ruined city, their broken windows like sightless eyes overlooking a view they could no longer see. Ell sat down on the stone railing on the far side of the balcony. He leaned back against the wall behind him and looked down at the sickening drop to the city beside him. Good thing he wasn't afraid of heights.

He closed his eyes to rest. Ell had slept well enough last night, but they had arrived late and he was accustomed to rising early. Therefore, the solid few hours of sleep he had acquired were welcomed certainly, yet not quite enough to erase the exhaustion he had accumulated during the last week of running, training, fighting. Not to mention the time spent simply realizing that the reality of his life had been shifted forever.

A splatter of light rain sprayed his face. It was a guttering spray, not enough to really get Ell wet. It was the sky's reminder that it contained rain, even if it was only a small amount. After the torrential downpour of the night before, the heavens were mostly rained out. Only this light sprinkle remained, sufficient just to land on his cheeks and give him a chill when a gust of breeze touched his face. It was strangely comforting. Ell knew not how he would manage to learn to control his power, or if he ever would at all, but that didn't change the fact that he looked at things differently now. Water. It had always represented life, and growth, and springtime to Ell, yet now it had an even greater meaning. Water was the symbol of his newfound ability; it was the source of his power. It reminded him, that he was different, that he was special. However, despite the comfort it provided, it nevertheless also was an annoying tickle in the back of his mind that he had not yet mastered his craft. *I will learn to water call*, he promised himself. The determination to succeed firmed within him daily.

He opened his eyes and watched the city below. It spread out in a ragged mess of streets and alleys, trees and streams. It was nature mixed with architecture. Copses of trees with streams trickling through them abutted dome ceilinged cathedrals and houses. Meadows met courtyards, and statues were overgrown with moss and lichen. It had always been this way, even before the fall. The city was the pinnacle of elven society and architecture in the north, yet at its basest level it was still grown out of the mountainside behind it, birthed among the rocks and trees of the land.

Ell loved it. He let his mind wander. It was good to forget about the present for a time. He imagined the city at its peak, elves dancing lithely from markets to houses to storehouses to palaces. His imagination grew, and he could see the perfect balance of Legendwood within and outside of the walls, the great forest cultivated to improve Verdantihya, not overrun it. He could hear the laughter and see the smiles of the people living here. His parents had been some of those people. His uncle, as well. Maybe Arendahl had lived here also, although Ell didn't really know all that much about the old elf's history.

As if on cue, the two of them stepped out onto the balcony with him. Arendahl gazed stonily out over the scenery in front and below him, while Dacunda at least managed a look of fondness for his old home.

They walked silently over to him. Ell prepared himself for a serious conversation—the two older elves had a serious look about them. His moment of respite was over. It was time to return to the matters at hand.

"You cannot avoid your future," Arendahl rasped harshly, he had never been one for tact.

Ell pursed his lips in a sour grimace, "I'm not," he muttered, "I'm just clearing my head." He glanced up at the grey sky above them. It didn't have the thunderous, midnight colored clouds of yesterday, yet it threatened more rain than the tiny sprinkles that still sputtered about. Drops of water floated here and there on the wind.

"I've seen that look before," the old elf said, his eyes narrowing dangerously, "it's the look of a youth attempting to dodge his responsibilities. You should be practicing with me instead of lolling about this empty balcony."

Dacunda placed a restraining hand on his mentor's arm as if to tell him, enough. "I know it cannot be easy, the reality you face, Elliyar. But you must look at it as a gift, not a curse." Dacunda shook his head, a look of wonder on his face. "To think, the records we possess say that our people haven't witnessed a Water Caller among us for nearly half a millennia and now there are two in my lifetime. One, my own nephew." Ell's uncle spoke the last sentence with pride and Ell felt the warmth of that approval.

Ell spoke then. "It's not that I wish it were otherwise, or," he glanced at Arendahl and rolled his eyes, "that I wish to shirk my responsibility." The old elf, the recipient of Ell's eye rolling snorted in typical fashion. "It's just that everything feels so… different now. Like my old life is disappearing."

"Nothing is disappearing, Nephew, you are just building your life, adding to it, not removing anything." Dacunda placed a hand on his shoulder.

Ell wasn't so sure. "What about them?" he nodded back towards his sibling and cousins in the mansion. They were talking and laughing, and making jokes at each other's expense. Or rather, Rihya and Ryder were joking and laughing while Dahranian managed to muster up a quiet smile every so often as he observed their jesting and casual mockery of each other.

"What about them, boy?" Arendahl interjected his way into the conversation. He appeared no longer willing to restrain his leathery tongue. "Get to the point." Patience was not his strong point.

"Well," Ell wondered aloud to them self-consciously, "won't they look at me, sort of, different?" He concluded the question rather feebly. Not sure exactly what to say.

Arendahl snorted again and then spat off the edge of the balcony. "What, boy? Afraid they are going to treat you like someone special, someone *better* than them?" He grinned widely and then laughed. "No need to fear that. You still need to eat, sleep, and breathe like the rest of us, and you still need a bath after a week on the trail." He wrinkled his nose.

Ell pursed his lips in annoyance. The old elf was rather fragrant himself, who was he to complain? But the statement had served its purpose to lighten the mood. What was Ell so concerned about? His family loved him, they would treat him the same, wouldn't they?

Dacunda laid a hand on his shoulder again. "Don't worry, Elliyar, it will all be fine."

"Do they know yet? About me, I mean," Ell asked.

"No. I wanted to wait for confirmation from Arendahl before I spoke to them about it. I didn't want to even voice my conjectures about your ability until I had heard Arendahl's report of how the events of the past week transpired." He paused thoughtfully. "I did not think it would do to heighten your concern or raise your hopes of this mysterious power until we knew for certain whether or not you truly possessed it."

It made sense. Ell understood the thought process behind it. Arendahl nodded along silently as if he understood and approved, as well.

"How long had you speculated that I might be a Water Caller?" he directed his question towards his uncle.

Dacunda gazed at him solemnly. "I began to suspect very strongly after witnessing you fight during the ambush. The way the air misted, and the power with which your blade struck. It was… unnatural for an elf of your young age and ability." He paused as if wondering whether to continue and then spoke further. "However, there were other hints of what you possess inside of you, which in hindsight I should have been able to recognize." Ell wondered what those might have been but his uncle did not elaborate. If he had intended to share them, he would have done so already, so Ell did not press him for further information.

"No reason to beat yourself up," Arendahl said gruffly. "You turned him over to my keeping as soon as you found me, and it was the best thing you could do."

His keeping? Ell didn't retort this time to the old elf's bothersome way of referring to Ell, but there was no denying the fact that Arendahl had a way of annoying Ell to the ends of the earth and back. He gritted his teeth. It was not as if he was a little child. Arendahl smirked as he watched Ell's face, as if he knew exactly what Ell was thinking.

Ell decided to ignore the comment and pressed on. "What did you tell them?" he asked his uncle.

"I just said Arendahl wanted some company on a personal quest and you would rejoin us here at Verdantihya. They know nothing. But that will have to change." Dacunda looked at him earnestly. His uncle was almost always serious it seemed.

Ell nodded reluctantly. He was beginning to realize it would be all right, that his relationships would not change over night. However, it didn't alter the fact that a part of him still wished he could keep them in the dark for just a while longer. It was his fear talking though, and he was not accustomed to doing what fear dictated. Besides, they would see him training with Arendahl as long as the old elf continued to travel with them, and they would inevitably have questions. It would be best to answer them as much as possible beforehand.

As if reading his thoughts yet again, Arendahl spoke. He had a habit of doing so to Ell's extreme annoyance. "We will be needing to train over the next day or so, while I am still with you, and the others will surely be curious. It will do no good to hide it from them." His reiteration of Ell's prior thought brought to mind another question.

"How long will you be with us?" Ell asked the old elf.

"Only shortly. We must make the most of our time. I have matters to look into." The old elf spoke mysteriously. "Matters of importance. Once we have refilled our water skins from the Source we must be going. I shall not be able to tarry long here."

Ell remembered something he had wanted to ask his old teacher. "There is something I've been meaning to ask you, Arendahl." The old elf inclined his head to welcome the question. Ell continued. "Our power, the ability to water call, it stems from the Source, yes?"

Ell watched as Arendahl's eyes clouded with thought. It was a moment before he responded. "I suppose you could say so, yes. We, as a people, were birthed into the land, and the Source is the lifeblood of the land. We are tied to it. I suppose you could say that all of our power, both the normal abilities of the Highest and our extra abilities as Water Callers, stem from our bond with the land, and the Source is the symbol, the physical representation of that covenant from which our powers flow." Ell wasn't sure that was exactly the response he had expected from the old elf. It sounded complicated.

"So, I have been wondering," he began again, "if our power stems from the Source, from where would the powers of the dark creatures have stemmed? The Unsired, for example, how did they gain the powers to control the other evil creatures of the time before they were exterminated?"

The two elves before him grew very still. Dacunda's face became impassive. Arendahl's eyes were frozen agates. They were silent as they waited for Ell to finish.

Ell chose to do so, although he got the distinct sense that their walls were up and they were not likely to reveal much of the information Ell was seeking. He asked anyways, "Is it possible that there is another *source*, an opposite source from the one here at Verdantihya?" His voice dropped to a whisper. It was hard to even speak of something so strange. It felt almost sacrilegious to think about the idea of another Source. How could the land have more than one source of life? Unless the other wasn't a source of life, he speculated idly.

"It would be best if you dropped this line of thought," Arendahl spoke gently to him, but firmly nonetheless.

"Why?" Ell did not understand.

His uncle answered this time, after sharing a strange look with his mentor. The old elf let Dacunda speak. "You will paint yourself a fool in the eyes of most of our people by just mentioning this, and those who do not think you a fool will be unnecessarily frightened. Are either of those goals worth achieving?" The explanation wasn't much of an answer, but Ell could see it was all the answer he would receive.

Arendahl changed the subject briskly, speaking in his stilted voice. "Come. Time to train," he said, and he turned towards the middle of the balcony, clearly expecting Ell to follow. Ell groaned inwardly. He wanted to gain control of his powers, but he also wanted a moment to rest. It appeared it was one or the other in Arendahl's mind, however. Ell slipped off the stone rail and onto his feet.

They stood face to face as always, eyes open, hands hanging loosely at their sides. Ell had seen Arendahl reach down and place his palms on the ground when trying to call upon the water. The old elf had allowed Ell to do this once or twice, but in general, he treated it the same way as when Ell closed his eyes in attempt to practice. Arendahl wanted to do everything in his power to make sure that Ell didn't rely on any sort of mental or physical crutch when it came to water calling. Although it was frustrating at times to not be able to do what he wanted, Ell still had to agree. It would be better in the long run, if he could access his abilities any time, anywhere, and in any manner. You never knew what life or war would throw at you. Ell's goal was to learn how to access his power, that much had to come first, but he also desired for his water calling abilities to become second nature, an instinctual action developed by the constant use of his abilities. He wanted this, because from his experiences in battle, he had learned that instincts did more to save one's life than anything else.

Ell breathed in and out, attempting to slow his heartbeat and feel the world around him. Arendahl muttered the usual platitudes, instructing Ell to feel the land, to feel the water around him in his typical, gravelly voice. Ell pushed his awareness out from himself. Sometimes, it almost felt as if he could feel some of what the old elf desired him to sense, as if he was on the cusp of a breakthrough, but the breakthrough never came. Ell certainly never felt the sensation he had felt the other day as if he had dipped his fingers into a well of power. He was beginning to wonder if he hadn't imagined the experience. Arendahl had said the experience was unique to Ell, since the old elf himself had never encountered it in that manner. It was a statement, which didn't inspire confidence in Ell. He wanted something concrete, something substantial for him to grab hold of, not the continual assurances the old elf gave him that one-day, sooner than later, it would all become clear. Arendahl constantly said that Ell's powers would manifest regularly, and Ell would understand how to access them. He said it impatiently however, and the combination of his impatience and Ell's own frustration drove him nearly mad. He just wanted to be able to grab hold of something, anything, that would be a tangible clue as to how he could take control of his ability and actually begin to be a Water Caller. Right now, he felt like a child trying to learn to do something they had never heard of or even seen. He felt like he was groping around a dark cave trying to find his power in the dark, and the sensation was maddening.

They concluded their short training session, fruitlessly once again. Ell turned away from the old elf, feeling a measure of self-disgust. Why was it so hard for him to touch his power? If something was a part of you, and you had used it before, then how could it be so difficult to find. It felt like he was searching for a specific pine needle in the midst of an entire forest.

"Sooner or later, boy, it will happen. Sooner or later." Arendahl laid an uncharacteristically comforting hand on Ell's shoulder. Normally he griped about the time they were wasting, all the while telling Ell how it had taken him years to master his own ability. It made no sense. It was like he was contradicting himself. One moment he was expecting speed of learning from Ell, and the next he was relaying how it had taken him the opposite to do so when he was younger.

Dacunda had stayed to watch them train. He had a look of slight disappointment in his eyes. Not with Ell, but with the fact that it was proving tough for his nephew to reach the ability. Ell knew his uncle was likely chafing to get back to raiding and he would love to have the advantage of a trained and experienced Water Caller at his disposal. He knew Dacunda was beginning to realize—after his initial excitement at the revelation that Ell possessed the latent ability—that it was going to take much more time than he had anticipated to develop the skill.

Ell's uncle masked the frustration and smiled genuinely. "All you can do is practice, Elliyar. It will come."

Ell nodded. How else was he to respond? He turned toward the door back into the interior of the palace and stopped. His cousins and his sister stood watching him from the doorway, curiously.

Ryder broke the odd silence. "You two must really like each other, gazing into each other's eyes for so long." He smirked as he indicated his comment was directed at Ell and Arendahl. The old elf snorted derisively and muttered something about Ell's cousin being a youthful idiot. Ell supposed it indeed must have looked comical, or at the very least strange, to see them training face-to-face. Ell laughed and the awkwardness of the moment was broken. One could always count on Ryder to lighten the mood. And suddenly, Ell knew it would all be all right. No matter what happened with his powers, whether he gained control of them or not, his relationships with his family would not change.

They had questions of course. Ell answered the ones posed to him as best he could but the majority of the questions were directed at Arendahl or Dacunda, who knew more on the subject than Ell. Ell watched the eyes of his family members widen briefly as they found out he was a Water Caller, or rather, that he would become one. Ell couldn't quite bring himself to think of himself as an actual Water Caller until he learned, at the very least, to summon his ability on command. Dahranian appraised him silently, respectfully. Dahranian respected strength and power and the ability to extend your prowess in battle. Ell's abilities would do just that. Ryder joked and teased him, earning more reproving frowns and muttered comments from the stoic, stony-faced Arendahl. However, it was Rihya's response to it all, which surprised and touched Ell the most. She didn't jest or look at him differently the way the others did.

"I've always known you were special, little brother," she said firmly, confidently, as if the entire discussion had only confirmed what she had suspected for many years. "You have always been a bit… different, somehow *more* than most people." She smiled as she said it. It was a high compliment coming from her. Rihya's tongue was fiery and she did not hold back its lashings and scathings when she was angry, yet neither did she allow it to speak words of flattery. If she stated an opinion, she meant it. Ell nodded his thanks with a somewhat shyer smile than normal as he accepted her high compliment. It meant a great deal to him, coming from her, his sister, and the closest blood he had to him left on earth.

They wrapped up the conversation and then talk turned to what lay ahead. They were to go back to raiding. Dacunda was convinced it had been a long enough rest for them all. Ell had to agree. It was necessary to begin pricking the enemy again. There were undoubtedly other bands of the Highest doing the same thing all throughout the Lower Forest and along the plains near the human camps, yet it was important to lend their strength again, as well. Pinpricks they might be, but enough pinpricks together could injure a person. Yet, a part of him and it was a part, which was growing larger and larger by the day, wanted to return to Indiria's Emerald, to Little Vale, the valley along the Westrill. Ell missed Miri fiercely and longed for her company. He longed to see her face and feel her hand in his. He desired to kiss her and brush her hair back from the sides of her face, exposing her slim, dainty ears, the tips delicately pointed. However, he knew now was not the time. He had an obligation to his people, to his family, and he would not abandon it. Miri understood. She had to.

"Back toward the Camps?" Dahranian inquired of his father.

Dacunda nodded soberly. "Arendahl will travel south with us for a day or two at most and then will continue on his way further down into the Lower Forest as we turn east towards the Camps. I want to hit the humans hard again." His voice was harsh as he spoke of the raids, a stone grinding another stone to dust.

"Where is Arendahl going?" Ryder asked, ever curious.

Arendahl made a sour face. "None of your business boy. I have matters of my own to which I must attend." Ell laughed inside. He was glad he wasn't the only person on the receiving end of Arendahl's leathery tongue, nor that he was the only one being referred to as 'boy.' Ryder shrugged his shoulders. He let the retort slide off his back. Ryder had always been good at ignoring all sorts of provocations towards him by other people. He had thick skin.

"We'll spend the remainder of the day resting and then leave early on the morrow," Dacunda said. They all were fine with the decision. They were used to spending only a night, maybe a few at most, in any one location.

Ell, his sister, and cousins spent the rest of the day catching up. Ell told them of their adventures in the north, though for some reason he left out the bit about the Stone Ogre. It felt personal somehow. Although they knew of his ability to water call now, for some reason he didn't feel like talking about it in depth and that encounter would inevitably raise comments or questions. After all, none of them had ever seen one of the fearsome ogres of old, let alone fought one and survived. Ell wondered idly how many types of ogres there were. It was a question to ask Arendahl before they parted company.

However, Ell did speak of the fight with the Ghouls in the Barren Maze and the travel south again to catch up with them at Verdantihya. His family recounted their version of the week apart and it appeared their journey had passed in relative peace. Mundane events such as hunting, running, setting up and breaking down camp had occupied all of their time.

It was good to see them again. Ell enjoyed Ryder's joking, Rihya's sharp retorts to his jests, and Dahranian's quiet, stable presence. Ell wasn't the jokester of the family and he didn't laugh all the time, tending toward the serious side of life, yet today it felt good to let loose. He quipped with the younger of his cousins and then swapped stories with his sister. They sparred also, keeping their blades and reflexes sharp to prepare for the next fight, the inevitable return to battle that they all knew would come. It was a fitting last day of rest before reality set back in. War was the reality. This day of peace was nothing but a fleeting glimpse of the future for which they were all hoping, the future for which they were fighting. The Andalayan sky remained grey all day and into the evening, but the rain did little more than spatter weakly, occasionally. It was not the harsh downpour of the previous night. Ell enjoyed the day and allowed himself to be rejuvenated. There was a storm brewing, he could feel it, and it wasn't necessarily a physical storm. Something in the air, the atmosphere, told him that before long everything would be stood on its head. He was determined to be prepared for when the storm finally came. He steeled his resolve and sharpened his blades. He would train his body, his mind, and his ability. He would be ready.

Chapter Nineteen

The North Crag was visible to the eye after going not quite a day's journey south of Verdantihya. It was a rocky spire sticking straight up into the air. As tall as a small mountain but with none of the bulk and width of one, it was a striking feature of the landscape, a landmark which all would use as a guide while setting their course. The North Crag had a twin, natural tower, leagues and leagues to the southwest. The South Crag was far from here, but Ell had seen it once in the Lower Forest. The southern spire was even more impressive since it was not surrounded by hills and mountains, but instead rose unparalleled out of the ancient forest of oak, elm, and the many other assorted species of trees in the lowland woods.

They ran lightly past the North Crag on the trail south. It was probably almost a half-day's trek to the North Crag from the path on which they now traveled, maybe less if one pushed very hard to cover the intervening distance. The stone pinnacle rose up, rugged, narrow and crooked, like a gnarled, old finger of the earth poking the sky in its eye.

Dacunda saw Ell gazing at the slender peak as they ran. "Icari made its nest there recently," Ell's uncle spoke between deep, measured breaths as he ran. "We crossed paths with another band of the Highest on our way to Verdantihya to meet you. They were making their way north after raiding the Camps. They lost one of their company to the winged demon, not knowing it had laid claim to that territory." He grimaced as he relayed the information.

"It's just wrong," Ell said quietly, sadly. All the effort, the blood, the lives lost so long ago during the First Days to quell the tide of evil rampaging across the land had been for nothing. It was returning. He was just thankful that unlike the rest of the dark creatures of that era, the Unsired had been wiped out, never to return. It was a small consolation, but a consolation nonetheless. Ell shivered at the thought of those dark, mythical, evil beings. It hurt him to see how his land, his Andalaya, was returning to unruliness. Yet he preferred Ghouls, Ogres, and Icari to the Unsired, the warlords of old who had been able to bind the darkness to themselves and bend it to their will. Any number of creatures needing to be disposed of over and over again was better than that predicament.

His uncle nodded grimly. He was aware of the dire circumstances, which Andalaya and the Highest currently faced. He was, after all, the person who had finally driven the reality home in Ell's own mind.

The sky was still a damp, grey cloak, mist and fog swirling about one another on the eddies and currents of the air. Spring sunshine would not peek its head through the barrier of grey anytime soon. Dacunda spoke again.

"The Icari are the foulest of creatures I have ever seen." Dacunda was almost talking to himself. He added in a quieter voice, almost under his breath, "And quite possibly the most dangerous."

"Do you really reckon them to be the most dangerous thing you have faced?" Ell questioned his uncle as they ran at the head of the company. "After all of your battles and duels over the years?"

"Yes," Ell's uncle responded soberly. "Obviously the mayhem and chaos of a full-scale battle is unparalleled and hard to compare to a single enemy. Yet of all the beings I have seen, an Icari is by far the most fearsome, lone combatant I can imagine. Simply the advantage of flight gives them the edge, not to mention the speed, power, and size of them. They are at least three times the size of an elf."

Ell reflected on his encounter with the Icari. He was inclined to agree with his uncle. It had indeed been a ferocious beast. He was willing to admit that he had only escaped with his life by the narrowest of margins and no small amount of fortune.

"Have you ever fought one, Uncle?" Ell asked curiously. Meeting Arendahl and realizing his uncle had led a different life previous to the constant raiding and running after the fall of Verdantihya had made Ell particularly inquisitive about his uncle's past.

Dacunda appraised his nephew before answering. "No," was all he said.

It was a brief response, and Ell had learned to differentiate between his uncle's tones of voice. Sometimes a one-word answer was just that, a simple answer. Other times it concealed more information, information for which Ell was often forced to dig.

"What aren't you telling me, Uncle?"

Dacunda narrowed his eyes with a look of annoyance. "When did you become so good at reading people?" he questioned in a half-joking, half serious voice.

Ell responded, running a hand through his wavy, shoulder length, blond hair, "After spending a week having to dig deep and claw hard for every scrap of information I could get from Arendahl," he said in mock disgust.

Now Ell's uncle did bark a short laugh and then agreed. "He is tightlipped, that one."

Ell waited silently, looking at his uncle. Dacunda ran quietly for a moment before finally speaking. "Alright, Nephew, much has changed in you, and perhaps a bit more information about the world around you won't hurt, or go to your head," he added afterwards as almost an afterthought.

Ell kept his stride next to his uncle's as he waited for the information to come. The chattering of Ryder and Rihya behind him filled his ears, as well as the odd conversation between Dahranian and Arendahl. The old elf spoke in his stilted, rough, even course, manner, while Dahranian conversed with measured, slow, and courteous responses. They were opposites of one another.

Dacunda finally answered him, "Icari began appearing again a few years before the human invasion. Nobody knew why, or how. It had been thought they were extinct, having disappeared for centuries." He growled in disgust. Dacunda hated the dark creatures and what they represented. They were a symbol of their people's, the Highest, fading power, their waning control over the land that had once been under their dominion.

Ell's uncle continued, "At first it was just the odd sighting, from so far away and with them flying so high in the sky, or at night time when it is hard to perceive things clearly, that we were not even sure it was the return of the Icari we were witnessing. Yet over time, it became clear." He paused to organize his thoughts. "Our people began seeing scenes of their crimes. The aftermath of their attacks was gruesome. Blood spattered ground, with only the bits of a body, perhaps an arm or a leg left behind. The rest had been carried back to their terrible aeries, a feast for later. It was not long before they grew bold. They even began attacking in daylight at times, or in the sight of a group of elves rather than just hunting solitary prey. Oh, they were still cautious, even as they are now, yet it was a foretelling of things to come."

Ell was just a bit confused. "They still remain fairly careful predators, don't they, Uncle? I mean, after all, the one that attacked me was hunting at night and there were only two of us."

His uncle nodded soberly, and ran on in emphatic silence for a time before returning to the conversation. "Yes. But there is a distinct difference between the occasional sighting like we had years ago, where there was an uncertainty in what we were seeing, and now where they attack openly and drag their prey away to their lofty deaths."

The land was green around them as they traveled. Dew dropped from the leaves of trees, wet from the left over water from the spring squalls of the past few days. Their soft, leather boots grew damp around the soles. Eventually the wet section crept slowly upwards, climbing gradually up the leather from the moist earth and low-lying plants against which their boots brushed.

"What was the point of all this, Uncle? I am still uncertain as to what piece of information you were trying to convey to me specifically."

Dacunda answered stoically as he ran lightly, effortlessly. "You asked me if I had ever fought an Icari." He reminded Ell of the start of this conversation. "The answer is no. A resounding no. I have never known anyone to have crossed blades with an Icari and lived to tell the tale. Perhaps, there might be some who have survived in a large group, fending off the winged beast. But never alone. Nobody I have heard of has ever stood their ground to an Icari and survived." Dacunda glanced at Ell out of the corner of his eyes, appraising his nephew's reaction. "Until you, that is. You are the first person of which I have ever heard to stand against an Icari alone and escape with their life."

Ell pondered the statement. His fortune at escaping the Icari so many weeks ago on the way back from the Cliffs of Anover with Miri had been apparent to him even then, and now it was even more so.

"Just because you have never heard of another surviving an Icari attack alone, does not mean it has never happened, Uncle."

Dacunda smiled at Ell's humility. "True. But word travels fast among our people. I believe I would have been made aware of such a story. I suspect Arendahl would have to regale us of a tale from the First Days to find a legitimate account of when an elf of the Highest last accomplished such a feat."

Now Ell was feeling a bit self-conscious. It had been luck more than anything else that saved his life that night. Grit, yes, but more than anything, fortune had shined upon him.

"I did have my bow and was able to loose a shaft into the Icari before the beast mauled me," he debated back, not willing to concede the fact that he might be special, different, in yet another way. "It is not as if I stood alone with my belt knife and dagger against the creature."

Dacunda nodded agreeably. Conceding the point. But there remained a smirk on his face betraying the fact he did not truly believe what Ell was saying. Ell dropped it. If his uncle wanted to think him special, then so be it. *You are special*, the voice inside his head said, *why try to deny it?* It was true. Not everyone had the ability to water call. Arendahl only knew of himself and Ell, who had the potential. What was a little thing like surviving an Icari attack compared to being a Water Caller?

They paused for a rest and a meal. A handful of dried berries, a few nuts, flatbread, and some dried meat was their fare. They could hunt for food along the way, but the farther they went towards enemy territory, the less they would want to have a fire. So meat hunted for and dried weeks previous, was often midday meal or dinner along with the firm, portable flatbreads made from the natural grains of the land. The number of cold, dismal nights Ell and his family had spent huddled together in whatever shelter they could find or construct, without the warmth of a fire, were many. Safety and caution came first on raids. Deep in the heart of Andalaya, it was different, but south of Verdantihya in Legendwood and then the Lower Forest, it was best to avoid notice.

"Ready, boy?" Arendahl wolfed down a fistful of meat, his strong, old teeth making quick work of the tough venison.

Ell nodded his acquiescence. They stood across from each other. The breeze coasting down lightly through the branches of the trees overhead teased their unbound hair playfully. Ell's own shock of wavy, blond hair billowed with a particularly stronger gust. This portion of Legendwood was not so dense. The grey-blue sky could be seen above between the limbs of the canopy. Ell and his family were deep in a valley, the mountains rising around them, and the woods creating a shady haven for elves and animals alike. A wild hare darted through the bushes and into the undergrowth from one side of the trail to another. A songbird sang somewhere not far distant.

"Focus, Elliyar," Arendahl spoke firmly. "I will be parting ways with you as soon as we start moving again, therefore this will be our last training session together. Well, at least for now. Who knows, our paths may cross again before long."

The last session. The news rocked Ell slightly. He wasn't ready for the old elf to go. How was he supposed to practice? What could be so important, preventing Arendahl from staying a few more days to teach him? Wasn't instructing another Water Caller important enough to be worth his time?

"Why are you leaving so soon? Why not stay, keep instructing me, and then raid with us for a time?"

The old elf answered Ell, "I have told you all already, I have matters to which I must attend." Arendahl jerked his head in a nod at Dacunda. "Your uncle isn't concerned about me leaving. He trusts my judgment. Why don't you? Perhaps your lack of trust in me is the reason I have had so little success in teaching you." The last bit was spoken lightly, acerbically, and yet Ell knew he did not intend it too harshly. It was just his way. Arendahl was a demanding instructor and he spoke plainly. It was true. They'd had little joy in seeing Ell's ability develop. So far, it had been slow going.

"I suppose that will have to be enough," Ell responded. "Although, I would like to know what these important matters of yours are." He tilted his head hopefully. No information was forthcoming. Arendahl could clam up with the best of them when he did not wish to speak. And just now, he definitely did not desire to give Ell any more information.

"Enough, boy, let us begin." He spoke the familiar litany smoothly, calmly. "Feel the land. Feel its air, woods, rivers, and streams. Focus on the water. Feel its power. Stretch out your consciousness and tap into that power."

Ell stretched and stretched his mind. He felt nothing. Ell was acutely aware of the extra sets of eyes watching him train. It made him feel awkward, with his family watching him like this. He tried to push through. Ell attempted to somehow connect his consciousness with the land, with the water that he knew to be in everything and all around him. No luck. It was yet another useless session.

"This is a waste," Ell rubbed his hands through his hair from his forehead to the back of his mane in disgust. "I cannot seem to do it." He felt weary from his training. Almost like he did in the aftermath of accidentally accessing his abilities all those times earlier. It felt like he could only feel the fatigue of his powers and nothing else.

"Do not be so quick to call something a waste, boy. We are getting closer, I can feel it." Ell tried to believe that was true. It was hard to do so at times. "Unfortunately, I must depart now," Arendahl spread his hands, his regretful manner belying his previous statement about his leaving being of the utmost importance. "I expect you will continue to train, even by yourself, when we are apart. Eventually you will have a breakthrough."

El nodded. He would keep trying, even by himself; however, he did not have high hopes for any change in the near future. But what was he to do other than agree when someone as forceful as Arendahl expected it of him?

As they walked back towards the rest of their company, Arendahl continued to speak. "You will feel discouraged in the coming days. You will feel alone." The old elf spoke with a certainty that chilled Ell. "It is something unavoidable. There are areas of your life in which you will not be able to find comfort, understanding, or solace from the others. Simply the truth of what you can do sets you apart as different." Arendahl gazed deeply into Ell's eyes as if willing what he said to penetrate into his young pupil's heart.

The old elf went on, as they neared Ell's family, who had been watching the training session curiously. "You must find a way to hold on to the determination you feel now as we train. Fix your mind on the goals you have set for yourself. They will help to sustain you. Why do you want to learn how to master your ability to water call?"

Ell was startled for a moment as he realized the question was not rhetorical. He paused to think a moment before answering. "It drives me near to distraction that there is a part of me, a part of who I am, which I do not understand and cannot access at will. I want to be able to control this power, to help our people fight, of course, but also just for me. I want to take control of who I am completely and without limitations."

Arendahl nodded his agreement. For once, the old elf seemed quite pleased with Ell's response to one of his questions. "Good, that is very good. Personalizing your desire to win this battle within yourself will help. Having a cause for which to fight, like our current war against our enemies, is vital to helping one achieve their goals. However, making a personal reason, as well, sometimes brings matters closer to the heart. It is good that you have a reason to want this more than just to be able to add to your skills and prowess as a warrior." Arendahl's face was serious as he gave his advice.

Ell pondered what he had said. It was good to feel the old elf's affirmation, even if it was only about the emotions driving him, rather than any tangible success.

Arendhal wasn't finished. "But most of all, boy, you have to hold on to your hope." He punctuated the sentence with a gnarled, old finger poking Ell's chest as they turned to face one another. "Keep your hope high and all things are possible. There will be times when you doubt yourself, but you must try and hold on to your belief and your faith that you can actually accomplish the task to which you set your mind."

"I will try, Arendahl."

"Good. You will learn to call upon the water. You will master your ability and in doing so master yourself." The old elf spoke the words like a declaration. Ell felt the power of them as he listened, and in hearing them, a part of him truly did begin to believe. He had worried before about what would happen when Arendahl left. But now the seed had been planted. Ell did believe. He knew he would someday access his ability at will, instead of at just an accidental, instinctual level. One day.

They walked back to the camp and were among the rest of his family now. Dacunda's eyes found Arendahl's. Ell watched the old elf shake his head slightly to the unspoken question on the face of Ell's uncle. *No, Ell had not tapped into his ability yet.* However, what would have once sent him into a spiral of self-consciousness, and a defeatist attitude, now simply fueled his determination. He smiled at the thought of the pleasure he would derive from proudly telling his uncle he had accomplished the goal to which he had set his mind and will. Even his uncle's slightly crestfallen face could not dampen Ell's resolve and self-belief. He silently thanked Arendahl for instilling confidence in him in this last lesson.

They had already eaten their last meal before the training began so there was no more time to bandy words about. Arendahl clasped forearms with each of the company, an especially long grasp when he came to Ell, as his eyes bored holes into Ell's skull.

The old elf exchanged a few quiet words with Dacunda before he left. "Keep your course, Dac. You are doing well." Ell watched his uncle's face buoy with pride. Even at his uncle's age, the compliments of his former mentor were still important to him. "Fight the fight, and make our enemies pay for Andalaya. Nobody takes our land for free." Arendahl whispered the last sentence in a harsh, gravelly voice.

Dacunda nodded firmly, resolutely. "I will," he promised.

"You know why I must go," Arendahl said mysteriously, and Ell's uncle shifted his feet uncomfortably, then nodded his understanding. "I do not leave you lightly," he paused and then glanced at Ell, "there is much work to be done here. Yet, you know the importance of my search for answers. We must know if it is true."

Dacunda sighed in resignation. "I know. Stay safe my old friend, and may your journey prove your suspicions false." He said the last like a prayer, and Arendahl nodded his approval. Ell was confused. *What suspicions did the old elf have, and why would he want to be proven wrong?* It made no sense.

Without another word though, and leaving Ell with questions aplenty, the old elf ducked in the forest heading away to the south and west into the heart of the Lower Forest. He moved silently and swiftly, hardly a leaf or a branch was left disturbed in his wake as evidence of his passing. Ell was surprised to feel a pang of regret as he realized the old elf was gone. It was more than just the need for Arendahl to teach him how to be a true Water Caller. After over a week of traveling together, and risking their lives for one another in the Barren Maze, a connection had been formed. The old elf was ancient and often rude and cantankerous. He had a leathery tongue and a rough manner of speaking. However, beneath it all, Ell could see loyalty, honesty, wisdom, and most of all, a fearless nature to take challenges head on and fight the enemy until his last breath. Those were characteristics Ell aspired to possess, as well.

"Well, time to move." Dacunda said matter-of-factly. Even the departure of his mentor could do nothing to shake him.

They gathered up their things, packs going over shoulders, weapons into holsters, and then ran on for a few hours heading due south. Arendahl had angled his path through the bush in a more westward direction. Ell and his family would go south and then likely turn east again, eventually to begin striking the human army's settlements along the eastern coast.

The afternoon passed uneventfully. A few bucks scattering off the trail were the most excitement they saw. However, as the afternoon drew to a close and the twilight began to set in, they came upon an abandoned camp. They all stopped to inspect it carefully. It was a few days or so old. The ashes of the fire were still visible. It had been a fairly large fire, which meant one thing.

"Only slavers would be arrogant enough to have a fire that big," Ryder sneered. He was the jokester in the family, the whimsical one, but his hatred of their enemies ran just as deep as the rest of them.

Dacunda nodded at his youngest son. No words were necessary. It was a sad statement that they could accept the truth of it so easily. The bands of slavers that pillaged and raped their fair Andalaya were all too frequent.

"Not more than a few days gone by the look of it," Dahranian said solemnly, touching his finger to the cold ashes of the fire pit.

"They look to have had a few captives with them," Rihya said in disgust, pointing out the churned earth on one side of the camp showing signs of a struggle at one point.

Dacunda responded grimly, "I am not surprised to see it. The slavers have become particularly efficient lately." He shook his head in frustration. "They come in larger numbers and with more frequency. The reports I have heard in the last month from our chance encounters with others of the Highest, indicate those numbers are only increasing."

They decided to set up for the night there. As much as none of them liked the idea of spending longer than necessary in an area that had been previously occupied by their bitter enemies, they could not escape the fact that it was a perfect location for a camp. A small hill rose from the earth and half buried in the hillside were two large boulders. The stones leaned against one another in the earthen hill and formed a shallow cavern, ideal for a camp. It was defensible should the need arise and would give shelter from a passing squall.

They set up their camp and pulled out their food for a dinner. It was early to stop, but they would not likely find another site so good as this before evening came. On the road, one developed a tendency to go out of one's way to make use of a decent campsite. It was almost as if they didn't want to waste it.

It was only as Ell was chewing his food, idly glancing around when he noticed something. It was a small item, partially covered by dirt near the area where it appeared a struggle had taken place. A bracelet? Something tugged at Ell's memory. He rose and felt his heart sink as he approached the object. It was a bracelet. He pulled it up from the dirt, the others watching him do so curiously. It was a small, thin object, woven from a few strands of thread, green and brown, with a few blues and purples wound in. Also woven in were a few tiny greenish stones, with holes bored through them making them into beads. Stones from the riverbeds of the western region of Andalaya.

"What is it, Nephew?" Dacunda asked him. Ell struggled to find the words for his emotions.

"It is a bracelet I gave to Miri, not long before we left Little Vale." His voice sounded dull, numb in his ears. *How was this possible? Had the village been raided?* But that couldn't be, the odds of that happening and then the party having time to reach this far south in the intervening time didn't make sense.

No, she must have been taken while outside the valley.

"Are you certain?" Dahranian asked quietly, intensely. Rihya came over to him and put her arm around his shoulders as he nodded his affirmative response to his cousin's question.

"It was the only gift I have ever given her. I could not mistakc it," Ell declared, his emotions still in a state of shock. *Miri. Taken. Slavers had the girl he loved.* Shock clouded his thinking for a time more and his mind blanked out. The questions they asked him fell on deaf ears as he thought, horror fogging his thought processes.

Then abruptly, all the feelings he had been suppressing since he found the bracelet burst forth. Rage controlled his senses. Then fear. Then anger once again. Pain at what might be lost. His eyes misted over and the air around him grew damp. Vaguely he realized something was happening, as the ground at his feet grew muddy and moist. A weapon was in his hand and then someone tackled him to the ground. He threw them off with unnatural strength drawn from the land around him, the power of the water coursing through the veins of Andalaya.

He leaped to his feet, still enraged, yet before he could do anything else, a fist crashed into his face. As he tried to shake his head to clear his thoughts and stay on his feet, another fist hit him, then one more, and the world went dark.

Chapter Twenty

It was night when Ell gained consciousness. The aching in his jaw was fierce and it matched the fatigue throughout the rest of his body. It was a familiar tiredness now and a two-edged sword. On the one hand, it comforted him, it was yet another reminder that he, in fact, could access his abilities as a Water Caller, and that there was still hope to learn to control it. On the other hand, the fatigue he felt after using his powers brought to mind, yet again, that this was another incidence in which he had tapped into his abilities by instinct and out of the depth of his emotions rather than out of a rational, reasonably thinking mind. Comfort and frustration all balled up into an odd set of emotions.

Curiously, he reached his consciousness out to see if it might be possible to tap his abilities yet again. He held out hope that after one of these incidents, something would just click in his mind and he would be able to access them at will. No such luck. He sighed. He would just have to keep practicing.

It was another few moments before Ell actually realized the strangeness of his situation. He lay slumped against a small rock, having only just regained consciousness. Ell glanced down and saw his hands bound together at the wrist in his lap. *Why was he bound? Why would his family do this to him?* Reality came crashing in again and he let out a groan. It was a groan of agony, as he remembered the truth of Miri being taken, but as the sound came from his throat it morphed into a moan of pain, as well. His face hurt, his wrists hurt. *Was it necessary to have bound him so tightly?*

"Awake finally." A quiet voice spoke from beside him, out of the darkness of the small cavern in the hillside. Ell grunted his assent although it had been more of a statement than a question. Dacunda walked out of the cave slowly, the moonlight shimmering down through the branches of the trees overhead and casting a pale, otherworldly light upon his face. He reached Ell's side and squatted down, his face now fully illuminated by the moon as he stepped into the clearing outside the cave with an opening in the trees above him.

"Do not look at me with such anger on your face, Nephew," he put his hand on Ell's cheek, fingering a bruise gently. "You were enraged to the point of endangering us all."

Ell grunted again, not yet willing to let go of his frustrations. "I hardly think that's true," he muttered.

Dacunda raised his eyebrows quizzically in surprise. "Do you not? How much do you remember?"

"I remember enough to be able to recall one or all of you hitting me so hard I lost consciousness," Ell grumbled. "How long have I been out?" He added as an afterthought.

His uncle chuckled. "Yes, Elliyar, we did at that. And a few hours. However, what you do not remember is throwing Dahranian into a boulder after you had pulled your blades. He struck his shoulder hard enough to require Source Water to heal the injury." Dacunda raised both hands in placation. "He is fine now. But it does not change the fact it happened. I also doubt you remember holding your dagger and facing me, your sister, and cousin down as if you were ready to use the blade on us instead of your enemies." He looked at the blank stare on Ell's face. Indeed, Ell could not recall doing any such thing. It was like trying to sift through memories in a haze of anger and fear and blackness.

"I thought not," his uncle said.

"I am sorry, Uncle," Ell said finally, letting his anger at his family fade. It was not they with whom he was angry in truth. They had just been the unmerited recipients of his rage. He would have to make amends.

"Don't worry, Elliyar." His uncle spoke calmly, caringly. "We understand. This time. But it cannot happen again. You *must* learn to control your abilities. Otherwise you will continue to be a danger to yourself and others, if you access such power in a fit of rage and an unsound mind."

Ell closed his eyes in frustration. "I am trying Uncle, but to no avail. I do not know how I will accomplish it without Arendahl to help," he finished forlornly, even a bit despairingly. It was as if all the determination he had felt earlier had seeped out of his bones. Gone, with the realization that Miri was gone.

Dacunda laid a hand on his shoulder. "You will find a way. I know it." He spoke confidently about a power of which he knew nothing. His confidence was in Ell, not in knowledge of the task at hand.

Ell changed the subject, as he squirmed his way into less of a slouch and more of a natural sitting position. "Are you going to unbind me?" He reached his hands upwards toward his uncle.

Dacunda reached forward to do so them paused a moment. "Are you sure you can control yourself?"

"I couldn't even tap my abilities if I wanted to," Ell answered a bit miserably. "I already tried and failed when I awoke." Dacunda nodded understandingly and untied his wrists.

"Did you have to bind me so tightly?" Ell asked a bit sourly.

Ell's uncle looked at him seriously. "You do not remember, but you snapped the first cords we used to bind you more loosely, without a moment's hesitation. As if the strands of cord were dried grass not our finest woven rope." He spoke almost wonderingly, mesmerized by the power which his nephew possessed. It had made their night difficult, and painful, but it also carried the potential to do boundless good and strengthen their cause against the enemy.

Ell looked away slightly ashamed at having been such a nuisance, a danger really. "I truly am sorry for last night, Uncle."

"Enough, we shall speak no more of it, lad. All is forgiven. We are family."

The others were huddled around a fire in the cave, kept small to prevent its light from shining outside the walls of their cavern campsite. Ell made his apologies once again to his cousins and sister and was met with similar forgiveness as he had received from his uncle. It was humbling really. Dahranian nursed a sore shoulder, and Ryder had picked up a small nick from one of Ell's blades while tackling him at the end, but all in all, they had come out the other side of the encounter none the worse for wear.

Ell ate a handful of dried meat, chewing slowly, methodically as he thought. "So what is the plan?" he finally asked, directing his question at his uncle.

"Plan?" Dacunda wore a confused expression on his face.

"Yes, the plan. Miri has been taken. What are we going to do?"

Pain flashed across his uncle's face and the rest of his family also looked at him grimly. "I am sorry, Elliyar," Dacunda answered softly but firmly. "There is no plan. There is nothing we can do."

Ell felt that same flare of rage in his chest. Perhaps more dully than earlier in the evening when he had flown out of control, but there all the same. "What do you mean no plan!"

"What he means, Ell," Rihya spoke up gently, her voice resembling an elder explaining something simple to a child even though she was only a few years older than him, "is that this site is a few days old. Even moving at as fast a pace as possible, we could not catch the slaver party before they reached the nearest Pillar."

"So?" Ell said indignantly. *What were they implying, that he just give Miri up for taken? Gone forever?*

Dacunda shook his head silently. "You know the Pillars are impregnable,

Elliyar. Tall towers with a single stair or sometimes ladder leading up to a wide platform on top with the holding cells. There is no way for a band of five," he indicated their small party, "to be able to breach the defenses. Even an army would find it difficult." He sighed. "Perhaps if there were more than one way up, but alas there is only a narrow stair or ladder on each Pillar. They were designed to be the perfect staging areas for captive slaves. Designed to be impossible to steal captives back," he spat. "In that endeavor the Departed accomplished their goals well."

"What would you have me do? Give up?" Ell asked honestly, his voice beseeching them for another answer than the one he saw on their faces.

Even Ryder, ever the optimist, looked at him hopelessly. "It is done, cousin," he said sadly, as he responded to Ell's question.

"I wish with all my heart it were not so," Dacunda said. "If anyone of us knows what it feels like to lose people they love to the slavers, it is I, but even considering the fact, I must tell you there is no hope."

Ell looked at him in confusion. *What did he mean by that statement?* "Uncle, our family members were killed long ago, not taken. What do you mean?"

Dacunda stared at him a moment. "I simply mean, I am older than all of you by many years and have witnessed this enough times to be even sicker of it than you," he responded passionately. It was true. Ell supposed after years of seeing your people enslaved and killed, the anger inside a person must increase dramatically. Still it had been an odd comment, the way he had phrased it. Ell let his thoughts move on from it, however, and back to the matter at hand.

"What if I am not willing to give up?" he asked quietly after a time. The thought of simply abandoning Miri to the horrors of a life of slavery was too much to bear.

"Then I would beg you to reconsider, Nephew," his uncle answered just as solemnly. They all became silent for a time—thinking their own dark thoughts. Ell imagined himself wringing the neck of every slaver he came across before finally rescuing his love. But it was entirely unsatisfying. In the end, the fantasies did not change the fact that Miri was still captive and the slavers still lived.

The fire died and they eventually took to their bedrolls. As they were about to fall asleep, Dacunda approached Ell for one more final word.

"Promise me, Nephew," he said, "promise me you will not do anything rash."

Ell paused and then nodded his agreement, feeling his bruised face flare into pain as it rubbed against the dirt floor of the cave. The pain was a reminder to him of the cost of not controlling his abilities. He had caused his family harm, even if it was only slight. He had to learn to control his abilities, not let them control him.

Appeased for the moment, Dacunda returned to his bedroll on the other side of the cave. Ell slept fitfully. It was difficult to fall fully asleep, and by the time his sister woke him for his watch in the middle of the night, he was glad to take it and give himself an excuse to sit awake and think.

He planted himself on a small rock at the entrance of the cave. The pale moonlight still shone, but a few wisps of cloud had blown in from the north and were clinging to the sky, half obscuring the pale orb of light in the heavens. It was a night with a mysterious, unknown look, bringing to mind tall tales and old stories. Lore from a different age. On a night like this, all of the old stories from the First Days seemed more believable. The wind rushed more forcefully than earlier through the trees overhead. Ell could imagine the wind was the voices of hundreds of the Ogre kin attacking the walls of an elven stronghold in the First Days. One could be forgiven for imagining the screech of an owl answered by another to be the distinct calls of Ghouls working in tandem, as they had in the First Days, as the evil creatures were starting to do again.

Ell ignored the strangeness of the night. He focused his thoughts on solving the problem at hand. Just because something had never been done, or was deemed impossible, didn't mean it couldn't be done. *Where there is a will, there is a way*, his uncle had always told him. It was time to prove his uncle right. Ell brooded in silence, the night loud with the sound of wind and branches rattling around him. He thought and thought, and as he did, the beginnings of a plan began to form. It was ludicrous at best—a half-concocted plan, which had more chance of getting him killed than of saving the love of his life—but at least it was *something*. Ell needed to cling to some vestige of hope.

Ell quietly grabbed his bow and quiver, and checked his blades in all their locations to make sure he was adequately prepared for the undertaking on which he was about to embark. He regretted the need to break his earlier promise to his uncle. Ell had affirmed he would do nothing rash. Well, on second thought, this plan was as well thought out as possible in such a situation as this. Perhaps he was not breaking his promise after all. Maybe his uncle should have just been more specific with the conditions to which he'd had Ell agree, asking Ell not to do anything dangerous or foolish. Rash implied that a plan was not well considered. Such was not the case here. Ell had had plenty of time to think it through, as he lay awake sleeplessly. Either way, Ell supposed his uncle would be sorely displeased with him. If Ell survived. Ell would be more than happy to face Dacunda's wrath if it meant he was alive and Miri was safe. And it would mean both of those circumstances together. He would rescue Miri or die trying. Of that much he was certain.

Ell set off silently, thanking the night for its noise to cover his escape. The trail of the slavers led south, towards the nearest Pillar. It could not be more than a few days in that direction, meaning his enemies would be already reaching the Pillar, their safe haven for the captives, by the time he would be able to overtake them.

If his scheme worked. However, he did not set his course to pursue them. He did not follow the trail south. Ell took a deep breath and stilled his nerves.

North.

He turned his course north through the forest. The plan was taking shape in his mind. It was crazy at best, but Ell was willing to place his faith in the most insane of plans if it gave him even a glimmer of hope that he might be able to save Miri. It shouldn't be much longer than a half-day's journey to his destination if he pushed hard. The wind picked up and before long, it was howling around him, a spring gale to shake the forest to its very roots. He ran hard into the wind, determination seething through him. He would save Miri. Or he would die trying.

Chapter Twenty-One

The North Crag reared its stubborn head directly in front of him. It shot skyward, a rocky spire, narrow, lean, and tall in the midst of short and squat mountains around it. It was taller than the tallest peak in its general vicinity, hence its ability to be recognized as a landmark while traveling. It had a similar twin, known as the South Crag deep in the southwestern portion of the Lower Forest. The two stone promenades thrust themselves into the air in their separate regions of Andalaya, almost creating a visual map for anyone wishing to journey near them.

This was the only way to reach the nearest Pillar in time. Ell had realized this while taking his night watch. The slavers had too many days head start on him, and once they reached the Pillar his uncle, Dacunda, was correct; assault would be foolhardy, a certain death. Pillars were the ultimate fortresses, designed to reside in borderlands and even enemy territory, yet remain unconquered. As soon as Verdantihya had fallen, the humans and the Departed working in unison had erected nearly a dozen of them throughout stretches of the Lower Forest and out onto the eastern plains. Ell had only seen them a few times, but even he had been in awe. Using some of the humans' architectural machines and slave manpower, they had built the Pillars. At first sight, the Pillars could only be described as enormous stone tables, as tall as a very small mountain with holding cells on top. One vast, central column of stone rose from the earth, wide enough to support the wide platform of stone at the top, which lay flat upon the cylinder below. Scaling the Pillars was impossible because even if you managed to reach the top of the stone cylinder by climbing, you could go no further since the immense, flat platform reached outward and over your head. There were no handholds on the underside of the platform with which to continue scaling the monstrosity of human and Departed construction.

No, the only way up were the solitary sets of stairwells and ladders arranged intermittently along the inside of the cylinder beginning near the base and reaching all the way to the top. A few good warriors could hold one of the Pillars against an entire army if they needed, so narrow and tight were the fighting quarters if an enemy army attempted to fight their way upward. In fact, there were sections of ladder interspersed throughout the climb that could be pulled up, leaving whole sections of the interior unassailable. They had been built to stand in the territory of the Highest, bastions of despair, a constant symbol and reminder to Ell's people how far they had fallen. Ell took consolation from the fact that at least the Pillars, themselves, were still necessary. This fact alone said that the enemy feared raids from his people enough to build these sky-high fortresses as waypoints along the route back to their own lands. It was a depressing consolation prize, that thought, but Ell clung to it nonetheless. Hope in any form was not to be despised. However, Dacunda was right, the Pillars were impregnable.

With this thought in mind, Ell reached the bottom of the North Crag and began to climb. He had spent half a day running hard to get here, making sure to outdistance any pursuit from his family should they have decided to follow. It wasn't that he didn't want their help in this venture, but their help would be useless. And, he didn't want to deal with them trying to stop him. They couldn't understand. None of them had loved ones trapped in the clutches of their evil, cousin race to the south. Ell grasped a handhold of the firm, rough, stone spire and thought about how much he hated the Departed. He had thought the bitterness inside him, the constant anger, was gone. It had begun abating during his time with Miri, and then as he focused on his lessons with Arendahl, it had fled his mind almost completely, lost amidst the hours of single-minded pursuit of a task other than fighting. However, as soon as he'd discovered Miri's abduction by slavers, it had all come rushing back at once. Bitterness, anger, frustration, and an overall rage at a life spent fighting from the shadows, and striking blows, which barely pricked the enemy, all to culminate with the one thing he cared about most in this life falling into the hands of his enemies. It was too much to bear. He felt the bile, the disgust, boiling in his stomach and his determination to save Miri, mixed with his hatred for the Departed, his hatred for the humans, forming a compound substance of grit inside of him. He would save her. And he would continue fighting. Somehow, some way, when this was all over, he would find a way to make a difference and turn the tide of the war. If he survived. Today was still young and there was a wealth of danger ahead of him. He grasped another handhold and pulled himself upward. The Pillars might be impregnable, unable to be scaled, but the North Crag could be climbed. His solution lay high atop its rocky peak.

The day was windy just as the night had been. The gusts of biting, northern wind threatened to pry him off the cliff face and dash him to the boulders below as he made his way upwards. He was only a quarter of the way up, the midday sun beating hard on the back of his neck, piercing even the cold wind to make its hot mark on his body. There was still a long way to go. At the top was the only hope he had of saving Miri, of rescuing her from the top of the Pillar and the horrific life that lay ahead of her. There was no turning back. Ell climbed steadily, occasionally having to readjust or back track if he reached an impassable portion of the cliff wall. When that happened he traced his way back down, slowly, carefully, yet steadily, and then picked another route and started back up again.

Ell did not ignore the terrible speculations about what lay ahead for his love if he failed. He did not turn a blind eye to the dark possibilities waiting in her future. Endless toil. Daily violation at the whim of evil elves or the madmen to the east. A living nightmare. He let the fire inside fuel him. Failure was not an option. He had to succeed. It was succeed or die trying.

He grabbed a fistful of rugged stone that threatened to cut into his palms and hauled himself upward, mentally defying the gale, which howled around him, whipped his hooded tunic about, and attempted to claw him from the face of the crag. Wind whistled in his ears and screamed violently. A storm was brewing. He grasped the rough face of the cliff again and pulled, finding footholds with his feet as he did so. Ell was a good climber, strong, lean, and lithe. He had always excelled at tests of his physical prowess such as this. When there was a particularly difficult position in need of scouting, Dacunda had chosen Ell more often than not to be the one to do it. It was one of his strengths, Ell's ability to move swiftly and dexterously, over troubling terrain. Whether the terrain was horizontal, or vertical like today, made no difference.

Hands. Feet. Hands. Feet. He moved smoothly, methodically. Ell climbed up the face of the North Crag with a nimbleness the likes of which even many of his elven kin would admire and envy. Slowly but surely his climbing pace ate away at the rocky spire left above him.

Halfway. The midday sun was just past its zenith, slowly beginning its gradual sink towards the horizon. He climbed. For a time he let his mind go blank as he lost himself in the rhythm of the movements. Upwards, steadily he continued.

Three quarters of the way there, Ell thought to himself as he pressed himself flat against the face of the cliff and peered upwards, estimating the distance left to climb. He glanced downward and for a moment, his vision swam sickeningly. This far above the earth everything looked different. He had been scaling the North Crag for hours. In the distance, he could just make out the passes leading into the valley where the ruins of Verdantihya resided. The city itself was obscured by the peaks surrounding it; peaks that today looked dark and brooding, as the storm around Ell grew in fury. Thunderheads blew in on a northeasterly wind, clogging the sky like a dark, puffy blanket. Ell tried not to think about the rain that would soon follow. It would make the last portion of his climb much more difficult. However, thousands of spans high in the air, he was already long past the point of no return. Onward was the only course. He scanned the cliffs above him, looking for his target goal. A dozen small promontories jutted out from the cliff face, any one of them possibly being that which he sought. It was difficult to tell. One of the ledges jutted out farther than the rest. It was the biggest. He would place his hope that it was the one for which he was looking.

Adjusting his course to swing wide and high around the largest ledge, he climbed further to his right, scaling the wall sideways for a time before returning his upward approach. He was on the other side of the cliff from the large ledge now, and would climb high and then make his way back to it when the time was right. Ell would need to come down upon the ledge from above, and swiftly, otherwise his plan to save Miri would likely end decisively before it had hardly even begun.

The rain began to spatter, striking the rocky spire with an infrequent rhythm. It grew in force, however, and by the time he was sure he had climbed high enough and was beginning to adjust his course back towards the front of the cliff where he had started the climb, the rain was in full blast. It poured forth like a torrent, the darkened, late afternoon sky an angry, celestial waterfall. It made his task much more challenging. Hand and footholds that would have previously been safe and easy to use became dangerously slick when wet.

Ell was making his way sideways again, back to his left towards the front of the cliff's face when he reached a gap. The rock wall to his left had a chimney-like rivulet running down it. To continue on his course he would have to find a way to traverse it. It ran from the top of the cliff to a good hundred spans beneath him. He had come too far along this route to retrace his steps. The afternoon light was waning more quickly as the clouds obscured the sun, making the climb even more hazardous. He could not afford to waste time. That meant he had to find a way across. The other side of the natural chimney was too far to reach, even if he stretched, although try he did. He grasped one hand precariously onto a slick rock hold, and balanced his right foot lightly, but firmly praying he wouldn't fall. The other arm and foot he dangled over open air as he leaned dangerously towards the other side of the inverted canyon. One second, two, three, and then Ell felt his fingers begin to lose their grip and he gave up and swung his body back into the safety of the tiny ledge upon which he balanced. The ledge beneath his feet was nothing more than an inch or so of a protrusion from the cliff face and it only ran a few spans long. A momentary resting point, nothing more. It was not safe to wait long.

Rains slicked his hair down to the sides of his face, and his hooded tunic was plastered to his body, heavier than it had been when he had first begun to climb. He had by now adjusted to the added weight, however. Ell leaned his face against the cool, moist rock. He just breathed, drawing air deeply into his lungs. He closed his eyes, silently cursing himself for not having been able to master his ability yet. *If only I'd been able to call upon the water, today of all days would be an easy one*, Ell thought angrily, feeling and hearing the wetness of the rain.

If he had been able to access his ability as a Water Caller, this climb and crossing the natural chimney before him would be simple with the advantage of increased strength, stamina, and agility gained from tapping the natural power flowing through creation's veins. Water. It always came back to his power. With it, he could do this easily.

Enough wishing, Elliyar, he told himself forcefully, *either you will be able to do this without use of your abilities, your powers, or you won't. Only one way to find out.* With that, he arched his body, right, leaning away from the chimney and then whipped his body back to the left, using the force of his motion to sling himself to the left and leapt sideways, all in one movement.

Time seemed to freeze and the moment dragged as he glanced down surreally at the forested floor of Legendwood thousands of feet below. While in midair, life seemed to pause for a moment of tranquility in the midst of a storm both physical and internal. Then as if to make up for the strange break in his thoughts and the world around him, everything came crashing back to reality all at once. Ell's body pounded into the cliff side on the far side of the chimney. His left hand grasped desperately for a handhold as his legs and other arm swung wildly in the damp, tempestuous, open air.

It was a moment that stretched a lifetime.

Ell felt his fingers slipping from their slick hold on the rock face. Despairingly he clung on, hoping they would hold long enough for the momentum of his swinging body to reach the wall again. As his fingertips reached the end of their grasp his body collided with the wall once again and his other hand and feet sought desperately for a secondary hold, another ledge or crack with which to balance his precariously swinging body. There. Finally his toe found something and his right hand wedged itself into a seam in the cliff face just as the fingers on his left hand lost their hold completely. However, with his right hand and left foot now balancing himself, he was able to correct his body again swiftly, and grabbed the handhold with his left hand.

Ell pressed his face to the cliff for an instant, breathing in the air. Life. He lived. Adrenaline coursed through his veins, the pulse of danger, excitement, and the thrill of victory over this natural enemy. The cliff face, in the rain of a spring squall, was a far more dangerous foe than anything he had ever faced.

Not wanting to wait long, and feeling his strength beginning to ebb, Ell continued on sideways, moving to his left and then slowly downwards as he steadily climbed his way back towards the front of the crag above the large ledge, which he had, targeted earlier. He prayed that he had chosen his direction correctly. If all of this had been for naught and he found himself thousands of feet above the earth and still far from his goal, Ell thought he might just break down and weep. Such was the wealth of adrenaline and emotions within him.

Ell climbed on. Sideways and downward now. On and On. Had he climbed too far, had he climbed too high? His thoughts were beginning to feel slightly muddled now with the beginnings of real fatigue setting into his body. He pushed through the exhaustion. He could not afford to give in to tiredness now. Not for Miri's sake or for his.

There.

Looking down he saw the ledge for which he had been aiming all along. The evening sky was a midnight blue now, dark enough that sight would have been difficult for a human, but luckily not for an elf of the Highest. His senses keen, he was still able to make out his surrounds clearly enough to continue. He might not see as well now, as he could during daylight, but it was nothing he could not handle. Ell had spent many nights scouting and on reconnaissance, not to mention the endless string of nights over the years spent raiding and ravaging the enemy's troops and supply lines. No, darkness was his friend as much as anyone else's. After all, he was Elliyar. Dusk Runner. Named for the onset of night, the beginning of darkness, when many people's eyes had difficulty adjusting to the changing light. Not Ell, he was born for the fight, born for adventure. Suddenly he felt invigorated. Remembering his name, his purpose, was enough to flood strength back into his limbs. He set forth directly downward now as he came in above the wide spacious ledge beneath him.

Just as he had expected, just as Dacunda had pointed out to him earlier the day before, there on the ledge, maybe twenty feet beneath him was the makings of an aerie, a peak-top stronghold. Perched on the tip of the ledge a few yards from where the ledge reached the cliff side was a bulky form. Large and monstrous it lurked, impervious to the rain, ignoring the elements. It was a relic of darkness long gone, a malady of the current state of chaotic affairs in Ell's tainted homeland. The beast screeched into the coming darkness, crying its defiance to the rain, the wind, and the storm that battered its cliff nest. Ell shuddered slightly. He knew it was only the deepest love, the love he bore for Miri that could drive him to seek out such a perilous situation and attempt what nobody had ever done before him.

Ell began quietly, picking his way closer, downwards toward the ledge.

His adrenaline was racing and his heart was thumping so loudly in his chest he feared the creature would hear it. It ruffled its ash-grey wings, wet from the rain and for a moment, he held his breath and paused, fearful indeed that it had become alerted to his presence. It did not look behind it however, and it did not look up. He continued stealthily to sneak up on the beast.

So, his uncle was right. Pillars were impregnable. They couldn't be climbed, not like he had scaled this most impervious of cliffs today. A Pillar was more difficult to scale than even one of the crags. How else to reach the top? Ell had been able to think of only one answer to that question the night before, as he sat his watch outside the cave, his family breathing restfully within the grotto. If an elf couldn't climb the Pillars, and the Pillars could not be taken by force, even by an army, then there was only one last solution to reach the slave cells atop the platform.

Madness surely. Ell knew this venture would more than likely cost him his life. But it was the only option. And so it was that Ell snuck up on the aerie. Ell crept closer to the beast. He was going to drop into the nest voluntarily, to confront an Icari.

And he was going to ride it.

Chapter Twenty-Two

Ell spun as he dropped the twenty feet down into the sky-high lair of the Icari, adjusting his body so that he landed with his back to the cliff. He landed lightly, quietly in a crouch, amidst the swirling air and rain of the storm. It was as wicked a squall as he had ever witnessed in springtime. This storm felt more like winter's fury rather than spring's calmer intentions to soak the land and rehydrate it. Thankfully, it was loud enough to cover the miniscule sound of his landing in the nest. Or so he thought.

However, the instant he dropped into the crouch, each hand pulling a blade free, the Icari swiveled its large humanoid head around and its reddish-orange eyes stared piercingly, viciously at the intruder in its aerie. At Ell. It must have even keener senses than an elf to have heard him in the midst of all the chaos and ruckus of the tumultuous storm surrounding them.

Their eyes locked for a moment. Ell's own clear, blue eyes met feral, fiery red, the fury of the First Days returned to wreak havoc on the earth again. The moment stretched as if neither being was ready to break the instant of tension, not quite ready for the climax of the moment to arrive. Then the gale around them ripped a cluster of small boulders free from the cliff above. The rocks plummeted sharply and crashed onto the ledge in between Ell and the Icari, sending sprays of pebbles into the air as they split asunder and rolled off the ledge again. Their momentum carried them toward the sodden forest floor thousands of feet further down, leaving only the remnants, the rubble of the boulders as loose gravel and scree, on the ledge. The impact and the crash of the boulders onto the ledge seemed to break the frozen moment and set them free to engage in the violent struggle that would ensue. The climax of Ell's climb had arrived.

Ell, holding his long, dueling dagger point down in his right hand and his small belt knife point up in his left, watched as the beast turned its body around fully, spreading its wings as it faced him. The wingspan was immense. At least the length of three elves combined head to toe, if not longer. The Icari screamed its rage at Ell's intrusion into its peak-top sanctuary and charged.

Well, in reality, it flapped its wings once and covered the distance between them in a ferociously quick glide. Ell sidestepped the beast as it flew at him, anticipating that would be its first maneuver. He slashed at a wing as it crashed into the cliff wall where he had been. It roared in anger at Ell giving it the slip.

Now for the hard part he thought. Ell had to do what no elf had ever done. It wasn't just killing the Icari in single combat, which he had to accomplish. No, it was a challenge much more difficult. He had to find a way to secure it somehow, allowing him to ride the beast south. The difficulty of the task almost overwhelmed him now that he was faced with the terror of seeing the Icari face to face from only a few feet away. It was immense. At least three times the size of a large elf. Its torso and legs resembling an elf or a human were thickly muscled. Its skin was an ashy charcoal color. The legs ended in a set of eagle-like talons, the claws scraping eerily against the stone of the ledge as it struggled to spin around from its first failed attack. *How long before it decides to leave this ledge behind and go fully airborne putting me at a serious disadvantage.* Ell knew he had to finish this encounter quickly somehow, before the creature wizened up.

It spun to face him. Instead of arms, it possessed wings. Its enormous wings flared wide again. They were dark. Ash colored to be exact, the remains of a fire long burnt out. Angelically they spread out in front of Ell, highlighting the difference between this vicious predator of flight and himself, an elf of the Highest. Mortal enemies since the beginning of time. It reared back its head, which also resembled that of an elf or a human although much bigger, and screamed again into the evening sky. It certainly was furious. As it voiced its fearsome cry, Ell saw the fangs. Row upon row of fangs lined its mouth, enough to rip an arm or a leg off something with hardly a second glance. It stared at him now, an almost cognizant look on its face before attacking again, and Ell wondered how capable were they of thought and speech. Or were they really just beasts like the mountain cats and wolves of Andalaya? Its roughhewn features, nose and cheekbones looking as if they had been hewn from the hard granite of the mountains themselves, regarded Ell for one last moment before it righted itself and flapped powerfully, sending it skimming low and fast across the ledge toward Ell, in another ferocious attack.

Ell's heart froze at the speed and power of the Icari, but fortunately for him, years of battle experience kicked his instincts into motion and he slid low and fast, underneath the beast as it skimmed toward him in flight. The blade-like talons of the beast passed just over his face, one actually clipping his cheek slightly, leaving a small gash. Ell could feel the blood begin to trickle down his cheek and onto his neck. He stood up swiftly and watched the Icari as it tried to slow itself on the ledge. It hadn't been able to turn its body, ungainly while on the rocky ground of the ledge. It swiveled its head around and glanced at Ell a few feet behind it, standing up.

It gathered its massive wings for a giant wing beat that would send it skyward, soaring, giving it the final advantage in this contest of wills and might. It had figured out what Ell was afraid it would. Once it took to the air, it could swoop in upon him time and time again. The aerial advantage would be one he could not stand against, particularly since he had left his bow and quiver with his family in the cave, realizing he could not climb the North Crag encumbered by it.

Now! Ell thought as he burst forward. This was his last chance before the opportunity passed, and his moments among the living became numbered. The beast flapped its wings powerfully, sending it up into the storm above and as it did, Ell gathered all of his strength and leaped as hard as he could, landing on the Icari's back as it rose into the tempest.

The Icari thrashed with a bestial strength that Ell could not hope to match by just holding on with his hands. Ell clung to the creature frantically, wrapping his arms around it as hard as he could, thankful that the beast had the wings that it did, instead of arms and hands. It screamed its fury, a storm all on its own.

Ell glanced down and saw their battlefield, the rock ledge, disappearing into the dark of the storm as they rose and flew jerkily upward and away from the North Crag. The Icari bucked and flung its body this way and that hoping to shed its unwanted passenger. In one surreal moment, Ell realized he was making history. The creature probably had no comprehension for what was happening because such a thing had never occurred before now. It spun and twirled with speed, hoping to dump Ell thousands of feet up in the air. He hung on for his life.

As the moments stretched, Ell realized that he was losing this fight; he would not be able to cling to the flying demon forever. It simply wasn't possible with the frenzied movements of the beast. Eventually the Icari would buck him loose and then death would meet him swiftly and surely as he fell to the hills below. It would mean his death, and Miri's as well, if that were the case.

Thinking fast, Ell plunged his long, dueling dagger into the Icari's side just below the ribs, hoping the anatomy of the creature was similar to an elf's and that the wound would not be mortal. Only excruciatingly painful. The other blade, his short, belt knife he reached up and pressed to the throat of the beast as he used that arm to clasp the creature's body close. The Icari let out a roar of pain and then froze as it realized what was occurring. Apparently, it could think rationally. Then Ell spoke, as he held on tightly, his blades sunk into the creature and leveraged against its throat to provide handholds of sorts with which to keep himself on the Icari's back as it flew.

"You feel that blade in your side," Ell hissed, his anger aroused at the evil spreading in his land, at the evil this beast represented by making its nest in Andalaya. "It is not seeking your death. At least not yet. Although by all rights it should!"

Ell paused and breathed for a moment, collecting his scattered thoughts. "I know not whether you can understand me, Icari, flying demon of the night," he continued, "but if you can, then understand this. I *will* ride you. Or we both shall die together." Ell put all the force he could into the declaration, tightening the blade against its throat, emphasizing his commitment, the ultimate commitment. Success or death. Both of their deaths together if it were necessary. He could slit the beast's throat as quickly as he wanted now that he had the belt knife pressed against it.

The Icari bellowed in pain and rage. Ell wasn't sure if it could understand speech. Then something surprising happened. A different garbled sound began coming forth from the Icari's mouth. Ell leaned his head in closer to hear the noise.

Finally, it became clear to him. The Icari was trying to talk. After another moment of struggling to speak through its gnashing of teeth and growls of anger, one garbled word was produced.

"Where?" the Icari asked in a guttural voice, latent with anger at being treated in this way. Fury at being ridden. It was a sound so strange coming from the Icari's mouth that it was almost unintelligible. Ell barely understood the growling question.

"South," Ell answered firmly. "To the closest Pillar. You know what a Pillar is I presume." The Icari didn't answer this time, but it swooped its path of flight down from the high heavens and back towards the storm swirling just beneath it, since they had risen so high in their earlier struggle as to be above the squall. The Icari dove back into the storm and Ell began to make out the shapes of the land beneath him. The North Crag, as a landmark, allowed him to see that the Icari had turned its course south as he wished, and the beast began soaring quickly in the direction Ell desired, covering ground at a faster rate than Ell would have imagined possible.

So, the creature does understand our tongue, Ell mused to himself as he witnessed it acceding to his wishes. *I wonder if they all do, or just this Icari?* He spoke again. "Take me where I desire and I will not slit your throat when I am through with you."

The beast growled and roared, not answering in the language of the Highest this time. But Ell now knew it could understand, since it had set its course south according to Ell's will. They would reach the Pillar. But how to survive getting off its back? It was a question he did not have long to ponder, before the solution would be necessary.

Air rushed by and Ell fought to keep his eyes open, though the droplets of water from the thunderheads around them spattered crisp and cold across his face. Despite the craziest of circumstances and the terrible fear twisting his belly into knots, his fear for Miri, it was hard not to marvel at what was occurring. Ell was flying! Soaring. Granted, it was from the back of one of the most despicably evil creatures in the history of the world, yet all the same, it was a magnificent experience. They rushed south in a whirlwind of wings beating powerfully, and then those same wings locking into place and soaring elegantly on the storm currents that rose and fell all around them in the sky. It was one of the most incredible experiences of Ell's life. He began to sense the air currents around them and feel how the Icari reacted to those different flows of air. *What would it be like to have wings of my own?* The thought was too impossible to even spend more than a moment's musing on it. He was an elf and his body, his form, was crafted to run swiftly and leap gracefully. The Highest were equipped to sprint, and dance, and lithely, agilely maneuver their way across the land. *Land, not air* he told himself. Yet he couldn't help but imagine a bit wistfully what it would be like if he had been created with wings. As terrible a being as the Icari was, by an hour into their flight, it had won a grudging respect from Ell, the way a mountain cat has the respect of a stag for its predictably ferocious and elegant nature. Flight was one of those things that merited respect, even if the flying creature itself didn't.

Ell pulled his attention from his mental wanderings and back to the moment at hand. It would likely cost him his life if he lost focus now. He brought his mind back to the present problem. How to dismount the Icari without falling prey to his fangs and claws? A vexing problem. Ell reached his consciousness out tentatively, attempting to access his ability as a Water Caller. Nothing. As usual, his mind came up empty, and he didn't want to push too hard, as he was worried that if he did, he might lose touch with the moment at hand and perhaps lose his grip on the beast.

They had been flying nearly two hours and had already covered a day's worth of travel by foot, when the creature made its first subversive attempt to dislodge its unwanted rider. The beast swooped low over the tree tops, not far from where Ell had left his family the night before, and inverted its flight pattern, skimming low enough that it hoped it would be able to brush him off upside down on the tops of the trees below them.

It happened so suddenly that Ell nearly lost his grip on the blades and the beast before managing to right his hold as he found himself diving across the forest and looking at his beloved homeland upside down. Ell grasped the beast hard and twisted the dagger in the Icari's side slightly, tightening his belt knife against the beast's throat convulsively, as well.

"Feel that steel, Icari?" He asked angrily. Ell was partially angry with himself for not anticipating this action and losing control of the moment. "Feel it? I will tear your side completely open and then rip your throat to shreds, if you don't end this madness at once."

The flying beast didn't immediately do as he asked, as if testing his resolve to end his own life for the sake of taking the others. Ell pressed his belt knife against the beast's throat and felt the tough skin begin to give slightly beneath his blade. It would be bleeding by now. Ell said a prayer and mentally committed himself to slash the Icari from ear to ear if it didn't listen. An elf was only as good as his word, after all. If he couldn't make good on his threats then he didn't deserve to reach the Pillar.

The Icari tensed as if sensing his commitment to slash and then quickly the moment passed and the creature flipped itself back over. It beat its wings and rose higher above the treetops continuing on their course south. Ell grimaced grimly in satisfaction. It had tested his resolve that was certain. He had found himself willing to pay the ultimate price—death. Ell wasn't quite sure how he felt about the decision. Death wouldn't save Miri.

They skimmed south over the Lower Forest. Ell kept an eye out for his family, expecting they would have kept their course south. He didn't think they would have followed him north. In fact, they might have suspected he had left in pursuit of the slavers and gone south. However, the darkness of the night setting, and the storm around them, made it difficult to see much. Besides, the many paths and trails of the Lower Forest were often obscured by the canopy of leaves and branches hanging over them. Instead, all he saw was the occasional giant, ash-grey feather that tore loose from one of the Icari's wings and floated almost peacefully downward. He imagined somewhat morbidly, that falling from the back of the beast to his death would be much more violent than the tranquil motions of the feathers as they drifted down.

The storm finally began to abate as they made their way south. Rain still fell, but not nearly so hard as earlier. Wind yet blew, but it was not the howling gale, which had enshrouded the North Crag hours before. They continued to soar. With his blades having bitten into the beast's flesh, controlling the Icari, it felt in a strange way as if they were one. It was almost as if Ell himself were somehow flying through the night.

They flew for hours more, and Ell recognized they must have covered the few days journey south towards his desired destination as he looked at the landscape around them. It was amazing how much ground could be covered by the winged creature when it decided to really fly for distance. Ell narrowed his eyes as he saw a shape looming up ahead. By the pale light of the stars, and the moon half covered by clouds, he saw the makings of a giant table-like shape rising out of the Lower Forest. The farthest north Pillar. If Miri were anywhere, she would be there.

The Icari rose high as it made its way nearer to the Pillar. It flew high enough so it would be difficult to see them from the tabletop platform, should any of the Departed be keenly searching the skies for danger. Perhaps, there would be sentries looking up, Ell conceded to himself, because the Icari flew as if it had done this before, rising high and then swooping down in a dive towards the goal. Maybe it had visited this or another Pillar previously, looking for an easy prey on a cold, hungry night. Ell found himself hoping this was the case. It made him sadistically pleased to think of one or many of his enemy Departed falling victim to the claws and fangs of the evil Icari. Evil deserved evil. It was as simple as that in his mind.

As they plummeted towards the giant tabletop, the platform full of holding cells and barracks for the soldiers and slavers, Ell realized he had still not formed a plan for dismounting. He knew the moment would arrive within seconds. Perhaps, subconsciously, he had known that no real plan could suffice. Once he leaped from the back of the flying beast, all bets would be off. Would it limp away in flight, happy to escape with its life? Or would it vindictively try to take vengeance on the elf who had ridden an Icari, the Highest who had made one of its kind into a beast of burden for the first time in history?

They neared the end of the dive and the Icari pulled up short just above the platform, opening its wings and slowing itself quickly and powerfully. Ell found himself hoping against hope that something, anything would go in his favor. If ever he needed luck, it was now. Miri's life depended on it as did his own. Ell held his breath and said a quick prayer for fortune and safety. Then he ripped his blades free and leapt from the Icari's back.

Chapter Twenty-Three

Even as Ell landed in a crouch on the stone deck of the Pillar, he could feel the power swelling within him. The air thickened with a slight mist around him, and he viewed the world through a milky, cloudy haze. As always, when his water calling ability was activated by instinct rather than on purpose, his mind grew slightly vague, and all of his actions seemed to be guided by the same instincts that had allowed him to access his powers. Ell wasn't sure if the experience would be the same whenever he finally accessed his powers purposefully. From the back of his mind Ell thanked whatever it was that had thrust his instincts to the forefront, forcing him to tap the land around him through his ability as a Water Caller. He supposed it must be the imminent danger proposed by the Icari hovering overhead, or perhaps the threat of the Departed, which he was aware, would be manning their stations all across the enormous platform-top of the Pillar.

Ell spun around, blades still in his hands held at ready. The power grew inside him and he felt his muscles strengthen. As always, Ell wasn't sure exactly how it happened, but it did. As he tapped into his powers as a Water Caller, he knew his reflexes would be sharper, his movements more graceful, more agile. Just watching Arendahl leap over twenty feet in a single stationary bound during one of his training sessions had taught him how powerful he might be.

The Icari screamed its rage. As if Ell's instincts, or whatever subconscious part of him it was that allowed him to access his abilities, had foreseen the dangerous future, the winged beast attacked. The Icari beat its wings twice to rise up and gain momentum for a dive back down. Even as Ell heard the dark, angry voices of the Departed reacting to the Icari's cries, the beast swooped. It dove hard and fast. Any rational, reasonable elf would have run and taken cover, but not a Water Caller. Ell knew, deep down, he had not truly earned the right to call himself a Water Caller yet. After all, he could not control his abilities by choice. Yet, in this moment, with the ability swelling instinctively within him, and the immense power he felt right at his fingertips, fear simply didn't make sense. As the Icari screamed, dropping low in a furious aerial assault, Ell stood his ground.

It flew hard and fast at his face and as it drew near, and its scarlet eyes reflected pure hate in the guttering torchlight of the platform. Ell saw its desire for retribution. Vengeance for the indignity it had been forced to suffer at the hands of its enemy. Him. The Icari's cry of rage revealed the rows of razor sharp, predatory fangs. It was the bane of elf and men alike, the scourge of the Northern Marches and the Broken Tree Range.

Ell stood his ground watching the beast approach in flight as if in slow motion, and then at the very last moment, when he saw the dirty gleam of triumph in the Icari's eyes, as it perceived its prey within its grasp at long last, Ell cocked back his arm and swung his fist.

The ability within him added incalculable strength to his arm, and the fist Ell smashed into the Icari's evil face might as well have been made of stone as much as flesh and bone with the manner in which it was adapted by his water calling ability. Ell connected sharply, abruptly with the beast's head and he could see the light of consciousness go out in the eyes of the Icari like the flame of a candle extinguished on a drafty night. Such was the power and might of an ability-enhanced fist.

Exultation and joy at the victory coursed through his mind and veins. Ell's heart gloried in the triumph of seeing his ancient foe plummet towards the earth, dropping like a stone thrown from a fortress wall. From the back of his mind Ell could sense that somehow his ability was holding the reins at the moment, it had seized his mind and was at the forefront. He felt the exultation, not his own necessarily, but the sense of a war fought from time immemorial. The feeling of triumph over an enemy as old as the mountains and as dark and black as a hidden cavern. He would almost describe the sensation as a oneness with his entire race, the Highest. The feeling of victory his people gained as the Icari fell, vanquished from the skies it claimed to dominate. The beast plummeted earthwards, careening toward certain death. At the last instant, the Icari seemed to regain consciousness, and as it awakened, it flapped its wings frantically trying to right itself. It did so, barely. Its efforts were just enough to slow its fall and save its life, but it still hit the ground harshly. Ell hoped it would stay down, dead from impact. He watched the beast struggle to rise, and heard from far below with his elf keen hearing, the whimpering as it finally managed to regain the air beneath its wings. It flew back north awkwardly, limping, if a creature of flight could be said to do so. Its screams were of pain now, not rage, although every so often Ell did get the distinct impression of anger interspersed in its cries. The sounds of the Icari fleeing diminished, as it had decided Ell too great a challenge for its already wounded and partially defeated body.

Ell watched it go and then disappear in the distance, his normal mindset merging with the strange control the ability had assumed over his mind earlier. He still felt the exultation, the joy of the fight and the thrill of victory over the ancient enemy, but he also felt the pressing need to find his love, to find Miri. He was a balance of concepts. Elliyar the normal elf was merged with the Elliyar who was a Water Caller of the Highest, come to wreak havoc upon the vestiges of the First Days come again.

He did his best to shake his head as clear as he dared. It was not something for which Ell struggled too forcefully because he did not wish to lose his access to the water calling ability. He had a feeling his power would be needed again before this night was over.

As if in answer to his thoughts, the shouts of Departed warriors came near. Soldiers began swarming the platform around him. There were at least fifteen of them he could see. There he stood, again making history on this night. Ell stood where no free member of the Highest had ever stood before. Well, at least none who was not a traitor.

Ell stared them down regally. He was no king, but he was not a slave either. They looked at him eagerly, another fresh fruit from soiled Andalaya, ripe for the picking. They were sorely mistaken. Ell knew that before the next few minutes had passed he would disabuse them of their preconceived notions.

The power flowed through his body like lightning. He could not ever remember holding onto his power for quite this long. In previous circumstances it had felt like a quick flash of energy, strength, just enough to survive in whatever situation he found himself. But this was different. With the Icari defeated and gone, he had assumed the ability to call upon the water would have left him. It had not. Ell stretched out his consciousness as Arendahl had taught him. This time, already having accessed his powers by instinct, the reaching out of his mind felt natural. He felt the streams and rivers of the land far below the Pillar. He felt the dampness of the air fresh after a storm and the droplets of water left behind on the deck of the platform after a rainfall.

Ell drew the energy, the substance of the water into him, swelling the power even more in his chest. The air misted around him and his blades grew moist and glistened with beads of condensation in the flickering torchlight. Ell stared at the Departed. Their lips were peeled back in feral grimaces of battle, anticipation at what was to come. Dark elves serving dark masters bent on dark and evil purposes. They deserved to be defeated. Ell looked at them as they stood there so arrogantly in their fitted dark hose, and sleeveless tunics and war vests. He would show them how mistaken they were. Andalaya was not completely broken, at least not beyond repair.

What must have been a senior commander gave instructions, and five of the dark elves, their faces tanned brown, their upper teeth filed to points and revealed through their expressions of war, charged. Ell moved fluidly between the forms of battle, his body mimicking the motions of the water from which he derived his power. His mottled, hooded tunic still damp from passing through the storm hours earlier clung to his body. It felt right. He drew upon the water around him, even the water from his own clothes.

Dagger held upright in his right hand, belt knife point down in his left, he slashed and spun and flayed his way through the five elves as if they were inconsequential. Blood patterned the stone of the platform beneath his feet. Such was his ability enhanced speed and agility, that not a single blade from the Departed soldiers touched him. The dead and dying lay around him, silent or groaning, depending upon their condition.

"Attack!" screamed the commander hoarsely, obviously rattled by how quickly and easily Ell had dispatched of five of the fifteen warriors the elf commanded.

The mob of the remaining ten Departed rushed at him. As during the ambush when he had fought Silverfist, and during the moment when he had struggled to survive the onslaught of the Stone Ogre in the north, Ell felt his limbs strengthen with untold power. However, this time it was more. The ability had stayed with him longer this time, and it also felt more tangible, a greater wealth of power at his disposal. He was a tornado of death.

One dark elf jabbed a spear at him and Ell dodged sideways, slithering in to gut the man with his dagger before spinning away to duck down and hamstring the elf beside him. *Two down.*

Three more came at him at once thinking to subdue him with a unified assault. They were wrong. He broke a kneecap with a swift kick, and the Departed bearing that injury crumpled with a muffled shriek, which turned into a full-fledged scream of terror as Ell then kicked him over the edge of the platform and off the table-like top of the Pillar to fall to the ground far below. His pitiful crescendo of horror ended abruptly as he struck the earth. The other two Departed snarled viciously at him, not much different in his mind from the Icari itself. He gazed at them intently through clouded vision, the misty presence around him coupled by the strange change his eyes always seemed to undergo as he accessed his ability. The two elves charged together. Idly Ell wondered what his eyes looked like when they clouded over, as he casually rolled into a somersault between the two rushing enemies and then spun to his feet to plunge his blades into their backs. *Five gone. Five more to go.*

Ell watched as the remaining five Departed approached him cautiously. They were determined, however, to finish what they had started since they were not deterred as they stepped over the bodies of their former brothers in arms. Throwing caution to the wind, one of them, a brutish, thick-bodied elf, even for one of the Departed, leapt forward swinging a war club with an ominous whistle. Ell leaned back slightly and felt the air move just before his face as the club passed. Another dark elf lunged in from the other side and Ell felt the sting of pain as even though he dodged, the spear grazed his back as it went by him. However, this attack he did not let go without retribution. Ell pressed the elf who had just lunged at him and slashed at the elf's face and then arm, leaving cuts on both the appendages and earning curses from the Departed warrior. The five soldiers formed up again and began advancing on Ell, swords and spears drawn. It was clear they hoped to force him right off the edge to join the Departed he had sent flying out into the air earlier.

As the unit of soldiers came forward, Ell gathered the power and strength within himself. He tensed. *Might as well see if it will work for me like it did for Arendahl.* As they got close, and he saw the relief in their eyes as they thought him cornered beyond saving, he bent his legs and leaped into the air with all his might. He flew over their heads in a flip and landed in a crouch behind their backs. Quick as a flash he turned and had them now with their backs to the empty air beyond. They tried to form up and regroup around him, but he pressured hard. His ability-enhanced speed and reflexes were too much for them.

As Ell rushed forward to meet their attack, he ducked low under a sword swipe and slashed an artery on an elf's leg while planting his belt knife in the foot of another, sending the dark elf hopping with screams of anguish. Ell rose up and kicked the hopping elf in the chest, watching him fall back, arms waving terrifyingly as he wobbled out into the empty air. The elf whose artery had been cut was laying on the platform bleeding out. Apparently, the artery had been an important one. *Only three more*, he thought with grim satisfaction.

Three remaining Departed seemed to know their doom was upon them, having seen twelve of their comrades dispatched within a matter of minutes by a solitary warrior. Little did they know that he was a Water Caller. He could see the fear in their eyes, yet to their credit, they did not flee. Ell was glad they didn't. He wanted to kill them.

He felt the thrill each time as his blades made quick work of the last three. Ell ducked, wove, and spun his way in and around them, leaving carnage in his wake. One managed to slice his arm shallowly with a sword before dying, but with his body strengthened by the power of the land, Ell found the pain easy to ignore. The last one down seemed to remember his duties and began sounding a horn over and over again, from the floor of the platform as he lay dying in a pool of his own blood, after taking a dagger in the gut. Ell cut off the sound of the horn by ramming his belt knife in the Departed's throat. Briefly he felt regret for the savagery of this encounter. Fifteen dead in what seemed like nothing more than a heartbeat. *No*, he told himself roughly, *all hope for quarter was revoked when they took Miri.*

Ell knew the horn would have warned the remaining soldiers on the Pillar. Those fifteen he had just killed wouldn't be the only ones manning this station. Yet surprisingly, he saw less dark elves on the platform than he expected as he slunk his way from shadow to shadow through the confines of the Pillar, leaving the battle in his wake. Find Miri. She had to be there. It was the only thing occupying his mind as he strode through the open air corridors of the Pillar towards its interior. Occasionally he met another of the Departed but they did not last any longer than their fallen brethren had before his ability-enhanced blades.

As the power swelled within him, he found himself wishing the dueling dagger in his right hand would start vibrating. If there was ever a time for vengeance, if there was ever a time to meet Silverfist and exact his revenge, now was the time with the power of the land, the ability of a Water Caller coursing through his veins. *No, focus! Miri is the only thing that matters right now.* He reminded himself of that truth as he searched. She had to be here somewhere. She had to. Nevertheless, Ell began to feel the nagging fear she might not. *What if she was taken elsewhere, to a different Pillar? A farther Pillar?* He hoped against hope that wasn't the case. He thought he might just go mad if all his effort to reach her had been in vain. Left to his thoughts he searched the halls and corridors of the Pillar. He opened doors cautiously, looking in cells only to find them empty of anything but old refuse and the stink of fear and pain.

Sometimes troops of soldiers responding to the earlier horn blast searched the Pillar as well, although Ell was fairly certain they did not believe they were looking for a solitary elf. Who would expect a single Highest to have been able to cause such carnage and commotion?

He could if he was a Water Caller.

When Ell heard the soldiers approaching, he would duck into a cell or a dark corner and hide until they had passed if they were many, or turn and slaughter them like their comrades if they were few. It was all about time now. He did not fear for his own life, but he worried about Miri. If he were to falter now, this far into his attack, her life would be forfeit. He could not bear for that to happen. So he worked his way cautiously, killing when necessary but searching for his love because it was his highest priority.

The Pillar was constructed like a military complex. A warren of corridors and passages, cells and barracks, with a few places for the commanding officers to recline and have drinks. Finally, he came upon a cell deep within the confines of the Pillar, from which the sounds of voices could be heard. He also noticed the lock on the cell door was fresh and rust free, unlike the old and crusted brown locks of many of the previous cells he had visited. This cell still stank of old refuse, but mingled with it was the smell of unwashed bodies. The living inhabited this prison cell, instead of just the memories of the previous victims who haunted the rest of this terrible place. He broke the lock with one massive blow from the hilt of his dagger. Ell took a deep breath, said a prayer, and opened the cell door.

Chapter Twenty-Four

The cell was dark, like the rest of the Pillar. It was dank, smelling of unwashed bodies. Some of those bodies no doubt were the people huddled in the far corner. However, Ell knew the smell had also built up. It was the residue of over a decade's worth of slaves being held captive in this holding cell before being transported to the human camps or to Dark Harbor for their life long sentence of enslavement. It sickened him. It was like all the filth of the last two decades since the fall of Verdantihya had accumulated here. The smell of fear and human waste was prevalent. It was a miniature hell, constructed for the victims of the slavers and the humans. Ell wanted to tear the entire room apart. No, he wanted to tear the whole structure from its hinges and then cast it into a faraway sea, never to be seen again. Could water calling enable him to do such a thing? Ell wasn't sure how much power he could summon with his ability; he only knew that the desire to rip this place apart was just a fancy. It would require far, far more strength than what was currently streaming through his joints and muscles.

She was in the corner, her hair bedraggled, her clothes torn and dirty. Ell hated the Departed for doing this to her. Miri looked up, disbelief on her face. Ell took a step forward. There was no light, but perhaps if he stepped closer she would be able to recognize him.

"Ell?" Miri's voice mirrored the disbelief on her face. "How is it possible?" Then fear shone from her eyes, small sparkles of terror in the depths of the dark cell. "You must go before they find you. I cannot bear the thought of you chained like us. There is no key nearby. You must go before they catch you." Her voice was frantic, and her logic clouded. He loved her for her worry on his behalf, but she wasn't thinking clearly, fear had clouded her mind. If he was here where no free member of the Highest had been before, then sound reason dictated there must be a reason.

"It's alright, Miri," He calmed her down with a hug, dropping to one knee in front of her. She clung to him tightly, still murmuring that he needed to be gone from there before they took him too. Ell breathed in her scent. Miri's personal aroma was mixed with the sweat, grime, and refuse caked onto the walls and floor of this cell over its years of use, but it was still her. Beneath all of those other smells, Ell could still smell the scent that belonged totally and completely to Miri. He let himself suck in air through his nose, sifting out the bad smells and letting only her aroma assail his nostrils for a moment longer, then he released her.

"Pull your hands back and expose the chain," Ell commanded urgently. Miri did as he said.

"How do you propose to free us, Ell," she questioned in confusion. "The chain is inches thick and made of steel."

With one hammer blow from the hilt of his knife, he shattered the bonds, which held her hand completely.

"Oh." Miri said startled at his strength and looking at Ell in a new light.

Quickly he worked his way to the other elves who were similarly shackled. One chain link for each elf, meant only one wrist was chained. It made Ell's work quick and simple. With his ability-enhanced strength, Ell crushed the shackles one by one, freeing four other would-be slaves. Two of the Highest Ell recognized from Miri's village, however, the other two were strangers and had looked to be in the cell for quite some time.

The two strangers had even dirtier, grimier skin and clothes than the others, and their faces showed the marks of persistent beatings at the hands of their jailors.

"Who are you?" Ell questioned roughly. Then changing his mind he spoke again, "Never mind that. There's no time for questions now. We must be going!" He grabbed Miri by the hand and led her toward the cell door. Miri made comments about who he was to the others as she walked. The other elves followed him eagerly into the shadowed corridors of the interior of the Pillar. The hallways were dimly lit with torchlight. However, the torches were hung from the walls at far enough distances apart, that shadows stretched long and dark in between them. They were not nearly so quiet a group exiting the interior of the building as Ell had been while entering it alone. Tired, stiff legs from the captives shuffled slightly as they walked. No doubt, they had been run hard, underfed, and generally maltreated by their captors up to this point. Also, their shackles had been split, but the cuffs around their wrists still had a link or two attached that would clink together at times. Speed would be their ally. Getting out of here alive was going to be more difficult than Ell had imagined. He had only thought of the difficulties of reaching the top of the Pillar, which indeed were troublesome. However, he had woefully abandoned his planning of any type of exit strategy.

Follow the torches. The brighter and closer together they are, the more used those passages. Ell focused on getting them out. Although his instincts shrieked at him to stay in the dark and avoid those very well lit passages he was beginning to take, logic told him he would need to do just that in order to find his way out of this maze of corridors. They had to reach the stairwell leading down, and to do so it would necessitate they enter the well-used areas of the Pillar.

Voices, angry and coarse, sounded from a nearby passage. Ell pressed his followers against the wall and ensconced them in shadows as best he could while he peeked his head around the corner to take a look. Three Departed warriors were coming their way. They would be on them in a matter of moments. Ell ducked his head back to his hallway and spoke to Miri.

"Three Departed. I'll take care of them. Don't worry about me. Just keep the others out of my way." He indicated the four other would-be slaves. Two were female, and although they looked competent, they did not have the look of a fighter about them as his sister, Rihya, did. The other two were males, but one was young and the other elderly. Ell had a feeling that right now he would operate best alone.

"Are you certain?" Miri asked him, fear showing in her eyes. "I could try and help if you gave me a knife."

Ell flashed her a smile filled with bravado. "Trust me. Things are a little… different now. I can more than handle these three." He could tell her about his ability as a Water Caller later. Now was not the time for explanations.

His confidence seemed to reassure Miri and she smiled, a bit wanly, but still it was the first look of hope he had seen on her face. *That's it, love. Believe. We are going to get through this.*

Ell heard the dark elves about to approach from around the corner and turned to ambush them. The element of surprise was hardly necessary with his limbs strengthened as they were by his power as a Water Caller, yet old habits died hard. Ambush was always preferred to a frontal attack.

He gripped his blades tightly and leaped around the corner in a somersault. As he rolled between two of the three Departed soldiers, he slashed viciously at their legs and heard their desired screams of agony. In a flash, he was on his feet. The third, unwounded dark elf was large and he swung an axe at Ell. Ell ducked the swing and the axe crashed into the stonewall, chips of rock and sparks spraying everywhere from the impact. Ell feinted one way, watching the big Departed shift his balance as he tried to adjust to Ell's movement, but then Ell darted back the other way and in close. With a powerful thrust, he rammed his belt knife into the elf's thigh, and then with a quick flick of his wrist sent the tip of his long, dueling dagger up the front of the dark elf's bare stomach. Blood fountained out of his abdomen and the elf dropped his axe, hands attempting to keep his entrails inside his body. The dark, leather vest the elf wore over his bare torso quickly soaked with blood from the gushing wound. The elf was too stunned to even scream.

The other two Departed, hobbled towards Ell, already wounded from his initial assault. The look of fear in their eyes as they walked toward what would surely be their death was a satisfying sight to Ell. He liked to feel like the predator instead of the hunted. After so many years of fighting from the shadows and then running away, after years spent trying to stem the flood of slaves being harvested from his wounded homeland, it felt right to be the aggressor now.

In response to his emotions, Ell sprinted at the two, dodging swipes of their blades and ending with his dagger and belt knife planted in the two chests of the Departed. Ell yanked his blades free and watched as the bodies dropped to the floor.

Miri poked her head around the corner and upon realizing Ell had cleared the way for them, brought the rest of their party around. Six Highest were going to escape from a Pillar tonight, Ell told himself determinedly. For the first time in history, it would happen.

"Quickly," Ell motioned Miri and the others to follow him as he turned and moved decisively in the direction from which the Departed had been coming. They followed him. They trusted him to rescue them. The responsibility was a new weight on his shoulders, but with his ability to fuel him tonight, he found himself welcoming it. *Tonight at least*, he thought. *I don't mind it as long as I am a Water Caller*. But tomorrow would be different, who knew if he would be able to even touch his power tomorrow?

Blood dripped from the tips of his blades. He had not had time to clean them after the last skirmish. Continually they worked their way deeper into the common areas of the Pillar. They must be near the headquarters by now. Twice more Ell had to dispatch groups of Departed warriors. First, it was a pair of hulking, mace wielding brutes that fell to Ell's ability-enhanced speed and agility. Next, it was a group of four more Departed. The second group tested his limits as he found himself beginning to grow tired. He was still much stronger and faster than he would have been in a normal fight, but it was almost as if Ell could already feel the effects of his power draining him, a foresight into what was to come. Each time he had accessed his ability as a Water Caller, he had ended the experience completely exhausted. This time he had been using his ability for far longer than the past experiences. Ell was almost afraid to let go, worried that the wave of fatigue would fell him like a storm of arrows. He couldn't afford for it to happen until long after they had escaped this death trap. Ell clung to his ability for dear life. It fueled him now, but the exhaustion was waiting, lurking on the fringes of his consciousness. He fought to stave it off.

Other than the two groups of dark elves who he had fought, they encountered no others, instead hiding in the shadows or slipping into side passages until the danger had been averted for the moment. There were still many Departed roaming the halls and corridors of the Pillar, but not as many as Ell had anticipated.

"Where are all the rest?" Ell questioned Miri as they moved ever farther into the well-used passages. They had to be nearing the entrance to the lone stairwell down. It was bound to be guarded, but Ell would deal with that when the time came.

Miri quirked her head at him in response to his question. "Where are the rest of whom?"

"The other Departed," Ell answered, keeping his eyes focused on the way ahead and his ears peeled for any sound of pursuit from behind. So far, they'd had tremendous fortune to encounter so few of the enemy's soldiers. "I was expecting more than this."

Miri understood now and her face dropped. "They've gone north," she said sorrowfully. "Borian has betrayed us. They will no doubt tattoo the red tears of a traitor on him after they complete their mission." She saw Ell's confusion. "He was captured with us as we were returning to Little Vale from Verdantihya with a fresh supply of Source Water."

Ell shook his head in disgust as he continued to lead the rest of them onwards. Borian, the young hunter from Miri's village, was despicable. Traitors were the worst type of coward. It was one thing to run from battle, but it was an entirely different sort of gutless elf that succumbed to fear and betrayed his entire people to a race of diabolical slavers.

"I'll kill him," Ell grunted angrily. "What did he offer them?"

Miri shook her head again sadly, as she limped along beside Ell, her old wound making it look as if she had suffered some sort of injury in the skirmishes of the past quarter hour.

"He is guiding a host of Departed to Little Vale, to our home." Against her will, a tear trailed its way through the grime on her face. She wiped it away with a half frustrated, half sorrowful look on her face. "Some sort of special traitor was leading them. I think it was *him*." She looked at Ell meaningfully.

"*The* traitor? Silverfist?"

Miri nodded. Ell clenched his fists around the handles of his weapons in frustration. If only he had dealt with Silverfist during the ambush. His family should have pursued The Traitor afterwards, instead of letting him escape. If they had, this might never have happened.

They kept moving. The rest of the elves, apart from Miri and Ell, seemed too traumatized to speak. The young and elderly male elves simply followed the orders Ell gave them, while the two women from Miri's valley cried despairingly as they followed him, as if they could not bring themselves to shed the terror of the experience and allow themselves to hope just yet. Ell understood. Nobody escaped a Pillar once caught. *Well, they would be the first.*

Finally, Ell peeked around a corner and saw a trap door that was guarded by two Departed. It was set in the center of a circular chamber. Ell estimated that they had to be near the center of the structure by this point and it made sense that the trap door might lead to the way out. Especially since it was being guarded.

Ell strode silently into the room and as soon as the two guards registered there was an intruder, he flung one blade and then the next at the two Departed. The first blade, his dueling dagger, stuck into one of the dark elves tan, bare shoulder, open to the air from the elf's sleeveless, leather vest. The second blade, his belt knife, flew more true. It blossomed from the throat of the second guard, who sank slowly to the stone chamber floor. The surviving Departed, pulled a horn to its lips and sounded an alarm, much as the dying Departed had done on the outer platform when Ell had first landed and fought the mob of warriors.

After blowing his horn, the Departed growled and charged furiously at Ell, flashing his filed teeth in a grimace. This dark elf was wounded, but he looked dangerous nonetheless. He wielded a sword and had a small round shield for protection. He was quick and agile, but not as quick as a Water Caller. He rushed Ell and thrust with his sword. Ell leaned sideways to avoid the point of the sword as it rushed past his side and then grasped his enemy's sword arm, pinning it to Ell's own side. With his other arm, Ell then brought the sole of his free hand down hard upon the elbow joint, breaking the bone. The Departed grunted in pain, but kept his wits and managed to bash Ell in the face with the small shield. The room darkened slightly. Ell stepped back, shaking his head and trying to clear it from the speckles of light and the darkening edges of his vision, which threatened to overwhelm his consciousness. Apparently, his ability, at least right now, did not actually enhance your health. The blow to his face had him reeling. However, Ell shook it off as best he could. He was forced to do so because the Departed dropped his shield pulled a dagger of his own from a sheath at his hip and came at Ell again. This time Ell focused, determined not to underestimate the dark elf. He watched warily, and as the dark elf slashed at his face with the dagger, he slipped to the side and then slunk in close to the injured Departed. Quick as a snake striking, Ell yanked his own dueling dagger, still embedded in the dark elf's injured shoulder, free from where it had been since his initial cast, and then plunged it into the elf's side.

Black blood fountained out of the elf's side, completely covering Ell's weapon and hand. Black blood. Elves did not usually have that color blood. Only Ghouls.

"You're still dead," the Departed gurgled as he died. "Won't matter that you've killed me. Won't matter... at... all." He paused to breathe, air filling his lungs in a labored fashion. Up close, his eyes were slightly glazed. Maybe it was death Ell saw in them, but either way, it reminded him of the sick Departed he had slain and then set on fire the last time he had raided with his family. Something was off about this elf. The elf continued, speaking his last words. "You'll never escape." Then he died.

Ell dropped him to the floor unceremoniously. His head ached fiercely from the elf's blow. Ell retrieved his weapons.

"Come on," he spoke to the others as they filed into the room after him. Ell made his way to the trap door. It was big. Big enough that it probably would have required a number of the southern, elven soldiers to lift it. Yet, tonight at least, Ell was a Water Caller. And that meant it was not difficult to pull it open. It was iron, and it clanged to the floor as he let it drop after jerking it wide open. No doubt, the Departed he had just killed had meant that there would be pursuit by his fellow dark elves. After all, he had blown his horn. Ell and his companions had little time to waste.

It was dark beneath them, with a single rope ladder descending into the dimness, and wide enough for only one person to climb at a time. It appeared that the architects of these Pillars had designed them to be steadfast in defense, stalwart fortresses in lands that were only marginally under their control. All of the Lower Forest was still in contention. True, the slavers and humans had greater access to it, and the Highest did not spend much of their time living there these days, but the elves who resisted, the ones fighting and raiding like Ell and his family, they lurked in the shadows of the Lower Forest, behind every rock and in the limbs of every tree. They were losing the war. There was no way around the fact. But they were making their enemies pay in blood each step of the way. The fact that the architects of these Pillars had created them to be so impregnable, was in a way a backwards compliment to the resistance of the Highest. It told them their enemies feared them. Ell took a measure of pride in a truth even as small as that, as he led his small, rag-tag band of escapees downwards.

Ell climbed down the ladder carefully, it was dark below, and he assumed that whoever used the ladder normally had someone with a torch above and a torch below to light the way.

"I remember coming up this way," the young boy finally seemed to break out of his shock and speak. Or perhaps he hadn't, because when Ell glanced upwards at him, the young elf's eyes still carried that glazed look of disbelief. "I screamed as they brought me upwards. I fought. I kicked. But they were so strong. And their teeth were so sharp." He was rambling now, and as Ell and his company reached the small landing at the bottom of the ladder, the elder elf, the other one who seemed to have been held longer in captivity than Miri and her female companions from Little Vale, placed a hand comfortingly on the young elf's shoulder. Perhaps they were family. Was the elder one the boy's father? Or maybe it was just a protective bond created, the elder feeling responsible and caring for the younger. Either way, Ell was glad to see it. It seemed the elves he was leading were finally beginning to shake the stupor and shock of being held by their enemies. When he had first entered their cell he had been worried they would slow him down, make it more difficult for him to rescue Miri. Their reactions had been sluggish, and their expressions vacant, as if they had blocked out the terrible ordeal as best they could by shutting down their emotions. It seemed they were finally coming out of their traumatized condition.

Ell put his finger to his lips and quieted the boy gently, then motioned them to follow again. He wanted to hold Miri's hand, keep her by his side, never let her go again, but he couldn't. He needed his hands free to fight should the occasion arise, and he focused his wits and mind on the task at hand—to do the impossible, and escape from a Pillar.

The landing, to which the ladder had led them, was actually a small chamber. Darkness stretched above, since they didn't have a torch to light their way, but Ell's eyesight was keen as per one of the Highest, and in a moment his eyes had adjusted to the lack of light. He looked around. The small chamber was rough stone. Small and cramped. If an enemy made it this far, they would find themselves hard pressed to successfully break into the Pillar above as the ladder could no doubt be pulled up, and the intervening space was not close enough to reach. Defenders could easily fire arrows, throw spears, or pour any sort of nasty boiling concoctions down upon the heads of invaders. Assaulting a Pillar would be a grisly business. Ell supposed the rest of the descent to the base of the Pillar would look similar.

There was a door in the wall. Ell placed his ear against it, listening for any sound of soldiers on the far side. The horn call might not have penetrated down through this central core of the pillar, as the structure looked to be a cylinder with many chambers and passageways heading downwards. Sound wouldn't reach far when it came from above Ell suspected. He also doubted they'd had the presence of mind to send someone down to warn them. The danger had been above on the platform, at the top of the Pillar and in the barracks and cells, not down here in these dank, dim, narrow passageways leading to the outside and freedom. At least he hoped that was the case. Ell did not relish the idea of fighting his way through each chamber.

"Do you hear anything?" Miri whispered nervously. She seemed the only one who was thinking clearly, like a normal person, albeit a slightly more anxious one. Ell didn't know why she was the only one who seemed to have retained her wits and cognitive ability during imprisonment, but he was glad of it.

Ell shook his head. "No. But it doesn't mean there isn't anyone." He turned to whisper to her and to the other four elves he led. "I'll go through. Don't follow until I come back to get you." And with that he thrust open the door in a flash of ability-enhanced speed and entered the next chamber, leaving his followers behind.

Not knowing what to expect, Ell had his daggers out and ready in his hands. However, this chamber was indeed empty. It was another small, easily defensible position. There was a trapdoor in the floor with a few murder holes around it for pouring all kinds of hot liquids down on invaders. He pulled it open to investigate and looked down into the darkness below. Once again, an invader would experience difficulty in reaching this position, as it was also a rope ladder hanging down into darkness, one that could be hoisted up at the mere sign of danger. Ell was growing impressed with the Pillar's construction. He understood why his uncle had told him it was impossible to breach the defenses of a Pillar. Even a besieging army would not likely be able to assault it and prevail due to the series of close quarter, extremely defensible positions from the base of the Pillar to the top. Only an extended siege was likely to bring a Pillar to its knees. Well, that or a Water Caller who had ridden an Icari, Ell thought wryly to himself, still able to find a drop of humor in the circumstances. He returned through the door and motioned for Miri and the other captives to come.

"Safe for now," he murmured to them, "beyond the next chamber, however, I cannot say."

They followed him onwards, each of the former captives wearing their anxiety on their face. Their eyes darted to every corner of the room and there were startled jumps at every sound they heard. It was better than the vacant expressions they had worn earlier. At least worry was an emotion. However, Ell couldn't wait for this night to be over. It would be good once they were all free and he and Miri could rejoin his family.

Ell led the group onwards, ever downwards. They passed through three or four similar chambers with rope ladders hanging down. After the chambers with ladders, the following landings and chambers were often separated by a spiral staircase, clearly an effort by the builders to conserve space since the staircase was able to revolve upon itself as it twisted downwards. Twice along the way, Ell was forced to slaughter a handful of guards standing watch at their position. However, it became increasingly strange to him that there weren't more guards. Many of the landings looked to have been more commonly used, some even having torches burning in sconces on the wall, providing light. The torches gave enough light to see that many of the chambers were well used even though they now were empty. It was peculiar how there were so few of the Departed manning this Pillar. *Where are all the soldiers? Heading north with Silverfist?* It was a question to ponder later.

Every chamber was narrow, tight, and even those lit with torches felt dark somehow. Ell supposed it was the residue of what happened here, the death, the murders, and slavery, which managed to superimpose itself on his image of the Pillar. Darkness and evil had a way of clinging to a place, soiling it, tainting it for all time. Ell had a feeling that even if these Pillars were ever truly conquered and order restored to his homeland, they would never be free of the horrific scar that slavery left on a place.

"What was that?" Miri tugged on his sleeve, causing his hooded tunic, still damp from flying on the Icari through the storm, to cling to him in an unpleasant manner. Ell cursed for having lost concentration for a moment. Miri spoke again. "Did you hear it?"

Ell cocked his head and then nodded to Miri. The other elves looked on in concern, their faces clearly showing they were straining their own ears to catch any hint of whatever it was to which Miri's keen hearing had been alerted. Ell did hear. The sounds were distant, far above them, but they were there. Rough, harsh voices of the Departed, and they were growing closer, slowly but surely, moving downward. Someone above must have discovered the dead guards near the trap door at the top of the Pillar. Ell swore in frustration. The time for stealth was at an end. The enemy was most likely in front of them, but it was also certainly behind them.

"Slavers above," Ell said in answer to Miri's previous question. "There's no time now. We must be free of this maze of chambers before they catch up to us." Ell paused, appraising the architecture around them. They had been going down now, steadily for a while. They must be at least nearing the bottom of the central core of the Pillar. They must be close to the forest floor. He spoke to Miri, but let his gaze flicker to the rest of the company of escapees in order to include them.

"Speed is essential now. I don't know how many are above us, but once they realize we have found the exit point they will be hard in pursuit. Once we get free of this place we will have to out run them." *They would get free*, Ell promised himself. "I know you're all exhausted from your ordeal, but if there was ever a time to find strength buried deep within yourselves, now is that time." His stare was penetrating. A few of the elves shied away from it. He supposed his abnormal, cloudy eyes must look strange to the elves. His eyes always shifted in appearance when Ell was accessing his ability.

They all nodded their understanding. Ell led them forward and downward again. One more spiral staircase, and then a door to another chamber. Ell pressed his ear to the thick, oaken plank of a door dividing the two rooms. Departed voices sounded from beyond it.

"—Don't know what the ruckus is all about above," one voice was snarling in anger, "but it can't be good. Stay alert." The voice of the Departed on the other side of the door had the typical sound of one who was chewing their words as they spoke. Ell supposed it had something to do with the way many of them filed their teeth to points. Changing the structure of one's mouth and vocal instruments must somewhat alter the way a person spoke.

"Of course," another voice spat back from the next chamber, "what do you take me for, fresh meat straight from the capital's docks? I know my business." Ell thought idly about how nearly every Departed he had ever heard speak sounded angry. It was a strange cultural observance.

Not wasting another moment in contemplation, however, he burst through the door, kicking it down with a monstrous surge of force from his ability. Mist swam in the room around him as he drew deeply on his ability. Ell felt the room around him. Water, old and stale, sat in a few cups on a table in the corner. Sweat was on the brows of his startled enemies. And yes, there it was. Beyond a door on the opposite side of the chamber, Ell could feel the moisture, which could only be emanating from the outside air. Freedom lay close enough to lay hold of now. Ell drew upon all those sources of liquid, which he had just felt, sucking moisture from even the air on the other side of the door and spinning it through his body. He did it instinctively, still not understanding how he knew how to do it. Either way, it worked. Strength flooded his arms and legs. The cloudiness of his eyes, which had abated since less of his power had been required as they progressed downward through the inner core of the Pillar, returned in full. Ell let out a shriek of fury, a primal release of the energy inside his body and mind and leaped into action.

More than just the two voices he had heard speaking occupied the room. One dark elf raised a warning horn to his lips and blew a short, furious blast. Those horns were beginning to annoy him. Four other Departed turned to face Ell with their hands going straight to the handles of their weapons. They were well-conditioned warriors. Even an attack from within, from the interior of what should have been a place of safety for them, didn't slow their reactions. Snarling they strode forward to meet his attack, arraying themselves around him in a semi-circle.

Ell struck the point of the semi-circle, and one dark elf fell immediately to the blur of Ell's blades. Ell sheathed his daggers and grabbed the fallen elf's scimitar. It was massive, and slightly curved, dark iron, spotted with old blood. It should have felt heavy in his grasp, but it was light, extremely light. Ell relished his ability. He felt the strength of the land, of creation, flowing through his muscles and he swung the scimitar in a wicked arc, decapitating the soldier to his right, the head full of pointed teeth spinning off to the side in a bloody mess to slap the wall and then fall to the floor. The head left a sticky pool of dark, red-brown liquid on the floor.

The three remaining Departed advanced on him warily, yet relentlessly. He had to give them credit, they were determined if nothing else, and they met their deaths bravely. However, courage wasn't the only way you judged a person. Ell's enemies were often brave, it did not change the way he viewed them or the atrocities they committed in his land. Ell waited for their attack with an imposing silence, the scimitar held low and to the side, point toward the stone floor of the chamber, dark blood dripping to the ground. He was coiled to spring and the first to come within his range of movement would die. It was already settled.

One Departed feinted, hoping to draw Ell's attention while another attacked from the opposite side. Ell heard Miri gasp in fear as she watched him in combat. One Departed turned as if just realizing there were more people in the room than just Ell. Fearing for the safety of his love, Ell sprang into action. He would end this now, not wanting to gamble on the chance that one of the dark elves might focus his attention on the unarmed captives Ell had led to the base of the Pillar.

By taking just one step toward the elf who had looked at Miri, Ell was in range for a swipe of his long blade. It caught the Departed in the shoulder, biting deep, and the elf screamed in rage and pain, his attention back where Ell desired it. The three dark elves attacked at once and Ell moved with the silken grace of a lion on the plains. He thrust left under one arm in a sudden, surprising motion, and one elf died with a length of steel buried deeply in his gut. The Departed clattered to the ground and Ell left the scimitar planted in his dead enemy's stomach. The remaining two did not back down, but they seemed to know they would meet their deaths shortly.

Ell pulled his belt knife and flung the blade at one rushing attacker, felling him with a knife in the heart. The last Departed got in close and actually managed to slice Ell's arm as he attempted to dodge the elf's swing. The blade cut shallowly but painfully, yet Ell was able to ignore it. He slithered in close, and with ability-enhanced might, he grasped the Departed's throat and ripped.

The throat came free of the neck in a showery fountain of blood, spraying Ell's face and hair. He discarded his enemy's body and turned to the captives.

Miri had a look of horror on her face, and in a moment of clarity, Ell realized what a mess he must look. He hadn't just killed five Departed warriors; he had demolished them in a matter of moments, ripping the last one's throat from his body in a feat of supernatural strength. However, there was no time to worry about that now. Horns sounded from higher up in the Pillar in answer to the short blast by one of the fallen Departed from a few moments earlier, and shouts and curses from above told him they were being pursued in earnest.

Ell motioned once again for the others to follow and opened what was the final door to the outside world. It was an extremely narrow, defensible door in unison with the rest of the architecture of the Pillar. Defensible, rock solid, and built to repel an enemy. It was only wide enough for one person to fit through at once. Ell stepped out of it, onto a short lip on the outside of the building. The central core of the Pillar, which ran from the earth floor to the wide, table-like platform above, resembled nothing so much as a giant tower structure. Ell saw the wisdom in the building of this fortress. Not only did the series of chambers, separated by drop ladders and narrow spiral staircases, take up little room, allowing for thick, solid stonewalls able to repel any type of siege engines, but they also were tight quarters. One or two elves could hold many of the chambers for a long time, especially if they defended in rotations.

This last, or rather first, line of defense was just as good. Ell peered down at the forest floor nearly fifty feet below. Instead of stairs or a ladder leading up to the outside entrance of the Pillar, a drop cage with a rope pulley system was in place. There was no way up without the defenders lowering the cage down to the ground and allowing people entry to the fortress.

Fortunately for Ell and the escaped captives, the cage was already up and waiting. Miri and the other elves of the Highest looked out the narrow doorway, a cluster of heads protruding from the darkness beyond. It was almost dawn, and the landscape was just beginning to fill with the seeds of morning, grey light sending its early tendrils over the horizon.

"This is it. We're here," Ell declared. "All of you get in, quickly. I'll lower you down." Ell spoke through the haze of his ability. He had drawn deeply to fight the last five Departed, and at times, when he accessed his ability as a Water Caller in a more powerful fashion, it felt hard to stay in touch with his emotions, and in a way, with reality. He had to fight to think like himself, like Elliyar, instead of someone—*something* else. Ell wished Arendahl were around to answer his questions. Not that the old elf had really answered much in the first place, Ell thought wryly as the elves huddled into the cage to be lowered down, but any sort of aid at this point would be helpful.

Ell grasped the rope in one hand, then reached his other hand through the bars to grab Miri's hand and hold tight. "As soon as you touch down, lead the rest away as fast as you can. I'll climb down the rope and follow as soon as I have you safely on the earth below," he promised.

Miri pressed his hand, damp with the mist of his ability, to her face in a silent, desperate acceptance of his promise. She was dirty, ragged actually; her clothes in shambles, filth and grime caked to her skin from the days on the trail and then her time spent in such a horrible cell. Yet she was still beautiful. Hair bedraggled and fingers covered in the refuse of imprisonment, she was still the most striking elf he had ever been around. It wasn't strictly her looks. It was her manner, her bearing, as well. She was a blend of beauty and earthiness, grace and imperfection.

And she was almost free.

After days of torture at the thought of his love being a slave for the rest of her life, the simple thought that she might soon be safe and free was enough to send a jolt of elation through Ell's body. Free. There was no price on freedom.

Standing on the edge of the Pillar, Ell began lowering them down, at first gradually, but more swiftly as he gained confidence with the motions of the cage. He could hear the sound of pursuit not long behind them. By the sound of it, there were at least twenty Departed clamoring viciously as they made their way downward through the Pillar's core. The Pillar may have been nearly deserted in appearance as Ell had noticed, but there were still enough there to cause him and his escapees trouble.

Almost there. One last hand over hand. Finally, the cage touched the ground below and Miri opened the contraption. As promised, she began heading towards the forest proper. The Departed had clear-cut a space of maybe one hundred yards around the Pillar, enough to see any nearby enemies. Miri began making her way with the rest of the escapees towards the forest, her limp unmistakable. She glanced back once in worry at him standing resolute on the lip of the entrance to the Pillar fifty feet in the air.

Ell could hear the approach of the enemies behind him, and suddenly his ability began to fade. Out of nowhere, it felt as if his strength was leaving. His ability-enhanced reactions, senses, and might, were ebbing away like a receding tide. Ell could feel the difference. Even his thought was growing sluggish as he fought to stem the flood of exhaustion threatening to overwhelm his consciousness. He didn't know much about how to activate or control his ability, but even with little knowledge, he could tell he had pushed his power to the limits. He would not be able to hold onto the ability to water call much longer. That meant the Departed would kill him, or even if he ran they would chase him down, and the rest of the prisoners also. Miri would go back to that horror of a cell, which was unacceptable.

The voices were close. Ell saw a gleam of eyes peering down through the gloom of the Pillar's interior. Ell stood on the outside lip of the entrance looking through the chamber behind him. Departed warriors, dark elves with their flashing swords and teeth filed to points grinned in excitement as they finally saw their prey in sight. He couldn't fight them. Not with so many. Not with his ability draining from him like sand in an hourglass compounded with the exhaustion and fatigue to follow. The mist stopped its gradual swirling around him, ending the manner in which it had accompanied him for the last few hours since he had landed on the Pillar. Ell's eyes unclouded. His ability was almost completely gone now.

In a last desperate attempt to stave off the inevitable capture of his love, his Miri, should he fail to slow the Departed down, he did the only thing he could think of. With the last vestiges of his ability-enhanced speed, he drew his dagger and in one movement slashed the roped attached to the cage, disabling the pulley and contraption. Then he flung himself from the lip of the Pillar.

Ell clung desperately to his ability. He would need it to survive the landing. Everything seemed to slow down. Perhaps it was just his mind or the exhaustion setting in. Perhaps it was reality, he didn't know. Arrows released from the Departed warriors' short bows rained around him, one piercing the flesh of his arm near the shoulder and sticking as the barbed head hooked into his body. He screamed in pain, and he screamed in fright, as the ground loomed close.

Grasping around him for water, grasping at his ability with his mind, with his senses, with any way he could think of he tried to strengthen his body for the impact. Ell prayed, and then landed on the earth of the Lower Forest. As he struck the ground in a spray of soil, his ability vanished like a puff of smoke. It was gone completely and the exhaustion he had fought to stave off tumbled over him like a wave crashing on a rocky, windswept coastline.

As his ability left him, so did his strength, and with it red-hot agony shot through him. Flames of pain licked up his arms from a shallow cut sustained in the fight above, to the arrow now buried deeply in his shoulder, the barb gripping flesh and tearing as he moved.

Ell climbed unsteadily to his feet, gritting his teeth in pain. Arrows landed around him from above and he stumbled towards the safety of the forest. Through the fog of pain and fatigue, he knew he had accomplished his aims. The Departed wouldn't have water-calling abilities, to allow them to survive the jump from the entrance. They would have to replace the rope to climb down. It might not take them long, but Ell knew it would buy himself and the other escapees enough time to gain a head start. It had to, otherwise it was all for nothing.

Miri screamed his name in fear and he saw her limping gait as she sprinted his way and reached him. One arm under his shoulder she helped him move a little faster towards the safety of the woods, away from the clear-cut and the rain of arrows.

"Miri," he gasped, tired beyond belief. He tried to tell her to go, to leave him that he would follow. But he was too tired to even finish his train of thought. Blackness crowded the edges of his vision, and Ell prayed he would not lose consciousness like he had after the ambush of Silverfist in the north. They had to keep moving, they had to escape.

Ell could hear the shouts of the angry Departed from above. They would no doubt, be already working on a solution. He could hear Miri trying to get his attention, trying to say something to him or get him to answer some question, but it took all his focus, all his remaining energy just to remain conscious.

They half walked, half ran, stumbling north through the forest. The other escaped prisoners, took turns helping him move and keep up, as Miri was not strong enough to do it alone. After a time, horns sounded from behind. Through the haziness in his brain, Ell realized that the Departed must have reached the ground and would now be in hot pursuit. *All for nothing,* he thought vaguely. *I did the impossible. I rode an Icari, I stormed a Pillar singlehandedly, and fought my way out, but it was all for nothing.* They were going to be captured again. They would return to prison, to slavery, and there was nothing he could do to counteract their capture. His limbs felt numb. His mind was nearly blank. It was hard to summon even emotions through the exhaustion.

They struggled on for a time, the horns growing louder behind them. Then, piercing the darkness enshrouding his mind, a familiar voice spoke.

"What's wrong with him? Is he injured?"

"Yes," it was Miri's voice in answer, "but I don't think his wound is the problem. It's almost like he is... too tired to stay awake, although I don't understand why that is, since he hasn't had time to lose enough blood for that to be the case."

The quiet, calm, assured voice spoke again, "I will explain it later. Hurry, we must find a defensible position, the best we can manage. You will all have to fight." The voice was determined. Ell knew the voice, finally recognizing it even as he lost consciousness.

Dacunda.

Chapter Twenty-Five

Somebody was slapping his face. "Wake up!" The voice was urgent. "Wake up, Ell!" *Rihya.*

Ell came to groggily. He glanced around not fully understanding what was going on. The arrow was gone from his arm, and he was vaguely aware of the fact that he had not been conscious for its removal. The wound was already closing, faster than normal, indicating at least a few drops of Source Water had been sprinkled over the wound.

"Drink," his sister's voice was urgent again. "Source Water will help with the exhaustion. At least I hope," she added under her breath. She held the flask of water to his lips and Ell let a mouthful, then two gulps, flow down his parched throat. He hadn't realized how thirsty he was after the past night's exertions. His head cleared immediately after drinking the restorative Source Water. The fuzziness left his thinking. Miri sat next to him, clutching what had been his limp hand worriedly. He squeezed hers reassuringly.

"One more sip, sister," he asked for another mouthful from her. Leaning forward towards his sister, he grasped the flask from her. She was crouched on her heels and watched him intently.

"Just one more," she warned him. "We must save the rest for after the battle. It will be needed."

"Battle?" Apparently, his head was still foggier than he realized since he wasn't aware of an upcoming battle.

She snorted, finding humor even in a dire moment. "Yes, you numbskull. Or don't you remember bringing the entire Pillar down upon us in pursuit like a swarm of hornets leaving the nest?"

The Pillar. Miri. The rescued slaves. He remembered now. Ell nodded. Yes, he remembered indeed. All the dead, all the dying Departed from the night before. He remembered the feeling of victory, the exultation in destroying his enemies. He was still glad of the outcome, for saving Miri's life, yet the pure enjoyment of the massacres the night before at the top platform of the Pillar made him slightly sick to his stomach. He hated the Departed. He would kill them gladly, but last night he had butchered them. It hardly seemed fair, considering he had been tapping his ability as a Water Caller.

"Yes," he murmured. "Of course, I remember." The strength slowly reentered his limbs. He was not revitalized, not by a long ways. He felt like he had run for two days straight without a night's sleep. However, it was a far cry short of the exhaustion he had felt upon leaping from the Pillar's entrance when his abilities had abandoned him.

Dacunda approached. "He's awake." It was a statement more than a question.

"How long was I out for, Uncle?"

"Minutes." The response surprised Ell. Part of him was relieved it had not been longer, the other part of him wanted to slip back into restful oblivion. *No!* Ell rejected the thought. Rest was certain death. A horn call pierced the still morning air, dulled by the fog that hung low. It was thin fog, not enough to fully obscure one's vision, just enough to make the entire world appear as if seen though a grey lens.

Dacunda peered at him, hopefulness painting a strange picture on his usually solemn, serious face. "Can you access your abilities?"

Ell reached out silently in answer. He stretched his consciousness out. Nothing. Crestfallen he was forced to shake his head in a negative response to his uncle, shame flaming his face crimson. Miri clasped his hand tightly. Somehow, she understood his frustration, even though she knew nothing of his ability or his struggles to control it. He fell in love with her in that moment all over again. His uncle wore a look of disappointment, but not condemnation.

"Well, at least you can still hold a bow." Dacunda extended Ell's black yew bow to him. The long bow felt firm and right as it met Ell's callused hands. Ell groaned as he pushed himself to his feet. "Stay in the back for now, as a marksman. I don't want you engaging in combat unless it's absolutely necessary. You look like you've spent a week drinking honey mead with a Wood Ogre and fighting all of its cousins." Ell grunted in wry laughter at the illustration. Dacunda smiled then and clapped him on his unwounded shoulder. "Good to have you back, Elliyar. You've managed to stir up a hornets nest yet again, but I'm so astounded you actually managed to do it that I can't even bring myself to be angry." He paused and shook his head in disbelief. "If we survive the next hour, you will have to tell me the story in full detail." Ell nodded his agreement, and Dacunda turned to walk away and ready the rest of them for the confrontation. Dacunda looked at Rihya at the last moment, "Oh, and patch up that shoulder of his already, would you niece?"

Rihya tossed her head and snorted in mock disgust. "That's what I was doing when you interrupted. Get on with you." Ell's uncle strode away, grinning despite the grim hour at hand.

Rihya bandaged the wound in his shoulder as Ell stood patiently, wincing slightly as she bound it up. "We'll have to stitch it later, Ell. There's no time now."

Ell grunted his assent. One more scar, more or less, wouldn't change much about his looks.

"How did you manage it?" Rihya whispered in genuine amazement. It was spoken almost to herself as if she was afraid to ask him how he had reached the top of a Pillar and freed slaves, afraid of what his answer might be.

He stared at her long, intently. "Later, Rihya," he said fondly but firmly. "Let's focus on the matter at hand." She nodded, flourishing her knives flamboyantly, ever seeking attention. He smiled as she walked away following his uncle.

Ell turned to Miri as he surveyed where they were. Dacunda had chosen as defensible a location as possible. It was a tight copse of trees in the middle of the Lower Forest. The Lower Forest was more spacious and less of a tangle of bushes, trees, and creepers as Legendwood was to the north. This copse was on a slight rise. Someone, probably Ryder and Dahranian, had dug up some boulders from the surrounding hillside to place between the trees on the outskirts of the copse to provide a slight bulwark between them and the enemy. It was a measly defensive wall, but Ell had to admit it was better than nothing. At the very least, it would provide some minimal cover from which to loose arrows as the enemy approached. From the sound of the horns and the Departed shouts, the time of arrival would be very soon indeed.

"I want you to stay back," he cautioned Miri, "let those of us who know what we're doing do most of the fighting." He spoke with a mixture of confident command and the pleading of a worried lover.

Miri gazed at him adoringly. He could see the love in her eyes. He could also see the inability to agree to his request in her eyes, as well.

"I can't, Ell. Your uncle spoke to us. Dahranian scouted back quickly and saw what we're facing." She paused, slightly fearful but determined to show courage. "There's at least thirty Departed coming. If we don't all fight, none of us will make it. All of your efforts last night will be for nothing. I won't allow that," a steel entered her voice.

Ell sighed. He knew the truth. Ell's family—Dacunda, his boys, and Rihya were the only four seasoned warriors. Add Ell, an exhausted, hobbled veteran, and then five other of the Highest fresh from captivity and likely not experienced fighters, such as the Departed were, and he understood that even if fortune did shine upon them most brightly this day, they would still be lucky to survive the battle.

“Alright, Miri,” he condoned, “but please, be careful.” He grasped her hand. “I cannot lose you again.” They shared a glance then joined the others at the ring of trees and uprooted boulders at the edge of the copse.

Dahranian and Dacunda stood in their familiar silent, resolute stances, their hands on the pommels of their swords, which were already drawn and upside down, placed tip deep into the moist soil. Ryder was beside them, swinging his arms, stretching, and loosening up.

Ryder turned to look at Ell as he heard them approach from behind. “About time you woke up. I was worried you were going to miss all the fun.” He grinned mischievously. “We haven’t faced odds this poor for quite a while. It’s about time we had a last stand. I was beginning to think we weren’t taking enough risks anymore.” Ell loved the way his cousin could bring levity to a moment of utter despair. As if to punctuate Ryder’s sentence, the Departed came loping into sight, weaving their way through the trees of the Lower Forest in a loose formation. Ell smiled tightly in response to his cousin.

Rihya twirled her knives idly as if the thirty approaching, bloodthirsty, dark elves were the least of her concerns. Only the four strangers seemed to show their nerves. The two female Highest, Miri’s companions from the valley, had been given spears. Ell prayed they would survive. The male elves, one too young to have had much training and the other past his prime, held a sword and an axe between them. Dacunda had distributed the assortment of weapons from their packs to the new arrivals.

The Departed saw them, bellowed ferociously, and began sprinting, their speed allowing them to cover the remaining yards in an intimidating manner. The battle would soon be upon them. As one, Ell and his family members unslung their bows and in a fluid motion had arrows knocked, sighted, and then loosed onto the oncoming hoard of dark elves.

Ell’s arrow flew true. It struck one Departed in the shoulder, dropping him to the ground. The elf groaned in pain and rage and then yanked himself back to his feet, continuing to stagger on. Ell and his family fired arrow after arrow for the next half-minute, bringing down perhaps eight of the attackers and wounding two more. Odds were still against them.

The dark elves rushed up the hillside to meet the Highest in the copse of trees, their faces leering with anticipated victory in the confrontation to come. Dacunda, Dahranian, and Ryder hopped lithely over the edge of the boulders, forming a rough wall around the belabored northern elves and met their foes with ferocity.

“Stay behind the walls!” Dacunda shouted back to Ell and the rest of them. It was agony to watch his family fighting without him in the mass of Departed coming up the hill. Yet Ell knew in such an exhausted state, he wouldn’t last minutes in the sea of dark elves. He was still too weak and tired. Instead, he continued to fire arrows, trying to pick off Departed who were attempting to close in behind his family members. Or, rather, he did until the Departed gained the hill and spilt their forces. Half of the Departed continued to fight Dacunda and the others while the other half of the remaining enemy forces headed towards Ell, Miri, and their new companions who were attempting to hold behind their flimsy fortifications.

Ell was forced to bring his bow to aim against foes who were nearer and posing a more immediate threat to him and his love. He would have to trust his family to take care of themselves.

The older elf who had escaped with Miri and Ell was doing his best to swing his axe against two attackers who were scrambling over the boulder to Ell's right. The young elf, was also attempting to help defend. Their efforts were next to useless. They were clearly not trained in the arts of war. The older elf did manage to wound one of the Departed, burying his axe in the dark elf's leg, slowing it enough for Ell to feather his neck with an arrow. However, the other Departed swiftly followed his downed companion, bloodlust showing in his eyes. He kicked the young elf in the face, and then promptly decapitated the older elf who Ell had just rescued from slavery, sending him to his grave.

Frustration welled up in Ell, anger at the fact that the elf had tasted freedom, regained his liberty for only a matter of hours before it was robbed from him by death. Ell fired an arrow at the dark elf who had just killed Ell's newest companion and the shaft buried itself in the Departed's shoulder. The elf spun away from Ell and his deadly bow, taking cover behind a tree in the copse. Ell glanced around him, appraising the battle. The two female elves from Miri's valley were hard pressed by a lone Departed. They had managed to kill one dark elf between them. The dead one had been small. The other, however, was smiling viciously as it toyed with them, dancing one way and then the other, avoiding the tips of their spears with agile grace, and inflicting a score of slashes and cuts upon their arms and faces. If they survived the battle, they would not leave this copse of trees without scars. Ell fired an arrow at the Departed and missed. It was enough to send him into retreat for the moment, however.

Every bow pull and release was agony to Ell's aching muscles. The fog in his brain, briefly banished by the drink of Source Water, was fast threatening to return. He willed himself to stay alert, keep vigilant. Miri, determined to do her part in the fight, was somehow holding her own against a Departed warrior. By sheer luck, she hadn't been killed yet. Ell, in a ferocious burst of energy he didn't know he possessed, lunged forward, tackling the dark elf. He pulled a belt knife and brutally rammed it into the Departed's eye, sending brain and blood everywhere. This Departed bled black like the dark elf at the first trap door on top of the Pillar. Ell didn't know what it meant.

Curses and screams tore through the morning air, the typical sounds of battle. Ell gazed about him. Dahranian disemboweled a Departed warrior, but sustained a slash to the shoulder and switched his blade to his off hand. Another Departed died at his blade, even though the wound had noticeably slowed Dahranian. Dacunda fought valiantly, fending one Departed off to his left and another to his right, blade clanging against blade, steel meeting steel, to send flashes of sparks into the dawn. He felled one with a thrust to the leg, not a mortal wound, but an incapacitating one. He focused his attention on the remaining foe and went on the offensive. The Departed swung wildly to fend off Ell's uncle, but silently and deadly, Rihya slipped up behind the dark elf and hamstrung him with one of her knives. Then she effectively sawed through his windpipe as he fell to the ground in a cry of anguish. The cry was cut short as she accomplished her goal.

Of all of them, Ryder seemed the only one unconcerned by the enemy. He swung two long handled axes as if they were light as feathers. He must have picked up the second from a dead enemy. He wielded them accurately and with swift agility, yet with the power and strength only he possessed. Enemies came and fell, wounded or dead around him. The Departed swarmed nearer, sensing him as a major threat, finally beginning to overwhelm him with their numbers. Ell was forced to return his gaze to the forefront of his vision as a few of the Departed closed in around the copse of trees to get closer to the defenders. He wished he could send a shaft or two to help Ryder, but he could not take the time, instead having to send one arrow zipping through the air towards a Departed soldier who ducked and caused Ell's arrow to bury itself into the tree behind him. The soldier grinned wickedly and advanced. Ell's aim was growing poor with exhaustion.

Luckily, Dacunda and Rihya came to Ryder's aid, and Ell focused his attention on the warrior at hand. Miri beside him, he let the soldier come close, feigning exhaustion. Perhaps it wasn't entirely a ruse, the exhaustion was real after all, and it did not take much acting to make the Departed believe him to be easy meat. Just as the Departed warrior lunged for his throat, Ell sidestepped, just enough to dodge the blow. He swung around behind the soldier and plunged his blade into the back of the dark elf's neck, severing the spinal cord. His enemy dropped limply.

Just then, a blow hit him on the back of the head, and he fell hard to the ground. Someone must have snuck up from behind their defenses he thought fuzzily. Ell tried to shake his mind clear. He heard Miri scream in pain and fear. He managed to get to his hands and knees to see Miri in the clutches of an angry Departed soldier. She had managed to nick him with the knife she held, but not being a warrior, she had not been able to fend him off. He grasped her by the hair, tilting her head back and had a knife to her throat, ready to slash. The Departed began to do so slowly, as if he was taunting Miri with her imminent death. Blood trickled out from the shallow cut on the side of her neck, and the Departed began to draw his blade across even further. Blood began to flow freely and in a burst of rage and terror at seeing the love of his life meet her death, Ell's hand grasped desperately at the ground around him, and upon finding a fist-sized stone, he cast it at the Departed. It struck the Departed in the elbow, causing him to drop his knife as the stone hit the joint awkwardly.

His attention drawn off the girl for the moment and focused on Ell, the Departed dropped Miri. Ell staggered to his feet. He met the soldier's vicious attack weakly, barely able to fend off a dagger swing at his face. Miri lay gasping painfully for breath on the ground not far away, blood flowing much too freely from her neck. She might die yet. Anxiety gave Ell strength. He summoned the last vestiges of his might, willing his limbs, his muscles, to function and work as normal. He pulled his long, dueling dagger and met the Departed soldier's advance. Blade rang against blade. The soldier drove his fist into Ell's injured shoulder, nearly forcing Ell to his knees in agony. But Ell managed to stay on his feet, for a moment more, long enough to fend off another swing of the dagger, and then all energy gone, he tripped, stumbling weakly to the forest floor over a stone behind him. The Departed looked down upon him from his standing position with a black glee, the joy of murder written clearly on his face.

Then all of a sudden, a spear point emerged from his chest. He gurgled, punctured lungs sending bloody wheezes from his throat. The spear was ripped free, and was then again rammed into his back, this time to burst through his stomach. The dark elf died as painfully as he had intended for Ell to perish, and then crumpled to the floor. One of the female elves Ell had rescued stood where the Departed had been. Blood covered her face and ran down her spear and onto her hands. Ell sighed in relief, then nearly wept in frustration and sorrow as an arrow lodged itself in her neck, then another and another bristled from her chest. An enemy archer had begun taking aim. Normally, the Departed fought to capture if they could, but Ell must have spooked them with his prowess on the Pillar. They appeared to be taking no chances and no prisoners. Ell thanked the dead elf silently for saving his life and did his best to honor her sacrifice.

Ell scrambled through the chaos of the battle to reach Miri's side. He looked around as he did and saw everyone, everywhere, hard pressed to survive. Ryder fought three Departed, but had sustained a number of wounds.

Dahranian was limping badly, but was appearing to come to Ryder's assistance. Dacunda had an arrow shaft protruding from one shoulder, and was locked in combat with one Departed, another Departed waiting to take his companion's place should he fall. Rihya, her blades still flashing as she weaved her way in amongst the enemy, was wreaking havoc left and right, but a grimace of pain had replaced her usual look of focused excitement. A Departed cut her along the ribs with a swipe of his blade and she rolled to the side with a grunt of pain. It was madness all around.

The other female from Little Vale lay bloodied against a boulder, Ell wasn't sure if she was dead or alive. The young Highest, was still on the ground from the kick he had received earlier. Ell hoped he had just been rendered unconscious. Yet none of it mattered when compared to Miri wounded and bleeding out on the dirt in front of him. Ell grabbed the flask left behind by Rihya and hoped there was enough Source Water in it to save Miri. There had to be. Desperation fueled his efforts.

He reached her side. Miri was gurgling soundlessly in her own red blood. Her throat was not completely cut, but a good quarter of her neck had been slashed, a wound that started shallow and ended deeper as it went. Ell didn't think twice. He emptied what was left of the flask of Source Water on her throat and watched as the wound began to close up around itself. He poured enough that the cut was almost completely closed, pink flesh forming a fresh scar. Ell then shook the last few drops from the water skin into her mouth. Miri's eyes were still wide with shock, not registering that her wound was slowly healing. Ell prayed it would be enough to stave off death. He hoped against all hope that she had not bled too much before he reached her.

Ell looked around and finally the tide of the battle seemed to have turned. His family was bloodied and wounded but they were alive. The enemy was slowly being finished off, little by little. Eventually, what was left of the Departed soldiers, only a mere three were left, turned to run, but the second they tried to break away, Ell's family was in pursuit. *Finish the enemy off completely whenever you can. Leave no foe alive behind you*, Ell's uncle had always said. There was nothing for Ell to do but clutch Miri's hand and wait in exhaustion for his family to finish it. Thirty Departed warriors dead. Ell marveled at the accomplishment. His family members truly were a force with which to be reckoned. The victory had not come without a cost, however. The two female elves and the elderly Highest seemed to be dead. Ell still held out hope for the boy, but as of yet, he had not regained consciousness, which did not bode well. Not to mention the variety of wounds and injuries sustained by Ell's family. Yet, they were alive. They had won for now.

He hugged Miri close, whispering softly to her. He didn't even know what he whispered; he just let his voice flow out over his lips in whatever words came. He whispered of his love for her, that she would be all right. He told her they would make it back to her valley and he told her they would be Joined one day. One day soon, he hoped.

Finally his family came striding back, limping in pain, but gloriously alive. Ell saw blood dripping from his sister's side. Dacunda still had an arrow in his shoulder. Dahranian and Ryder both had a handful of cuts between then. Ell hoped they had enough Source Water to go around.

"She's not...?" Dacunda began to ask in weary sorrow as he saw Ell clutching the motionless form of Miri to his chest.

"No," Ell answered shaking his head. "I had enough Source Water to stave off the immediate fatality of her wound. Yet, I do not know how much more she needs to recover. I have none left." Ell tipped his flask bottom up to illustrate his complete lack of Source Water.

Dacunda, paying no heed to his own wounds, knelt down and freed a flask from his hip. He poured a mouthful of Source Water into her dry throat, forcing her to swallow. "There," he said seriously. "That should be enough." Ell looked at him gratefully but did not release Miri. Her breathing eased against his chest, as she seemed to fall into a wounded sleep.

The rest of them began checking the others. The three strangers of the Highest whom Ell had briefly rescued were indeed dead. However, the boy eventually awakened once he was shaken, only to cry pitifully over the elderly elf without a head.

"Was he your father or uncle?" Ell asked compassionately. The boy shook his head disconsolately.

"Well, who was he?" Ell asked.

"Don't really know," the boy sniveled. "I met him in the cell. But we were there for days, maybe even weeks. He... cared for me as best he could, kept my spirits up." The boy went back to crying over the elf. Ell let him mourn in peace.

Ell's family set about patching up wounds. Rihya had the most serious injury, a slice that ran deep into her side where a sword had bitten sharply. She writhed in pain as they stitched her up and poured a bit of Source Water over the wound. It was just enough Source Water to keep the most serious of injuries at bay, but they couldn't waste it. They only used enough to stem the wound and initiate healing, letting the body carry out the natural healing process on its own. They had to make their Source Water last.

Dahranian and Ryder refused attention until they had been able to extract the arrow from their father's shoulder and had administered the Source Water and the required stitches. Then they received treatment themselves. They had survived. Everyone who lived was in one piece, but Ell knew they were in terrible shape.

They sat there for a time, Ell cradling Miri in his lap, and the rest of them resting. Nobody had the energy to speak more than a few words. Ell supposed they were all just glad to be alive.

Finally, Miri awoke. Maybe an hour had passed since she had fallen unconscious.

"How are you feeling?" Ell asked in concern.

"I am not really sure," she croaked, her voice cracking in painful fashion. It would probably be days, maybe even weeks, before her vocal cords were back to normal.

Ell hugged her close. "I was so worried," he whispered fiercely. "Just rest now. Just rest. We aren't going anywhere for a while."

Miri struggled to sit up and look him in the eyes. She was weak but determined so he finally let her rise to her knees. "That's just the thing," she said, "we must go on. We must go *now*."

Ell looked at her in a nonverbal question. She answered, "Borian has led them north. They are going to Little Vale."

"Who is going?"

"A whole band of slavers. A large one. That is why there were so few guarding the Pillar, they had all started north." Miri was growing exhausted just by speaking, he could tell.

"Who is taking them north?" Ell asked, vaguely remembering her mentioning something about this topic as they were escaping last night. His memories were fogged by exhaustion and pain.

Miri responded. "Borian no doubt has the red tears tattooed on his face by now. He has turned traitor." Pain flashed across her face at the memory of the betrayal of her old friend. He had never been a friend to Ell. "He is leading *him* north to take the whole village captive."

"Him who? Who is Borian leading north?" Ell felt a morbid fascination. Something told him the answer would be important. He was right.

Miri responded, "Silverfist."

Chapter Twenty-Six

It was a damp day. The battle had been over for an hour. Ell was still resting with his arm around Miri, both of them really just catching their breath after the ordeal of the night before and the fight this morning.

"So explain to me," Ell continued their conversation from earlier, "what exactly happened? What is going on?"

Dacunda and the others gathered close to hear Miri's tale. She began softly, her voice reminiscent, as if the events she was retelling had taken place years ago instead of days or weeks. Ell supposed that even a short time spent in captivity could make a person feel farther removed from their past, make them feel as if more time had elapsed than what really had.

Miri ran a hand through her hair. "Elder Larsil cut his hand deeply, to the bone. He is very old, and we, in Little Vale, decided to give him a bit of Source Water to speed his recovery, make it less painful," she paused as if thinking of the decisions made by the village, their actions. "It was a good decision. The elder needed it. However, how could we know that shortly after using the Source Water on Elder Larsil that there would be another bad injury to one of our hunters, and then a sickness to hit half the village? Before we knew it, we were completely out of our supply of Source Water. It had to be replenished."

Ell nodded his understanding, as did Dacunda. The rest of them, the strange young boy Ell had freed included, sat quietly, patiently waiting for her to finish her tale.

"They decided to send a few of us. Myself," Miri pointed to her chest, "Elaris, and Semira," she indicated her deceased companions, lying cold on the damp soil of the Lower Forest after being killed in the attack, "and Borian." Ell could hear the note of anguish and also anger at Borian's still fresh betrayal.

"Go on," Dacunda said gently, as Miri stopped a moment to hold back the tears after mentioning her two dead female companions.

Miri nodded. "We were on our way to Verdantihya, to fill our flasks to the brim with Source Water, when we were ambushed by slavers. They must have known we were coming because they hit us hard and quickly. They were waiting for us."

Ryder spat at the mention of slavers. "Probably had scouts in the area and caught sight of you," he said. "They do like to stay vigilant for fresh captives."

Miri nodded again. She knew all that. "We were down before we knew what hit us. Ropes around our necks at the end of catch poles. Wrists bound. They led us south for days. We pushed hard, they were eager to get us to the Pillar. Once we reached the Pillar, they threw us in the cell and left us to rot for a few days. No food, no water, nothing."

Ell grabbed her hand and held it tightly, trying to silently reassure her through his close proximity, of his unspoken affection. She felt the pressure and squeezed back. Ell let her finish her story.

"A few days passed and then they came back. Threatened us, beat us." She pulled the hair back from her face again, and now Ell really looked, he could see the faint bruising around her eyes, impossible to have seen in the dim interior of the Pillar. Anger flared anew in his chest. Nobody had the right to touch her like that. Nobody.

Miri seemed eager to just finish the telling of events, to recount the story of her capture and move on. "Borian was frightened. He offered them information; he mentioned the village, our valley. We begged him not to say anything, not to disclose its location, but he didn't listen. They removed Borian from the cell, I heard them talking as they left the cell, telling him there might be a way out for him." She paused and covered her face with a hand. Ell forced himself to see it from her perspective. Borian and he had clashed, and Ell felt nothing but disdain for him, for any of the Highest who chose the route of betrayal and disgrace for their name. Yet Borian's decision did not exactly surprise him. He remembered the young hunter's temperament. It had not exactly been friendly, honorable, or even particularly moral. However, as much as Ell had disliked the elf, Borian had still been Miri's friend and companion for many years. The betrayal must cut Miri like a knife.

"When he returned, they had him prove his loyalty by killing another of the prisoners who was in the cell with us, another young man who had refused the same offer. Once he committed the murder, it was done; Borian had sealed himself to them."

"And so he is leading them north to the valley now, isn't he? It is his final act of betrayal, the end price for his freedom, and their allowing him to serve them." Dacunda spoke almost to himself as he finished the story for her. Miri nodded in response, affirming his guess.

Dacunda put his hands to his head. He was thinking hard, Ell could tell. Ell knew his uncle. Dacunda was trying to decide what to do with the information.

"Uncle," Ell spoke up, "we must do something." Ell felt an obligation to

Little Vale, to Miri's village. Not just because of Miri, but also because they had treated his family well. And when you looked at the basics of the decision process, it came down to the fact that they were northern elves. They were his people, even if it was ill advised for them to be staying so long in one location.

"We are wounded. Exhausted, Elliyar," his uncle retorted in frustration. "We are at least a day behind our enemies. Even if we push hard enough to reach the valley before the slavers, which," he held up his hands, "I am not sure is even possible considering our unrested state; we would reach it in no fit condition to fight." He paused to let his statement sink in. "I am not sure it is possible to save the village."

A tear rolled down Miri's cheek slowly. "Please. We must do something." Ell heard the begging note in her voice. It was her family, her village, which was now in danger. After about a week in captivity, she would want nothing more than to prevent the same fate from happening to those she loved most.

Ell's uncle gripped the handle of his sword so tightly his knuckles went white. Ell knew his uncle would do what he thought best, what he thought was right. Dacunda was not afraid. He never avoided a fight he thought was necessary or morally right. But he was also not one to be swayed deeply by his emotions, relying more on rational thought and logical process.

"Uncle," Ell said again. "We can do this. Two days ago you told me it was impossible to save Miri," Ell indicated his love sitting beside him on the cold, moist forest floor, "yet here she sits free. With your help, of course, we could not have survived without you." Ell admitted freely, "Still, she is free. Free."

Dacunda narrowed his eyes. "Yes, Elliyar, but at what cost?" Dacunda eyed the dead Highest and Ell's wounded family. Ell's Uncle continued, "And since we are on the subject, you still haven't told me how you accomplished that feat, Nephew." It was a half statement, half question.

"Time for explanations as we go north," Ell wasn't ready to abandon his argument that they should pursue the slavers. Now was the time to push his uncle, to get him to commit. His own tale could be recounted later as they ran. "And north we must go. We can do this. Uncle, we can save the village, I know it." Ell let his passion infuse his voice. Silverfist was leading the band of slavers. Ell wanted another chance at avenging his father's death.

"Elliyar, we do not even know how many Departed Silverfist is leading north. It may be a small army for all we know if he thinks to capture an entire valley's worth of elves." Dacunda was still resisting. Ell understood. His uncle's responses were logical. Yet Ell could feel deep inside of him, this was a battle they had to fight.

Ell shook his head. "We will not be able to live with ourselves if we avoid this fight."

His nephew's comment gave Dacunda pause. Ell knew he had struck a vein with his uncle. Dacunda thought everything through thoroughly. He was logical and rational much more often than emotional. Yet he did still take his emotions into account. If Ell could convince him that letting this moment go would be too much for his conscience to bear, then it would likely begin to outweigh the other arguments.

"I know you, Uncle, I know what moves you. If we do not at least attempt to protect the village, people who gave us shelter, rest, and peace, a valley where there are many of our people who will fall to the enemy, you will not be able to bear the memory."

Again Dacunda stopped to think after listening to Ell speak. "When did you become so persuasive?" Dacunda asked wryly. Then he held up his hands to show he was joking. "No, it's not that I disagree necessarily, Nephew, but this is big." Ell's uncle looked around at the whole family. "Even if we over take the slavers, we will most likely face longer odds than we did in battle today. And we barely survived this fight." Dacunda motioned around at the carnage of bodies lying bloody and untouched on the dirt and loam of the forest floor. The blood scented the air with a sickly smell, and it assailed their nostrils. The bodies would be left to blend into the forest, decomposing until they were all gone except for the bones with moss and plants growing over them. "There will be no ambush for us to set in the valley, since the slavers already know of its inhabitants. If I ask you to face those odds, it will have to be a decision made by each of you alone. We will take a vote."

Fair enough, Ell thought. *A vote will be good.* "Well," Ell said, seeing no reason to waste time, "all in favor of pursuing Silverfist and doing everything in our power to defeat him once and for all, and defend the village." His and Miri's hands were the first up. Then, surprisingly the young boy they had rescued. Ell had not even remembered he was there.

"I agree with you, Ell, this is something we must do." Ryder spoke jovially, yet seriously, somehow managing to blend those two emotions and make them seem normal together.

Rihya and Dahranian were not long in adding their agreement. Dacunda looked around and then sighed, raising his hand. "It is settled then," Ell's uncle spoke, ending the vote and reassuming command of the situation. "We leave in one hour. Rest, sleep, and bury our dead companions. They deserve a decent burial at least," he said motioning to the dead, older elf and Miri's two female friends from Little Vale. "They spilled their blood on our behalf, as well as their own, and deserve to be honored." Ell nodded his agreement solemnly. He remembered Miri's female companion saving his life during the recent struggle, just before she was riddled with arrows. He would bury her himself.

They set about the task, tending to their dead as quickly as possible, and then resting as best they could before heading north. Miri told them that Borian had not been converted to the cause of the slavers more than a day's time before Ell's rescue, so the slavers could not be much farther than one day's hard journey ahead of them. If they pushed, perhaps they could overtake the slavers and save the village. Ell and his family were tired, wounded from the battle they had just narrowly survived, yet they were fewer in number than the slavers traveling ahead of them, led by Silverfist. Ell did not know how many slavers were ahead, but it would be many times more than the seven of them following. Even exhausted as they were, there was still a chance they could overtake Silverfist and mount a decent defense of the valley and the village. Small groups made better time than large ones. It was a proven military fact.

The hour Dacunda had allotted for rest passed more quickly than Ell had hoped. No sooner had he lay down, his head on a natural blanket of moss next to Miri's, than Dacunda was nudging them awake. Ell couldn't have slept for more than thirty minutes, perhaps, but even that minimal rest made him feel better. He was still exhausted, still recovering from the night spent utilizing his abilities to rescue Miri from the Pillar, but any rest was better than none.

He leaned in close to kiss Miri discreetly. She responded in surprising fashion, pressing her lips fiercely against his. It appeared she cared not for who was around to see her burst of passion. Ell understood. Life, death, battle, and chaos could do that to you. It could make you realize what was important in life and cling fast to those things you held dear. He responded to her just as passionately. Her lips were warm against his, her hair hanging loosely off the sides of her head and draping over his own as he rolled onto his back and she leaned over from her place beside him. They kissed with abandon a moment longer then Ell pulled her close in a tender embrace.

"I must prepare to leave," he murmured, his mouth close to her ear. She nodded her understanding into his chest. Unlike Ell, she had nothing to pack, no gear or weapons to secure before leaving. When one was in captivity, they typically had nothing more than the clothes on their back.

Ell left Miri lying in the moss, looking like nothing more than an earthy princess, catching a few more precious moments of rest. He turned to begin gathering his belongings for the journey north. They would have to travel extremely light if they wished to overtake the slavers. Traveling light meant only necessities would go with them. Ell refused to leave his weapons behind. He slung the long bow of black yew over his shoulder, fastening the quiver of similarly black Dreampine arrows, to his back. Both his belt knife, and his long, dueling dagger, inherited from his father Adan, went into their usual places. He placed the belt knife into a sheath at his hip, and the dueling dagger in a long, slender sheath strapped lengthwise down his outer thigh. Ell picked up his short spear and decided he would strap it to his back as well. It might look like too much to a bystander, but Ell had been accustomed to traveling with these possessions his whole life. Weapons were his tools of trade and he required different ones for different purposes. Other than these items, he would not take much. He wrapped his light travel blanket and strapped it to his pack, the pack his family had brought with them south on his behalf. They had known he was pursuing Miri, hoping to rescue her, only they had not known how he had planned and been able to accomplish that feat. Either way, Ell was thankful they had brought his things.

"What should I bring?" An unsure voice asked Ell from behind him. Ell turned his head and saw the young elf, the only other surviving escapee other than Miri. He had a bruise on his head from the Departed who had kicked him in the face, knocking him unconscious during the battle.

"Well, are you absolutely certain you want to come?" Ell still didn't know how he felt about this boy accompanying him and his family on what might end up as a suicide mission. It seemed beyond ironic, and slightly fatalistic, that the young elf should be rescued from a Pillar and a life of enslavement only to be facing the same reality should they fail to defend the village. "Do you have any family?"

The boy shook his head solemnly. He appeared a serious elf. Slight of build even for one of the Highest, he couldn't have had more than twelve namedays. "They're dead. Killed when I was captured."

Ell felt a moment of pity for the boy. It was not an uncommon story these days. Not many of the Highest could claim to have been untouched by the struggles of late, most having experienced a death or enslavement of a family member or two. Yet the simplicity of the boy's statement, the acceptance with which he gave the information, at once, tugged on the strings of Ell's heart and also drove him near mad with bitter frustration that the plight of his people should be so dire as to make news such as this common.

"Well, you're welcome with us..." Ell extended the phrase abnormally long, inclining his head, waiting for a name to call the elf.

"Artorious. But everyone just calls me Art."

Ell smiled kindly. "Well, Art, you are welcome with us. However," Ell narrowed his eyes seriously, "I must confess, we lead dangerous lives. Occasions such as today," he motioned to the remains of the battle, "are not entirely uncommon. Should you choose to stay with us for any length of time, you will need to study a weapon. You will need to learn the... art of it... shall we say." Ell smiled again at the pun, but the boy did not. He seemed a very serious sort, understandably so.

The boy nodded solemnly. “I can learn.”

“Alright, well then, why don’t you grab that spear,” Ell indicated the short spear, which lay to one side of the grave belonging to one of Miri’s female companions from Little Vale. “Spears are a good weapon for beginners. Less complicated. Also, find a knife, as well, to go at your belt. Nobody, even a person who does not consider themselves to be a warrior, should exist in this land without a knife. Such a useful tool even if you do not use it as a weapon.”

Art dutifully went off in search of a knife, as Ell had admonished he should. Ell went back to packing his belongings but there was not much to pack except a few odds and ends and his blanket. He still had a small pouch of dried meat from a few days earlier, and he put it into an inner pocket. A few fresh herbs to be used in the making of poultices should his Source Water run out. His cloak for colder weather.

“You were good with him, you know.” Ell knew without looking that it was Miri’s voice. He turned his head and looked at her, with her eyes open, and her body on its side propped up on her elbow with one hand holding up her head. She still resembled the regality of the wild, in Ell’s mind, the epitome of what it entailed to be an Andalayan, one of the Highest.

She continued. “You spoke words he could grab hold of. Something to give him purpose, hope. A skill to learn. Practicing the spear will take his mind off his losses.”

Ell didn’t know if that were true. He had just spoken words necessitated by practicality. If he had comforted the lad, so much the better, but it had not necessarily been his intention.

“I am glad,” Ell was quiet for a moment, phrasing his thoughts. “But my intentions were simple. Necessity states he will need to defend himself again. Learning a weapon will save his life. If it lends itself to his mental well-being also then so be it, I will take pleasure in knowing that. But,” Ell stared at Miri seriously, “this is my normal life. This battle, long odds, dire circumstances. My family and I face this regularly as we raid and fight. We bleed in the dust and dirt for the sake of our people, our land. With the boy, of course, I seek to be kind, but more than anything I seek to prepare him for the world he will meet. Life is not gentle to those unprepared to defend themselves.” Ell trailed off. He and Miri did not exactly agree on ideals surrounding this topic.

He was of the impression that all people should at least know the rudimentary skills of a weapon and how to defend themselves. Miri did not agree. Her lameness causing her pronounced limp, and perhaps even more so her upbringing, lent her to believe not all were able or created to fight. Ell had been more inclined to agree with her line of thinking when he had been in Little Vale. Before she had been taken, things had been different. Everything had changed since then. The bitterness, the anger he had felt his whole life bubbled inside him, again threatening to brim over the exits of his soul. For a brief moment in time, Miri had tempered that internal fury, with her cool, quiet love, her simple belief in good and the ability for some to avoid war. Not so any more. Nearly losing her had made Ell revert to his former set of core beliefs. Even more pronounced perhaps, after having nearly suffered such a great loss. Nobody could avoid the war. It was impossible to do so. The world was ensconced in a conflict so brutal, so terribly graphic to those who confronted it on a regular basis, that Ell had realized that until something changed, until his people were safe, the Highest and most importantly his own loved ones would never be truly free. Living in a constant state of fear changed people, even if you thought it wasn't so. No, Miri's ideals were for a future time, or maybe not even then. Maybe her ideals belonged to a time long gone, an era long past. The best he could do was temper his emotions with love also, so that he fought for a better future. The anger he felt at the circumstances of his people was still present, it would not go away. But he would use it as fuel.

"Well," Miri answered with a faint smile, "either way, you gave the boy hope. It was a kindness." They both avoided the discussion that Ell had just had internally within his mind. Neither wished to disagree with the other in an argument so quickly after being reunited.

Miri pushed herself to her feet, and Ell was once again impressed with the amount of grace she managed while maneuvering through life, considering the old wound she bore in her leg. He watched her familiar limp as she strode away to help Rihya consolidate her things. Ell was glad Miri got on well with his family. These were all the people he had in the world and it was good to realize they could all coexist as one, even with their differences.

The next few minutes were a hustle and bustle of last minute preparations. Gathering their weapons and equipment took time. While checking the dead Departed for anything of use, Dacunda found a handful of extra supplies. Some of the dark elves had kept pouches of food and flasks of normal drinking water at their hips at all times, accustomed to being called to leave on slaver raids at a moment's notice.

Before long, they were ready to go. Dacunda looked at them all as they gathered in the center of the copse of trees, their makeshift hill-fort from the morning's defenses.

"Ready." He was not an elf of many words, leastwise not those words he deemed unnecessary. Everyone nodded their affirmation. Ell's uncle turned and set their course at a quick pace north. It was time to tempt fate once again. Ell had just finished doing the impossible and rescuing slaves from a Pillar, albeit with help. Why not add overtaking a small army of slavers and mounting a successful defense of a largely unfortified village to that list also? Ell found himself grinning with a feral desire, a wolfish look on his face to match the anticipation he felt at the challenge ahead. For some reason, his emotions reminded him of Arendahl and the way the old elf had seemed to relish the idea of battle and confronting his enemies. Ell could think of worse people to model in life.

They set their course north and slightly west. It was time to put an end to Silverfist once and for all and strike a true blow for the Andalayan resistance. Ell hoped the swirling destiny of the battle ahead would spin his own personal course to cross that of the infamous traitor elf, the one who had murdered his father.

Something had changed inside him, Ell realized. He had always been competent, quietly efficient in battle. Now Ell found himself more confident than ever. Ell relished the idea of once again testing his blade against Silverfist. Something told him he would get the chance again and soon. Ell certainly hoped it would be so.

Chapter Twenty-Seven

They ran fueled by need. Ell ran beside Dacunda at the front of the company. Miri, kept pace as best she could near the back, Art beside her. They were talking together, and Ell could see that Miri was having as little luck getting the boy to crack a smile as Ell had had earlier. Well, if anyone could bring the boy out of his misery it would be her. Miri had a way of bringing perspective to situations. Not many people could find something positive in just about anything.

"They are slowing us down," Dacunda said quietly. "If we wish to accomplish this mission, we may have to push on ahead of them." He spoke critically, yet respectfully. Ell was not offended by his uncle's appraisal of the situation. It was only the facts. The truth was, Miri's limp, while she managed it extremely well, prevented her from maintaining the pace over long periods of time, a pace they would need in order to reach Little Vale before Silverfist and his slavers. Art, as well, slowed them down. While he ran hard, he was still just a boy and would not be able to keep up. It would require days of running to reach the valley along the Westrill.

"I know," Ell said in agreement. "But what are we to do, leave them behind, alone?"

"Yes." The simplicity of Dacunda's statement took Ell aback. Miri had only just been freed after suffering a terrible ordeal for weeks. How could she understand being left to fend for herself all alone, and with a young elf in her care no less? "Otherwise, we will not be able to reach her home in time. All her family and friends will certainly pay the price then."

Dacunda spoke the truth, Ell knew. It was just hard to stomach. He didn't want to be separated from her for even one moment after what had happened, let alone the days, possibly weeks it would be before he saw her again, should they push onwards without her. Ell mulled the thoughts over in his head. It was hard being in love he realized, sometimes it was magical, an experience beyond any others he'd ever experienced, but at other times, the pain was almost unbearable. Thinking he had lost Miri to a lifetime of servitude and torment had nearly drove him insane. The agony while she had been captured had been almost beyond Ell's ability to overcome. He felt particularly protective of her now. The thought of leaving her and running on ahead, even if it was to save her home, made his teeth clench subconsciously, and his fists ball up at his sides. But Dacunda was right.

"You are correct, of course, Uncle. As you usually are." Ell had finally accepted the truth after a few moments of silence, time that he'd spent mentally wriggling and writhing around, trying to find any way to avoid this reality.

"I will speak to her shortly. For now, they are keeping pace. We don't have to leave them until it is clear they are holding us back. Perhaps, tonight, or even tomorrow morning," Ell finished hopefully. Dacunda nodded his acceptance, although it was clear by the impassive look on his face, he expected to have to leave them behind sooner than later.

They ran on together, smooth, deep breaths, in an out as they pushed north. It felt like Ell had spent his entire life running next to this elf. His uncle was a great person. A strong warrior, a loyal friend, and courageous leader. There were worse ways to spend one's life, Ell reflected idly. He could hear Miri now carrying on a conversation with Rihya behind him. They were opposites. His sister was quicksilver, the sudden storm that created flash floods and drenched the valleys, then was gone the next moment. Miri was the meandering river, appearing to lazily curl and wind its way down towards its destination. A river, which seemed slow and steady, and it was. Yet, what could not be seen from the surface were the diverse currents swirling beneath, much stronger, more powerful than you would ever imagine just by looking at it. Ell loved them both, but there was no denying the two girls were extremely different. He grinned at the comparison of them.

"Something funny, Nephew?" Dacunda asked curiously.

Ell shook his head. "No, not really, Uncle, just a passing thought. But it is not of great significance." Ell's uncle made an understanding face and let the comment be for a moment before changing the subject.

"Elliyar, I have held off asking, figuring you would have told the entire group the tale of the past two days if you wished it. However, I feel like I must ask now. How did you manage the impossible?" Dacunda ran steadily beside him, an implacable force, the unrelenting warrior. "I have seen entire bands of elves throw themselves against the walls of a Pillar in the early days of the war and do nothing more than break their bones and chip their swords. Not to mention wind up dead."

Ell sighed. He knew the questions would come. One could not do what he had done and expect to avoid those questions; he had just hoped to avoid them for a time longer. It seemed that he was always the focus of attention these days, with his abilities manifesting so recently. It would have been nice to stay in the background for a time. However, Ell supposed talking to his uncle in a private conversation would suffice for now.

"I don't really know where to start, Uncle. It was a... strange day." Ell paused in the middle of the sentence searching for the right word. Even the word strange didn't really seem to do justice to what he had experienced. Climbing the North Crag, riding an Icari, fighting his way single handedly through a Pillar to rescue Miri. What he had achieved was almost too much to believe.

Dacunda seemed to understand. "Well, how about at the beginning. What happened when you left us in the night?" Dacunda's eyes narrowed dangerously, and he added, "Which by the way, if you ever leave us near enemy territory without a sentry again, I will personally see to it that you learn a very pointed lesson." He lowered his eyebrows and created the most menacing face he could as he stared at Ell. Ell understood. He had left his family exposed by abandoning his place on the watch while the rest were sleeping. Any enemy might have been able to advance upon them and slay them in their blankets.

Ell held up his hands in apology then answered the first question. "I left you in the middle of the night. I am sorry for doing it, Dacunda, but I was beyond distraught. I thought I might go mad with the idea of Miri as a slave." Dacunda peered at him, apparently accepting the apology although he still didn't look like he had entirely forgiven Ell for endangering the family. "I left you and headed north."

Ell had expected his Uncle to be surprised but the level look he received told him that perhaps his uncle had already guessed as much. "Continue," Dacunda said. Ell did.

"North, to the Crag. I... climbed it." Ell fought for words to describe the experience. Hanging for his life by a few fingers, thousands of feet above the forest floor. It was not the sort of thing one merely put into words.

"You climbed it," Dacunda said flatly. It was not a question.

"Yes. I climbed it. Then I found an Icari's nest and I rode the beast," Ell stated it matter-of-factly. How else could one speak of such incredible events? It was almost a disservice to try to make them sound amazing. The truth was, just claiming to have ridden an Icari was enough of a shock to most people. He wouldn't need to dramatize the discussion any more than it already was just by virtue of the subject.

Ell's uncle closed his eyes and shook his head. Then he finally let out a bark of a laugh. It was almost a groan really. "You would have given your father more headaches than he could have counted. Instead, I am stuck with you." Dacunda was not one to joke, so when he did, as he was now, Ell knew he was truly shaken.

"It really wasn't too bad, Uncle." Ell realized the ridiculous nature of the statement the moment it left his mouth. It had been dangerous. He had nearly died just trying to reach the Icari's peak-top lair, let alone subduing it in combat.

Dacunda shook his head. "I cannot condone any accord with the creatures of darkness, Elliyar," Ell's uncle was very serious again now, "no matter what the end result." Dacunda glanced back at the now, free Miri.

Ell thought of the fight on the top of the North Crag, of the wind howling, the gale thrashing the peak and tearing stones from its rocky walls as the rain pummeled their struggling bodies. No, it had not been an agreement of any kind he thought grimly. It had been a matter of dominance, one over the other, and he had come out on top that time.

"No, uncle, it was more of a… forcible arrangement," Ell finished with a dark chuckle.

Ell's uncle peered at him for a time, as if to make sure he spoke the truth. Finally, it seemed he was satisfied. "So you flew?" Dacunda said, his face showing his amazement. "How ever did you manage it?"

"With a dagger planted deep in its side and another at the Icari's throat."

"A precarious situation," Dacunda wiped a hand across his brow although there appeared to be little sweat there. Ell supposed he was feeling his 'fatherly' worry, as Ell recounted his dangerous excursion. It was understandable. "Did you at least activate your abilities as a Water Caller?" Ell's uncle asked hopefully, as if it would make the aftermath of the situation a little easier to handle, were it the case.

"No, well not at that point. I rode it normal, just me," Ell amended, and pointed to his own graceful, muscled body indicating he had not been anything unusual while riding the Icari.

"Which makes the feat even more incredible," Dacunda murmured almost to himself. "I shall have to rethink what I consider to be within or outside the realm of possibility from this point onwards."

Ell nodded. He supposed it was true. After a day like he'd had, one had to rethink a lot of things. Nothing ever stayed the same in life, but some events were even more a catalyst for change than others.

"Uncle," Ell remembered something important. "I feel the need to tell you, I was able to communicate with the Icari. I spoke to it to tell it where to go and it understood me, since we reached my desired destination, the Pillar." Ell paused. "Does that mean anything?"

Dacunda narrowed his eyes. "Maybe. Perhaps it means something, perhaps not. I, however, am not the one to answer that question." However, Ell could see his uncle's response was careful, cautious, as if not wanting to entertain any more discussion down that idea path. Ell decided not to press his uncle further. Dacunda would speak about something when he was ready, and not a moment sooner.

"And so…?" Dacunda motioned with his hand that Ell should continue his tale of how he had rescued Miri. And so Ell did. He told of riding the Icari in the storm during the night, nearly falling off at times. Ell spoke of landing on the Pillar's platform and how his abilities had instinctively activated. He spoke of felling the Icari and then slaughtering the guards. Ell told of searching the dank, dim interior of the small fortress atop the Pillar and then of finding Miri, with Art and the other slaves. It was a long story, but Ell shortened it when he could, minimizing the events when possible. Dacunda seemed to know when he was underselling his accomplishments but he didn't correct Ell or dig deeper, accepting the story as it was.

Ell finally wrapped it up. "And so that's when I cut the rope, jumped off the Pillar, and then blacked out. The next thing I knew, I was waking up and the enemy horns were sounding and we were readying ourselves for battle," he trailed off, not really knowing what to say.

"It is quite a tale, Nephew," Dacunda said in admiration. "I am proud of you, you know." Ell felt a rush of warmth flood his body. Dacunda continued, "I don't say it often, but I am. Not many could have done what you did. Well," Ell's uncle amended, "actually nobody I know could have done that, except perhaps Arendahl. I expect it is the type of story we would be telling our children around the campfire had the events occurred during the First Days. I suspect centuries from now, the 'Tale of Elliyar and the Icari' will be a favorite of most young elves." Dacunda smiled. Ell felt pleased that his uncle deemed his accomplishment worthy of such an honor, but deep down he hoped it would not be so. Fame was not something for which Ell pined. He was perfectly happy just to do his duty, take care of the ones he loved, and enjoy life as best he could. History could tell the tales of others all it liked, but he would be just as happy to be left out of it.

Dacunda seemed to read his thoughts. "You know, you will do great things, Nephew, feats that will be spoken of for generations to come. I know it in here," Dacunda tapped his own chest above the heart. "You might as well just get used to it."

Just get used to it. Coming to terms with being different was easier said than done, but Ell had a feeling it was something he was going to have to confront over and over again. He wasn't normal anymore; there was no getting around it.

Ell grunted noncommittally. He wasn't ready to get used to it yet. "I'm going to have a word with Miri and explain the situation." Dacunda watched him drop back until he was running beside Miri.

Rihya gave Ell a pointed look, as if to say it was about time he had paid some attention to Miri, but Miri just smiled pleasantly as she always did.

"Rihya, would you mind giving us a moment alone?" Ell asked between breaths as he continued to run. They all were pushing themselves hard, and Ell could feel his lungs beginning to burn just a little bit. He hadn't fully recovered from tapping his abilities the night before. *I have to figure out a way to use my abilities without growing so exhausted afterwards*, he thought. It was a problem for another time, however. Rihya switched places with Ell and went forward to strike up a conversation with Dacunda. Likely, she was trying to get their uncle to do something, or adapt his plans ever so slightly to what she thought they should do. Rihya liked to be in control.

"It's good to have you by my side," Miri said happily. That was one thing Ell loved about her, it did not take much to make her happy.

Ell agreed, "Yes." He was not an elf of many words, and at times, it felt better to not speak at all. Miri always understood those moments when he wanted silence. They ran on side by side, their shoulders rubbing together as they ran. For a time Ell forgot it all. He forgot the mission at hand, he didn't think of Silverfist or the slavers, nor the war or even the events of the past day.

For now, he just smelled her fragrance. She had found a stream to bathe in before leaving the copse of trees, and while it hadn't been able to remove all of the grime of the cell, and her captivity, it had helped. Somehow, she had even managed to maintain the faint scent of lily that always seemed to accompany her. Ell didn't know how she did it. If you breathed in his own scent, it would probably resemble nothing so much as sweat, and steel, and the leather and cloth of his clothes. He supposed there were worse things to smell like.

After a time, Ell broke the silence, "We will not make it to the village in time. Well, at least not the way things are going." He started the conversation ambiguously, as tactfully as possible, not wanting to offend.

"I know," Miri said simply.

"You do?"

"Yes, I just said so, didn't I?" She smiled again to take the sting out of the words. "I've had this limp for a long time, Ell. It's not as if I don't know my own limitations."

Ell felt a tremendous sense of relief, a weight lifted off his chest. At least he wouldn't have to convince her of the problem. He should have known it would be easy with her, it always was.

"What are you going to do about it?" Miri questioned him directly, almost as if she wanted to hear him, wanted to see his ability to make a tough decision.

Ell sighed. He didn't want to say it, but he must. "We will have to leave you behind. You and Art." A pleading note entered his voice. "If we do not, we won't reach your village in time, and your people, your friends, your home will suffer."

Miri nodded and smiled faintly as she looked straight ahead, still running as best she could. It never ceased to amaze Ell, the amount of grace with which she managed to navigate her life, considering the severity of her limp.

"Are you alright, Miri?"

"Of course, Ell. How could I expect anything less? I was already wondering when you and your uncle would reach this conclusion. Besides, how could I live with myself if I were the reason holding you and your family back from the defense of my home? I could never live with those consequences."

Ell nodded to himself slowly. Indeed, he should have foreseen her ability to think rationally. Miri had always been the optimist, the one who could see the good in any situation, the positive in any set back. However, she also had a very practical side and Ell was thankful for her logic right now. It would have been even more difficult to leave her side so soon after her captivity if she had not been able to understand his motives.

"When will you go?"

"Soon," Ell answered her, "our pace is already beginning to lag just slightly because of you and the boy. We should break away soon."

Miri just nodded. She reached out silently and clasped his hand as they ran. It was a bit awkward, the motions of it, trying to run with hands together, but it felt right. Ell could sense, however, that there was an element of fear residing beneath her calm exterior. She was putting on a brave face, but she grasped his hand more tightly than usual, and held on for longer than she normally would have done. She was fighting the terror of being left alone so soon after her release and Ell loved her for it. He was proud of her.

The next hour they passed together. It was bittersweet. So wonderful to be together, but so hard to think about how soon they would need to part ways. The company finally came to their first resting point. They had left the copse of trees in late morning and run through the midday without stopping. Ell could see Miri was exhausted, both from her previous ordeal and from this run so soon after. She sank wearily to the mossy ground. They had chosen to stop in a small glen. The terrain was hilly through this portion of Andalaya, making its way slowly but surely towards the mountainous Legendwood in the north. The trees of the Lower Forest were just beginning to thicken, and underbrush was growing more bunched together. Trails were more necessary. The Lower Forest, in general, was more spacious, the distance between trees great enough that often a precise path was not needed. In the Lower Forest, the tree canopy was still there, the spreading limbs of oak and elm and many more, reaching out and providing shade. But the farther north one went, as they were now, the canopy grew thicker, and the forest denser. The part of Andalaya where the Lower Forest met Legendwood was the densest part of the forest. Thick spreading branches covered the sky and met the underbrush, the wild brambles and the beginning of many types of pine, and spruce mixed in as well. It was a medley of colors. A collage of greens, and browns, yellows and blacks, lights and darks. It was beautiful and it was home. Ell loved the way the moss grew on the rocks and stones, the way lichen hung from branches and trunks of trees in the thickest, dimmest part of the woods where the shining light of the sun hardly pierced. It was dangerous these days, yes, but it was still beautiful and it was still his home.

"Tired?" Ell asked his love the obvious question. Miri nodded wearily. He held her hand and squatted down beside her, resting his weight on the heels of his feet and his back against the same boulder where she slumped.

"No time, Elliyar," Dacunda said as he saw Ell slide down to rest beside Miri. "If we hope to reach the valley before the slavers we must go now." Dacunda paused, his gaze flicking to Miri. "Have you spoken with her?"

Ell nodded is response, then followed with words. "Yes, she understands."

"And the boy?"

Ell shook his head this time. He had not spoken to Artorious yet. What did one say to an orphan you had just rescued and now were leaving behind?

Art furrowed his brow, the serious expression looking normal on his young face. "Told me what?"

"You're slowing us down, lad." Ryder spoke up in a friendly manner, trying to break the news as nicely but directly as possible. "There's no way we can reach our destination in time to save the villagers if we continue at this pace." Art just stared at Ryder, waiting for more. "Well lad, can you run faster, without any breaks. We'll likely be setting a faster pace than this for days, without rest. Can you keep up?" Everyone knew the answer.

The boy bowed his head, "No," he said in a small voice. Serious, simple, and not an elf of many words. He would fit in just fine with our family, Ell thought wryly.

"No need for shame, Art," Ryder continued. "I'm taller, faster, stronger," he flexed his large, right arm and held it for Art to feel in a joking manner, "and that's only because I'm older. Practically ancient compared to you." His jesting managed to pry the tiniest of smiles out of the boy. Ell was again amazed at how amiable people found Ryder. He was the funniest of them all, and his humor could sometimes unlock a closed mouth or a heart that had shut itself away.

"So... what should I do?" Art asked.

"You'll stay with me and keep me safe," Miri spoke up, giving the boy a purpose. "We will follow as fast as I can manage and catch up with them when we can."

Art nodded his acceptance, looking relieved to have some sort of task. "Alright."

"I'll be staying too, so when we take rests I'll teach you how to use that knife at your belt," Rihya said. Ell was surprised and a bit confused. He looked at his uncle for confirmation, and his uncle stayed silent, showing he did not necessarily disapprove of the idea. Ell stayed silent, as well. They would miss her knives during the battle to come, but he would not say a word to deprive Miri of extra protection. Miri was brave, and she was one of the Highest, trained in the art of living off the land and surviving in the wild, yet there was no getting around the fact she was lame, and not a warrior. Ell would feel better indeed, knowing his sister accompanied her.

"Really?" Art asked Rihya, perking up a bit at the offer.

"Really," Ell's sister answered. "But only at the rests. We will still be moving as quickly as we can to follow." Art nodded vigorously. It was fine with him. Ell knew the boy would run his hardest just to get the chance to practice daggers with Rihya.

Everything settled, they said their goodbyes. Ell hugged Miri fiercely. No words were necessary, their bodies pressed together, and their hot breath on each other's cheeks, lips, and mouth said it all. He kissed her then pulled away. He could not afford to second-guess this decision by giving in to his emotions.

Ell pulled his sister close in a hug, as well, and whispered in her ear, "thank you."

She didn't answer but squeezed him tightly in response. She was staying with Miri for him, for her love for her brother and what was important to him. It was the only thing that could get Rihya to pass up the opportunity to participate in a battle.

"Take care of them, especially her," Ell pointed towards Miri as he bent down to say goodbye to Art. Miri smiled as he said it, but Art nodded solemnly. Ell liked the boy already. He had a sincere manner about him. Ell had no doubt he would do his best.

With goodbyes said, they were off. Ell, Dacunda, Dahranian, and Ryder left the three of them sitting in the small, mossy glen catching their breath. Ell prepared himself for the run of his life. He knew they would hardly stop between here and the valley along the Westrill where the village lay. He prayed his body would hold up as he still felt the drain of exhaustion about him.

However, he was accustomed to pushing through and push on he would. There was a job to be done, a battle to be won, and a traitor to be killed.

"About time we got a chance for a little bit of male bonding," Ryder quipped with a grin as they ran on. Even Dacunda and Dahranian chuckled a bit at Ryder's remark as they all matched strides, running in unison to the north.

Chapter Twenty-Eight

The journey north was arduous, difficult beyond almost any other trek to battle Ell had ever experienced. They stopped infrequently, and when they did, it was only for short moments during the day or to catch a few hours of sleep at night. Dacunda had been the last to accept this mission as a good idea, but after he was won over to an idea, he set his heart on it like nobody else. Once Ell had convinced his uncle initially, that not only was it possible but also morally necessary to attempt to warn and save the village, his uncle had embraced the mission entirely.

Dacunda pushed them hard and they often ate what little food they had while running. They filled their water flasks at the streams and rivers they forded, and hunted on the run, weapons ready to bring down any flock of birds or group of varmints they surprised and scattered out of the underbrush as they went. It was tough going. Ell was not sure he would even have the energy to fight once they reached their destination in the valley; such was the pace Dacunda set. It usually would not have been as difficult; however, the trek so quickly after a rigorous battle and not having had time to rest before hand, made them all very weary. Yet, Ell knew it was necessary. The slavers had at least a full day's head start on them, if not more, and to make up time Ell and his companions would need to draw deeply upon their reserves of energy saved for special situations such as this. It was really more of a mental challenge, a matter of will. Certainly, his body was tired and would grow more so as the days passed without time to fully rest. But, Ell had experienced that the body could endure much more than the mind thought it could. Often it was the mind, which gave way long before the body ever did. Ell willed his spirit to stay focused and refreshed. He kept the goal of their journey in the forefront of his mind at all times. This was about Miri. He was not rescuing her this time, but it was still her for whom he was fighting. He ran to defend her home, her family, and her friends.

Of course, there was more to it than just being a rescue attempt. Silverfist was leading the slavers. Ell was itching to get another chance to kill Silverfist,

The Traitor, who deserved to die. Avenging his father's death would be a sweet victory to place on top of the success of repelling the slavers and saving the village. Ell paid close attention to the dueling dagger on his thigh. He would be ready. This time he would know what it meant when the slight vibrations began, the hum saying the weapon's twin blade was near. He would use thc weapon to identify where his enemy was.

The days blurred as they ran. Morning dawned clear and they were running. Sunset grew near and they were running. Evening and then night ensconced the world in darkness and they slept for a time, but mostly they were still running. Ell felt like he would never want to run again for the rest of his life after this. Eventually they stopped talking, all energy and strength was reserved for the fitness required to complete this quest. Elves, especially the Highest, were created to run for nearly endless periods of time without strain, yet this taxed even them to maximum capacity. Ragged, uneven breaths and stooped shoulders replaced the smooth, measured breathing and normally impeccable posture of the northern elves. Each of them focused solely on the run, one foot in front of the other. Left foot, right foot. Left. Right. Over and over again until the landscape changed around them. Ell got lost in a haze of motion, and his wits were dulled by the fatigue, the cost of the journey. Operating in that fog of exhaustion, it almost seemed as if the land changed between one step and the next. What had once been the clogged, dense mixture of the hilly environment of the Lower Forest as it met the beginnings of Legendwood, became pure mountains, rugged and mammoth. The mountains dwarfed the sky, peaks crowding upwards, the earth's giant claws reaching up to rip the heavens and tear them down to the land. This was home. This was the heart of Andalaya.

Before too much longer they reached the Westrill and adapted their course to follow the river. Sometimes they ran on the high, cliff top trail as the path went over the mountainsides looking down at the Westrill as it flowed through the deep gorge below. At other times the path dipped low, running along soggy, muddy banks where the plants grew right down to the water's edge, with trees and vines and creepers overhanging the flowing water like a mother bird hovering protectively over her chicks.

They kept a close watch over their shoulders, in case they should already have passed the slavers at some point and be set upon from behind. But they also scouted ahead, one at a time, in order to make sure they did not run upon them either. It was nervy not knowing exactly where the enemy was.

Ell and his family began having to take a few more breaks during the course of each day. They had pushed hard and fast for many days, and their bodies would give out if not allowed a chance to breathe. It was necessary. Ell also felt like it was a good idea considering that at the end of this trek there lay the possibility of a battle with long odds against their favor. They would need their strength. It was a precarious balance between trying to push hard enough to reach the village in time, and not to push so hard that upon reaching the village they were of no use to anyone.

The closer they came to their destination, the less they talked. It was as if the reality of the task they had accepted had begun to sink into their heads. They were planning to help a small village escape, or maybe defend itself from what would most likely be a small army of slavers. If they survived what was ahead, it would be due to their wits, their strength of arms, and most likely more than a little good fortune.

They paused to rest at a point on the trail mid-way up the cliffs along the gorge. The forest was not so thick as to completely obscure the sky or the surrounding environment. It was more open here than other sections of Legendwood. However, tall trees still reached upwards, swaying in the wind, the tops of the trees moving back and forth. Mushrooms of all shapes and sizes grew in the resting area, some even leaving the mossy floor of the forest and climbing up the trunks of the trees, as well. Flat, wide mushrooms protruded from the sides of the trees like small ledges upon which insects could rest. Tiny, round mushrooms clustered at the base of rocks and bushes. Even the strange Stilt Mushrooms, mushrooms that grew tall and thin like huge, white, spongy blades of grass, grew out of the tiny streams running through the small alcove in the forest and cascading down the cliff sides. The miniature waterfalls were more like vertical streams rather than actual waterfalls, as the water seemed to cling to the walls for dear life and drip and trickle down the sides of the gorge instead of gaining separation from the walls the way a larger, more active, waterfall would.

Dacunda left the three of them to sit for a short while and eat their lunch of dried berries, nuts, and dried meat, while he scouted ahead. Ell's uncle was pushing himself to his limits, resting less, scouting more while the rest of them took time to eat and sit. Ell knew better than to say anything. Dacunda was an elf on a mission, they all were really, and once his uncle made up his mind to do something, there was no swaying his decision. Dacunda had decided it was up to him to do the scouting as they drew closer to Little Vale, where Miri's village lay, and even if Ell or the others had offered to take his place, he would likely have turned them down. It was the reason he was a good leader—he pushed himself farther and harder than he ever asked of those he led. There was not a hypocritical bone in his body. Yet, it was also a weakness. Even the strongest of leaders wore out eventually, and Ell worried that Dacunda's efforts would drain too much out of him.

Dahranian pulled out his sword as they finished eating, and began to sharpen it with a whetstone. Ryder, in typical fashion, grabbed at the chance to close his eyes. Ell's cousin Ryder was infamous for napping whenever he had even a moment without something to do. Ell supposed it was the life of a warrior, a soldier. You never knew when you would be called upon to fight in a battle or run hundreds of miles in a few days, such as they were doing now, and it was important to grab rest when you could. All the same, Ell had never been able to simply close his eyes and fall asleep the way Ryder could.

Instead of sleeping, Ell pulled out his dueling dagger and turned it about in his hand, occasionally tossing it end over end, idly catching it by the hilt without worrying about the blade. He was used to handling weapons. What might seem dangerous to a bystander was not necessarily so to a trained warrior. Besides, he was an elf, one of the Highest. His reflexes were sharp.

"You are going to wear out the dagger just by staring at it," Dahranian commented in an uncharacteristically jesting and sarcastic tone. "Give the poor blade a rest, why don't you?"

Ell smiled in realization. It was true. He'd been pulling out his father's dueling dagger every chance he got, at each resting point or campsite for the night.

"I guess I am just anxious to get to the battle. To actually do something other than run," he responded to his cousin.

Dahranian quirked an eyebrow quizzically as if he didn't quite believe Ell. "Is that it? Just eager to fight? Or are you eager to fight someone in particular?" He directed a meaningful look at the dueling dagger. "You know the elf who wields the twin to that blade is dangerous, far more dangerous than most of us would like to admit. I would urge you to exercise caution, Cousin."

Ell's face tightened. "Maybe," he said in a reserved voice. "And even if I am looking forward to a confrontation, is that wrong?"

Dahranian shook his head, and lifted his hands slightly as if to say he meant no offense. "None, Ell. I am just reminding you that Silverfist has been a traitor for nearly two decades. You are hardly the first of the Highest to feel a personal vendetta against him. Yet, here he is, still kicking and breathing, leading an army of slavers in the north, the heart of Andalaya. Many have already tried to vanquish him and failed."

"Well, it's time somebody didn't fail," Ell retorted. "Besides, I doubt many of those who failed could claim the title of Water Caller." Ell still felt almost guilty calling himself a Water Caller. Until he could truly master his powers it didn't feel right.

Dahranian nodded complacently. "True, Ell. Just don't forget that Silverfist is wily beyond measure. Only the craftiest of adversaries could have orchestrated the capitulation of Verdantihya such as he did. To do so took incredible skill and wits. Do not underestimate him." Dahranian ended his warning and was clearly done talking as his gaze left Ell's face and he went back to sharpening his blade and staring at the steel, checking for pits and nicks he might have missed and would need to polish.

Ell sat staring into the wilderness, brooding on the recent conversation. Ell had to admit, Silverfist was not a normal elf in most senses of the word. True, other than his metal hand, his anatomy was no different from one of the Highest. But the way he thought, his ability on the field of battle, it was proven. Ell had just escaped a Pillar, done the unthinkable, yet he had done so with the aid of his powers as a Water Caller. In the back of his mind, he worried that those same powers would not be available to him in this coming battle. He had so far, not been able to choose when they arose. Without his abilities to draw upon the strength of the land, the life source of creation, water, would he be a match for Silverfist? Ell had the nagging feeling of doubt that without his abilities the answer was no, he was not a match. *Only time will tell*, Ell thought determinedly. However, he would not avoid the traitor on the battlefield, that much was certain.

Dacunda returned and his report shed light on their current circumstances. There were good tidings mixed with bad.

"I crested the rise as the path meets the ridgeline and there is a party of Departed not far ahead. Some leagues at most. We should be able to pass them by soon." Dacunda blinked slowly as he sat down on a rock, his fatigue showing.

"That is good news, Father," Dahranian said with his characteristic sincerity.

Dacunda cocked his head and made a face, showing his uncertainty over the truth of his son's statement. "Yes and no, Dahranian. True we have nearly accomplished our goal of overtaking the party of slavers, but I fear we may be faced with an even more difficult task than we had bargained for."

"Oh?" Ell asked for more information.

Dacunda stared at him solemnly. "It is as we feared, a small army lies ahead of us. There must be a few hundred of the Departed, maybe more."

Ell closed his eyes and rubbed a hand over them. Hundreds were indeed many with which to contend. "Silverfist must have emptied almost three quarters of the force inhabiting the Pillar to bring them here."

"Yes," Dacunda responded, "and I would not be surprised if he added numbers along the way, by signal fires to attract more slave bands in the area. You know how there are always one or two roving about." It was true; slavers were a constant threat. Often only numbering in the tens or sometimes twenties, however, a band of slavers many hundreds strong was not something to be taken lightly. Andalaya was under populated and her people scattered about the land, living their lives in nomadic hiding. All except for this village. This one village had rejected the safe option and tried to resume life as it had been before the fall of Verdantihya. It was an admirable sentiment, but unwise. Dacunda had predicted this dilemma, this danger when they had first visited the village months ago.

"What's this?" Ryder asked leaning up on one elbow after his nap. "Are we facing a hopeless situation again?" He barked a laugh. "It's about time. We haven't faced one of those in days. I was beginning to wonder if we were on the right track." He finished his quip with a wink at Ell. Ell wished he could mimic his cousin's lack of regard for the severity of the situation. Ryder had a way of looking dire moments in the face and responding with a wink and a smile as he just had now. It was an admirable quality, and one that Ell simply did not possess. Oh, Ell had courage, and grit. The events of the past week, his flight on the Icari, and rescuing Miri and Art proved that he did, if nothing else. Yet Ell could never manage to face situations, such as those, with the positive outlook on life that Ryder possessed. Ell said a silent prayer for Miri's safety as his thoughts fell upon her. He cared for his sister's safety, as well, and Art for that matter too, yet he trusted his sister to take care of herself. She had been doing so for all of her life. Miri had also, yet not in the same manner. Besides, she was so freshly freed from bondage that Ell felt an unusual protectiveness when he thought about his love. Now was no exception.

"Can you not take anything serious, Ry?" Dahranian asked with a shake of his head.

"Oh I can, brother dearest, I just choose not to. Life is serious enough as it is. I don't think I'd be able to face these types of situations if I didn't keep my smile strong." Ryder grinned his widest smile at his brother as if to emphasize his point. Dahranian ignored him and moved on to sharpening a new knife with his whetstone.

Dacunda motioned for silence. "Hush, you two. We must now begin to think of a strategy."

"What's there to think of?" Ryder asked his father. "Seems simple to me. We slip around those southern bastards, warn the village, get them away if we have time, and if not, we hole up somewhere in the valley and make these slavers pay dearly for every drop of Andalayan blood they spill." Ryder emphasized his point by jamming his belt knife hilt deep in the soft soil upon which he reclined. Apparently, he wasn't so calm or relaxed about what lay ahead as he had implied earlier. *Good*, Ell thought, *there are few people more intimidating or ferocious in battle than Ry when he's fired up.* They would need his passion when the battle began.

Dacunda nodded silently to his son's question. Then he responded, "Yes, I suppose your assessment seems about right."

"Don't overthink it, Father." Ryder waved his hand dismissively, earning a faint smile from Dacunda.

"Alright, Ryder, I won't." Dacunda began addressing Ell and Dahranian again as Ryder lay back down and closed his eyes. Whether he was actually sleeping or just feigning it was hard to tell. "So, we slip around them, avoid the sentries and scouts, which they have no doubt posted, and then push hard to reach the village with enough time to prepare." Ell's uncle spoke seriously, his tone and expression conveying the gravity of the situation.

Ell nodded his agreement, as did Dahranian. "Alright then, let's move," Dacunda said, clapping his hands softly to symbolize the end of the conversation.

They spent the next minute or so, gathering weapons, which had been set aside while resting, and picking up whatever else had been set down during the break.

"Remember, from here on out, we move silently. Don't compromise stealth for speed." Dacunda directed his words at the three of them.

Ryder again brought levity to the situation by rolling his eyes. "Really Father, as if this were our first raid. We've been through this sort of experience before. Relax."

"Very well," Dacunda responded gruffly, "but if that's the case, don't let me catch you making a mistake. I expect this to go well. If it doesn't, we'll likely be dead," he muttered.

They set off running, swiftly but silently. Dacunda had said the slavers were a league or two ahead, so Ell and his family had to leave the trail. The path would lead them right up to the rear of the slavers war party and that would be a disaster. Any confrontation had to be avoided at all cost until they reached the valley. They didn't want to alert Silverfist and his dark elves to their presence.

In order to leave the well-cut trail, which ran along the cliffs overlooking the river, Ell and his family had to climb the steep mountainside sloping upwards. It was slow going. They had to half climb, half crawl, steadily up, hand over hand until they reached the ridgeline far above the trail. They then continued on their course, traveling towards the Indiria's Emerald where Miri's village lay, on just the other side of the ridge to hide themselves from sight.

"Traveling like this will slow us down," Dacunda spoke what they all were thinking as they moved through the trail-less forest, picking their way around trees and over logs instead of running lightly on a path free of obstructions such as the slavers would be. "If we hope to overtake the slavers before they reach the pass into the valley, we'll have to travel through the night."

It would be trickier going at night. Some of the hillsides they traversed were steep. The river and the gorge were on the other side of the ridge, and so there was no giant cliff of which to be afraid, yet at night, even these smaller slopes to ravines and gullies would be steep enough to necessitate caution.

Dahranian answered his father's comment as they ran further, "We will do what we have set out to do, whatever it takes." His response summed up how they all felt. Resolute, unmoving in their resolve to stand up to Silverfist once and for all and save the village. Ell nodded his agreement to his cousin's response.

They continued onwards and nightfall slowly crept closer. The evening sun was fading on the horizon, golden and warm. It lit up Andalaya strangely, lending one last flash of brilliance to the land before it would slip beneath the mountains and sleep for the night. The golden light was reflected in the tiny streams playing their way down the ridgeline. The streams were small, and would sometimes trickle into nothing, or at other times form small pools, which would not grow large because the ground around them absorbed extra liquid. The water turned gold in the fading light, like veins of metal mined forth from the mountains of Andalaya. It was a strange juxtaposition, such beauty on the course leading up to what was sure to be a harrowing defense of Little Vale. Ell reflected on that truth. Andalaya, herself, was really one of the greatest contradictions of all. Gorgeous beyond measure, the land's wild beauty was a thing of wonder. It had stunned generations before with its glory and would continue to do so for future generations. Yet, at the same time, it was the scene of great injustice. Its people splintered, scattered in every direction, most of them living the lives of nomads in order to survive. And that was only the few who still remained. The rest had been taken captive and carted away to serve a life sentence of brutality in a faraway land. It was unfair, that such a wonderful place as his homeland should be linked also with a great sense of despair.

Ell fought the feeling of hopelessness threatening to consume his thoughts. Things could change. They had to. If one person had taught him to see life with a positive perspective, it was Miri. Ell strove to do so. He wasn't sure if he really managed to win the battle in his mind. At times, he felt he had, but at others, the despair crept in again, seeping its dangerously seductive tendrils deep into his mind and heart. Either way he pushed forth, running, leaping lithely across the landscape. He would fight. He would fight to the end, to whatever might come.

The night was almost upon them, the evening glow was fading and the dusk was setting in. *Dusk Runner*, Ell thought, reflecting on the meaning of his name, Elliyar. It seemed fitting to be running towards a battle on the eve of night, like the way his name depicted. In a way, he felt comfortable in the shadows. Yes, he longed to one-day fight with an army against his enemies, in the light, in the open without the familiar need to strike and then slink away. Yet, he had practically grown up as a warrior in the dark. All his earliest skirmishes and raids had happened at night. Strike and move, ambush and then leave the enemy licking their wounds and afraid of the darkness from which you had attacked. It was classic guerrilla tactics. Ell ran on, for once embracing the shadows he had long resented.

Suddenly, just as the last of light was fading, Dahranian shouted as he saw a form cresting the ridgeline not twenty feet above them. Everything happened fast. In the waning light, Ell saw sharp teeth flash, and a guttural, angry growl of a curse. One of the Departed. Ell reached for his bow, and struggled to unsling it from his shoulder and knock an arrow to loose in order to bring down what must be an enemy sentry. However, Dacunda was quicker. His longbow, dark and heavy, was off his shoulder in a flash and Ell was impressed to see that before Ell even had his arrow knocked, his uncle was releasing his own. The arrow flew true, and it struck the dark elf in the throat, preventing the Departed scout from blowing a warning blast on the horn it had been raising to his lips. Instead, the only sound emanating from the dark elf was a gurgling cry as he drowned in his own, dark blood.

As they rushed up to check the body, Ell strained to see if the blood was the typically dark brownish-deep red usual of the southern elves. Or if this elf, too, had the black blood Ell had seen on two occasions earlier; first in the Departed he had killed months ago, the one he had feared possessed a sickness, and the second being the dark elf he had slain in the chamber atop the Pillar protecting the trapdoor. Ell tried to see, but he couldn't tell if the blood was rusty brown as usual or the abnormal, inky black.

Dacunda checked the body for items that might be important. Missives from a commander, good weapons, and in general, anything at all that might be useful or give clues as to the plans of the scout's leader. Ell watched as the dying Departed's eyes flicked back and forth across their faces, as if struggling to memorize his killers' appearances while choking on his own blood and fluids. A few more moments longer and then the life went out of the dark elf's eyes. Ell was abnormally grateful for his death for some reason. It had felt strange to have the dying elf's fading gaze upon his face.

"This changes things," Dacunda murmured seriously, as he found nothing of import on the dead elf. He ripped his arrow free from the dead enemy's throat, leaving a gaping hole in his neck. "Silverfist is a traitor, someone to be despised. He is even a coward, at times," Dacunda admitted, "running from a battle he knows he cannot win. Yet, he is very clever, an astute commander. This missing sentry will not go unnoticed and Silverfist will know something is amiss." Dacunda rose quickly and motioned them to follow with the same urgency. "We must proceed quickly and pass the slavers, then press on to the village. Else I fear Silverfist will sense something in his plans is awry and will look to speed his arrival to the valley by pushing harder. We must reach the village in time to prepare it against his arrival."

Ryder spat on the body of the dead slaver. "Cursed, sentry. He had to complicate things, didn't he?" Ell's cousin asked the question of no one in particular, rather addressing his angry question rhetorically to the darkness enshrouding them.

They ran hard, almost recklessly, even for an elf of the Highest. The darkness made the ridgeline upon which they ran tricky. It was full of crevices and cracks between the boulders and rocks on which they stepped. Vines and creepers threatened to entangle their feet and roots of trees attempted to trip them in the night. But Ell and his family strained their senses to the extreme, not lessening their pace even though slowing down was advisable. Sometimes you had to do things, which went against sound counsel. Ell had learned the truth of that in the last few days after climbing the crag and riding the Icari.

On the trail-side of the ridgeline, Ell and his family could see the campfires of the slavers far below. Silverfist was among them, Ell was certain. His dueling dagger was quivering ever so slightly as he reached down to check it. He wouldn't have noticed it while running or while doing any movement. It was only barely vibrating. Ell only noticed because he knew what to feel for, and was expecting it, checking for it. He prayed that Silverfist was not paying nearly so close attention to his own dagger. Ell hoped it was in the traitor's sheath, and that the traitorous northern elf, turned slave commander against his own people, would not notice the vibration as Ell had. Their safety and ability to reach the village likely depended upon it. However, Ell still thought they would go unnoticed. After all, Ell had anticipated the vibrations when his own dagger came near its twin. His enemy had not known the counterpart was nearby, and would likely therefore, not be paying as close attention to the miniscule shakings of his own weapon.

They pushed on along the ridgeline, none of them talking. Silence was best at a time like this and they all knew what needed to be done. Run on the ridgeline, pass the slavers, and then rejoin the trail ahead of the small army camped below, and make one final push to the valley.

Eventually the lights of the slavers camp faded into the background and then into the far distance until the twinkling, flickering torchlight could no longer be seen. Yet even then, Dacunda would not let them rejoin the path.

Ell's uncle had them push on, along the ridgeline, through the night until dawn was almost breaking. They had not stopped to rest once, such was the urgency. Ell hoped they would have enough strength to sustain this same pace through the next day, as well.

Finally, Dacunda made the sign for them to begin their descent, as the grey light of morning crept over the mountains. The sun had not yet risen, but its light pierced the darkness, sending wisps and rays of light cutting through the clouds that clung to the sky. They reached the trail and immediately increased their pace.

"I know I have asked a lot of you. This was a difficult night and I know you must all need rest as badly as I do. Yet we cannot afford to do so. The slavers will surely be upon us if we stop even for a moment's break." Dacunda spoke apologetically even as he continued to run.

"We have asked a lot of ourselves, Uncle," Ell answered stoically. "This is not a mission to be taken lightly, and we have not come expecting anything other than challenges, difficulties, and danger."

Ryder and Dahranian voiced their agreement and they all continued to run through the morning sun as it crept up over the tops of the mountains and began its slow but steady job of warming the land beneath their feet.

Hours passed and they ran as hard as they could. Sometimes it almost felt as if they were sprinting rather than just running, so taxed was Ell's body from the days since they had left Miri, Rihya, and Art. Finally, when total exhaustion seemed almost upon them, Ell and his family saw the rise of the path as it ascended towards the last pass into Little Vale. The river would crest the pass and fall into the enormous waterfall, spilt in many directions as it fell to the valley floor. They had made it.

They ran up the pass, panting breaths, with heavy legs, and glimpsed the valley below. Smoke trailed lazily from a left over fire from the night before, a fire that should have been put out even in a village. The elves of this valley had definitely grown careless. They would be in for a rude awakening. Ell, Dacunda, Dahranian, and Ryder paused a moment at the top of the pass to look over the valley in which the Westrill flowed far below.

"Are you ready?" Dacunda asked softly.

"Ready for what, exactly?" Ryder asked curiously.

Dacunda's face was grim as he responded. "Are you ready for the fight of your life? Never have we faced odds as long as this. Not in all my years of raiding."

"We will survive, we always do," Ell said as Dahranian just stared out in his typical silent fashion.

Dacunda didn't look convinced. "We said Verdantihya would hold," he whispered, "and yet it did not. It fell indeed, and when it did, it did so tremendously, in a terrible fashion." He continued, "We said for decades that a Pillar couldn't be taken, couldn't be breached, and yet here you are Elliyar, to prove it isn't so." Ell's uncle shook his head. "I am no longer certain at all of what will or will not be. I have seen what were considered to be impossibilities, both good and bad, to be overthrown in my lifetime." Dacunda appraised the valley and then turned to stare at the three of them. "However, I do not know what will come of these next days. Recently, I feel as if I know nothing at all." He spoke solemnly, seriously. Ell felt the weight behind those words. It was true, the world was changing and reality was shifting. What was once impossible might not be so any longer, yet what had once been strong and held firm against the darkness in the land might also yet prove to fail.

But not this time Ell thought hopefully. He clung to hope, to the possibility they might still survive this battle, for if he didn't hold on to that, he did not think he would have the will to fight.

Chapter Twenty-Nine

Little Vale was tranquil like the calm before a storm. Ell dreaded what would happen to this place when the slavers arrived. The Departed had no care for nature or the preservation of the land. In that way, they were very similar to the humans with their machinery, logging, and overall gutting of the earth to serve their purpose.

"Keep your wits about you," Dacunda cautioned. "I know we are ahead of the slavers, but the valley is too quiet, something is off here." Ell's uncle spoke as they reached the bottom of the pass dropping into the valley. The descent, normally easy, had been difficult on their tired legs. Ell was worried about the battle ahead. How would they be of use to the villagers if they could not fight effectively?

The village was on the far northwest side of the valley along the north bank of the Westrill. The river flowed lazily, another contradiction to the fury and violence, which Ell knew would soon descend over the pass behind them. Hundreds of slavers might not seem like many when compared to the thousands upon thousands of humans who had crushed Verdantihya so many years ago like a nut between two stones, yet, it was all about perspective. The village could possess no more than seventy people at the absolute most and not a few of those were children or elderly. The numbers of worthy, battle-tested warriors were small.

Ell, his uncle, and cousins crossed the valley as swiftly as they could, although fatigue had long since made their limbs weary and heavy. They finally approached the village, only to see it was empty. No smoke curled through the holes in the roofs of the small cabins. No game was turning on the giant spit in the center of the village. No children played and laughed, and there were no friendly calls of welcome or recognition from one elf to another. Instead, silence greeted them. It was strange to see the village with such a hollow, ghostly feel to it. Ell remembered the way the village, upon his first arrival, had felt like something out of the tales of old. It hadn't been a swiftly erected nomadic camp such as every other settlement he had seen before. Instead, it had been lively, warm and full of life. Most of all it had felt settled, firmly in one place. That alone had been the most astounding aspect of the village. Aside from meeting Miri, of course, and how she had exposed him to an entirely new philosophy on life, one that was not entirely linked to war. Ell had grown up at war. He had cut his teeth in raids and battles. The idea that there could truly be something more to life had been completely foreign to him. Miri, and in a more general way, this village, had showed Ell he fought for a reason, he fought for a purpose, not just revenge, but a greater cause. He struggled and bled on behalf of freedom, the freedom to live a life not requiring blood as payment for survival. Ell felt sadness to see the village, which had provided him with all of those knew ideas and thoughts, looking so lonely and abandoned.

"Are we too late, Father?" Ryder asked anxiously. He was a jester and presented a carefree attitude most of the time, but his passion ran deeper than most would expect at first glance. The welfare of this village, these people, meant a lot to him. Ryder cast his gaze around the surrounding area, searching along with the rest of them for any sign of life.

Dacunda looked around for a few more moments before answering. "I do not think so, Ryder," he responded finally, speaking deliberately. Ell knew Dacunda well enough to know his uncle would not make such statements without reason.

"Oh?" Ryder questioned, waiting for more information.

Instead, it was Dahranian who answered. So like his father, Ell didn't doubt he took the words right from Dacunda's mouth. "Look around. There is no sign of struggle. No sign of items being gathered in a hurry in order to flee. Therefore, we can effectively rule out an attack already having happened. Besides, we know that Silverfist and his slavers are behind us. We passed them in the night and saw their fires. No," he continued thoughtfully, "I believe this to be a calculated decision. Maybe not long deliberated over, but neither was it an urgent choice to leave."

Dacunda nodded approvingly of his eldest son's ability to deduce the situation. "Yes," Ell's uncle agreed, as the sun returned briefly from behind its covering and illuminated his face for a moment, before the breeze carried a cloud back in front of the sun to obscure it once again. "I believe we will find what we are looking for there." Dacunda pointed up the slope behind the northern edge of the village. The clearing extended up along the mountainside. Ell could clearly see where his family had helped oversee the building of a last ditch fortification, over a month ago now.

The grass around them was the bright green of late spring, only slightly dulled by the dimness of the day, the clouds today depriving their surroundings of the ability to be lit up completely by the brilliance of the sun. The day was grey all around. Occasionally the sun poked its head through the clouds but it was always for a moment only. Today the sun was the unwelcome visitor.

They made their way up the slope and neared the top, the points of the sharpened stakes placed into the ground to impede an advancing force causing them to weave their way in and out as they climbed.

As they neared the top, where the earthen bulwark was erected, a voice called out. "Halt. Do not come further until I receive word of whether or not to admit you."

Ell's uncle glanced sideways at his family. His mouth quirked into a small, wry smile as he waited. "Well, at least they have made some changes around here in the last month. Maybe not everything I would have hoped, but still, even one guard is an improvement."

Ell and his cousins smiled with their uncle. It was true. The last time they had arrived here, they had been greeted with open arms. A peaceful setting was not something to be looked down upon. Of course, hospitality was a quality to strive for, yet during dangerous times, a little bit of caution did not go amiss.

Only a few minutes passed before the sentry called out again, "Advance." The elf kept his bow in his hands ready and an arrow knocked, although not drawn, as they entered the compound. The defensive structure was small and simple, but Ell knew it would prove to be more effective than having nothing at all. It was the same series of earthen walls, the making of which Ell's uncle had overseen over a month prior. Sharpened stakes protruded from the defenses as well, which would force any enemy to slow their advance while trying to climb over the obstacles. As an enemy slowed, the defenders could fire arrows and pick them off with whatever other weapons they had to defend themselves. The first wall was maybe twice the height of a male elf. Not enough to hold off an army by any means, but it would be better than nothing.

Dacunda nodded approvingly at the sentry at duty on the wall, along with his four other companions. The defending elves all straightened their backs at the approval from Ell's uncle. They remembered him. The wait for entry had been a formality, a necessary step of decision making along the chain of command.

Along the way to the cavern mouth, they'd had to pass over three more earthen bulwarks, each one about twice the height of an elf. It was not an impenetrable fortress by any means. But attackers would indeed be slowed down and have to bleed in order to take it.

Ell and his family were led into the small caverns, naturally carved out of the high slope of the mountainside. The caves penetrated deep into the mountain. Rows of pallets lined the walls, along with food stores and a few weapons. The Dimness of the interior of the mountain was a shock in comparison to the hazy, grey light of outside. The rough stonewalls were irregular, with stalactites dropping down from above. The remnants of stalagmites protruding up from the floor of the cavern were apparent. The rocky spines had been broken, and only the flattened nubs at the base of the stalagmites were left behind after having been cleared to create space and comfort. The whole cavern reminded Ell of the mouth of some unholy beast with jagged teeth, the bottom row of fangs knocked out.

As they entered the caverns, one of the elders met them. “Welcome,” he said, “I did not think we would have the pleasure of your company again so soon.”

Dacunda didn’t bother with pleasantries. Ell’s uncle had always been blunt. Speaking directly was better in his mind. Ell tended to agree with him.

“There is a small army of slavers less than a day behind us. I assume you know something of this as you have retreated here,” Dacunda waved a hand at the caves around them. The caverns were faintly lit, torches spaced at far intervals, in order to find the balance of being able to light the caves as well as possible, yet spaced far enough apart so as to conserve their resources.

The elder closed his eyes painfully at the news and then nodded gravely. “We feared something was seriously wrong. Our usual scout who goes west did not return two days ago, and the second we sent did not return either. The second should have returned by yesterday evening at the very latest. We knew something was wrong, so last night we gathered everything important, and in an orderly fashion, retreated to this place of safety.”

“That was wise,” Dacunda said. The elder inclined his head at the compliment. “There are hundreds of slavers, close on our trail, and we will need every spare moment to prepare. It is good you have gathered already what is needed.”

“Is there no time to run?” The elder questioned. He was clearly worried. “I do not expect we have enough fighters to survive against so large a force.”

“They are too close, I think, to run,” Dacunda disagreed. “Besides,” Ell’s uncle paused as he searched for the right words to say his next piece of information, “they are led by someone who is a good tracker, not to mention aided by one of your own.” Dacunda said the last part quietly. “I do not expect we could hide our trail from the two traitors should we choose to flee.”

The female elder Ell remembered from before had arrived and she had caught the majority of the conversation with her keen elf ears. She placed a hand on her heart and spoke. “Do you truly mean to say that one of our own has led them to us?” Her voice quavered as she spoke what, to her, must have been the most difficult news of all.

“I am afraid so,” Dacunda responded. “It’s what we were told by Miri.”

"The girl is somewhere nearby?" She asked in earnest excitement. Clearly, she was fond of Miri. Ell was not surprised. Who wasn't?

"She is not here. We had to push hard to reach you before the slavers since they had a head start on us. We were forced to leave Miri with my niece and another lad, who could not keep the pace."

The elder smiled, her eyes moistening up. "Perhaps her lame leg has finally turned a blessing if it has kept her from reaching this place with you. I expect the odds of our surviving are long." She spoke practically. Dacunda just met her eyes. No response was necessary. Hundreds of slavers. No more than seventy of the Highest to defend this primitive line of defense. The numbers spoke for themselves.

"Come," the male elder said, "You must be tired, hungry."

Ryder opened his mouth to agree enthusiastically, no doubt about the proposition of something to eat, but Dacunda shot him a glance and he shut his mouth with an exaggerated glumness.

"We would be glad of a bit of food, and a moment of rest, but it cannot be long. We must see to the defenses." Dacunda was business as usual.

"See to the defenses?" the female elder said in surprise. "You are staying? This is not your home. If I remember correctly, you did not even approve of our staying here. Which I must admit, in hindsight, seems like more folly than it did at the time." She ended with a sigh. "Why are you staying for a fight that is not yours, for a battle you could have avoided?"

"I do not run from the enemy of my people and neither does my family." Dacunda's back was straight, and he spoke proudly of his own ideals and of his family. "If this is the place to make our stand and enter the next reality, then so be it. Besides, there is always hope. Fortune may yet shine upon us."

"You are a good person," she answered Ell's uncle simply.

The next few minutes consisted of finding them the first hot meal they'd had in days. It was venison fresh from a spit. It was juicy and full of flavor as the grease from each bite flooded Ell's mouth and often ran down his chin. He wiped his face with the back of his hand as he finished one piece and thanked the elf who handed him another to replace the one he had just eaten.

Dacunda hardly rested or ate, before he started overseeing the defenses. There were hunters and even a few veteran warriors here in the valley, but none had experience like Dacunda. His history of fighting in the armies before the fall of Verdantihya, and even being present on that catastrophic day, not to mention the past two decades spent raiding, made him the obvious choice to assume command of the defenses. He had scouts run out to the western pass; a pair to watch each other's back. They would return when the enemy was sighted, bringing an estimate of how long before the enemy would reach the village.

"I expect they shall only be there a handful of hours at most," Dacunda admitted to his family as they spoke of the scouts and their plans together in a quiet moment. "However, every little piece of information we have is important. We do not have any advantage right now over the enemy other than weakly built fortifications. We shall have to conjure up some sort of advantage for ourselves over the Departed."

"Understood," Dahranian agreed. "Archers behind each bulwark, when the enemy does come, yes?" Dahranian continued when his father nodded to him. "Right. We'll have to find a way to arm everyone with the exception of only the very youngest and oldest here. Male, female, warrior or not, it makes no difference." Dacunda agreed again with a nod, although this time a bit more reluctantly. No doubt, Ell's uncle was recalling their most recent fight; the one after Ell and Miri had escaped with the others from the Pillar. The female elf companions of Miri, and the elderly male elf, had hardly stood a chance in the battle against the Departed. It had been necessary to arm them, just as it was now, but it didn't make the decision any easier. It was difficult knowing you were asking someone to do something, to put their life on the line, by fighting when they were not skilled in combat. There was no avoiding it, however, so why dwell on it? Ell told himself to squash the bile threatening to rise in his throat when he gave too much thought to the number of dead that would likely litter this mountainside over the next days. Dead warriors were one thing, it was sorrowful to see a comrade in arms fall in battle, yet fallen civilians were even harder for him to stomach. Ell prayed a prayer of thanks that Miri was safe and that she was anywhere but in this valley.

As the afternoon rolled on, the sun eventually won its battle with the clouds and the afternoon light burned through the grey covering for good. It was a pleasant reminder in the face of the battle to come that one could still find peace even in the midst of struggle. Ell rested, his hands placed together over the pole end of his shovel, his chin resting on the knuckles of his hands, just drinking in a moment of sunlight. A line of sweat trickled down his cheek from his brow.

Dacunda had ordered the bulwarks built as high as possible. And so the four rudimentary, earthen walls grew. With sharpened stakes poking out of them, the bulwarks resembled giant, dirty versions of the small Spinebacks, the little rodents that roamed the forest, their backs covered with tiny spines. Ell lent his strength to the task alongside Ryder. Dahranian was overseeing the arming of the less skilled fighters from the village. The females and youths, even the elderly who could still hold a weapon, which many could do since elves didn't age the way humans did, were with Dahranian. Elves grew old, but their strength didn't wane as much as one would think. However, usually in a short burst of physical decline, extremely old elves went from being fairly healthy, whole individuals to being on their deathbeds. Therefore, in this case, only the children were excluded from the battle strategy, since most of the elderly could still contribute to the defense.

Dahranian was the perfect candidate for arming and teaching them what he could during the intervening hours between now and when the slaver army showed up. Ell's eldest cousin was learned and a good weapons instructor. Yet, he was not arrogant or proud as a warrior. His sincerity would provide a safe environment for the villagers to practice and learn the spear, the knife, and even the sword, or whatever other weapons were lying around. Of course, there were hunters and skilled fighting elves residing in the village—this was a gathering of the Highest after all. However, there were not nearly as many as Ell had hoped. There were, perhaps, twenty elves in all who could be considered adept with a bow or a spear, and half of those were more hunters than warriors. There was a difference between killing game and taking life in battle.

All the same, Ell fought to keep his hope. He told himself he would see Miri again. That somehow, someway, they would wriggle out of this tight spot just as his family had managed so many times before. They had a habit of being survivors. *Besides, I didn't fight my way through a Pillar's worth of slavers and ride an Icari, as well, just to die in some forsaken massacre*, Ell thought to himself, half wry, half angry. Sometimes it was difficult to keep a finger on his emotions lately. They seemed to jump around and alternate so much. Ell even seemed to feel many emotions at once, where as in the past he had felt fairly steady in his thought patterns, his emotions predictable and rational considering his circumstances. Not so anymore. Love did that to you he supposed. It set your head back on your body upside down. It shook loose all the strange emotions lining the cracks and foundations of your consciousness. Where you once felt only anger and resolve in battle, now you felt fury, battle-rage, fear for others, sorrow for the dead, and even pity for your enemies at times. It was like a flood of different emotions had been released inside of him when he met Miri. His emotions had been a dam, but falling in love seemed to have opened the floodgates of the dam, almost the way Verdantihya's gates had been burst open so many years ago. Ell shoved his thoughts aside and kept working.

"Daydreaming again, cousin?" Ryder smiled mischievously. "She will be safe with your sister dearest." Ell nodded his response, not taking the bait to engage in conversation with Ryder. Ryder fancied himself an expert on love and females, even though Ell could not remember a single time he had seen his cousin speaking with one. Ryder could ignore facts such as that easily, however. Ell had no wish to hear him droning on about girls as they worked.

A horn blast, one of the villages hunting horns, saved Ell from having to listen to his cousin. The two scouts were still far across the valley, but the note carried. Ell could just vaguely see their outlines moving steadily towards the caverns on the mountainside. *One horn blast.* That meant the enemy army was approaching Little Vale.

Ell finished his section of the bulwark as quickly as he could, piling the loose dirt where it needed to go and packing it down with the flat end of his shovel. Then Ell walked over to stand with his uncle who stared impassively out over the valley, a commander surveying his troops and his position. It seemed fitting if this should be the end, that Dacunda should go out with an actual force of elves, albeit a small one, under his command rather than just a handful of family members mucking up the enemy's supply lines. His uncle deserved that much at least. *No, this is not the end!* Ell scrubbed a grimy hand through his similarly dirty hair angrily. He had to stay positive.

But it was hard to do so. They stared east, towards the pass at the end of the valley. It was afternoon and Ell and his family had arrived only a few hours earlier. Ell saw the sun beginning to drop in the sky. The orb of light cast its hazy glare directly upon its opposite, eastern horizon. The waterfall reflected the sun's light, glittering and sparkling; Ell could see it do so even from afar. One couldn't make out specific shapes or people, but before too long had passed, Ell could just see the darkness of a mass of Departed spreading over the pass and down toward the basin. The slaver's army had arrived, and if possible, it looked even bigger than it had last night by torchlight when he and his family had looked down upon it from the ridgeline above their heads. Ell supposed it was possible that another few bands of slavers might have been in the area, had been attracted by the fires, and joined them. It was a grim sight.

They rolled over the pass, like a small wave of darkness. The intervening ground between the caverns on the mountainside above the village and the pass seemed pitifully small. The enemy would arrive shortly.

"Time to take your positions," Dacunda said gruffly. "Ell, you are our best shot. I want you in command of the archers. Ryder, your axe and your natural tendencies are more of a brawler, so I want you at the bulwarks and in the trenches leading the defense of our makeshift walls." Ell's uncle smiled to cushion the statement, and Ryder grinned showing no hard feelings. He was at home in his own skin. He was a brawler and he relished the fact.

Ell's uncle wasn't finished. "Dahranian, I want you in command of the reserves, those who are not officially trained as warriors and fighters, though I do not expect they shall be reserves for long," he finished with a grim murmur. "You, Son, are adept at giving confidence to those who may be lacking. The villagers here will need encouragement badly." He placed a fond hand on his eldest son's shoulder. Dahranian nodded, resolutely. He would do whatever Dacunda said. It was natural for him to follow his father's orders. He was the perfect soldier. It was also what made him a great leader, because when the occasion did arise for him to assume command in Dacunda's absence, he expected absolute submission the same as he gave to his father. His expectation that his commands be followed tended to result in his orders being executed with great efficiency. Confidence, Ell had learned, was essential to being a good leader and commander of troops. *Or any other aspect of life really,* he thought to himself.

"I shall direct the battle, although likely my blade will be needed soon enough." Dacunda was almost finished. "Ell, your archers will begin firing when the enemy is 100 yards away, no further. We have the slope and the arrows will carry, but we cannot afford to waste any either. Make them count." He spoke firmly, impressing his point to Ell. Ell understood. This was a life or death situation. A battle true. Ell realized he had mostly raided his whole life. This sort of confrontation was a new experience for him. Usually, you just fired the arrows you had, and when they ran out or the enemy closed the distance, you engaged in hand to hand combat until it was time to cut and run, disappear into the shadows as they always did until it was time to repeat the process and raid again. There would be no running this time.

"All will go well, Uncle." Ell tried to make his voice sound confident. Dacunda smiled and placed a hand on his shoulder like he had with Dahranian.

"Of course," Dacunda said simply. His lack of other words implied his belief that it would probably be the opposite. Dacunda leaned in close and spoke quietly in Ell's ear. "Will you be able to access your ability? It could be the difference between life and death for us."

"I will… try, Uncle." Ell attempted to sound confident again, but knew he fell short. "It has never come by choice, though, I must admit. It seems to only come by accident."

Dacunda nodded in understanding and said no more. The disappointment was clear on his face, however. Ell felt a burn of shame once again. What was the point of being a Water Caller if you couldn't access your abilities at will? What was the point of having the power of the land, creation itself at your fingertips only to be unable to grasp it if your life and the lives of those you loved depended on it? Ell felt the familiar, sour taste of humiliation in his mouth as they all clasped hands and then set out for their posts. Would he ever master his power?

Ell was in charge of the archers and they were posted on either flank of the battleground, which admittedly was very small. Four earthen battle works had been erected and a trench dug in front of each to make the wall even higher.

Each constructed wall of dirt was separated from the next only by a short distance of maybe thirty feet. Ell and the elves under his command set up their positions along the second wall. Ryder would be leading the defense along the first earthen rampart, dug out of the mountain, with stones and boulders jammed in its dirt to make it stronger. There was no need for the archers to be in the middle of the fray. Their job was to slow down the enemy's assault, break it if they could, and then pick off the enemy soldiers that came close to breaking through the fortifications.

The naturally formed caverns were near the top of a mountain. The slope leading up to them was steep, which was Ell and the villagers' biggest advantage, that and the way the slope narrowed at the top. On the western edge, the slope tapered drastically and fell off into almost a cliff. It would be extremely difficult for the enemy to attack from the west. Due south, a straight charge up the slope, was the most obvious route of attack. Ell hoped their efforts to create a hasty defense would prove to be enough to stem the enemy. The sharpened stakes would help tremendously, as they would force the enemy to slow down or else be skewered on the wooden spears jutting out from the mountainside. This would allow the archers free reign to pick them off. At least he hoped it would be so simple.

The small army advanced across the valley, and Ell surmised there was still about an hour until they would reach the village below the caverns. Ell took the moment to reach deep within himself. *Search*, he told himself. *Find something of which to grab hold. Your life, everyone's life, could depend on your tapping into your ability!*

He pressed himself, sweat breaking out on his forehead. Ell stretched his consciousness; he tried to feel the land the way Arendahl had always said. It was futile. He shook his head in disgust. *What use were his abilities if they were outside his reach when he needed them most?*

Ell blinked. Had reaching inside for his abilities really taken that much time? The enemy was almost there, meaning an hour must have gone by. Training sessions with Arendahl had passed likewise at times, but Ell hadn't expected it to happen right now.

He glanced around at his archers who were looking at him strangely, likely they didn't have a clue why he had been pressing his eyes shut and sweating for an hour. Ell didn't bother to explain, it wouldn't do to give them a hope he couldn't fulfill. It looked like he was on his own, without his powers, unless his ability decided to appear of its own accord.

"Ready?" He asked his archers. Dacunda had deemed the archers important and had allotted him a grand total of eight. The rest of the able bodies would be defending the wall, or held as a second line of defense to refresh the first line when they grew exhausted. It was ironic really that only eight bodies could be spared for something his uncle thought extremely important. But such was the case when you were attempting an undermanned defense against a larger force.

The elves under his command nodded silently. Some seemed steady, but a few looked nervous. Ell didn't really know what to say to them. He had never had to lead people in battle. His wealth of experience had always involved doing what his uncle gave him to do, and raiding small numbers of the enemy then melting into the forest again. There was no disappearing from this battle. Their backs were to the mountain, and although the caves might provide some shelter, they would not do so forever.

Ell turned his gaze at the mass of enemy soldiers gathering at the base of the slope hundreds of feet down. There certainly did appear to be more Departed than he had previously thought. By a quick estimate, there looked to be over four hundred dark elves at the base of the mountain. Ell sighed inwardly. It would take a miracle to survive this. They would bleed the enemy certainly, but in the end, numbers usually won.

The small slaver army under the command of Silverfist seemed content to wait out the afternoon. They set fire to some buildings in the village, and raucous laughter could be heard faintly, drifting up, wafting on the breeze in the direction of Ell and the villagers. They must be waiting for darkness he realized. It was not a bad strategy. The archers under Ell's command would find it more difficult to pick off their targets at night. Defense would be much more difficult without the archers at full ease. However, it wouldn't be easy for the slavers either. Those stakes jammed into the mountainside on the approach to the first wall would slow a person down in full daylight, and even more so in the darkness. It was a trade off really. Silverfist must be gambling that the darkness would impede Ell's archers more than it would aid them as they chose their dark elf targets. They would find out before too long whom it would end up benefiting. Ell tried to wipe the grim expression from his face. People needed to see hope when faced with dire odds like this. He wasn't sure if he succeeded, because the archers around him wore even grimmer expressions than his.

And so they waited.

The light faded gradually. It felt like the longest afternoon of his life. In a way, Ell wished the enemy would just get it over with and attack. He supposed it was just another part of Silverfist's strategy. Make your enemy nervous, anxious. Finally, the evening came and the light truly was almost gone. Ell could see the slavers vaguely in the shadow light. They appeared to be milling around, preparing for some action, an assault no doubt.

Finally, as night set upon the valley, a horn blew loudly from below. It wasn't the short warning blasts Ell had heard near the Pillar. This was a long, deep note from a war horn. The battle was beginning.

Chapter Thirty

If the slope leading up to the caverns had not been fairly narrow, with a small cliff on one side and sharpened stakes more densely situated around the outside edges funneling the enemy inwards into a killing channel, then the battle would have been over long ago. As it was, they were barely hanging on by their teeth and no more than half of an hour could have passed since the battle began.

Silverfist had whipped his slavers into a frenzy. An initial attack force had charged upwards. The first enemy contingent had been about one hundred warriors strong. It was most likely a test. One quarter of his troops to test the villagers' mettle, to see if they could hold their ramshackle defenses for even five minutes. And they had. Ell and his companions had held the defenses for half of an hour. It had been bloody, and the villagers had already taken casualties, but they were still holding.

Ell released another arrow and feathered a Departed warrior whose head had just popped up over the top of the earthen bulwark. The dark elf fell backwards, dead, an arrow through one eye.

At first, Ell and his eight archers had simply loosed small flights of arrows as the enemy charged up the hill. They had brought down a few. But there just weren't enough archers to really send a hail of arrows upon the slavers. Ell and the archers under his command were more precise now. The enemy contingent had been whittled down; maybe twenty of their number deceased. The enemy dead were lying on the ground, riddled with arrows or stabbed full of wounds. Some of the recently dead Departed rolled or slid slowly back down the steep hill, impeding the progress of their living compatriots trying to move upwards.

The village archers now targeted any enemy warrior who looked to be about to make his way over the bulwarks. Ryder and his companions held the earthen wall. They defended it sloppily, slipping and sliding in the dirt made muddy with blood. Ryder cleaved with his long axe. He used the blade at one end to relieve the attacking enemies of a limb here or a head there, and with the haft of his long axe, he cracked skulls and broke wrists. He was a force to be reckoned with, a fury of pain and death. Dacunda had withheld from the actual fighting at first, but quickly his instincts had over taken his ideals and truth be told, he realized there was not a lot of strategic maneuvering to do at this point. Once the battle had commenced, it was clear what everyone's job was. The archers fired arrows and picked off enemy Departed who looked to break the line of defense on the wall. Either the rest of the villagers were at the wall as a first line of defense led by Ryder, or they were part of the reserve crew led by Dahranian, waiting for their turn to step in and allow the first line a rest. There was no third line. The reserve line also finished off any dark elves who managed to break through the lines and avoid the archers' arrows, as well. A few children, much too young to fight, carried small flasks filled with the vital Source Water to heal the worst of the wounds. So far the strategy had worked. Time would tell if it would continue to do so.

Ell fired again, killing a slaver who was about to attack Dacunda while he was focused on fending off two other dark elves that were trying to climb the wall. Ell's arrow took the slaver in the throat and the elf fell off the wall, knocking down two other enemy warriors who were trying to climb, as well. Ell's archers did the same as him, loosing arrows and providing cover for the first line.

It was desperate fighting. Ell saw one villager run through the gut with a spear, a wound too devastating to waste Source Water on. It was a fine line, determining when to utilize Source Water. Small wounds were too insignificant to heal, but terrible ones like the elf who was speared through the gut required too much of their precious water. It was a brutal decision, but Dacunda had made everyone understand before the onset of the battle. Only those who were too injured to fight, but could be cured with minimal application of the Source Water, were to be aided first.

Another villager, a female of the Highest, her face streaked with sweat and her golden hair clinging to her once fair, now dirty face, screamed in terror. Ell saw a catchpole loop its noose over her head and drag her over the wall to the enemy side. The Departed were slavers. They wanted living slaves, not dead bodies. Nobody leaped over the wall to save the captured female. Another elf from the reserve line simply stepped up grimly to take her place. Ell felt a pang of anguish that she had experienced exactly what they were fighting to prevent. Ell shuddered to think of what might happen to her as the lone captive slave in a small army of dark elves. He imagined if it had been Miri and his anger flared.

Ell fired arrow after arrow into the enemy attackers. The dark metal tips of his arrows glinted in a sinister fashion in the makeshift torchlight illuminating the battlefield. Silverfist had held his attack until nighttime to make the defense more difficult, because the archers would have a harder time seeing targets. However, Dacunda had countered the tactic by simply ordering large stand poles with torches at the top to light the night as best they could with their guttering, flickering light. It was a bit of a draw tactically, neither side really gaining an advantage from the circumstances.

Arrows began firing from below, as well, and most of those arrows began targeting Ell and his archers. The enemy knew that if they could kill the archers then the wall would likely crumble much more easily. Resistance was difficult without someone watching your back. Which is exactly what Ell and his crew of eight archers did. They watched the backs of their companions from above, picking off Departed warriors in a bloody mess. Ell and his companions loosed arrows, ducked behind boulders to take cover, and then popped up to quickly fire another shot before ducking back down again. It wasn't a perfect process but nothing ever went exactly according to plan once the chaos of battle began during war. And this was war. Ell harbored no doubts about that. Mayhem reigned. All a person could do was keep their wits about them and remember the fundamentals of battle. In this case, for the archers, it was simple. Duck, reload, find a target, loose. Then repeat.

An arrow grazed Ell's shoulder and buried itself in the chest of one of his archers behind him. Ell saw the hunter's eyes glaze over in death. There was no need to bring Source Water for that injury. Rage filled him even stronger and he fired more arrows and faster, picking off targets left and right. Ell concentrated his cover for Ryder and Dacunda. It might sound callous to ignore the rest of the defenders, but Ell knew that however his family faired, so went the defense of this location. The caverns would fall if they fell. The first line of defense would certainly falter if Dacunda and Ryder died. So Ell protected his family, feathering Departed with arrows. He lost track of how many dark elves he killed in the dim light of the torch-lit night. Loose, draw, loose. He repeated the action over and over, his black Dreampine arrows lodging themselves in the enemy. Ell fired his customary dark arrows as he always had, feathering targets with his typical deadly accuracy, the only difference now was that this time the enemy knew his arrows were coming, rather than being taken by surprise in an ambush. It was a strange turn of events from the way he had been living his life, always fighting from the shadows, from hiding. Not anymore.

Exhausted and worn, bloody and broken, the first line of defense gave way on Dahranian's command and the reserve line stepped forward. The two lines of defense essentially traded functions, reserve line becoming defense line and defense resting and becoming reserve.

Another catchpole looped over the top of the wall, and the noose hooked another elf, this time a male, some kind of artisan if Ell remembered correctly.

The elf had helped make the small log houses. The elf whimpered pitifully as the enemy dragged his kicking, moaning body over the side of the wall. Ell loosed an arrow to try to sever the rope that hooked the villager, but he missed. The villager disappeared into the mass of bodies clogging the hillside.

The night wore on. Ell didn't know how long he loosed arrows. Eventually he ran out, and so did the rest of his archers. When that happened, they just took up arms and joined the defense at the bulwark, bolstering the lines as best as possible.

Departed died, the dark elves screaming and cursing in pain as they did. Villagers were lost, as well. Some died, but more often than not catchpoles came in close, hooking elves and dragging them over the wall unless the elf being captured or their defense companions had the presence of mind to cut the rope immediately. It was pandemonium, utter confusion at the wall. Eventually, Ell and his family were forced to fall back with the villagers to the second bulwark. The second earthen wall was smaller, since the slope narrowed as it went higher up the face of the mountain in the direction of the caverns.

Ell fought with a spear, fending off Departed, their vicious faces snapping their filed, sharp teeth in the light of the torch flames overhead. He killed and killed. And just when he felt his limbs were too heavy to fight any longer, surprisingly, another lengthy horn note sounded in the night. The enemy gradually disengaged and the dark elf troops fell back down the hill, carrying their catchpoles and axes, their swords and bloody spears with them. Ell panted for breath. *Why had the enemy stopped the attack? Why did Silverfist not press them further?* They had been dangerously close to breaking. Ell didn't understand, but it couldn't erase the elation he felt. They had held, against the odds, for most of the night against the first force sent up from below. It had been a tight confrontation, and Ell wasn't convinced they could have lasted much longer, but it didn't change the facts. Somehow, they had held. Ell let a smile spread on his face.

He turned to one side and saw Ryder grinning behind him, blood and dirt and ash from the fire of a torch smudged on his face.

"Not bad, cousin! Fun little skirmish that was." Only Ryder could refer to the life and death struggle, the all or nothing defense of the bulwark as a skirmish. Ell smiled to himself wryly. That was Ryder for you.

Ell threw back his head and laughed, letting the wind grab at his wavy blond hair as it whipped to and fro around his head. High up on the mountainside the wind was strong. Ell welcomed it. For some reason, the wind reminded him he was free. Improbably, against the odds, they had survived the night. Suddenly all he could do was drink in the moment. Air tasted sweet. The smell of their sweat was more pungent. His muscles ached from the strain of a night spent taking part in the last ditch defense of their position, and the ache was beautiful; it told him he was alive.

He collapsed against Ryder, one arm slung around his cousin's shoulders. "It never felt so good to just be alive, Ry." Ell tilted his head back and just breathed. The dawn was breaking and the sky began to reveal itself as stars winked out across what had moments before been the night sky. Morning came quickly in the mountains.

"Yes, indeed," Ryder answered. His face had a serious look to it even though he smiled. He must feel the weight of what they had just done, as well.

Dacunda flanked by Dahranian strode up. As they did, they clasped hands and patted the shoulders of their troops, boosting morale as they went. They came to stand beside Ell and Ryder.

"This stinks of something strange," Dacunda muttered to them. "We were inches from breaking, why would Silverfist have his men withdraw?"

"Perhaps they think to wait us out, siege format." Dahranian offered his opinion. "He wants slaves, after all, not a bunch of dead bodies. You saw the Departed using their catchpoles whenever possible. There must have been three or four of ours dragged over the mound last night."

Dacunda appraised his eldest son. "It is possible," he conceded. "That could make sense, I suppose." He shook his head, however, still confused. "Yet, slaving aside, simply in regards to battle tactics, it made no sense for him to withdraw."

Ell felt a chill run through him. They had survived, but it had been at the whims of a traitor. They lived at Silverfist's mercy. His euphoria from a few minutes before disappeared. He answered his uncle's statement.

"That's because to them, this isn't a battle." Three heads turned to Ell, disbelief written on their faces. And certainly, they had cause to think him wrong. After all, when one looked downslope you could see the mountainside littered with dead bodies. All signs indicated it had been a battle.

Ell ignored the bodies of the Departed who had been caught in the rush of the attack and skewered on the stakes protruding from the slope leading up to the bulwarks. He ignored the villagers scavenging vital arrows from the dead bodies of the slavers left to rot beneath the defenses. He pushed on to speak his mind.

"Well, at least not a battle in the proper sense of the word," he amended his previous statement. "To him, Silverfist, this isn't a real fight. It's just a large-scale quest for slaves. A slave hunt. That's the sole purpose of his expedition up here. Forget the number of Departed clogging the village below. Forget the fact that there is a small army of our enemies to contend with down there. If you just look at the facts, we have around seventy people here all told.

Silverfist summoned a small army of just over four hundred by the looks of it." Everyone was listening now. "That's nearly six to one odds, give or take. It's not much different than the twenty plus slaver bands that capture three or four of the Highest and cart them back to a Pillar."

"This really is just about slaves," Dahranian agreed solemnly with Ell's logic, reinforcing his own earlier appraisal of the situation. He spat. "Bastard. It's not enough to betray and then kill us, but he has to take our people away, as well."

Ell's blood ran cold as he heard Dahranian agree with him so matter-of-factly. Ell glanced around at the villagers gathering arrows and nursing their wounds. It was true he realized. There were a few dead villagers from the night before, but in reality, most of their injuries had not been mortal. Silverfist had likely instructed his first wave of attackers to wound but not kill. Dead slavers were no cost to Silverfist, but dead *slaves* on the other hand brought him no money. The greedy traitor would sacrifice his own men for money. The first wave of attackers had been an attempt to overwhelm the defenses with as little loss of life on both sides as possible. That hadn't worked out well for his men, since Ell could see many dead Departed littering the mountainside, but in terms of wanting to keep the majority of his slave-to-be population alive, Silverfist had succeeded masterfully. The traitor had sacrificed many of his own warriors, already captured a few of the villagers with catchpoles, and weakened the villagers' defenses considerably enough that another strong push might be enough to overwhelm them without too much loss of life. *Is that what awaits us?* Ell thought bitterly. *A life of enslavement? Not for me,* he determined in his heart. He would rather die than live his life as a slave.

The same realization seemed to be sinking into the minds of his cousins and uncle. "So," Dacunda said grimly, "this is truly a slave hunt. Well, they will find it the most costly hunt ever." He punctuated the sentence by clenching his fists. Dacunda was usually a formidable foe, but when he grew angry, he was terrifying indeed. Ell saw the look of fury growing in his uncle's eyes. Dacunda was old enough to remember what it was like for the Highest, as a people, to be strong and proud, to have a real army, not just scattered, rag-tag bands of raiders. It must be more difficult for him to come to terms with how far the northern race of elves had fallen, than for Ell and his generation who had never known anything but the current plight of their people. There was a small feeling of shame, which simmered in his heart every time he struck and then ran away. It had been with him his whole life, Ell realized. But not so with Dacunda, he had needed to adjust his thinking much more to adapt to the existing circumstances. Ell was glad that today and always, he fought alongside Dacunda as he saw the look of anger harden in his uncle's eyes. The slavers would pay dearly indeed.

The next hour was spent retrieving arrows, rationing out tiny portions of Source Water, and throwing the dead Departed who had managed to breach the makeshift walls before they were killed, back to the outside. Many of those dead slavers were cast over the small cliff on the western edge of the slope. It was easy disposal. The villagers, under Dacunda's guidance, made certain to clear away all the dead bodies just outside the bulwarks, so as to be ready when the next assault came. And it would come, Ell was certain. They could not allow the dead bodies to provide stepping-stones for the enemy to climb upon when that happened. All the while, Dacunda had appointed a few sentries to keep a close watch on the dark elves gathered below in the burnt out husk of the village and to raise the alarm if they showed signs of readying themselves for another attack.

Ell sat against the earthen mound of the secondary bulwark. It was a rare moment of rest and he reclined gratefully. The sip of Source Water he had drunk had done only a small amount to replenish his energy, yet he could drink no more because the remaining Source Water would be needed when the next attack came. Dacunda squatted beside him, a spear lying crosswise on his bent legs.

"What happens now, Uncle?"

Dacunda looked at Ell wearily. "Silverfist has decisions to make, Elliyar. Depending on those decisions, we will see what happens."

Ell cocked his head waiting for an explanation. Dacunda obliged. "Silverfist threw only a portion of his forces against us; he hoped it would be enough to overwhelm our defenses. Yet, he clearly instructed them to try to capture and wound rather than kill. Even his archers focused only on you and your archers, Elliyar. Silverfist clearly only wanted to neutralize what he perceived to be a threat making it difficult to penetrate our walls. He didn't want his archers killing our lines of defense along the bulwarks."

Ell sighed. He saw where this was going, but asked the question anyways. "So, what are the different scenarios?"

"One scenario is that Silverfist continues as he has been doing. He commands his people to attack with catchpoles and to wound not kill. We will bleed them very badly if they decide to do so, as you can see from last night." Dacunda spoke gravely.

"And?" Ell drew the word out, not really wanting to hear another scenario, since he could see it would likely be worse than the one prior to it. Yet, he needed to know, needed to hear it.

Ell's uncle smiled grimly at him. "His second option is to abandon his desire for slaves and treat this like an actual assault and just focus on taking this ground. He can instruct his soldiers to capture when possible but over all to focus on killing. This scenario is much more practical. You neutralize a threat and then see what advantages can be taken from the situation afterwards. Less slaves captured, but he retains more of his soldiers. The gains are perhaps less, but so is the risk. We would fall quickly should he decide on that option, I think."

"What do you think he will do?" Ell asked.

Dacunda shook his head. "I do not know. I have not spent time around the traitor for many years. But I do know he has always been greedy, leading me to believe the first scenario is possible. Yet, he is also a crafty and practical battle commander as shown by the countless confrontations he has survived and won. Therefore, the second scenario feels just as possible." Dacunda sighed. "Truth is, I just don't know, Elliyar."

What did it matter, anyways, Ell realized. "Either way, both result in the same end, don't they, Uncle? One just takes longer for us to be killed or captured than the other." Dacunda's silence was answer enough. Ell continued. "It appears that all we can hope for is to bleed them grievously before this is over."

Dacunda took a deep breath. "I will not argue otherwise, Nephew. What you say is most likely true. Just look at their forces in comparison to ours." Ell looked and saw what his uncle meant. The Departed were much more numerous and the villagers and Ell's family had even less numbers with which to defend than they'd had the night before. Not to mention the dark elves were all soldiers trained for war, and blood, and violence. Apart from Ell, his family, and a few of the hunters, this group of Ell's people was remarkably unskilled in combat. A fact exemplified by their decision to revert to a more peaceful and antiquated way of life, building a small settlement as opposed to the nomadic lifestyle of hunters, refugees, and raiders.

"I see what you mean, Uncle. So this is it then?" It wasn't as much of a question as Ell made it sound. He knew the eventual outcome of this battle.

Dacunda surprised him, however. "The odds are certainly stacked against us, Elliyar. And I cannot tell you that I expect us to survive. But," Ell's uncle held up an admonishing finger, "miracles have happened before. The impossible has been done at times and I will not completely give up hope of emerging victorious, somehow or some way. Even though it be only the slimmest of slim chances that we win, I will fight as if that is a possibility."

Ell nodded silently. His uncle clapped him on the shoulder and then moved on to continue overseeing the work to be done between assaults. *Miracles have happened before, as well as the impossible.* Ell heard his uncle's sentiments echo in his head. He shrugged off the responsibility he felt. The weight was unbearable. Those impossible feats accomplished recently had occurred because of Ell's abilities. Well, not entirely, Ell corrected himself. He had climbed the crag and ridden the Icari on his own natural merits, but everything else was due to his powers as a Water Caller. What Dacunda had really been implying, whether that implication was conscious or subconscious, was that unless Ell somehow managed to tap his ability deliberately, then they were doomed.

Ell ran his fingers through the dirt of the inside wall of the bulwark. He let the bloody mud, now dried to a crust in the late spring sunshine, crumble between his fingers. Blood. More of his people's blood would be spilled unless he could access his ability. Ell was exhausted, but he tried anyways. He reached out his consciousness; he tried to find the source of power, which should be at his fingertips. He angrily muttered a curse as he grasped at nothing. Nothingness. That was all he felt. He didn't deserve to be a Water Caller. His uncle would have been a better recipient of the power, more worthy of it or Dahranian possibly. They both had the discipline, the self-belief to control it. Ell couldn't even control his temper at times. That had been evidenced during multiple raids, not to mention the latest ambush of Silverfist over a month ago now, and his rash plan to free Miri. Granted the last example had succeeded, but only because his family had been waiting to bail him out once he escaped the Pillar.

Ell didn't deserve to be a Water Caller. He was a warrior, nothing more. A gift of power and prestige, which required such preparation and education to access, it just wasn't for *him*. Ell was a simple elf. He hadn't even reached his twentieth name day.

Dahranian came and snapped him out of his reverie. "Something is happening below." As if on cue, Ell noticed the slight vibration of his dueling dagger strapped to his thigh, reminding him that somewhere below, Silverfist lurked. The elf who had betrayed his people and caused the downfall of the last great, northern stronghold. The Highest who had ruined Verdantihya. The elf who had killed his father. The silent litany of Silverfist's wrongs repeated itself in Ell's mind almost by rote.

Ell hoisted himself up to lay on the top of the wall, ignoring the filth and grime, which had collected on his long-sleeved, hooded tunic, and his dark hose. This was battle, war, and war was never clean. Down below, in and around the village, bodies were moving first one way and then another. It was almost as if there was a conflict of some kind as Ell observed the Departed swarming around each other, looking like nothing so much as hornets stirred from their nest. They didn't appear to be fighting, but there was movement and shouting. A disagreement of some kind. Then one dark elf charged up the mountain, and all of a sudden, another followed. Before Ell knew it, half the slavers below had followed suit and were running wildly. Ell could hear the snarling, growling of their curses as they made their way swiftly up the mountainside.

"Battle ready!" Dacunda shouted the command. Ell looked behind him to the second bulwark where his archers waited, ready to fire the arrows they had collected after the first assault had finished. They would know what to do now. It was simple really. Ell had a feeling he would be needed more at the front this time. Ell rushed to the first bulwark and took his place in the first line with his cousin, Ryder, and his uncle. Dahranian stood behind to command the second line as before. Ell glanced around and saw how pitifully small their forces were in comparison to the small horde of dark elves charging up the hill and gnashing their teeth filed to points.

After a few moments of running, the other half of the Departed warriors below must have decided that if half their comrades were running to battle then they all might as well do so. The rest of the enemy forces committed themselves and Ell stared down the hill as hundreds upon hundreds of angry dark elves, filled with battle rage, sprinted up the hill brandishing their weapons. It was easily three times the numbers Silverfist had committed in the attack the night before. And they were fresh while Ell and his companions were exhausted.

"No catchpoles," Ryder murmured.

"So, Silverfist made his decision," Ell directed his comment to his uncle. Dacunda nodded once, grimly. It would be a full on assault, no quarter, no need for capture. It appeared the slavers had abandoned their original intent and were now seeking to conquer first, capture second. *Perhaps we bloodied them enough to make them think twice about their initial strategy last night.* Ell felt a grim satisfaction at the thought, even as near certain death charged up the mountainside. It had been strange, however, the way half the force had attacked first and had then been followed by the second portion of their enemy forces almost as an afterthought. Was there division in the enemy troops? Had Silverfist lost control? Ell was confused. He didn't have long to be baffled, however. Arrows started raining down from his archers behind the second bulwark, peppering the enemy. Yet the few archers could hardly do much to slow the progress of a force of hundreds.

Ell leaned forward on the mound upon which he stood next to Ryder, who was hefting his axe in a deliberate fashion. Dacunda held his spear at the ready, his sword in the sheath at his hip for later use. Ell readied himself also, spear held tightly and body braced for the impact he knew would surely follow in the next few moments. Time seemed to slow down for a moment, Ell flashed back to good moments with Miri. Holding her hand, kissing her, seeing the Wandering Mist on their last night together in the valley when they had gone to the falls. He fought for her. He fought for his people. No longer did Ell only fight for fury and vengeance, although those emotions were still strongly within him, but he also fought for love. That truth strengthened him as he faced his death.

The impact was immense as the bodies of the slavers hit the wall and were then trampled and clambered over by their rabid comrades from behind. The Departed were whipped into a blood frenzy. Battle had been joined once again—perhaps the last battle Ell would ever fight.

Chapter Thirty-One

Ell ran a slaver through with his spear. They had only been fighting for a few minutes but already it felt like hours. The weight of the full mass of the Departed army storming the earthen walls pressed in on the defenders. Ell feared they would soon buckle. It did not feel like they could hold this first bulwark for very long. A few arrows from Ell's archers feathered the dark elves as they fought their way up to the brink of the wall but there was a disappointingly few number of arrows. What did he expect when there were only a handful of archers?

Ell kicked the dead body of the Departed elf and yanked his spear free, letting the body fall back towards the outside. It hit two dark elves on the descent, knocking them to the ground. They grunted and then growled furiously sounding more like animals than elves. Something was strange about the Departed in the first wave of the attack, the ones who had broken free and led the charge up the hill. They reminded Ell of something. He couldn't put his finger on what, however, and the mayhem surrounding him made it hard to think.

Instead, Ell just reacted. He dodged an upward thrust of a spear by one of the slavers attempting to scale the small earthen wall. Then Ell jammed his spear back down at the dark elf, slicing deeply into the Departed's face as he did so. The Departed screamed in rage, his eyes bearing a glazed expression. Ell rammed his spear at the screaming dark elf again and his spear entered the sharp-toothed mouth of the Departed, the point bursting through the back of the elf's skull. The scream ended abruptly in a bloody gurgle.

Dacunda had discarded his spear after having it snapped in two by a particularly powerful Departed. Ell's uncle laid about with his sword. He was death incarnate. A determined expression painted his sweat and blood streaked face. Dacunda decapitated one Departed who crested the wall, then lopped off the arm of another, sending the dark elf into a screaming fit of shock.

Ell saw Ryder and Dahranian, fighting side by side, brothers in arms as well as by blood. Ryder's long axe was sopping wet. The entire blade was dark with blood of the Departed. Even the clumps of moss, which grew on the haft of Ryder's axe, were soaking up the blood like wartime sponges. Ell was grateful, once again, that Miri and his sister had escaped this tragic circumstance.

Ell used the butt end of his spear like a stave and clubbed a dark elf who had reached the top of the bulwark. Ell knocked the hand axe from the elf's grasp and then stabbed with his spear. The Departed blocked the thrust with his small shield, but then an arrow from one of Ell's archers took the Departed in the neck and he toppled back to his bloodthirsty comrades below.

On and on they fought. Ell lost track of time. At some point, the two lines of defense merged into one. You couldn't have two lines of defense when enough people died. Female Highest fought and died alongside their male elf counterparts. Ell felt the same stab of anguish at the villagers' deaths as he had felt in the fight after rescuing Miri from the Pillar. Something felt wrong about those who had only sought peace and quiet falling in such a violent manner.

Someone sounded a retreat, and Ell and his family led the line of defense back to the second, and then shortly thereafter, to the third bulwark. Each earthen wall was successively smaller in length around the mouth of the caverns and therefore easier to defend. However, the waning number of defenders made the outcome inevitable.

Slash, stab, kick, block. The motions of battle became routine. Screams and shouts filled the air, both of pain and anguish and of the dark joy of victory when an enemy was vanquished. Ell looked to the side and saw a Departed warrior sink his teeth into the neck of a village girl as she attempted to heft her spear. Apparently the rumors were true, the Departed really did use those filed upper teeth for more than just appearances. Ell felt a sinister chill when he noticed the dark elf didn't spit anything out after biting the girl. Instead, he just swallowed without chewing. Blood and elf meat found its way into the dark elf's belly. The girl wailed in pain, but the sound was cut off sharply as the same dark elf who had taken a bite from her neck swung his wicked scimitar and eviscerated her in one slash. The girl toppled backwards. Ell leaped to avenge the dead elf. He was too late to save her, but the fury of battle and the bitterness of years of oppression spurred him onward.

Ell discarded his spear recklessly and ripped free his long dueling dagger from his thigh and the knife from his belt. The dagger quivered at his touch, it sensed its twin nearby. *Silverfist. No time for that now, providence might make a way for our paths to cross at some point before the end, but for now, I'll have to settle for this one.* Ell rushed the dark elf who had blood on his lips and teeth, the dark elf's tongue caressed its mouth as if savoring the flavor. Ell's dagger sang with strength, it flew fast and true as he swang, somehow aided by the nearby presence of its sibling blade giving it added energy. Ell slashed and cut, opening a vein in the dark elf's arm. Blood, black and dark, like the sick Departed from months ago, spurted out. Ell ducked the swing of the scimitar wielded by the Departed and then promptly opened up the dark elf's guts with his belt knife. An ironically fitting end, considering that it had just done the same thing to the girl. Ell kicked the body off the wall and it fell in a lump on the ground to be trampled by the rest of the slavers pushing onward. Black blood. Ell still had no answers as to why some dark elves bled the normal, dark, reddish-brown, and others the sickly, inky black. Ell realized he might never know. He looked out. There were no more catchpoles, no more searching for captives. The Departed were in a frenzy and there had to be nearly two hundred still out there compared to the paltry few villagers who remained with Ell and his family to stand against them. The defenders stood, attempting to hold the hastily constructed dirt wall. The odds must be five to one against the villagers.

Ell fought on. Blood gushed from a slaver he impaled with his long dueling dagger; this elf's blood was the typical deep, reddish-brown. Thrusting his puzzlement aside, Ell dodged and slid his way through the bloody muck of the earthen bulwark, ducking low to slice hamstrings, opening veins in arms and legs. He fought dirty. War was never clean, but Ell took it a step further. He fought like a wild wolf, which wounded its prey, crippling it before going in for the kill. Elves screamed around him, as he shattered bones and slit throats.

Arrows had long been forgotten in the chaos that had ensued since the clash of the two forces. But Ell felt a sword slice his thigh as he attempted to slide out of the way. He was not quick enough though, as he felt the blade open up his muscle and pain riot in his leg. Ell swung around and then slithered in close. He was near enough to embrace his enemy, inside the range of the dark elf's sword. Ell crossed his knives and in one swift motion swung them apart opening up his foes throat with an outward swipe of both of his blades.

The swirl of battle raged around him, but for a moment, it was as if Ell was in the eye of the storm, as if he had been given an instant of rest to see where to go, what to do next. Ryder decapitated a slaver, and blood the color of midnight poured out black from the wound, like refuse from a rotten corpse. However, a second later, a spear thrust caught his cousin in the arm and Ryder fell back clutching his shoulder.

Dahranian and Dacunda swung their long swords together, cleaving a swath of enemies around them but they were both riddled with wounds and blood flowed freely from both of them. They would not last long. None of them would Ell realized. They had fought well, made the enemy pay in blood, but they were steadily being overrun. Dirt walls and wooden spikes in the earth could only protect you for so long. Eventually your strength flagged and your forces diminished.

The battle raged, but Ell couldn't shake the strangeness of the enemy at times. Some of the Departed acted and fought normally as any elf would, dark or light in skin color. Those Departed moved with speed and surety, graceful if not quite as fluid as the northern elves. They fought and killed, but many died, as well. The ones that died did so with dark, red blood, almost brown dripping from their bodies. Yet, there were other slavers, other dark elves who differed. Ell had a hard time figuring out what it was. Their movements were a little less graceful, a little jerkier. They lacked none of the speed and strength of the swarthy southern elves, but the litheness that accompanied most elves, the ability to fight, run, and kill as if they were part of some terrible dance was gone. Instead, they hacked and rampaged, in their erratic manner, bursts of speed and energy with no tact, no subtlety to their movements. They did not lack for effectiveness, however. They still killed with similar efficiency. Ell stared longer. It was the eyes also, the glazed expressions, devoid of emotions other than madness and frenzy. Ell even saw one that looked to be on the verge of disease like the Departed he had killed on the raid months ago. It made his blood run cold. Something was wrong.

Wind assailed Ell's nostrils. The stink of blood and guts, of bowels released as a person perished and lost control of their bodily functions, brutalized his senses. Yet that smell was the stench of new death, fresh kills. Another scent lingered on the wind, also. It was a dusty, old smell, the sensation of ancient death and disease and evil. It hung on the air like a pervasive cloud, floating just at the tips of his senses. Ell's subconscious recognized it as it had months before.

Bonewinds. The fabled breezes of old, spoken of in nearly forgotten lore. The wind, which heralded death and decay, and the opposition to all that was good and right. It had been said that during the First Days the original enemies of the Highest, their ancient foes, had joined battle with this wind at their backs. Ell forced down a feeling of revulsion. He would not waste time by sicking up. There was still fighting to be done, even if his brain didn't quite understand who or what he was fighting. Ell's instincts made him certain something was off about his enemies. Some of the Departed made the tiny hairs on the back of his neck stand up.

The eye of the storm passed him, and Ell was cast back into the depths of battle. He fought fiercely, a cornered, wild lion fighting against a host of foes. He opened up skulls to the bone with vicious slashes of his knives and gutted Departed in a primal manner. But he sustained more wounds also, in addition to his injured thigh. A sword nicked his cheek and left a trail of blood on his face. An axe was swung by one Departed, and Ell ducked but the dark elf was powerful and quick and he jerked the trajectory of the axe back towards Ell swiftly, and the haft of the weapon struck Ell in the shoulder, jarring his entire arm. Ell almost dropped his belt knife but managed to cling to the blade long enough to open the veins in the slaver's arm, which held the same axe that had just struck him. The injury he gave to the crazed slaver was a mortal one. The vein he struck would eventually bleed out, even if the elf didn't realize it immediately.

The press of battle forced Ell's family and the villagers to fall back one final time to the last, earthen bulwark. It was even shorter in width across and Ell fought in unison with his companions. Everyone was wounded, their bodies near to exhaustion. Ell could see the life, the hope fade from the eyes of the villagers, even the seasoned hunters who were veterans of a few skirmishes from long ago. Ell didn't blame them, but he did wonder if his eyes carried that same look of despair. He hoped it didn't. Ell hoped his own eyes had the spark of fire in them, telling his enemies that they would pay dearly for his life.

In the midst of what felt like the end, Ell looked out. Over a hundred and fifty Departed had to be out there still. Ell was amazed at how much it had cost them to get to this point. The defenses and the villagers fighting alongside Ell and his family had acquitted themselves well. Sure, without Dacunda to lead them and without Ell and his cousins to hold the lines strong, the villagers likely would have fallen long ago. Yet, it spoke of their character. They could follow a leader like Dacunda and rise to the occasion. Ell felt a newfound sense of respect for the people who he had once secretly looked down upon as inferior, yet who at the same time he'd envied for their choice to avoid battle. It was sad to think that this was where their courage would be destroyed. Ell swung his flask of Source water up to his lips and swallowed the last tiny gulp of the precious liquid to aid his muscles and wounds as best it could. If this were the end, he would meet it with as much vitality and strength as possible.

Suddenly, a body dropped down onto the top of the earthen bulwark from the cliff side above the cavern mouth. Ell stared in astonishment as an old elf with gnarled hands and lank, grey hair knelt in the crouch in which he had landed, palms pressed to the earth with his eyes closed as he reached out for power. The battle froze for a moment, everyone startled, foes and friend alike, then the ancient elf rose to his feet, drew his sword and whipped it in a deadly arc as he stood up, nicking the throats of two nearby slavers. The two slavers dropped back, choking on blood as they died. The battle resumed with a renewed fervor. Slavers pressing and pushing forwards, sensing the end of the Highest they had come to claim. Yet the old elf stood his ground and somehow held the wall by himself, earning a respite for the weary villagers within. *Arendahl!*

Ell felt a surge of hope from deep within as his mentor and teacher displayed with true vigor and passion what it really meant to be a Water Caller. The ancient elf did not fight as if he were the oldest elf on the mountainside. He covered ground like nothing Ell had ever seen. Ell supposed it was how he must have looked to his enemies when he had fought the slavers atop the Pillar on his way to rescuing Miri.

Arendahl decapitated Departed and severed hands. His sword strokes were fluid and decisive at the same time. He was grace, power, and incisive action all joining together in one collaborative effort. Departed warriors died, in droves. But even Arendahl with his ability-enhanced skill in combat could not stem the swell of dark elves attacking. Arendahl swept the wall clean and then stepped back, letting the line of defense step forward once again as the old elf caught his breath. The line of defense led by Dacunda, Dahranian, and Ryder fought with renewed vigor. Ell stepped up beside his mentor and looked him in the eyes. Milky white, they gazed back at Ell in the fashion of a Water Caller tapping his power.

"Surprised to see me?" The old elf smirked a grin, his eyes alight with the fever and excitement of battle. "No, don't answer that, I know you are. Can see by the dumbfounded look on your face." As Arendahl spoke with his stilted speech, Ell realized how much he had missed the old elf and his odd quirks the last few weeks.

The old elf barreled forward. "Come now, there's not much time."

Ell cocked his head in question. Arendahl snorted in typical fashion to show his exasperation. "Well, I'd think it's pretty obvious boy, if you and I can't break through your mental block and get you to access your abilities then we're probably all doomed. I can't fight this battle alone, you know."

"But I tried, I can't," Ell protested dejectedly as the sounds of battle raged right beside him. "I'm not even worthy to call myself a Water Caller. I cannot even help my family, my people, when they need it most!" Ell's self-disgust pushed through, surprising even himself.

"Shh, boy," Arendahl said with astounding gentleness given the circumstances and the moment. "Forget about everything. Forget about doing things and deserving things. Don't worry about what you can or cannot do, or what you think you should be able to accomplish. You don't earn the ability to be a Water Caller. You just are one. You think I did something to deserve this?" The old elf scoffed a laugh, "I was an idiot of a youth, yet here I am."

Ell was listening now, unsure of what to make of it all. If you didn't deserve something or earn it, then what worth could it have?

Arendahl pressed on in a rush. "Forget everything Elliyar, and just breathe. Just close your eyes. Don't try to do anything, just breathe. Just *be*."

Ell did so.

The sounds of the battle around him didn't quiet, in fact, they grew louder, but that was fine because he was Elliyar, Dusk Runner, a child of war, a student of battle. It was who he was. He welcomed the sound of war. He noticed the feel of the earth, soft but at the same time hard beneath his feet, as the soles of his soft leather boots felt the different types of soil and rock. Elliyar was of the Highest, born of Andalaya, bred for the mountains and valleys, the rivers and peaks of this land. He could smell the fresh pine and spruce, the tang of weeds and grass from the valley far below with his keen senses of a northern elf. He sifted out the scent of the Bonewinds and the blood and guts of battle, and just focused on the liberating beauty of the fragrance of the world around him. Elliyar was a warrior, yes, but also a lover of beauty and grace, one who cherished the pure, the pristine. His mind flashed to Miri as an example of those ideals.

Out of nowhere, everything changed. Where once Ell had clawed and scrabbled to find his power, where he had fought to grasp control of his ability, he now stopped and rested. He just was. All of sudden as he fully accepted who he was, one of the Highest, a warrior, a lover and yes, a Water Caller, whether he had earned or deserved that ability or not, the power of creation flooded his body. He felt the *oneness* with the land around him of which Arendahl had spoken of during their training sessions. The sensation flooded his awareness as he accepted who he was. Surrendering and allowing himself to become fully who he was meant to be, helped to forge that all-important link with creation.

Ell felt power like he never had before. This was more than what he had experienced when he had fought Silverfist in the ambush, or when he had fended off the attack of the Stone Ogre. This was greater even than his night of unparalleled prowess on the Pillar. The immensity of the power within him stunned him, yet it felt right, as well. It was like the day training with Arendahl when he had briefly touched a well of power deep inside himself. This was like a lake of water, of ability, a never-ending wellspring of power.

Ell pulled the strength into him from every hint of water and moisture from the surrounding land and air, and he felt the mist begin to cloak him, the tiny droplets of water dampen the cloth of his tunic and hose. Ell's eyes were still closed but he knew that once he opened them the familiar yet strange cloudiness would have invaded his sight, allowing him to see as one with the ability to pull on the strength of creation. Ell drank the power in, readying himself to return to the battle.

Ell heard Arendahl mutter something in a tone of exaltation to himself as the old elf saw what was happening. Ell felt his limbs and bones and head all refreshed by the power of the ability at work within him. Ell was now ready to engage the enemy once again. This time he felt an odd sense of pity for them. It was only a small emotion, but it was there. The Departed were about to face not one but two of the Highest imbued with power, which had been passed down through the ages. Lost to the northern race of elves since nearly the First Days, but regained now. Ell looked deep within at his reservoir of power and he knew that between the two of them, Arendahl and he, the remaining slavers would be hard pressed to prevail.

He realized now that he hadn't done anything to deserve this gift in the first place, and therefore he needn't feel like he had to do anything to earn its continued use either. What was given freely could be used freely. He understood that now. Ell had fought so hard to prove to himself he could learn to use his ability that he had clogged his mind with unnecessary thoughts and emotions. His powers were not something he had to fight to acquire. Rather, they were just something he already *was*.

He was Elliyar. Dusk Runner. Son of Adan the Green. And he was a Water Caller.

Chapter Thirty-Two

The tide of the battle turned in a heartbeat. Ell and Arendahl, filled with power, leaped into the fray. Ell didn't stay on the wall for long. He felt the strength of many elves in his legs and the force of creation in his arms. Ell bent his knees and burst upwards in an impossible jump. He left the wall and its ragged defenders behind as he soared through the air and then landed in a puff of dirt in the center of the battlefield. A second later, Arendahl landed beside him, after having executed the same incredible leap from the bulwark.

"Ready, boy?" The old elf grinned wolfishly as he often did before a contest of arms. Ell was ready. He could feel the pulse of the rivers in his blood, the ceaseless crash of waves on the distant shore pounding in rhythm with his heartbeat as he felt the entirety of Andalaya from her mountains to her coasts swelling within him. This was what it felt like to be a Water Caller. This was what it meant to rise up and meet the potential inside of you. For so long he had underperformed in regards to his potential. No longer.

The stunned silence of the battlefield, as the enemy had watched the two of them effortlessly bound a distance of fifty feet from the wall, evaporated amidst enemy war cries. They were the center of focus. The bulwark was forgotten; all attention was on Ell and Arendahl.

Three dark elves rushed in and attacked Ell at once and he turned to engage them. Ability-enhanced speed and agility allowed him to weave his way through the three blades swinging for his head, neck, and torso. Like a dancer in the midst of a misty performance, Ell ducked the first swing and opened up a wound on the slaver's chest with his dagger, droplets of water flicking off his blade as he fought. Ell slid sideways to avoid a downward chop, and then backwards a step to avoid another swing. Then he stepped forward, his knives finding guts and entrails as he nipped in close to open up his enemies' bellies, one blade for each stomach. In an instant, three Departed had fallen.

Arendahl lashed about with his sword, parrying thrusts and responding with cuts of his own. He was like whirlwind, all spinning and action. He moved so quickly that his opponents didn't know what to do at times. Ell saw the old elf cut down four slavers at once with a grand, powerful, diagonal slice of his sword. The four dark elves were dead. The first with his face split and the second his throat opened up. The torsos of the last two were ripped open by the strength of Arendahl's blow.

Ell focused back on his own work. He fought with impossible speed. He saw a movement made by the enemy and reacted almost before the motion had been actualized by the attacker. It was like fighting underwater, only he was not impeded by the water, only his enemies were. It almost seemed as if their motions slowed down. Ell cut and slashed until his weapons were covered with blood. He glanced down at his blades and saw that they were a strange mix of the brownish-red blood and the odd, new, black blood that some of these Departed bled when injured. It created a mottled coloring to his steel.

The sunlight of the early afternoon illuminated the battle, and Ell felt the long awaited exhilaration of finally being able to confront his enemies directly. No shadows, no skulking and hiding and striking from a distance. This was war, and Ell fought the war, he took it head on. He struck and struck until his normal arm would have long been exhausted, but his strength hardly flagged. Ell could feel his body was strong, fueled by his homeland. He was even stronger than the night on the Pillar, because on that night, he eventually had begun to tire, but Ell felt no fatigue now. He felt invincible. That wasn't to say that he didn't take wounds. No, it was nearly impossible not to do so when you took on tens of enemies at once. However, the wounds and injuries felt like nicks and scrapes, and could hardly do more than inflame his psyche with a newfound aggression. These Departed were just bugs for the swatting, annoying and taking up his time.

At some point, he and Arendahl found themselves fighting side by side, and then even back to back, as if they fought some desperate, last stand scenario. Yet, this wasn't a last stand for them, not by any means nor any stretch of the imagination. This was slaughter, and Ell and Arendahl just happened to be at the center of it. The Departed rushed in upon them like slavering beasts. Ell saw the madness, the glazed look in many of their eyes as they attacked relentlessly, meeting their deaths. Yet, in some, he saw fear, the normal emotions present on the faces of many warriors who found themselves facing a foe they never thought to encounter. Ell once again felt a small stab of pity. He squashed it. There had been no mercy for the villagers all night, nor the first half of this day.

Ell slashed and cut, his clothes dampened by the haze of mist, which swam around his body as he drew upon his ability as a Water Caller. A spear thrust managed to snake its way in and slice his left forearm, causing him to convulsively drop his belt knife. Ell instead grabbed the spear and yanked hard, jerking the slaver in close. Ell swung his fist with the might of a hammer blow and sent the dark elf reeling with pain and clutching his face. The dark elf collapsed to the ground and didn't move.

Ell picked up a sword from the dirt to replace his dropped belt knife and then he sheathed his dueling dagger, wielding just the sword for a time. Arendahl and he were death incarnate. The two Water Callers stood back to back on the battlefield and slayed the enemies who came within their reach.

"Nothing like it, eh!" Arendahl commented excitedly in his gruff voice. "The feel of the sword in your hands and the strength in your limbs. This was what we were made for. We are creation's response to the sickness that abides in the land, just as it was in the First Days."

Ell didn't know what to say exactly so he just fought on, relishing the feeling of added grace and power to each and every one of his movements. A Departed, a particularly quick one, darted in with a spear and Ell sidestepped the thrust and sliced upwards with his sword as he did, shearing the wooden haft in two. Then Ell whipped his sword, slick with blood and water droplets from the mist, back the other direction and chopped through the forearm of the dark elf, sending a spray of reddish-brown blood and a howl of anguish as the dark elf fell back injured. Four other Departed stepped up to take his place, scimitars and axes hovering dangerously, waiting to exact revenge for their wounded comrade. They all attacked at once and Ell fended them off simultaneously, his borrowed sword a blur of motion and action as it parried and blocked, defended and then thrust. The four Departed fell to his ability-enhanced speed and strength of arms.

Ell glanced around and saw that a few of the Departed had begun to assault the bulwark once again. But with their numbers lessened, Dacunda, Dahranian, and Ryder seemed to be having no difficulty in leading the rag tag bunch of villagers in their defense. Ell and Arendahl had drawn the Departed's full attention for a time and given the villagers a much needed few minutes of rest. They would be fine. Ell went back to killing.

Arendahl and Ell stepped out from the protection of fighting at the other's back. The Departed were thinning, their numbers couldn't be more than fifty now. Some of the dark elves were still in a frenzy, a few even frothing at the mouth, foam and spittle dripping from their top row of sharp teeth. However, Ell could see the hesitation in others. He could practically see them weighing the circumstances in their heads. Two northern elves had just killed over half their numbers in a matter of minutes. Ell and Arendahl had been a tornado of steel and blood and skill. A person would have to be in the middle of an absolute blood frenzy or dedicated to the point of madness to continue fighting them without good reason.

First one, then another, began to break away and run south, down from the mountainside. Ell jumped again, in an incredible leap and landed about twenty feet down slope, his lithe grace accentuated by the power of the land around him. His strength drawn, energy channeled, from the river below and the undetectable moisture in the air. The mist surrounding him was like a tiny cloud dampening everything nearby. Ell turned up hill to confront a few of the fleeing slavers. He ducked low and swung a powerful blow with his sword, shearing the leg off one at the knee, sending the elf tumbling in pain to roll down the slope of the mountain. The other two attacked together. Ell saw through the haze of mist, the milky clouds that formed in his eyes when he tapped his abilities. It was the familiar sensation, too difficult to really describe, where all at once it was harder to see through the haze of mist, yet easier, as well, as if he had been created to look through that mist every day of his life.

Ell swirled close to the two would-be-fleeing slavers, a shower of mist and water droplets flinging into the air as he cut with his sword. As he engaged the enemy, they fell with ease to the strength of his arm. A single swing of his sword shattered the upheld blade of one of the dark elves and a kick to the chest sent the other flying over the side of the small cliff on the western side of the slope to fall to his death below. The one with the shattered blade, pulled a dagger free with his now injured arm and tried to repel Ell's next attack but couldn't. The Departed fell with a crunch as Ell's blade bit deep into his skull. Brownish blood oozed from the wound. A normal bleeder. Not a new, black-blooded one.

More slavers began to flee; half the remaining dark elves seemed to realize the battle was lost. Ell noticed a blond haired slaver running with the rest. Borian. The sight of his blond hair disappeared, as he became part of the mass of fleeing Departed. Ell watched him go. He couldn't spare the time for that traitor just now.

A handful fought on, still in the midst of a bloodlust the likes of which Ell had never seen. Most slavers were vicious, cruel, and even brave at times. But they were not courageous to the point of certain death. The ones who continued to fight, fought with an unusual fervor, and also bled dark, sickly, black blood from their wounds. It was peculiar and Ell couldn't believe it was due to coincidence, even though as of yet, he had no theories allowing him to surmise its cause.

Arendahl seemed to have the few remaining Departed well within his skill to defeat. Indeed, he almost toyed with them now, as there were only a few remaining, zealous Departed wielding their weapons aiming for his demise. The old elf would be fine. He had done this far longer and was likely much more adept than Ell was himself.

Ell turned to return to the earthen bulwark to aid his uncle and cousins there, but then a vibration from his thigh caught his attention. Suddenly, it all came crashing in on him.

Silverfist.

Ell hadn't seen him in the battle. Where was he now? He must still be close for the dagger to be vibrating. Ell looked down hill and he saw a lone fleeing form, heading in the opposite direction of the rest of his Departed comrades. Clever. The traitor thought to avoid the trail set by his companions should Arendahl and Ell chooses to pursue.

Ell took one last glance at the bulwark to assure himself that his family could handle their task there and felt convinced they could. There were only a few of the last, feverishly fighting slavers, the ones bleeding black not brownish-red, and Ell had no doubts the villagers holding the walls would be enough aid for his uncle and cousins. No, they did not need him. It was time to end it. It was time for some long awaited vengeance. Justice for his father.

Ell discarded the sword and picked up his belt knife from where he had dropped it earlier. He was more comfortable with his two short blades, the daggers. Ell could fight with any weapon, sword included, as he had done so, wreaking havoc on the field of battle here today. Yet, the dueling dagger, coupled with his belt knife was his preferred mode of close combat. There was something personal, intimate about fighting with knives. It could get messy, true. But you were so close to your enemy that you felt their deaths more when you killed. Some people might not want to experience such a thing, but Ell didn't want to distance himself from what he did. He killed because he had to. He fought and slew his enemies because it was right to do so to protect his people. But he did not want to forget the pain he caused either; he didn't want to become callous. It was his personal way of making sure his own soul did not grow dark and black inside like his enemies.

Ell grabbed his two blades, gathered his strength, and leaped in giant bounds down the slope. It was not flying, not by any stretch of the imagination. Riding the Icari had shown Ell how true flight felt. But Ell landed fifty feet down the hill in a spray of rocks and dirt then he burst upward again in another huge leap. No, this wasn't flying, it was something else entirely. But the freedom he felt using his powers to do what would have previously been impossible for him, was akin to the wild sense of excitement and exhilaration he had felt while flying on the Icari's back.

Ell jumped once more to reach the flat ground at the base of the mountainside and then sprinted south and west, in the opposite direction of the fleeing Departed. He was chasing Silverfist. The rest of the slavers, the few still fighting, could be dealt with by Arendahl, his family, and the villagers.

Silverfist's slender frame could be seen disappearing into the woods on the other side of the river. Ell ran hard to cover the distance between them. Best to gain as much ground as possible before Silverfist realized he was being chased. The traitor's fleeing form was gone from sight, but as Ell bounded across the river in an ability-fueled leap, he picked up the elf's tracks and followed the signs of his passage. Silverfist was moving quickly, but Ell was even faster now because of his power. He followed the traitor, using a broken twig here, a carelessly placed footprint there, to guide his pursuit. It wasn't long before Ell's keen senses picked up the sounds of heavy breathing and branches cracking under foot from up ahead.

Then all sounds stopped, and Ell could hear that Silverfist had ceased moving. Here, in the far west of Andalaya, Legendwood was dense and full of underbrush. Pines, spruces, and firs dominated the landscape, but unlike many of those higher altitude forests where the space between trees was open, this section of the land was full of underbrush. It was much like where Legendwood met the Lower Forest in many ways. Spruce and Pine, abutted brambles and briars. Occasionally an oak or an elm filled the space. The sky penetrated sometimes, its light shining through and speckling the forest floor with an alternating patchwork of light and shadows. There was no trail here. Ell had followed Silverfist through the underbrush. On the ground lay all manner of dry, dead wood perfect for building a campfire. It would make for shifty footing when the fighting began. Ell would have to pay careful attention to where he placed his feet.

He pushed through a last stand of bushes cautiously. Silverfist had obviously stopped for a reason. Ell did not want to be taken by surprise. With his long dueling dagger, quivering with unrestrained energy as it did when near its twin, held tip up in his right hand, and his belt knife blade down in his left, Ell left the bushes and entered what was a small clearing. The glen was sheltered, and gorgeous, the perfect place to escape with Miri for a romantic seclusion. Silverfist stood with his back to Ell, panting in the center of the glen. The traitor was a stain on this perfect little corner of paradise. Ell wanted nothing more than to eradicate this blemish that marred the surface of his fair land.

"That was quite the show you two put on there, boy," Silverfist snarled angrily, a hint of jealousy in voice. He still stood, breathing heavily, his back to Ell, shoulders straight.

Ell warily approached, holding his daggers tightly and at the ready. Power coursed through him. He had slain over forty dark elves just moments before on the mountainside. One elf, even one as infamous as the original traitor, would not be able to stand against him now.

"Just doing what was necessary," Ell responded carefully.

Silverfist threw back his head and laughed bitterly. "Always talking of duty and honor and what must be done, what is necessary. Same as your father. You are just like him."

"Thank you."

"It was not a compliment, boy!" Silverfist spat venomously as he turned around. "I hated your father. He was too weak to do what was necessary, for all the blather he spouted about duty and honor."

Ell felt his anger boil. Who was he to slander the name of Adan Wintermoon? "I hardly think you are one to comment on what does or does not make one weak."

"What do you know?" Silverfist asked. "You know nothing of what it was like back then. I had foresight. I could see what was inevitable. Andalaya was bound to fall eventually. All I did was speed up its process and join the winning side."

Ell shook his head in disagreement as he continued to close the space between them, placing one foot in front of the other, slowly but surely. "You are a coward as well as a traitor," he said to the elf in front of him.

Silverfist laughed. "I don't deny it, boy, fear of being on the losing side drove me to betray Andalaya. But it does take a certain grit, a boldness if you will, to turn your back on your entire race." The traitor laughed again, reveling in himself and his accomplishments, the red tears tattooed at the corners of his eyes, moving whenever his face shifted as if they were actually falling. "I may be a coward, but you must admit, I am a brilliant one."

Ell sneered at the elf. "I admit nothing, Traitor." Slender, lithe, just like all the rest of the Highest, Silverfist stared at him. Pointed ears, perfect blond hair. The only difference was that it was shaven on the sides of his head in the manner of the Departed, a waterfall of flaxen hair, like a horse's mane. How could Silverfist be so similar to the northern elves yet at the same time be so different. Ell despised this elf, this betrayer.

Silverfist seemed angry that Ell would not give him the satisfaction of saying he was special. "Once again, what do you know, boy? Have you ever chopped off your own hand to escape? I did, then I plunged it into the Source Water to heal it right before I released the dammed up reservoir." The traitor held up his marvelously crafted metal hand, formed into the shape of a fist.

Ell continued to circle the elf. He was growing tired of the banter. Time to be done with it. "I don't care what you think I do or do not know," he responded to Silverfist. "You killed my father," Ell lifted the dueling dagger that was vibrating with pent up energy. "That is all I need to know. Let us finish this."

Now it was Silverfist's turn to sneer. "Fine, boy. Have it your way. But are you really going to fight me with that freakish power of yours?" He laughed at Ell's surprised look. Ell had to give him credit; he was the bravest coward Ell had ever encountered.

"Yes," Silverfist went on, "I know something is different about you. Nobody could fight like you just did. Besides, mist clings to you like a cloak, droplets of water on your blade. Not to mention your eyes. It's something old, isn't it? Something talked about in the ancient lore." The traitor had a feverish, power-hungry look on his face as if he coveted the abilities he had seen Ell display.

"You know nothing of it," Ell commented. Now it was his turn to point out how much his opponent's information was lacking.

"Use it if you wish, but even if you kill me, you know it won't be a fair fight." Silverfist's tone of voice changed. It was a strange, cajoling sound now. "You won't really get your revenge that way." His soft, silken voice crooned in Ell's ear.

Ell paused. Everything in him screamed to ignore the traitor and the scarlet tears that danced upon his face every time he spoke. Yet, deep within another voice whispered. *I do want to kill him*, Ell thought, *but I want to do it the right way. For Father. This is personal.* Ell knew it wasn't wise. Ell knew his uncle and Arendahl would berate him for doing it later. If he survived. Yet, Ell would not have his vengeance unbalanced by his powers. Silverfist really had spoken one word of truth. It wasn't fair like this.

"Very well," Ell said after a moment of silence had passed. "Have it your way. I'll fight you fair, head on. Nothing extra involved. I will let go of the power, the ability within me. And I will still kill you."

So Ell stopped tapping into his ability. Ell let go of his connection with the land, and the power within him winked out.

Chapter Thirty-Three

Foolish. Silverfist thought to himself. *Youth and their sense of right and wrong, their sense of honor.* The boy should have just finished him off quickly. Silverfist had seen him kill five of his slavers in the space of ten seconds during the battle on the mountainside. He was a realist, Silverfist. You didn't survive where he lived, for as long as he had without being clever. He knew that the boy could have killed him in an instant with whatever power he had used on the hill. But if he really had let it go, well then… anything was possible. Silverfist would bet on himself in an even fight against anyone he had ever encountered. Except Half-Mask. The Prince of Darkness was not to be trifled with. He would kill anyone who confronted him within a matter of moments. But then again, a fight with Half-Mask could never be called equal. The Prince was… formidable. In many ways.

Silverfist closed the space quickly, not wanting to give the boy a chance to renege on his promise and utilize his special powers again. *What were they?* Silverfist lusted after the power he had seen. What would it be like to be so powerful, to be able to slay your enemies while hardly blinking?

The boy's weapons were already in his hands, ready for fighting. Silverfist drew his sword with his good right hand. He could feel the dueling dagger he had won so long ago, quivering in his sheath at his hip. The craft of forging dueling daggers was a strange art. Lost now, for the most part. Odd things happened when dueling daggers fought against one another. Silverfist used his sword instead.

He whipped it at the head of the boy and the elf—*what was his name, Elliyar?*—danced backwards lithely, frustratingly. He was quick. Wintermoon. Until the boy and his family had ambushed him over a month gone now, Silverfist hadn't expected to hear that surname again in his lifetime. It was a name of the past. Old history. An old hatred. Once again, Silverfist felt the familiar surge of pleasure as he recalled defeating the father of this elf with whom he now fought.

The boy attacked hard and strong, but Silverfist was quick too. One slash of a dagger narrowly missed Silverfist's cheek, and Silverfist reciprocated by attempting a blow with his metal fist. If only he could make connection. The fast acting poison in the ridges of the metal fist was as dangerous a weapon as the sword in his hand. However, the boy ducked out of the way, snakelike, a spring coiled for action. Vexed, Silverfist pressed the attack.

Now he went on the offensive aggressively. He worked his sword forms rapidly, one motion smoothly blending into the next. His sword was barely deflected by the boy's dueling dagger and the sound of steel on steel rang out violently, sending sparks into the late spring air. Silverfist's eyes lit up at the prospect of killing the boy and winning the twin to the dagger he already claimed at his hip. What a coup that would be! He almost laughed at the idea of it. *Like father like son.* The madness inside of him was close to bubbling over now. It had been brewing for many years, lurking beneath the crafty, rational surface above. But after watching a scene like he had witnessed on the mountainside, his madness was close to bursting forth completely. Seeing nearly over a hundred of your soldiers killed by two elves could turn that simmer of insanity into a boil. Silverfist fought to keep himself under control and his mind focused.

Silverfist swung his sword again and again, but the boy blocked him adeptly, almost every time. Yes, Silverfist sliced him on the shoulder of his left arm, but the wound was a shallow one, not likely to slow him down very much unless the duel lasted long. Silverfist intended to make sure that wasn't the case.

He lunged at the boy, but the boy ducked and then slunk in close, his wild locks of wavy blond hair shining golden in the sunlight. The boy slashed and cut with a ferocious venom and it was all Silverfist could do to avoid taking serious harm. He deflected one cut with the hilt of his sword and another with the back of his metal fist, sending another shower of sparks into the air. Even with his defense, he still took a cut along his chest to match the scar already there from the assassin months ago.

They danced back and forth, their violent game of cat and mouse seeming to go on forever. It could have been minutes or hours. Silverfist was an experienced enough fighter to understand that the passage of time felt different during combat. One didn't focus on the length of time you fought. What was important was how you felt. It didn't matter if you fought for an extended time, as long as you didn't grow exhausted. Similarly, it did not matter if you fought but a short while if you quickly grew too tired to fight effectively. The moment was all that mattered.

Silverfist threw everything he had into those moments. He slashed and cut. He wove his sword forms endlessly, fighting for any sort of opening in the boy's tactics. Whenever it seemed he would gain an advantage over the boy, the elf managed to escape the intricately woven trap, or even more improbably, he would turn the tables on Silverfist, gaining the advantage somehow and putting the slaver on his back foot.

How was this possible? Silverfist grew increasingly frustrated, and as he did so, increasingly erratic. How was the boy matching him blow for blow? Silverfist had crossed blades with some of the most feared warriors in the land and emerged victorious. Even the boy's father had been defeated at Silverfist's own hand. The boy was too fast. Too quick. Even injured from the battle he was smoother and more graceful in his motions than anyone Silverfist had ever faced. Silverfist began to have the sneaking suspicion that he had been duped. The boy must not have abandoned his powers. He must have only dulled them, lulling Silverfist into thinking they were on even footing when they really weren't. *That has to be it*, Silverfist thought with incredulity. *It's the only answer*.

The Original Betrayer—that was how he often thought of himself—began to grow angry. Why couldn't he have those powers? He would be ten times the elf this boy was if he possessed them.

They fought on, trading blows, striking viciously at one another until finally Silverfist made a mistake. He swung his sword too wildly, enflamed by the passion of the moment. *Fool!* He thought to himself even as the stroke of his sword was still in motion. The sword arm and the blade carried wide and Silverfist tried to correct his stance and bring the blade back in to defend himself, but the boy lunged close in a burst of speed and energy. Before Silverfist could rectify his mistake, the boy had his long dueling dagger at the slaver's throat. Silverfist made to move but the slightest motion pressed his vulnerable neck to the edge of his young foe's blade and a tiny trickle of blood ran down from the nick.

Silverfist froze.

* * * *

Ell found himself, improbably, with his blade to the throat of his most hated enemy. Accessing and then subsequently releasing his abilities by choice had made all the difference. The usual fatigue that hit him when the power left his body had not come, allowing him to fight the duel on fair footing with Silverfist. Sure, Ell had felt the wounds he had sustained in battle more keenly after letting go of his water calling ability, but determination to avenge his father had fueled him and brought him to this point of victory. Still, even he was surprised at the outcome.

Stunned, he forced himself to maintain his concentration in the moment.

Don't lose focus. This is the craftiest elf in the entire land. He spoke to himself almost nervously as he kept the blade there. Why didn't he just kill him? Why did he have his dueling dagger to the traitor's throat?

Against the odds, Ell had defeated his enemy without using even a hint of his ability as a Water Caller. Part of him, a large part, was extremely glad that he had managed to do so. Ending this feud once and for all was something best done as the youth who had been wronged, rather than a Water Caller who had realized the extent of his potential and power.

Silverfist licked his lips nervously. "What are you waiting for, boy?" The traitor didn't quite speak politely, but he wasn't discourteous either, now that Ell had a knife to his throat. "Isn't this the moment you've dreamed of?"

Isn't it? Ell wondered the exact same thing to himself. Then why did he feel so empty? What was the matter? Why was his hand stilled from taking the killing blow? *Would you execute him?* A small voice whispered in the back of his mind. *How are you any different from him if you kill someone in such a defenseless position?*

Ell dashed the thought away angrily. This elf had betrayed his entire race, caused the downfall of Verdantihya and put his own people on the run. Then, as if that wasn't enough, he had led the hunt for their capture, profiting greatly from the gains he made from selling his own brethren. Yet, Ell's hand wouldn't make the move to end his life. Something wouldn't let him. *Would you kill a captured prisoner in front of Miri?* The same voice whispered in his head. But this was the most dangerous of captives, and in truth, the traitor was still far from unarmed. Besides, Miri was not here to witness it. Why had he thought of her now?

Silverfist seemed to sense Ell's hesitation and pressed whatever advantage he had left. The advantage of Ell's mercy.

"I have information," the slaver half stammered, seeking to save his own life. *He really is a coward* Ell thought. "I can tell you about Half-Mask. He's planning something. Something big." The slaver continued, "Something is different about his troops these days. Didn't you notice during the fight?" Silverfist spoke rapidly as if fearing that if he slowed down or stopped Ell would execute him on the spot.

"What information do you have that you could possibly offer me? What do you think would make up for my father's death?" Ell said in disgust. If he did spare the traitor and take him prisoner, it would not be for whatever information he possessed. It would be because of her, Miri. She had taught him that hatred and killing weren't the only way. Love made a way for true justice to occur. This traitor had wronged not just Ell, but all of Andalaya. Didn't the rest of Ell's people deserve a say in his judgment. A trial maybe?

However, at Ell's last question, a light of hope crept into Silverfist's eyes, and the slightest of sly smiles moved onto his face.

"Death," the slaver murmured silkily now, regaining confidence for some reason. "Who ever said anything about death? Your father still lives." Silverfist said those words with a dramatic whisper.

Ell almost dropped his dagger at the shock of those words. Then fury poured forth like a raging flood. "Liar!" he screamed. "You think to trick me by telling me that which I long to hear most. Your plans will not succeed." Ell shoved the dueling dagger against the slaver's throat in an even rougher manner, and the trickle of blood began to flow more freely. The dueling dagger quivered as if it had a mind of its own and it too longed to quench its thirst on the blood of its enemy. Idly in the midst of all this, Ell noticed that Silverfist still bled red like one of the Highest. For some reason Ell had expected him to gush forth black blood like those of the Departed who strangely bled the dark, inky color.

Fear entered Silverfist's eyes again, real terror. "No, no. I swear it. It is true. Or at least, I believe it is true." In the midst of the panic in his enemy's voice, Ell somehow heard a spark of something. *The slaver spoke the truth*, Ell realized in amazement.

"Tell me," Ell commanded harshly. If there were something he didn't know, then he would find out now.

In a fearful tone, Silverfist obliged. "I never killed your father, whatever you may believe." He went on, speaking rapidly, "We met, we fought, I *did* beat him," Silverfist flashed a hint of his former animosity which had been lost in the midst of the terror he now exuded, "but the other slavers and I rounded them up and took them captive. They are slaves now."

"What? So you just kept the dagger as a trophy?" Ell demanded angrily. How could one of the Highest do such a thing, sell his own people into slavery?

"It was my greatest victory. I hated your father." Madness flared in the traitor's eyes. Silverfist seemed to forget the knife at his throat and began to rant. "Adan the Green, pride of the army, best of all of us. Well, there are other measures of an elf's worth than his skill with a bow or his ability to order people around. There is cleverness, craftiness. Do you think just anybody would have been able to engineer the destruction of Verdantihya like I did?" Silverfist was lost in the past now.

The slaver continued while Ell listened, sick to his stomach at the betrayer's twisted mind. "Cut off my own hand to ensure my survival," he cackled with a dark glee to himself. "My only regret was that Andalaya's precious Adan wasn't killed in the battle. But no matter, I rectified the mistake when I captured him singlehandedly before the war was over. He and his family." Pleasure outlined the elf's face.

His family. Ell was shocked again. Was it possible? Part of him couldn't even begin to imagine it as truth. The pain, if this were some terrible lie concocted by Silverfist, would be too much. Yet, another part of him couldn't help but hope against hope that there was a grain of truth to the slaver's tale.

Suddenly the slaver snapped out of his babblings and back to reality. A sick expression was on his face, as if he realized just how he had sounded, glorifying in the sale of someone's family. It was never a good idea to do so when the person had a weapon at your neck.

"The point is," Silverfist corrected his ranting hurriedly. "The point is, I sold them but did not kill them. Have mercy on me like I had on them." A pleading note entered his voice. "I could even help you find them." Silverfist must be desperate, Ell realized if the traitor thought Ell couldn't detect the false tone of friendship underlined by slyness in his offer of aid. Yet, Ell somehow found that even with the falsity in the slaver's voice, he did not want to kill him. He wanted him to go on trial. Andalaya, as a whole, deserved to determine what happened to him. His crimes were larger than just his offenses against Ell's family.

Ell eyed him in consideration. "If I do not kill you, it will only be to take you captive for a trial, to see justice done."

"Fine, fine," Silverfist agreed hurriedly.

"Alright then, drop your sword," Ell said.

The slaver opened his slender but strong elven hand and the sword fell. Ell glanced to the side as he watched the blade clatter to the ground, to lie on the broken branches, grass and moss of the meadow.

It all happened at once.

Out of nowhere, Silverfist, now unarmed, swung his metal fist and rammed it into the forearm of Ell's hand holding the blade to his throat. Ell felt his bone shatter and his dagger dropped lifelessly from his hand. *Idiot!* Ell berated himself for dropping his guard, even as he attempted to fend off the slaver's most recent attack. This was the moment Silverfist must have been waiting for the entire time.

One arm useless, Ell still had his knife in the other hand and he swung it in a downward arch plunging the blade into Silverfist's chest even as the traitor barreled into him with a tackle. Pain exploded, erasing thought from Ell's mind as his broken forearm hit the ground. Ell fought to remain conscious.

Silverfist lay on top of him, Ell's belt knife in his chest. Blood bubbled from his mouth, but he fought on. Ell must have punctured one of the slaver's lungs.

Silverfist swung his silver fist again and smashed it into Ell's exposed face much more viciously than Ell would have imagined possible after sustaining a wound to the chest as he just had. Ell's vision threatened to go black at the blow, but he somehow held on to consciousness. Ell yanked his bloody belt knife free from the slaver's chest and rammed it upwards into Silverfist's gut, digging it deep.

Ell rolled over with the last of his strength and pinned the traitor beneath him, turning the tables. Ell's belt knife was hilt deep in Silverfist's stomach, and Ell could see the life flowing from his eyes.

"Wintermoon," Silverfist burbled through the blood that exited his mouth as he tried to speak. "You Wintermoons always thinking you're better than me. First your father and now you. But don't forget, I've had the better of things for nearly twenty years now." He gasped, "Sent your family to the auctioning blocks, and pillaged your land." His voice grew weaker and slurred, but the first traitor managed to giggle an insane laugh as he died. His last words before he passed spoke volumes as to what was important to him. "But you haven't beaten me, you know. Well, at least not really," he said and smiled a deathly smile. "I always have one trick up my sleeve that people aren't aware of. We'll call this more of a draw." And then the elf who had killed Ell's family, or perhaps taken them captive—Ell didn't know what to believe because he wasn't sure if the tale spun by Silverfist was one last twisted game—died.

He did not meet his end peacefully. It was a frightened, ugly death, as he gurgled and spit up the last red vestiges of his life onto his chin and chest. It was a death far from the eyes of any observers. Silverfist did not meet his end in a public spectacle the way he had lived his life. No legends would be told of his last stand. Ell felt it was the perfect end for an elf such as him. The lowest of his kind, the betrayer of his race.

Ell felt hazy. Not the haze of his ability to draw upon the land, the liquid-blood of the earth, as a Water Caller. No, this was the fog of pain and injury. Ell nearly swooned as he pulled his knife free from his dead enemy's belly and tried to clean it. Ell grasped the dueling dagger that had been his father's before this traitor had stolen it from him, and pulled it from the dead elf's sheath. Now Ell had a matching pair, the way they were supposed to be used, in tandem.

He left the body and stumbled back towards the valley in the direction of the village. He needed Source Water. Something was wrong. Blackness clouded his sight. This felt different from anything he had ever experienced. What had Silverfist meant by tricks? Ell's cheek burned. He reached his good hand up to touch a scrape on his face made by the ridges on the knuckles of the silver fist. He had a similar scrape on his broken forearm. The wounds were minor but burned like the fire of a terribly infected wound.

Ell struggled to move a bit further before collapsing onto the dirt not fifty feet from where he had left Silverfist's body. Was this the end? *I wish I could have seen Miri one last time. But at least I rid the world of Silverfist*, Ell thought as darkness took his mind. The pain ebbed as he blacked out and lassitude settled over him. His last thoughts were calm and quiet as his face pressed into the moist soil of the forest floor. *If this is death, then it comes much more peacefully than I had expected.*

A bird sang overhead and the wind in the trees was serene. It was the sound of the forest speaking of its wild beauty, speaking in its given tongue—nature. Elliyar Wintermoon, Dusk Runner, readied himself to meet the shadows of death and enter the next reality.

Epilogue

The wind blew gently across the valley known as Indiria's Emerald, along the Westrill, and up the face of the mountainside. The clean, soothing breeze was a strange contradiction to the scene in the valley below. A large funeral pyre still smoked to the west of the village by a good few hundred yards, even though it had been lit almost a week ago on the night after the battle finished. Arendahl wasn't sure how it was possible the pyre was still smoking. The flames had long since burned out. Perhaps it was just the ash being picked up by the Andalayan wind and wafting into the late spring air resembling smoke. If so, then that was disgusting. The remains of the dead should be buried properly. Arendahl was traditional in some ways, and putting a body into the ground after the life was gone from it was one of those ways. However, in this case, he hadn't objected to the people burning the hundreds of dead Departed on the pyre. Some of the dark elves had looked like they were falling ill with some type of plague. Nobody wanted a disease to spread, so burning the dead was the best way for prevention. He hadn't stopped them, even though he knew that it wasn't necessary. There was no plague. Thus far, only he knew the terrible secret of why that was.

Arendahl sat on the mountain above the caverns in which the villagers had sheltered. He had leaped up to the little ledge overlooking the mouth of the caves by tapping his abilities as a Water Caller. It was wondrous. After all these years, there was finally someone with whom he could share this burden, this responsibility. This joy. *I should go easier on him.* Arendahl harrumphed his ancient lips, dismissing the thought as quickly as it had snuck up on him. No, Elliyar Wintermoon needed a strong hand to guide him. Someone who could reign in his rash impulses and channel the wealth of energy and stamina the boy had. Arendahl snorted to himself as he remembered the moment he had realized the boy was not there when the battle had finished. It had not taken long to figure out where the boy had gone gallivanting. Pursuing Silverfist was rational on one level. However, discarding the power of a Water Caller, as if it were a cloak to take on and off whenever he felt the need to appease his idealistic sense of honor, was beyond ridiculous. Especially when you faced an enemy as dangerous as Silverfist. That rash boy would have been dead if it weren't for Arendahl, following his trail into the woods and discovering his body near to death on the soft earth of Legendwood. Paralyzein was a fearsome toxin when administered directly into the bloodstream, as it had been in the case of Elliyar. His face and his arm had been the entry points for the poison.

If not for Arendahl's abilities as a Water Caller, the boy would have perished soon after he had discovered him. Even as it was, the boy had been close to death. It had taken all of the Source Water in Arendahl's tiny, extra flask, as well as using up all the reserves of Arendahl's ability, leaving him drained and exhausted the next day. A close call. Death was a welcome old friend to him, no doubt a comrade Arendahl would meet soon enough. But not the boy, no the boy had to live for years to come. Arendahl would do everything in his power to make sure he survived.

Arendahl hopped off the rock ledge above the caves and landed lightly on the ground in front of the cavern mouth. The holes in the mountain ran deep, likely all the way down to the core. In the First Days, they would have been the den of Ghouls and Stone Ogres and others of their ilk. Not today. He prayed the world would not revert back to how it had been. He feared however, that it might.

As he strolled lazily down the mountain in order to reach the ceremony—he had to be there because he was officiating it, after all—he glanced at his surroundings. Earthen bulwarks and sharpened stakes painted a stark contrast to the beauty of the valley. Bloody, dried mud crusted on the mounds and crunched as he walked. The dark blood of the southern cousins—he preferred to think of them as estranged family rather than Departed as their name implied—clung to the stakes protruding from the earth.

Not for the first time Arendahl marveled at the fact that these pitiful defenses had somehow been enough. These villagers, and young Dac's family, should have been overwhelmed and killed or captured long before Arendahl's timely arrival. How fortuitous that he had encountered Dac's niece and the boy's lovely, female friend, along with Art, the random child accompanying them. They had been able to point him in the right direction and hurry him on his way to assist them. Sometimes, and this was one of those times, Arendahl couldn't help but believe in fate, destiny, or whatever else a person wanted to call it. Nobody could deny that fortune had shined upon the survivors of this battle. Oh, nobody would deny either that it had come at a high price, yet some had survived and lived free when by all odds they should have been dead or enslaved. Creation had a funny sense of what was possible and impossible at times.

He reached the bottom of the mountainside and stepped in among the shattered wreckage of what had once been a village. No matter, the people wouldn't have stayed even if the structures had survived. Some slavers had escaped and this quaint and ill-advised way of existence, had come to an end. At least for now. Arendahl was old enough to look at life practically, yet still hold out hope for a better tomorrow. Perhaps one day, the Highest would again be able to settle the land instead of roaming it like vagabonds. But today was not such a day. As it was, the buildings were destroyed. Some were burnt to a crisp, others only somewhat charred, but with parts knocked down. If the village had been a person, he would have said it looked like someone had disemboweled it and left the entrails strewn about. Such was the way the village looked with its broken pieces left scattered about the ruins.

His body ached as he walked. Water Callers tended to live longer than most elves, but not all. His abilities had allowed him to stave off his demise for a time, but he feared it would not last much longer. The end would likely come soon and swiftly for him. Within the next few years, he estimated. No matter. He had lived a long life, a good life. He had accomplished much in his time, and yes, he had seen many tragedies, also. The fall of Verdantihya ranked high among those. But he had a chance to leave his people with a tremendous gift before he died. He would leave them with the first, fully trained Water Caller the Highest had seen in nearly a millennia. Oh, he was a Water Caller too. But he had learned his arts alone, with no one to guide him. Therefore, there were many blockages and deficiencies in his abilities. Nothing would rectify those inadequacies. But he could do something about the boy. Leave him more prepared, more capable of serving his people well. It would be a fitting end to a long life. Arendahl, the mentor, the instructor, the advisor, would end his life teaching one final pupil.

The evening was coming and shadows were stretching across the valley as Arendahl made his way to where the ceremony was being held. It would be twilight by the time they were finished. He was the last one to arrive, even though he was officiating. He was late because he hated ceremonies and rituals, any kind of formalities really. He was not an elf of extra words or unnecessary phrases and ceremonies tended to be full of them. The thought crossed his mind and lent a grumpy attitude to him. At least it did until he saw the two elves he was about to Join.

The boy stood next to the girl. *Miriyah, was that her name?* Yes, he was almost certain it was. They looked happy in the way only two young romantics could manage. They almost made him miss the joy of youth and the vibrancy of first love. Almost.

"I was wondering if you were ever going to show," the boy whispered discreetly out of the corner of his mouth, so as not to be heard by the surviving villagers observing the Joining.

Arendahl grunted, as the girl covered her laugh at the comment. "Impatient as usual, boy," he muttered grumpily. The boy took on a slightly wounded look. So sensitive beneath his strong, capable exterior. *I really should go easier on him.* Arendahl rejected the thought quickly as he always did when it came. He was going soft. *Years ago, such a sentiment would never have crossed my mind,* he thought. *He'll need the strength I can instill in him for the times ahead.* Nevertheless, he did pat the boy's shoulder in a conciliatory way.

"Ready then, boy?" he asked with a rare, peaceful smile. Maybe he could summon up just a bit of his own patience for this ceremony.

"Yes," the boy said confidently, grasping the girl's hand firmly. They both wore their normal clothes, no special attire or frippery for the event. Arendahl approved of that, at least.

"Well, let's get on with it then," he said.

"Yes, let's," the girl said with a smile. She always seemed to be smiling.

And so the ceremony began. Arendahl kept it simple. Short and sweet. He spoke of love, though it had been a long time since he last felt its warm, romantic stirrings. Kelssari had died many years ago, before Dac had even been born. Arendahl felt a wistful twinge of regret and melancholy at her memory. He hadn't allowed himself to think of her for quite some time. Kelssari would have enjoyed being here for this ceremony. She had liked the romantic side to life.

Arendahl spoke of love and patience. He talked of trust and honesty. But most of all, he emphasized the strength the two, young lovers would need to lend one another as they began to share a life together. Eternity in the arms of one person. Only creation itself could have come up with a concept like that. It was perfect. Even his grizzled, old heart began to melt as he watched the boy and the girl do the ritual together. They faced each other, kissed the fingertips on both of their own hands as they held them face up, and then spread their hands wide in a simple motion to either side. They did it while kneeling. It was the traditional greeting an elf of the Highest did when he returned home to Andalaya, or more specifically to Verdantihya, after being gone for a long time. The two lovers did the ritual to symbolize their Joining. They were each other's home now. They welcomed each other home.

Then it was done. They hugged, kissed, and laughed as they realized with joy that they would share their entire lives together. The villagers cheered. Arendahl had never heard such a loud cheer from such a small group of people. The elves needed something to celebrate after the week they'd had. It had been beyond trying, full of grief, and they needed something beautiful, something hopeful of which to grab hold. Elliyar Joining with Miriyah was an event in which they could rejoice.

The boy and the girl thanked Arendahl. He wished them the best and then allowed them to gravitate toward the center of the party to receive their congratulations and begin the dancing. Even though the girl was lame, she somehow managed to dance with incredible grace. She was perfectly imperfect.

Arendahl's breath caught as he saw something he had only seen a handful of times in his long life. The Wandering Mist appeared in the midst of the partygoers. It circled the newly Joined couple, its wispy, winking, ever-changing lights dancing around them as if to bless their union. The Wandering Mist was also known as The Spirit of the Land. It was always a good omen. Creation's way of declaring its blessing.

It twirled and sparked in the air around them, blue and purple, violet and even a mix of those colors combined. It took all sorts of shapes, from dots, to flowers, to buds, to butterflies and stars. One light in the form winked on then danced an inch and winked out, while others did the same. Thousands of lights. It was like a misty, bluish-purple cloud of sparkles blinking on and off around them. A good omen indeed.

Arendahl's momentarily splendid mood at seeing the Spirit of the Land slipped back to his normal gruff demeanor as he watched young Dac approach. He had the worst kind of news to share with the boy's uncle, his old student at arms, Dac. The sort of news that put a sour taste in your throat and a chill up your spine, or worse.

"Proud?" He muttered the question to the boy's uncle. He already knew young Dac was pleased with his nephew. It was just a filler question.

Dac nodded tranquilly, enjoying the moment as he watched his family dance together instead of fight. His two sons, their female cousin, and the boy and his girl all laughed and danced amongst the Wandering Mist.

"They deserve a rest. Sometimes I think I push them too hard. They've been fighting battles since they were old enough to hold a weapon," Dac said, regretfully.

"They were born into war, what other life could you have given to them? They do their duty and they do it well, with honor," Arendahl responded. Dac just nodded not answering.

Finally, the boy's uncle spoke again. "He knows. About his father, his family, I mean."

Arendahl sighed, "I feared as much. We will deal with it later."

"I am afraid he will be terribly displeased with me," young Dac said.

"As I said, we will deal with it."

Dac nodded. "Well, we never had a chance to speak about your travels in the south. What have you to report? There is much to tell you on my end," Dac said. "The boy accomplished some incredible feats. Did you know that he rode an Icari?"

Arendahl started in surprise. Now that did astound him. The boy had potential. Guts, skill, and instincts all blended into one important combination. He did not answer the second question but addressed the first. "I fear that I have news of the absolute worst kind." Dac's face said he was bracing himself for whatever Arendahl was about to tell him.

Arendahl continued, not waiting for young Dac to ask the question. "I finally have my answer to many questions. I have answered the question of why the Ghouls will fight together now and range as far south as the Lower Forest, even into Legendwood. I know why the Icari returned and how it is possible that the Bonewinds blow once more. I now know why some of the southern cousins," once again he refrained from referring to them as Departed, "bleed black, and appear to be stricken with sickness."

A chill shot through his spine as if a cold ghostly hand had grasped his heart. Dac waited, his face growing grimmer by the moment. The few moments of peace and tranquility earned by the ceremony had well and truly passed now. At least they had for Arendahl and would soon for young Dac also, as soon as Arendahl opened his mouth to reveal to him what he had discovered in the south.

Arendahl stilled his breathing and spoke as calmly as he could, although a slight shiver still shot through his body as he delivered the news.

"In the south, I found the answer to those questions, and it was an answer most foul." He paused before he spoke again, partly for the dramatics. He was old and enjoyed a good tale. But it was also because he knew that as soon as he spoke the words, it would make real something, which he had hoped, to never witness. The First Days had come again. Black times. Evil times. He looked at young Dac, his gaze a penetrating glare, and then gave his information.

Arendahl gathered his strength as he said it.

"I tell you now, the worst of all things has come to pass. The *Unsired* have returned."

About the Author

Mathias Colwell grew up in far Northern California exploring redwood forests and cloudy beaches. He loves God, his family, and friends. Mathias has been a writer for most of his life, drafting his first stories as young as eight years of age. His desire to write fantasy was inspired by such authors as J.R.R. Tolkien, David Eddings and the late Robert Jordan. He is an avid traveler and all-around adventurer, having visited or lived in 27 countries. His travels have led him around the world to five continents including stays in Siberia, Spain, and Chile, and he attributes many of his passions and goals in life to these experiences. In his free time he enjoys reading, outdoor activities such as soccer, snowboarding and water sports. Mathias has a passion for issues pertaining to social justice and human rights and hopes to influence these areas in the future.

Other Works by the author at Melange,
And Fire and Ice for Young Adults

An Age of Mist
The Collector
A Burning Hope